THE COURSE O...
RUNS ...

They lay together silently. As the fresh sunshiny scent of the hay rose around them, they could hear rain strike overhead on the tiled roof of the barn.

"Ouch!" Ruark shot upright, grimacing in pain.

"What's wrong?" Juliana asked.

"That devil bit me." He pointed at Juliana's Brittany spaniel pup, who had tired of pursuing elusive game, and was now making a bid for their attention.

"Poor thing," cried Juliana. "He doesn't like being so neglected."

Ruark's black brows rose. "Poor thing? That dog? What about me? I'm injured, I tell you."

She examined the barely discernable red mark on his ankle, then dropped a quick kiss onto it. "Better?"

"Mmm, much," he replied, reaching out to draw her back into his embrace. Just as he bent his head to kiss her, the growling puppy pounced, backside high in the air, tail wagging.

Juliana began to laugh. "He wants to play, Ruark. Isn't he darling?"

The pup made another lunge at them, but this time, as he darted away, he grabbed an article of clothing and made for the door. He stopped and turned to look at them expectantly, hoping they would follow. It was obvious he expected a merry chase.

"Ruark, he took my chemise!"

Juliana hadn't even a moment to enjoy the sight of Ruark in all his naked splendor before the puppy ran out of the barn, dragging the undergarment with him.

The chase was on. . . .

TODAY'S HOTTEST READS
ARE TOMORROW'S SUPERSTARS

VICTORY'S WOMAN (4484, $4.50)
by Gretchen Genet
Andrew—the carefree soldier who sought glory on the battlefield, and returned a shattered man . . . Niall—the legandary frontiersman and a former Shawnee captive, tormented by his past . . . Roger—the troubled youth, who would rise up to claim a shocking legacy . . . and Clarice—the passionate beauty bound by one man, and hopelessly in love with another. Set against the backdrop of the American revolution, three men fight for their heritage—and one woman is destined to change all their lives forever!

FORBIDDEN (4488, $4.99)
by Jo Beverley
While fleeing from her brothers, who are attempting to sell her into a loveless marriage, Serena Riverton accepts a carriage ride from a stranger—who is the handsomest man she has ever seen. Lord Middlethorpe, himself, is actually contemplating marriage to a dull daughter of the aristocracy, when he encounters the breathtaking Serena. She arouses him as no woman ever has. And after a night of thrilling intimacy—a forbidden liaison—Serena must choose between a lady's place and a woman's passion!

WINDS OF DESTINY (4489, $4.99)
by Victoria Thompson
Becky Tate is a half-breed outcast—branded by her Comanche heritage. Then she meets a rugged stranger who awakens her heart to the magic and mystery of passion. Hiding a desperate past, Texas Ranger Clint Masterson has ridden into cattle country to bring peace to a divided land. But a greater battle rages inside him when he dares to desire the beautiful Becky!

WILDEST HEART (4456, $4.99)
by Virginia Brown
Maggie Malone had come to cattle country to forge her future as a healer. Now she was faced by Devon Conrad, an outlaw wounded body and soul by his shadowy past . . . whose eyes blazed with fury even as his burning caress sent her spiraling with desire. They came together in a Texas town about to explode in sin and scandal. Danger was their destiny—and there was nothing they wouldn't dare for love!

Available wherever paperbacks are sold, or order direct from the Publisher. Send cover price plus 50¢ per copy for mailing and handling to Penguin USA, P.O. Box 999, c/o Dept. 17109, Bergenfield, NJ 07621. Residents of New York and Tennessee must include sales tax. DO NOT SEND CASH.

SCOTNEY ST. JAMES
ROGUE'S LADY

ZEBRA BOOKS
KENSINGTON PUBLISHING CORP.

ZEBRA BOOKS are published by

Kensington Publishing Corp.
850 Third Avenue
New York, NY 10022

Copyright © 1994 by Lynda Varner

All rights reserved. No part of this book may be reproduced in any form or by any means without the prior written consent of the Publisher, excepting brief quotes used in reviews.

If you purchased this book without a cover, you should be aware that this book is stolen property. It was reported as "unsold and destroyed" to the Publisher and neither the Author nor the Publisher has received any payment for this "stripped book."

Zebra and the Z logo Reg. U.S. Pat. & TM Off. The Lovegram logo is a trademark of Kensington Publishing Corp.

First Printing: October, 1994

Printed in the United States of America

This book is dedicated to the members of my writers' critique group: Tammy Madden, Mary Pierce, Stacie Valdez, Stephanie Woody, and the recently moved and greatly missed, Renée Roszel Wilson. They are an incredible bunch whose friendship, help, and support have meant more than I could ever express.

"There's rosemary for remembrance;
pray, love, remember:
and there is pansies, that's for thoughts."
—William Shakespeare, *Hamlet*

One

Damn men, thought Juliana. *Damn all men. Damn my father and most everlastingly, damn Spencer Hamilton!*

She was staring out the rain-spattered window of a public stagecoach, not really seeing the luxuriant green vegetation of the English countryside that lay beyond. Her mind was relentlessly recounting the events of the day before.

The scene she was watching was nearly as real as it had been in the library of the Lowells' London townhouse. Juliana, plainly dressed, silent and withdrawn as usual, had been seated in the room reading when her father, Dodsworth Lowell, and her fiancé, Spencer Hamilton, had entered. Neither man had bothered to look about, so they hadn't noticed her curled up in the big leather armchair. Now, remembering their words, she shivered despite the heavy woolen cloak she wore.

"Sir, I fear I must broach a matter of grave importance," Spencer had said, accepting a glass of brandy from the older man. "It's about the wedding." Hamilton looked decidedly uncomfortable.

Dodsworth Lowell, flipping his coattails aside, lowered his bulky body into the chair at his desk and peered inquiringly at his future son-in-law. "What seems to be the trouble, Spence?" He reached for his own glass and, with a wink, said, "Let me assure you there'll be adequate food and drink for the wedding."

Spencer Hamilton shuffled his feet. "No, sir, it's nothing like that. It's . . . well, it's Juliana."

The other man's smile faded abruptly. "Juliana? What has she done now? Not more argument about bridesmaids or flowers?"

"No." Hamilton gazed into the contents of the glass he held. "It's very difficult for me to say this, Mr. Lowell. I just hope you will allow me to try and explain the situation."

"What situation?" Dodsworth Lowell was looking very worried.

"I can't marry Juliana, sir. I'm sorry."

Slowly, Lowell rose to his feet, his face purpling. "Now, see here, Hamilton. You're not going to back out at this late date and leave my daughter in the lurch."

"Please let me explain. I'm not trying to back out of the wedding." Hamilton withdrew a handkerchief from his pocket and nervously mopped his perspiring brow. "The truth of the matter is, I'm requesting a different bride. I've fallen in love with your younger daughter, Mariette. I'm asking your permission to marry her instead."

"Good God, man!" Lowell stormed. "You already have a bride, and the wedding is less than a fortnight away."

Spencer Hamilton had the grace to look embarrassed. "I realize that, sir, and I assure you, I never meant for this to happen. Juliana is a fine young woman, and I've a great deal of regard for her. But you yourself know she has been less than receptive to me. Sometimes I think she's only marrying me to please you and her mother." He turned and began to pace the floor. "But with Mariette, it's different. She seems to enjoy my company. She strives to make me comfortable. She sees to my every whim. Isn't that the way a bride-to-be should conduct herself?"

Lowell dropped back into his chair. "Mariette, you say? Yes, she would be more accommodating, I suppose."

At his words, Juliana silently closed the book she held and laid it aside. She removed the spectacles she wore for reading, folded them and slipped them into the pocket of her gown.

"Have you discussed this with Juliana?" her father continued.

"No, I haven't. I thought it might be best to seek your advice before saying anything to her."

"You know it's customary for the eldest daughter to marry first?"

"Naturally. But Juliana is so fond of flaunting tradition she surely wouldn't hold anyone to that."

From her concealed vantage point, Juliana gave in to the smile that was trembling on her lips. Spencer knew her better than she'd thought.

"I take it you and Mariette have been renewing your acquaintance behind Juliana's back."

"We haven't had to. Lately when I've come to call, Juliana has been preoccupied with one thing or another. I swear, it's almost as if she's avoiding me." Hamilton fussed with the lace on the cuff of his coat. "In her stead, Mariette has made me feel welcome. By comparison, your older daughter seems cold and unfeeling. I don't mean to insult her, but after getting to know the warmth and sweetness of Mariette, I simply don't think I could tolerate being married to Juliana after all."

"I can't fault you for that," Lowell admitted. "Mariette has a womanly way that somehow Juliana has never had.

But still and all, she is your betrothed, and I don't see how we can alter that fact."

Just then a knock sounded at the library door, and Juliana saw her younger sister enter the room. Mariette glanced anxiously from one man to the other as she glided to Hamilton's side. "Has Spencer told you, Father?" she queried in soft tones.

Clearing his throat uneasily, Dodsworth Lowell said, "Look here, Mariette, I should be very angry with you for stirring up all this trouble."

The girl's mouth pursed in a charming pout. "But I didn't set out to make Spencer fall in love with me," she protested. "It just happened. The day after I returned from the Continent with Auntie Lowell, he was here and we saw each other for the first time in years and years." She looked up at Hamilton, a smile lighting her heart-shaped face. "I remembered him as the big bully who used to chase us through the meadows when we were children down at Quarrystones."

Hamilton returned the smile. "And I remembered you as the little nuisance with tangled hair who used to spy on me."

Dodsworth Lowell waved a hand. "None of that silliness matters right now. What I want to know is, where was Juliana when the two of you were getting reacquainted?"

Mariette shrugged delicate shoulders. "Who can say? You know Juli, Father. She was probably off somewhere with her precious books or paints or flowers. She would rather be wandering alone through the park than entertaining Spencer. Really, she has treated him shamefully."

Lowell sighed and rubbed his forehead. "I know what you're saying is no doubt the truth, but surely you must see there is little I can do?"

"Father," Mariette cried, "you can't mean to go ahead with the wedding? It's impossible now. I love Spencer. I won't stand by and allow you to cause all of us to be miserable!"

"Instead, you just want me to make Juliana miserable?"

"No, I don't mean that. But consider this: Juliana will never be an adequate wife to any man. She's too bookish, too smart and opinionated for her own good. Though we are her family and care for her, even we have to admit that she's plain-looking. Perhaps she's one of those women destined to be a spinster. Have you ever thought that she might be happier as such?"

"Don't be cruel, Etta," her father admonished. "Besides, even if what you say is correct, I still have to think of Juliana. And to be honest, I see no way we can come to an agreeable solution."

Juliana chose that moment to make her presence known. Over the years, she had managed to cultivate a passable sense of humor about her shortcomings, but even so, there was a limit to the amount of verbal censure she could abide. Rising from her seat in the shadows, she said, "Really, Father, it's very simple."

Both men and Mariette turned to stare, as if shocked by her unexpected appearance. Before any of them could speak, Juliana hurried on. "I hereby release Spencer from our engagement. I wouldn't care to marry him knowing he's in love with someone else."

"Juliana, are you certain?" her father asked, obviously distrustful of her calm demeanor. "You have a legal right to insist upon the marriage, you know."

Juliana saw Spencer's intended protest, and her lips twitched. It would almost be worth it to make him think she was seriously considering such a reaction. "Yes, I realize that. However, I'll be happy to step aside and let Mariette become his bride in my place." She started to walk from the room, but paused at the door to turn back and say, "There's only one thing I ask."

"And what is that, Daughter?"

She drew a deep breath. "That you will permit me to have Quarrystones Castle even though I'm not to be married."

"Now see here, Juli, that's not fair!" exclaimed Mariette. "Father has promised the manor house as a part of the bride's dowry."

"Don't forget," Juliana reminded her sister, "I was a part of the bargain, also. If I'm to lose my prospective husband, then I wouldn't think it such a tragedy for you to lose title to a country estate you neither need nor want."

Quarrystones Castle was the Lowells' summer home, located in Kent, nearly a day's ride from London. In recent years, Juliana and her brother Jeremy had been the only family members who really enjoyed staying there. Because she loved it so passionately and had begged her father repeatedly, he had agreed to deed it over to Juliana and her new husband upon their marriage.

Dodsworth Lowell now looked from one daughter to the other, his ruddy face creased in thought. "I suppose Spence doesn't really need the estate, and Mariette, you've never cared for it. Perhaps it would be just compensation for Juliana."

"Sir, you know that your estate adjoins my own place, Moorlands," spoke up Hamilton. "I've already made extensive plans for combining the two. And shouldn't Mariette have a dowry of some kind? It's the custom."

"She can have money," Juliana said. "She'd prefer that anyway. She has always despised Quarrystones."

"It's true, Spence," her father affirmed. "Mariette hates being buried in the country. If you plan to marry her, I should think you'd invest in some city property."

Spencer Hamilton looked agitated. "Of course, I'd want to marry Etta with or without a dowry."

"Good, then you can have no objection to Father giving me the country house." Juliana smiled faintly. "If I am to remain a spinster, it's only fitting that I have a place of my own in which to live."

"Juliana, you're being selfish," Mariette objected. "Think of Spencer."

"I've agreed to end the engagement without a fuss, haven't I? That should be worth possession of Quarrystones. Now, I'd like to consider the matter settled."

With that, she turned and left the room, closing the door quietly behind her.

Juliana hastened upstairs, hoping to reach the privacy of her bedchamber before her composure deserted her. She leaned against the closed door and waited for feelings of misery to surface. The last two months had been devoted entirely to preparations for her wedding, and now she must suffer the embarrassment of being unwanted, of being pushed aside for her younger sister.

Instead of misery, however, she was experiencing a small, hopeful thrust of joy. Could it be that she was to be released from marriage to a man she really didn't care for, and given the one thing she wanted beyond all else, Quarrystones?

She stepped to the mirror and bent close to study her face. She thought it a plain, ordinary face, and wasn't surprised that Spencer had been so easily enamored of Mariette. Beside her dark, somber appearance, her sister must have seemed like some fragile fairy-child.

As she pictured Mariette's cloud of burnished gold curls

and sparkling aquamarine eyes, Juliana's level blue-grey gaze took in her own thick, brown hair pulled back into a severe knot and she smiled wryly. Nothing there to catch a man's eye.

Juliana's sister and brother were both fair, plump, and handsome like their parents, but as Etta had once told her in a high temper over something, she could easily have been a changeling, an orphan left on the Lowells' doorstep by some foreigner.

But Juliana was, above all else, sensible, and she had long since stopped feeling pain over her lack of beauty. At this moment, she was very nearly in a mood to celebrate it.

The bedroom door was opened and the impudent face of her younger brother peered around its edge. "Is it true?" Jeremy Lowell asked, grinning, "Is Etta truly going to marry Spencer?"

"It would seem that way," Juliana replied primly.

Her brother's yelp of joy rang through the room. "Oh, huzzah! I'm so glad!"

"Glad?" Juliana struggled to contain her mirth. "How can you be glad that I've been thrown over?"

"Because this means you won't be leaving home, Juli. I'll still have someone to play games and ride with."

Her laughter burst forth. "Why, you horrid wretch! You don't give a fig for my feelings, do you?"

Jeremy looked surprised. "I thought you'd be happy. Remember what you said about Spencer last week? That he looked like a terrier in a waistcoat, walking around on his hind legs?"

"But he is a very *rich* terrier, Jeremy, and at my age I should be getting married. I'd hoped the acquisition of a fortune might make a husband more tolerable."

"Oh, Juli, you're only nineteen. Mama says you won't really be an old maid until you're twenty."

They laughed together. "Then, of course, I must quit worrying about it," she said airily. "So, what do you say? Shall we go for a ride in the park to celebrate my continuing freedom?"

Jeremy agreed readily and dashed away to ask the groom to saddle their horses. Juliana had just gotten into her riding habit when Mariette marched into the bedroom.

Hands on her hips, she surveyed Juliana with blazing eyes. "How can you be so mean and grasping?"

"Mean and grasping? After I've disengaged myself from Spencer?"

"I want Quarrystones."

"Don't you mean that Spencer wants Quarrystones?" Juliana asked, her tone cool. "After all, you've never cared for it. We haven't been allowed to spend a summer there in two years because you wanted to remain in London, close to society."

"Spencer has plans for the estate. Naturally, I want to see my husband happy."

"Then I suggest you look for other ways to accomplish that."

"You're a witch," Mariette cried. Moving with the quickness of a snake, she slapped Juliana's face. "You're only being hateful because you're jealous."

Juliana rubbed her stinging cheek, her dark eyes sparkling in challenge. "Don't ever hit me again, Etta. You're no longer a sickly child that I have to indulge."

"Go ahead and slap me back. I know you'd like to."

"I'm not eight years old anymore, either. I'm past that sort of childishness."

"You hate me, don't you? You've always envied me because everyone says I'm prettier and more graceful. And because you know that men like me best."

"I don't hate you, Etta," Juliana said calmly. "The truth is, I've never aspired to being either pretty or graceful. And since I don't cultivate the friendship of men, it hasn't bothered me that they prefer your company. What does bother me is that you're acting like a spoiled brat over this."

"Spoiled brat?" Mariette's tone grew shrill.

"Yes. It seems very much as if you have coveted things you thought I had. It's the only reason I can think of that you'd want Spencer or Quarrystones."

"Oh!" Mariette stamped her slippered foot. "You don't need to insult me and think you're going to get away with it, Juli. That estate should belong to Spencer, and, I warn you, I intend to see that it does."

When Juliana and Jeremy had returned from their ride in the park, she was summoned into the library where her mother and father were waiting to speak to her.

"Yes?" she murmured, closing the door behind her. She tried to ignore the dread she was feeling.

"Juli," her father began, "I've been thinking about this business with Spencer. Are you certain you don't mind the change in plans?"

She sank into a chair. "I'm certain."

"You don't harbor any resentment toward Etta, do you?" asked her quiet, fair-haired mother anxiously. Eliza Lowell had never tolerated quarreling among her children when she could prevent it. All three of them knew that she preferred the surface of any situation to appear calm, for then she could blithely disregard whatever might stir below.

"I don't resent Mariette. After all, she can't help what happened."

Dodsworth Lowell cleared his throat, his double chin quivering with conviction. "Good. Now, Juli, about Quarrystones. Your mother has a suggestion that should prove suitable to all."

With a deepening sense of disquiet, Juliana raised her dark brows and waited for him to go on.

"I understand how much Quarrystones means to you. It was your summer home as a child and naturally you have fond memories of times spent there. But, my dear girl, as your mother has pointed out, it wouldn't be at all proper for you to live way down there alone."

"But the Cliftons are there."

"The Cliftons are getting on in age, may I remind you? Maybe they wouldn't want to be responsible for an unattached female."

"You have all your friends and family here in London, dear," her mother went on. "Why would you want to leave them behind? I've suggested to your father that he purchase a small townhouse for your very own. Something close by, so we can keep a watchful eye on you."

"You've all assured me I'm incapable of finding a man to take care of me," Juli said stubbornly. "Therefore, don't you think it would be best for me to start being responsible for myself right away?"

"Of course, of course," her father readily agreed. "But, here in London. Not in the country. It's too dangerous for a young woman alone. There are too many outlaws and rogues about these days. No, it really wouldn't do at all."

"You can hire a competent companion as soon as you are settled," Eliza Lowell said, unaware of Juliana's clenched jaw. "You won't be able to carry out any of these plans until Etta and Spencer have been married, but after they're off on their honeymoon, I promise that we'll get you settled in your own little house."

Juliana rose to her feet. "Do I understand this to be your way of telling me you're giving Quarrystones to Spencer Hamilton?"

"The fact is, Spencer has offered to buy the estate." Her father's gaze dropped. "You know that Quarrystones has become a financial drain, Juliana. We realize no income from it anymore, and now that the family doesn't ever go there to stay, it would be foolish for me to hang onto it. If I can get it off my hands by selling it to Spencer and make a profit in the bargain, then you have to agree that it's the thing to do. He'll put the land to good use, I've no doubt."

"But I love Quarrystones," Juliana cried. "I can't bear to see it go out of the family."

"Why, Juli, dear," chided her mother, "Spencer and Etta are family."

"You know how Mariette feels about the place. If an opportunity to sell it ever arose, she wouldn't hesitate. Father, please reconsider."

"Had you carried out our bargain, Juli, the estate would have been yours. But you chose to regard your forthcoming marriage as something less than desirable and Spence turned to another. I'm afraid that's your fault. He has come to me with a very generous offer, and I don't see how I can refuse to sell the estate to him. I'm first and foremost a businessman, if you'll remember."

"Yes, I remember," Juliana retorted. "When has anything ever come before your beloved business? Even your family?"

"Juliana Lowell!" Her mother was shocked, which, for some perverse reason, pleased Juliana.

"I won't tolerate being spoken to like that," growled Dodsworth Lowell. "I have tried to be fair to you, but right now, I find I'm seriously regretting my offer to buy you a townhouse."

"It doesn't matter. I would have declined it anyway." Juliana turned to leave the room.

"Where are you going?" he roared. "I haven't dismissed you."

Her chin lifted stubbornly. "There can be nothing else to say, Father. You're giving the estate to Spencer."

"Selling, not giving."

"And I'm to reside in your house until you declare otherwise."

"Precisely." He looked questioningly at his wife. "I don't think there's anything more we need to discuss. You may go, Daughter."

Juliana was furious. Never would she stand by and let her beloved Quarrystones be turned over to someone with so little regard for it. Spencer would strip it of any value, then sell it to the first man who came along and wanted it.

In desperation, she began to pace up and down the length of her bedroom. At first, there seemed no solution to her dilemma, but her quick, capable mind refused defeat and she soon concocted a plan of sorts.

With growing determination, she packed some of her clothes into a leather traveling bag. If her parents thought that, at her advanced age, she was going to simply accept their unfair edict, they were mistaken. In the morning she would slip out of the house and take a public conveyance to Quarrystones. Perhaps they might think differently about selling the estate to Spencer if they had to turn her out to do it. And once she was safely ensconced there, she'd refuse to leave, no matter what. If they sold it, they'd have to do so with her barricaded inside.

That night as she lay in her bed and stared at the ceiling, waiting for sleep to come, she started to doubt whether she would actually have the temerity to carry out her plan. Years of respectful obedience had taken their toll. She was afraid. Perhaps her family was right; perhaps she was destined to live out her years as a meek spinster under her father's protection.

But here she was, jouncing along in a stagecoach she shared with three other passengers. All it had taken to renew her courage was an early morning visit from Mariette, who came to gloat about the sale of the country estate to her future husband. Juliana had merely turned over in bed, as if too sleepy to argue, but when her sister had gone, she'd thrown back the bedcovers and leaped to her feet.

With a new burst of daring, she'd crept into her father's study and removed the deed to the estate from his desk; if it was in her possession, it would surely delay any sale of the property. Then she left a hastily scribbled note explaining her destination, but warning that if they came after her with the idea of making her return to London, she would create a scandalous scene that would have her mother taking to her bed in shame.

As soon as Juliana was out the study door, she paused, almost deciding to go back and retrieve the note. Dodsworth Lowell wasn't easily threatened and he would greatly resent her effort to do so. But then she remembered all she stood to lose, and, squaring her shoulders, left the message for her father.

Now she was less than an hour from her destination and

had already begun to experience excitement about the prospect of seeing the old country house again. Late April at Quarrystones was wonderful.

She glanced around the interior of the coach, wondering where her fellow travelers were going and whether they could expect to find a similar welcome at the end of their journeys. There was a middle-aged couple sitting across from her. They clutched several parcels wrapped in brown paper, so she could only surmise they had been in the city shopping. They looked fairly well-to-do, though a bit rustic.

Right beside her sat a young girl on her way to a job as a chambermaid in a large country mansion. Pleased by her ability to obtain such a coveted position, she had chattered incessantly for the first half of the trip. However, the older couple seemed disinterested and Juliana was lost in her own thoughts, so the girl had finally fallen into a petulant silence.

Juliana couldn't help but wonder with grave amusement what exactly she was doing there, in the midst of such ill-matched traveling companions. If she were back in London, she'd be sitting down to tea at that moment, listening to her mother and Mariette exchange gossip, winking at Jeremy as he slipped bits of cake to the dog. But her mood began to lighten as she realized they were drawing closer to Quarrystones. She leaned forward to study the countryside beyond the coach windows.

Gusting winds sent little fluffs of clouds scudding across the face of the springtime sun, lighting the rolling hills below with alternating sunshine and shadow. Occasionally, a quick spate of rain would strike the window, but the scene never lapsed into gloom because of the miles of yellow gorse lying like a bright carpet over the earth.

Unexpectedly, from the corner of her eye, she caught

sight of movement outside the stagecoach. She was startled to see two horsemen riding alongside, brandishing evil-looking pistols. At her gasp of surprise, the country man across from her lurched forward to look out the window.

"Highwaymen," he said in clipped tones. "Better hide your valuables, ladies." He himself drew a fat wallet from his pocket and began searching for a safe place to conceal it. He finally settled on stuffing it into a large crevice at the end of the seat. Juliana watched in fascination, unable to grasp the situation. Meanwhile, the coach lurched to a stop. A confusion of men's rough voices disturbed the stunned silence inside the coach.

She heard someone order the coachmen to step down, and she knew they were obeying because the coach dipped and swayed beneath their descending weight. Beside her, the young girl began to whimper.

"Hush," Juliana whispered. "Don't let them know they frighten you."

At that moment the door was thrown open and a masked man peered in at them. "Come on out, ladies and gentleman. We have a little business to conduct with you." A second figure stood close by, hefting the pistol in his hand menacingly.

As the passengers moved out of the coach, a strong wind blew rain in their faces, and Juliana pulled the hood of her brown woolen cloak over her hair. She was the last one to alight from the vehicle, and when the masked man put up a hand to help her, she shrugged away.

"I can manage, thank you," she said. Hearing a low chuckle, she glanced up to see a third fellow, this one seated on the largest horse she'd ever seen.

"Jesus, it's the Kentish Gypsy," exclaimed the stout country man in an awed voice. "I never thought to see the day."

Juliana took a closer look at the man looming over them. Indeed, he was dressed as a gypsy. He wore a snowy-white shirt, red cummerbund, and tight black trousers beneath a billowing black cape. His boots were black and shiny, rising to his knees. One long leg was casually thrown across the front of the saddle, and he affected an insolent pose, a hand resting lightly on the pistol at his side.

Juliana's gaze traveled upward to his face, but except for a straight mouth, square chin and strong jawline, it was covered with a mask. His hair was concealed by a red bandanna worn beneath a brimmed black hat. In one ear gleamed a small golden hoop.

"Shall we see if these folks have any valuables?" the gypsy asked, dismounting with ease and walking toward them. "Turn out your pockets, man."

Hastily, the traveler did as he was bid, handing over a few coins and a watch. The gypsy reached out a gloved hand and deftly removed the pearl stickpin he wore, and while the man made no protest, his wife gasped in anger.

"You animal!" she spat. "It's a fine thing when the gentry isn't safe to travel the roads of this country."

The smile on the masked man's face faded abruptly and with it went his air of jauntiness. Suddenly he seemed much more dangerous. The country woman shrank back and made no objection when he took her handbag from her.

Next he turned to the young chambermaid and as he did so, his charming smile returned. The girl gave him an answering smile, a bold look leaping into her eyes. Apparently, her terror was short-lived.

"You'll soon see I have nothing worth stealing," she said saucily. The gypsy laughed.

"Are you certain of that?" His voice was deep and a shade husky. The girl colored prettily as she interpreted the meaning behind his words, and one slim hand flew upward to smooth her fine blond hair in an instinctively provocative fashion. Her movement brought his attention to a gold locket she wore about her neck, and he reached out to touch it.

"What have we here, milady? I thought you said you had nothing worth stealing."

The girl's eyes widened. "Oh, heavens, not my locket! Please don't take it from me."

He smiled and tugged gently at the chain. "And, pray tell, why not?"

Tears sprang into her large brown eyes and spilled over onto her wind-pinkened cheeks. "It belonged to my mother," she said. "She died when I was born. It's all I have to remember her by. Please don't take it."

The gypsy seemed to consider her statement before he spoke. "Well, sweetheart, your tears seem genuine enough. Let me make you a proposition: I will allow you to keep your locket if you pay my price."

"What price?"

His smile was dazzling, showing perfect white teeth. "I should think a locket as lovely as this would be worth a kiss."

The girl's expression was one of relief. "Is that all?" She giggled. "I'd be most happy to oblige."

The highwayman stepped close to her and put one hand on her waist. The other remained on the butt of his pistol. He lowered his head to hers and kissed her soundly.

Beside them, Juliana stiffened. As if sensing her distaste, the man raised his head and gave her a piercing look. Behind his mask, his eyes glittered briefly, but the chambermaid distracted him by rising to her tiptoes to give him a second kiss. He laughed in surprise.

"If you should ever be interested," the girl said, "I'm to

be employed at Hexworthy Hall. I wouldn't object to seeing you again."

The gypsy backed away and made a sweeping bow. "I shall keep that in mind, sweetheart." He moved toward Juliana, coming to a stop directly in front of her. "And what do you have in the way of valuables, my lady?"

Without saying a word, Juliana handed him her reticule. It contained all the money she'd been able to scrape together, but she didn't consider it worth risking her life over.

As she started to withdraw her hand, he grasped it in his own and turned it palm-downward.

"What is this ring?" he asked abruptly.

"It's my birthstone. An opal."

"You were born under the sign of Libra?"

"Yes, I was," she answered, puzzled.

"I see that you wonder why I ask. It was merely because gypsies believe the opal is unlucky for anyone not born under Libra."

"Then I have nothing to fear," she stated calmly.

"Only that some rogue will steal the gem from you," he countered, a smile pulling at his mouth.

"It isn't valuable."

"Not worth the price of one small kiss to keep it?"

In answer, Juliana slipped the ring from her finger and held it out to him.

One of the other masked men laughed and said something in a strange language. The gypsy made a reply in the same tongue, then turned back to Juliana. He took the ring, tucking it securely into the cummerbund at his waist. Then, before she realized his intent, he quickly broke the slender chain of the necklace she wore and held out his hand for her earrings. In removing them, she pushed back her hood, baring her head. The outlaw stared at her for a long moment.

Again, his man spoke, but the bandit shook his head and Juliana surmised his answer was a negative one. She met his gaze as steadily as she could, hoping he would not guess how her heart hammered in trepidation.

Finally turning away, he called out, "Men, gather the coachmen's valuables and see to the luggage."

The two coachmen did as they were told, apparently unwilling to grumble too much. Their wallets were gathered up by the highwaymen, who then began rifling through the luggage. One of them climbed up onto the vehicle and tossed down the bags belonging to the passengers. A tarpaulin-wrapped roll came to rest at the gypsy outlaw's booted feet, and he looked down at it with interest. Kneeling, he began to undo the cords that bound it.

Taking a deep breath, Juliana cried out, "No! Leave it alone. It's mine."

Surprised by her outburst, he rested an arm across his knee and looked up at her.

"So, at last, something that elicits a reaction from you. I wonder what could be inside this bundle?" His long fingers busied themselves with the cords once again.

Juliana flew at him in a fury, pounding his broad shoulders with her fists. "Leave it alone, I said!"

He turned to grab her flailing arms and push her away, causing her to fall backward onto rocky, gorse-covered ground.

The gypsy rose to his feet and stood towering over her, hands on his hips. Juliana glared up at him, her eyes stormy. The wind had picked the pins from her hair and now dark brown strands whipped and blew about her pale face. Everyone grew silent watching the scene.

"I think there must be something very valuable in this

roll," the outlaw said slowly. "I plan to open it. I'd advise you to stay where you are and not interfere."

Juliana's head came up, but she didn't speak. Her fall had knocked the breath from her body, and she dared not trust her voice. Still, she met his eyes, refusing to show any fear.

The highwayman quickly opened the bundle and unrolled it on the stony ground. "What have we here?" he murmured, picking up a roll of paper. Untying it, he scanned the deed to Quarrystones with interest. "A legal document."

"It's nothing important," Juliana said. "If you don't put it away, it will be ruined by the rain."

He favored her with another long, contemplative look, but gave a shrug, rolled up the deed and tossed it back into the packet. Impatiently, he poked at the bundle's other contents. "Books? Paints and brushes?" Disbelieving, he rapidly searched every corner of the tarpaulin, then shook his head. "That's all it is. No jewelry. No hidden gold." He seemed amused as he turned to study Juliana once again. "Well, you surprise me, my lady. I've never met a female who'd hand over her jewelry without a sigh, then fight like a wildcat for books and paints."

"They're valuable to me."

"Aye, I can see they are." Swiftly, he did up the bundle again, then he reached down a strong hand, pulled her to her feet and placed the parcel in her arms. "They are, however, of no use to me. Therefore, I will return them to you. For a price."

Juliana backed away, coming up against the sturdy wall of the coach. "A price?" she echoed.

"Oh, indeed. The same price I asked for the young lady's locket. Just a kiss."

"Just a kiss! Are you mad?"

"You refuse?" He took the bundle from her. "Then you forfeit your belongings."

Juliana made a grab for the roll, but he held it away from her.

"I don't want to give up my books," she muttered. "They're valuable to me."

"Ah, so you *are* willing to pay the price?"

Juliana looked down at the yellow blooms of the gorse beneath her feet. It seemed the gypsy had won the argument.

"If I must," she said quietly.

She felt his finger beneath her chin and closed her eyes as he raised her face. She didn't want to have to meet the eyes behind his mask.

His lips were soft and warm as they closed over her own, and Juliana flinched at the sensation. Despite her intention, her eyes flew open and she stared into his glittering onyx gaze. His expression was still amused, so she shut her eyes more tightly than before, praying the kiss would end soon.

But the gypsy's mouth continued to cling to hers, and his hard body pressed her back against the side of the stagecoach. He rested one hand on the wheel at her side; with the other he held her bundle of books. Nearly faint from holding her breath, Juliana felt her knees begin to buckle. For a wild moment, she thought she might swoon there and then.

Instead, the gypsy pulled away and took her elbow with his free hand. Suddenly he was helping her back into the carriage and thrusting the tarpaulin-swathed package at her.

With a sardonic smile, he bent swiftly and plucked a sprig of the gorse at his feet. Handing it to her, he said, "As you English say: 'Gorse, like kissing, is never out of season.' "

Juliana knew then that he was completely aware of her embarrassment. Worse, he enjoyed it.

Her cheeks flamed, but since she didn't know what else

to do, she seized the sprig. "In the language of flowers," she countered, "gorse symbolizes anger."

The highwayman threw back his head and laughed, a richly mellow sound. "Most appropriate," he said, and for the first time, Juliana realized there was a curious lilt to his deep voice. She heard it again, distinctly, as he said, "Well, then, until we meet again."

He gestured for the other passengers to return to their seats within the coach, gallantly offering a helping hand to each of the ladies.

Then he turned and began issuing orders to his men. They scattered the traveling cases, then swung up onto their horses, pistols still cocked and ready. The gypsy mounted his black stallion and, with a mocking smile, rode close to the coach and said, "Now, good sir, if you'll toss me the wallet you thought to hide, I'll be off."

For a few seconds, the disgruntled traveler looked as though he was considering refusal, but then, with a resigned sigh, he retrieved the wallet and tossed it to the highwayman. With a quick salute, the outlaw wheeled and galloped away, followed by his henchmen.

When Juliana leaned forward to make certain they had gone, she saw the last of the riders disappear into a nearby tract of forest. She heaved a huge sigh of relief and hugged her bundle of books.

Then, remembering her mistreatment at the rogue's hands, she was again filled with anger.

Now, not only could she damn her father and Spencer Hamilton. She could also damn the arrogant gypsy highwayman!

Two

Nearly an hour later, Juliana stood at the turn-off to Quarrystones, watching the stagecoach rumble away. The driver had paused just long enough for her to alight and gather her luggage before going on his way, unwilling to suffer any further delays.

Juliana looked about her and took a deep breath of the fresh, damp air. How she detested the jarring noises and smoke of the city! She'd missed the feel of open spaces, the sweet-scented hay meadows, and shady forests whose silence was broken only by the singing of birds.

She shoved her traveling case behind a clump of rhododendron bushes to be fetched later, and, grasping the bundle containing her books and paints, started toward the castle. The lane wound downward from the top of the hill for nearly a mile through thick oak and beech woods. About halfway along the road there was a clearing where Juliana always stopped. From that vantage point, she had a marvelous view of the river valley below and, nestled in a circle of trees, her home. The sight never failed to thrill her. She loved to see the ancient forest and the glimmer of clear water, with the quarry-scarred hill and meadows beyond. Through the silvery haze hovering above the river rose the mellow stone tower of Quarrystones.

Juliana swallowed deeply. No, she would never give up

the fight for the old castle. It was unthinkable that she should ever lose her right to its beauty, its serenity. There could be no other place in the world that would provide such refuge for her.

She hurried on, anxious to see the house and the Cliftons.

After crossing a sturdy wooden bridge, the lane ended in a circular drive in front of the neat timber-framed stables. To reach the manor house, she had to cross yet another bridge, this one a centuries-old stone causeway that spanned the lily moat encircling the island on which the castle itself stood.

As she ran across the causeway, Juliana caught sight of Mrs. Clifton working on her hands and knees in the herb garden in front of the house.

"Essie!" she cried, dropping the bundle and approaching the other woman.

Essie Clifton rocked back on her heels, surprised to hear her name called. A look of shock passed over her blunt features for a moment, then she began to smile. "Oh, lud, it's Miss Juli! What on earth are ye doing here, child? Where did ye come from?"

She scrambled to her feet and, wiping her hands on the white apron she wore, she threw her arms around the girl and hugged her tightly.

"Essie, it's so good to see you." Juliana laughed, holding the woman at arms' length to study her. "You're looking well. How's Will-John?"

"The husband is fit, Miss Juli." Essie had referred to Will-John as "the husband" ever since Juliana could remember.

"I'm so glad. I've missed you both and wondered about you every day."

Essie tried to look stern. "Ye haven't yet answered my question, young lady. What are ye doing here?"

"I've come a long way, and I'm tired. I don't want to be scolded."

Essie's round black eyes snapped. "Ye've run away from your family, haven't ye? What have those butter-brains done to ye now?" She patted Juliana's shoulder. "I know ye well enough to know something's amiss. What is it?"

"Could we go inside and sit down? There's quite a lot to be told."

"Then a bracing cup of hyssop tea is what ye need. See, I've just been cutting some of the tops." She seized the small willow basket at her feet. "Let's go into the house."

The house. As soon as Juliana turned to face it, everything was suddenly right again. None of the things she dreaded and feared would ever happen here. It was as if the house itself opened welcoming arms to protect her.

Fierce pride overtook Juliana as she studied the faded brick of its Elizabethan facade. Climbing roses etched pretty designs across the brick, their curling tendrils gently overhanging the half-timbered balconies of the second story. A profusion of vines twisted their way up the tower, which rose from the edge of the moat and was reflected in its shimmering waters.

She sighed happily. "I'd nearly forgotten how lovely this place really is. Can you imagine?"

Essie gave a gentle snort as she pulled open the heavy door. "I shouldn't wonder. It seems nearly a lifetime since ye've been down here."

"I know. It seems that way to me, too. I should have come long ago. I simply didn't know it would be so easy."

Essie bustled on into the kitchen at the back of the house, tossing words over her shoulder. "I know it was yer family that didn't want to come down. Not enough fancy society to suit them, I suppose."

Juliana paused in the hall to look about her at the well-remembered entryway. Somehow, despite the fact that no fire burned in the little fireplace, the room seemed warm. A woven reed carpet covered the floor, and the plastered walls were bright with framed prints of country life. The old clock on the mantel ticked as loudly as ever, and a bowl of bluebells setting on a table near the wooden settle brightened the shadowy corner. Juliana ran a hand along the smooth banister of the staircase leading upstairs to the bedrooms. The wood was permeated with the sweet scent of lemon balm, which Essie always used to polish the furniture.

"Miss Juli, where are ye?" Essie called from the back room.

"Just having a look about. I'll be there in a moment."

Juliana stepped to the door into the parlor and glanced around. Though it was more formal than the entrance hall, it, too, had a comfortable, old-fashioned feel to it. A dark blue sofa and matching chairs were arranged in front of three, long leaded glass windows overlooking the front lawn. More chairs flanked the ornate stone fireplace in the back corner of the room, and there were wooden shelves filled with her father's books and a collection of old china cups and saucers once belonging to her grandmother. Beyond this room was the dining room, its large windows looking out upon the river.

Knowing Essie would have the tea ready, Juliana hurried back through the hall and into the kitchen. Many happy childhood hours had been spent in that very room where Essie had taught her to bake, and in the adjoining still-room, where she had watched in fascination as Essie had set herbs to dry or simmered strange-smelling concoctions in an old washtub for dyeing cloth.

"More than anything, I've missed this kitchen," she confessed, dropping into a spindle-back chair at the huge, round table.

Essie nodded. "Something must have told me ye were coming, child, because I took time this morning to bake poppyseed cakes." She placed an earthenware plate of the cakes on the table. "I know they were always yer favorite."

"Mmm, they're heavenly. I couldn't have asked for a better welcome home."

Essie poured out two cups of fragrant tea which she sweetened liberally with honey. Pushing one toward Juliana, she settled herself in the chair opposite and said, "Now, perhaps ye'd better tell me what has happened."

"First of all, the wedding is off," Juliana said, slowly stirring the tea. "No, that's not exactly true. The wedding will go on as planned, only I'm not going to be the bride."

Essie's thick grey brows drew together fiercely. "What are ye saying?"

Juliana smiled. "Don't look so menacing. I never felt that strongly about Spencer anyway. And I'm certain he and Mariette are far better suited to each other."

"Mariette?" The word was a hoarse screech. "What has that spoiled minx gone and done now?"

"It really wasn't anything Etta did. It was just that Spencer suddenly saw her again after all these years and was completely smitten with her. You've never been especially fond of Mariette, yet even you have to admit she's beautiful."

"There's some as say vipers are beautiful," Essie reminded her. "And ye yerself know the monkshood flower is lovely, but the plant is as poison as any growing."

"Nevertheless, Spencer has spoken with Father, and it has been decided that Mariette will marry him in my place. And I don't mind."

Essie's expression was doubtful. "Then what is it that

troubles ye? And don't bother trying to put me off, because I know ye too well. I can always tell when something's wrong with ye."

"I won't put you off," Juliana promised. "I'm counting on you to help me think of some way to solve the problem. You see, Father had promised to give me Quarrystones as a wedding gift, but now that I'm not to be married, he's going to give it to Spencer and Mariette."

"Mariette hates the place! Surely your father wouldn't see fit to turn it over to her."

"Not to her, but to Spencer. She feels it should be his because it adjoins his estate. He claims to have made extensive plans for combining the two farms."

"Oh." For a moment, the older woman's lips clamped firmly shut. Finally she said, "I won't say anything about that right now, but, child, there's things going on that ye don't know. Will-John and I have been worrying about how much ye knew and what ye were going to think when ye found out about . . ." Her gaze grew speculative, and she allowed her words to fade, as though she had reconsidered speaking.

"When I found out about what?"

" 'Tis a long story and one that will keep for a bit. First, I want to hear the rest of yer news."

"Well, I told Father I would release Spencer from our engagement on one condition: that he stand by his promise to deed this land to me. I think he would have agreed soon enough, but then Mother and Mariette interfered."

"Ah, of course," Essie muttered, dryly.

"And then Spencer offered to buy Quarrystones, and you know Father where business is concerned. He sees a chance to make a profit and thinks I can be pacified with a little house of my own somewhere near theirs."

"But that isn't what ye want, eh?"

"Essie, you know me better than that. The only place I've ever wanted to live was here at Quarrystones."

"Ye always said so as a child, but, my dearie, ye've grown to be a woman now. Ye'll surely be wanting a home of yer own, with a husband and children."

"You're right about one thing. I am grown, and it's time I faced certain things."

"Such as?"

"For whatever reason, there are some women in this world who aren't meant to marry."

This time Essie's snort was less delicate. "Oh, and I suppose ye be one of them? By the furry muskrat's tail, who has been filling yer head with such nonsense?"

Juliana couldn't repress laughter at the older woman's indignation. "It's not nonsense."

"Well, now, 'tis, and that's all there is to it." Essie got to her feet and drew herself up to her full five feet of height.

"It's not, Essie. Just look at me."

"I am, missy. And do ye want to know what I see? I see a lovely young woman who's been told all her life she isn't as pretty as Mariette, she isn't as friendly as Mariette, she isn't as fine a dancer as Mariette. It fair makes me shake with anger. Ye know, the sun does not rise nor does it set at the request of the fair Mariette."

Despite herself, Juliana had to laugh again. She rose from her chair and enfolded the small woman in a warm hug.

"You're a dear soul to defend me like that, but it isn't necessary."

"Someone needs to look out for ye. Lord knows, yer own parents can't be bothered." Essie frowned. "It's an everlasting pity Mariette was born such a sickly babe. By the time she outgrew her frailty, everyone in the family was used to letting her have her own way. She may look like an angel, but I swear she has a devil's heart."

"I wish I could disagree with you, but the truth is, Mariette would be a much nicer person if only she acted as pretty as she looks." Giving Essie's shoulder a final pat, Juliana sank back into her chair.

"I used to hate it when people compared me to Mariette, but it doesn't bother me anymore. I've realized there are qualities more important to me then social graces. I like having an analytical mind and the brains to find out things for myself. And I have a certain talent for painting that I'm thankful for."

"Juli, if ye'd only listen to me."

At that moment, the kitchen doorway was filled with the bulk of a short, rotund man.

"I saw a case on the causeway and brought it up to the house. I says to myself, could it mean Miss Juli's come home?"

"And sure enough, Will-John, here I am." Juliana flew into the old man's arms, hugging him tightly. "I've missed you so much."

Will-John Clifton patted her on the back with one hand and surreptitiously wiped his eyes with the other. " 'Tis mighty good to see you, lass. Mighty good."

"You don't know how wonderful it is to be back home," Juliana said, stepping away to have a better look at him. He was dressed in brown homespun with a battered hat upon his thinning white hair and wooden clogs on his feet. His dark eyes were like two melon seeds within the wrinkled breadth of his face, a face that was dominated by a rather large nose. It was a nose that some said had been made larger and redder by his well-known fondness for his own homemade beer.

"When will the rest of your family be arriving, Miss Juli?"

"They're not coming, Will-John. I was just trying to explain the situation to Essie. You see, we've quarreled and I've come down on my own. I expect Father will send someone after me in a few days, because he knows where I've gone. But I'll have to figure that out later. For now, I'm going to settle in for a nice, long stay."

He looked from her to his wife, clearly puzzled. He scratched his head. "I don't understand. Your wedding is so near at hand, why would you leave home?"

"Never ye mind that, Will-John," advised Essie. "Ye'll learn the truth of it in due time. For now, ye'd best get yerself on up the lane to fetch Miss Juli's other traveling case. I expect she's tired and would like a rest before supper. And when's she through resting, she'll want her things."

"Perhaps you could send one of the stable hands," Juliana suggested. "There's no need for you to go all that long way."

"Don't ye fret about it," said Essie. "If ye've finished yer tea, why don't ye go on up to yer room? I'll be along to set things to rights."

"You needn't bother, Essie. You always keep this house as if you're expecting company. I'm certain everything is fine." She started from the room, then stopped in the doorway and smiled. "I simply can't seem to find the words to tell you how splendid it is to be back at Quarrystones with both of you. Somehow I feel that everything is going to work out now."

"Of course it is," Essie agreed. "Go along with ye and rest."

Juliana had just set foot on the bottom stair when she decided to go back to the kitchen and make one last plea for Will-John to send a stablehand for her bag. As she approached the kitchen, she heard Essie's angry voice.

"Ye've got to get him out of here now, Will-John Clifton. It didn't matter so much before, but now that Miss Juliana is here to stay, he'll have to go."

"But where, Essie? There's no place else."

As she listened, Juliana smiled to herself. No doubt the elderly couple had given shelter to one wild animal or another. They'd done it many times when she was a child, rescuing wounded deer or badgers, once even a fox.

"Ye've got to find a place," Essie insisted. "We don't want to put Miss Juli in any danger."

"It may take some time."

Juliana turned away. Perhaps if she acted oblivious to their clandestine activities, they'd allow whatever poor, hurt creature they'd adopted to stay.

Juliana discovered she couldn't sleep after all. She was too restless to lay still, so after a while, she found an old pair of walking shoes and slipped out of the house. She could hear Essie banging kettles in the kitchen and something was already starting to smell good.

She decided to take the path that wound back over the causeway, behind the stables and around the small lake formed by the moat. Long ago some ambitious landowner had diverted the Quarry River to form the moat for the manor house, leaving it situated on a virtual island. At the east side of the house, the natural curve of the river formed the boundary, while along the west, it was a manmade channel. Where the channel flowed under the old causeway to join the river, careful damming had produced a lake, and at the south end of this, the water tumbled down over rocks, making a shallow waterfall before again following the river's flow.

There was a hump-backed bridge above the falls, and here

Juliana paused to look back toward the castle. It was one of her favorite views of the house. From that angle, the tower was foremost. She loved the way the still water mirrored it, casting back a perfect reflection of its vine-covered walls and the picturesque cupola with which it was crowned.

Suddenly she felt a chill and glanced quickly around. For an instant, she had the feeling someone was there, watching her. She experienced a tiny prickle of fear, the first she had ever known at Quarrystones.

Straightening her shoulders, she strolled on, unwilling to let her imagination play tricks on her. And it had to be imagination. What other explanation could there be? No doubt the arguments at home and then the arduous journey down from London had taken a toll on her.

Unbidden, the memory of the gypsy highwayman came into her mind. How ironic that the first real kiss she'd ever received had come from an outlaw! Her face burned with the thought of it. The worst part had been all those people looking on, the men with amusement, the married couple with disgust, and the young chambermaid with envy and undisguised malice, which had lasted until Juliana had alighted at Quarrystones.

And yet, she couldn't help but think, the kiss itself hadn't been nearly as unpleasant as she'd have expected. It'd had much more warmth than the chaste kisses on the cheek Spencer had sometimes given her. Spencer was always the gentleman, of course. Naturally he would show more restraint than a bold gypsy scoundrel. Still, she wondered how long Mariette would be willing to put up with such impeccable manners. She found herself smiling at the thought.

With delight, she spied a wealth of marsh marigolds growing along the swampy riverbank and soon forgot all thoughts of Spencer, her sister and illicit kisses. Unmindful of her long skirts, she knelt for a closer look, putting out a gentle hand to touch delicate yellow petals.

She had always picked the marigolds as a child, but they never lasted long enough to take home and put into water. One day her current governess had suggested that, instead of picking the flower and destroying it, she get her watercolors and paint it, thereby preserving it forever. That had begun her long fascination with painting flowers, something she had not tired of in nearly ten years. She'd presented that first effort to Essie, who framed it and hung it in the room where she and Will-John slept. It still hung there today.

Juliana got to her feet, promising herself that one day soon she'd take her paints into the garden and start a study of the purple pansies she knew she would find there.

Ignoring her damp and muddied skirt, she wandered along the sandy path, bordered on one side by the river and on the other by a sweeping tide of brilliant yellow daffodils, dipping and swaying in the sharp wind blowing off the water.

The path entered a grove of wild cherry trees, whose branches were laden with heavy falls of blossoms. The fragrance was dazzling, and Juliana stopped to breathe it in. Through the cascades of white blossoms, she had another, closer view of the house, this time the back portion. There on the end was the stone tower, but the breadth of the back, broken only by paned windows and the arched blue-grey door to the kitchen, was a brighter brick than the front side of the house. Built four centuries earlier, the house had been added to and remodeled, and each section had a character of its own.

As she watched, a pair of black swans sailed around the curve of the river and glided regally past the back door. She knew Essie often tossed them scraps of bread from the kitchen, but no such offering was forthcoming at the moment. No doubt she was too busy preparing an elaborate meal for Juliana's homecoming to spare a thought for the swans.

Juliana lifted her face, letting the scented falls of cherry blossoms caress it. There was nothing in London to compare with that.

Without warning, the feeling of being watched came again. She scanned the windows of the house, but could detect no one in any of them. Of course, the evening sun was beginning to set behind the wall of trees and the house was cast into gloom, so it was possible that someone might be standing unseen in the shadows. Juliana felt distinctly uneasy. Reaching up a hand, she broke off a spray of blossoms and, holding it to her nose, sniffed appreciatively. Again her eyes moved slowly about the edge of the lake and over the old manor house. If, indeed, someone was spying on her, she had no idea who it was or why he should be doing so.

From his vantage point in the old tower, the man watched her, absorbed by the way the wind whipped her skirts and seemed to blow her slight figure along the riverbank. How he wished he dared leave his dark sanctuary and go out into the sunshine to walk with her. Of course, Essie would have his head if he tried something so rash, and no doubt Juliana herself would have something to say about the matter.

There was an unusual courage about the woman, something he had rarely seen. He liked the straight way she'd held her body, the unmistakable challenge that glowed in her stormy eyes.

His laugh was soft on the quiet air. The old couple had been right: their Miss Juli was a treasure. One a discerning man would be wise to steal for his own.

* * *

An aggressive gust of wind chilled Juliana, sending her scurrying back along the path the way she had come. When she reached the house, Essie met her at the door.

"It's supper time. I was beginning to worry about ye, Miss Juli. When I couldn't find ye in yer room, I didn't know where ye had gotten off to."

"I couldn't sleep after all, Essie, so I went for a walk."

"Ye shouldn't be doing things like that," fussed the older woman.

Juliana looked surprised. "Why ever not? You know I've always roamed the grounds here. You never worried before."

Essie's eyes dropped. "Ah, I guess I'm just becoming an old fuss-feathers. Don't ye be paying any heed to me."

"It's nice to be worried about, but there's no reason for you to stew. Now, I'm going upstairs to change my clothes, and then I'll be right down for supper."

As she reached the second-floor landing, a thought occurred to her and, instead of proceeding to her own room on the third floor, she went into the large master bedroom where her parents slept when the Lowells stayed at Quarrystones. It was a lovely chamber, her favorite in the castle.

She crossed to the tall bookshelf in the corner where she rapidly scanned the titles looking for a worn book she had often borrowed as a child. Strangely enough, it didn't seem to be in its usual place. She'd have to ask Essie about it, she supposed.

After changing into a fresh gown, Juliana appeared in the dining room where the table was set for three. Essie and Will-John would be joining her for the meal, since the rest of the family wasn't present. Will-John had built a fire on the hearth to ward off the chill of the late spring evening, and the room was filled with candlelight and the pleasant aroma of baked chicken.

As she took her place, Juliana asked, "Does anyone know where the old flower book has gone? I can't seem to find it."

"Have ye looked in the usual place?" Essie asked, shaking out her napkin.

"Yes, in the master bedroom where Father keeps it. I didn't see it there."

Essie flashed a quick look at her husband, who silently shrugged. "I'll have a look myself later," she promised.

"You know, I've been thinking," Juliana said, accepting her plate from Essie. "Since I'm the only one staying at Quarrystones, I think I'll move my things into the master bedroom. It has always been my favorite room anyway."

Essie dropped the spoon she was holding and it clattered against the serving dish. "The master bedroom, Miss Juli? Why, what would yer father say?"

Juliana smiled blandly. "I'm already on his bad side, so one more crime shouldn't matter. If I'm to be allowed to own Quarrystones, I'd take the room sometime anyway. And if I'm to be thrown out, at least I'll have enjoyed it for a while."

Again Essie cast a furtive look at Will-John, who said nothing and began to eat, refusing to meet her gaze. Juliana was aware of their uneasiness, but could discern no cause for it. Ordinarily, they would have applauded her stand. She could only conclude that something odd was going on. Something very odd, indeed.

Later, after Will-John had moved her luggage downstairs to the larger bedchamber and lighted a fire in the fireplace, Essie brought her a glass of sweet wine and a biscuit.

"Ye see, Miss Juli, the book is there on the shelf where it's supposed to be."

Though the leather-bound volume was in its accustomed

place, Juliana was positive it hadn't been earlier. Instead of voicing her suspicion, however, she commented on the delicious flavor of the wine.

"Yes, 'tis from last year's blackberries. The husband nearly outdid himself on this batch, I'm thinking. A sip or two will relax ye and put ye down for a good night's sleep."

"I'm so tired I really don't need the wine." Juliana stifled a broad yawn. "But please tell Will-John that it tastes wonderful."

When the elderly lady had gone, Juliana set the wineglass aside and went to get the book. She crawled back into bed, taking her spectacles from the pocket of her dressing gown. Putting them on, she began turning the pages of the book. It had been written decades before and was a dictionary of the symbolic meanings of plants and flowers, as ascribed to them by the ancient Greeks and Romans. The subject had always fascinated her, and she had referred to the book many times since discovering it in her father's private library.

She ran a slender finger down the page until it came to rest below the listing for wild cherry blossoms.

" 'The white cherry blossom,' " she read aloud, " 'is a symbol for deception.' "

Deception? she thought. *Of course.*

The house had been as warm and welcoming as ever, but she couldn't deny that the Cliftons had acted rather strangely, as though they had something to hide. Something more than a sick fox or a wounded badger, she realized.

It was a matter that needed looking into. The sooner, the better.

Three

Pleased by her requisition of the master bedchamber, Juliana lay in the wide, curtained bed and stared dreamily at the orange flames dancing on the hearth.

Across the room the flickering light accentuated the stones of the curving wall where the outer tower protruded into the room. She'd always loved the odd shape of the chamber, though she regretted that the tower had been closed off and there was no longer any doorway between it and the bedroom.

Someday, she promised herself, *when this house is truly mine, I'll open an entrance into the tower.*

Briefly, she envisioned herself making the derelict structure into a small, private study, its walls fitted with curving bookshelves and a specially made desk to sit in front of the narrow window that overlooked the lily moat.

Gradually, she began to relax and drift into a restless slumber. Soon her regular breathing was the only sound in the room besides the crackle and hiss of the fire.

Slowly, quietly, a whole section of the stone wall moved, swinging forward to reveal an opening large enough for the tall figure of a man to duck through. He stood for a long moment, watching Juliana sleep, then crossed the floor to stand by the bed. When he walked, the firelight glinted off a single gold earring.

As he looked down upon her slender form bathed in moonlight streaming in through an ivy-framed window, one corner of his straight mouth lifted in a smile.

How pretty she looked. And how different from the prim miss in her somber traveling dress, with her hair tortured into that hideous knot. Now, with her body barely concealed by a thin nightgown and her hair spread in dark disarray over the pillow, she had the wild, sweet look of the gypsy girls with whom he'd grown up.

He studied the lovely planes of her face: the slight hollows beneath high cheekbones, the straight nose, the stubborn chin. Sweeping black lashes made heavy shadows beneath winged brows. Eased by sleep, her mouth was soft, the lips gently curved upward.

Something stirred within him as he remembered what it had been like to kiss that vulnerable mouth.

At the time, he had been unable to fully understand his reaction to the righteous young woman he'd encountered on the afternoon stagecoach. Ordinarily, he'd probably never have spared her a second look, especially in the presence of someone like the saucy chambermaid, so obviously willing to share her charms. But even as he had kissed that lady's eager lips, he'd been very much aware of the disapproval of the girl in the ugly brown cloak. Strange that it should have mattered to him, but it had. And then, when she so calmly turned aside his attempt at flirtation, he'd been completely intrigued.

He was filled with admiration for her spirited defense of her belongings. He didn't think he'd ever known another woman who cared more for books than jewelry, and since their meeting, he'd been haunted by a vision of her sitting among the gorse blossoms, hair streaming out in the wild wind.

Juliana sighed and turned in her sleep. Swiftly, the man stepped away from the bed, moving across the room to disappear into the darkness beyond the stone wall. The wall swung silently back into place.

Juliana awoke, experiencing the same unease that had plagued her since her arrival. A quick glance around the room told her all was as it should be. But as she closed her eyes, she was troubled by a fragment of the dream she'd been having. A dream in which a large, dark figure had leaned over her, watching her. Now the same figure drifted through her mind once more, and this time it had the masked face and mocking eyes of the gypsy highwayman.

In the morning, Juliana could think of no good way to approach the Cliftons about their odd behavior. She wondered if it could have been her imagination. After all, they had been the Lowells' retainers for as long as she could remember. They were more like family members than servants.

Perhaps her sudden appearance had upset them, especially since they, like she, knew her father would soon be making his disapproval known. They were no doubt worried that they'd be blamed in some way.

During the next few days, when no word was forthcoming from her father, she began to breathe easier and enjoy her stay at Quarrystones. Even the Cliftons seemed less on edge, helping her to forget her earlier suspicion.

One morning while getting dressed, Juliana realized she had been in the country for a whole week. It hardly seemed possible. She'd spent her time reading in the garden or taking walks along the river. Mornings were devoted to working beside Essie in the kitchen, or helping Will-John in the garden. Thus far she had found no time for painting and vowed to remedy that situation.

She filled a basket with her painting supplies and went in search of Essie. She found her in the kitchen shelling peas.

"Have you seen that old smock I used to wear for painting?" Juliana asked.

"Indeed I have, Miss Juli. I've kept it for ye. It's in the still-room."

The still-room was where Essie worked her magic, turning the herbs and plants she grew and gathered into food, medicines, and dyes. Bunches of drying herbs and flowers hung from the rafters, giving the room a pleasant, outdoors smell. The stoneware sink was filled with fresh vegetables from Will-John's garden, and at the opposite end of the room was a walk-in pantry with marble shelves and a quarry tile floor. More perishable foodstuffs were stored within its coolness, and it smelled strongly of smoked ham and bacon.

Essie took the smock down from a hook behind the door, and helped Juliana slip it on over the grey dress she wore.

"Although I truly don't know why ye'd care if ye got paint on that wretched dress," the older woman observed critically.

Juliana looked surprised. "It's a perfectly good dress, Essie."

"Be that as it may, it won't hold a candle to the new ones I've been making for ye." Essie grinned broadly.

"You've made me new gowns? Whatever for?"

" 'Twas a long winter, just the husband and me here alone. I had to keep busy. And anyway, I'd dyed up all that lovely fabric and wanted to use it for something special. It occurred to me that ye could use a change from those drab things ye always wear." She waved a thin, freckled hand toward the back door. "Now ye go on and do yer painting, and we'll look at the dresses later."

Juliana leaned forward to give Essie a kiss on the cheek. "You really are wonderful."

"Pshaw!" But she looked pleased as she hurried back to the kitchen.

Juliana went out into the backyard, one of her favorite places at Quarrystones. By the back step was the round brick fireplace Will-John had built for heating the washtubs of dye in which Essie simmered skeins of homespun wool. A flagged-stone path lined with rosemary led the way to the country garden, which would be a wild profusion of color before much longer. Beyond it, through a high hedge were two smaller and more formal gardens.

Turning in the opposite direction, Juliana crossed the smooth lawn that ran down to the water's edge. Around the base of an old beech tree that overhung the river was a bed of pansies, their large petals looking like midnight-purple velvet.

Dropping to the grass beside them, Juliana got out her paints. Most of the colors she used were homemade, the result of experimentation by herself and Essie. Favorably impressed by the unusual hues of dye the countrywoman could extract from the various plants she used, Juliana had decided the same plants could be used to make watercolors. Now, their method perfected, she was quite happy with the colors and thought them ideal for the botanical studies she liked to paint.

Instead of the customary canvas, Juliana preferred to paint on heavy ivory paper, which gave the finished picture an antique look.

She soon became engrossed in the beauty of the pansies and the quiet peace of the morning, and her brush skimmed over the paper. By the time she had completed the study to her satisfaction, her back was stiff from sitting so long and she decided she needed a brisk walk.

Gathering up her painting equipment, she went back to the still-room. She cleaned her brushes and left them and the painting on the pine drain board to dry. Then, removing the smock, she went back through the house and out the front door.

Drawn by the first roses blooming along the crumbling wall edging the moat, she rounded the corner of the house and came face-to-face with Will-John. He was halfway down the rickety iron staircase leading to the second floor of the deserted tower.

At one time nearly two centuries earlier, the tower had been a part of the manor house, with doors adjoining at two levels. But later those doors had been filled in with quarry stones, shutting off the tower and leaving it uninhabited ever since. Juliana's father theorized that some previous owner, during the days when the country had been beset with fevers and the plague, had most likely deemed the damp tower unhealthy.

It was possible to enter the bottom floor of the structure at the ground level, but because water from the moat often seeped in, it was usually wet and unpleasant. As children, the Lowells had played there when it was dry enough, but they had been forbidden to ever climb the stairway to the second floor because it was considered much too unsafe.

Now, seeing Will-John on the stairs was a shock. "What are you doing up there?" Juliana asked.

Will-John's face had frozen into a look of stunned surprise, but at Juliana's question, it turned beet red. He didn't quite meet her eyes as he lurched down the last few vine-choked steps.

"Why, Miss Juli," he muttered, "I was looking for vermin."

"Vermin? In the old tower? Why should you care about that? They can't get into the house from there."

He studied his feet. "You know Essie, miss. She hates vermin something awful."

"Now, Will-John, I know there's something strange going on around here, and I insist that you tell me what it is."

At that instant, Essie bustled around the corner, a determined look in her eye. "Will-John Clifton! I wondered where ye'd gotten to. Did ye forget that I need ye to go into the village and get some supplies?"

Will-John looked even more perplexed. "Supplies? What supplies?"

Essie threw up her hands in exasperation. "Men! Can't remember the simplest things!" She seized her husband by the arm and began virtually dragging him away, scolding all the while. "I swear, ye must be getting old, Will-John."

Juliana was amused, but she knew there was more to Essie's sudden appearance than reminding her husband of an errand he obviously knew nothing about. What on earth was happening? What were they trying to hide?

She stared at the iron staircase for some time before turning to wander across the causeway, lost in thought. After a few moments, she found herself walking beside the huge wall of rhododendron bushes that grew along the river. Several scarlet blossoms starred the glossy green of the leaves, bringing to mind how beautiful they would look in May when they reached the peak of their blooming season. Then they would be a solid mass of fragrant color: scarlets, mauves, and purples.

Idly, Juliana plucked a leaf and stood twisting it in her fingers. What had Will-John really been doing in the old tower? The question puzzled her, making her very much afraid of the answer. Intuition told her there was something seriously wrong, some very real threat to her home, or even the Cliftons themselves.

She tossed down the leaf. With sudden conviction, she decided she would see for herself. She marched back across the causeway and around to the tower. Grasping the wobbly railing with one hand, she clutched her skirt with the other and pulled herself up onto the narrow iron steps. Thick vines clutched at her hem, hampering her progress. At the top she cautiously opened the small door and stepped inside the musty-smelling room.

Light filtering in through the misted glass of the one window showed her that the room had recently been occupied. Spying a candle on a table beneath the window, she moved toward it, feeling about for the flint to light it.

With the soft glow of the single candle illuminating the area, she could see exactly how recently that occupation had been. A plate of meat, cheese, and bread had been placed on the table, next to a bottle of wine and a glass. Will-John must have just left it when she encountered him.

Along one wall was a cot with rumpled sheets and blankets, and a pillow bearing the definite imprint of someone's head. On the floor beside the bed were three books, which she suspected had come from her father's library.

Behind her was a scarred chest of drawers with a black cape draped over it. She pulled open the top drawer and there was the mask and red bandanna she had last seen the highwayman wearing. Juliana's mouth was suddenly dry as she put out a hand and picked up an object lying on the kerchief. It was a ring, the opal birthstone the outlaw had stolen from her.

"It appears I've been so careless as to be discovered,"

said the man standing in the doorway. Even as she spun about to face him, Juliana was again aware of the unusual lilting sound of his deep voice. "And I only ventured down to the stable for five minutes."

"What are you doing here?" she demanded. "No, don't bother to answer. I already know. You're using my house to hide in. You've forced my poor retainers to shield you from the law, haven't you?" Juliana's eyes blazed with indignant anger. No wonder the Cliftons had acted so oddly. Somehow they had been coerced into harboring a dangerous criminal.

"Since you've seen me," the man asked quietly, "what do you intend to do?"

"I have no choice."

He crossed the floor to stand in front of her.

"Meaning?"

Unwilling to show any fear of him, Juliana stood her ground, shoulders squared. Without the mask concealing his face, she couldn't help but notice that he was wickedly handsome. Had Mariette been there, no doubt she'd have been swooning at his feet.

And not, she thought with ill-timed amusement, *in terror.*

"I'll have to inform the authorities of your whereabouts," she said aloud.

"I'd rather you didn't."

"And I'd rather you didn't make a habit of robbing travelers and then using my home as your hiding place."

"Perhaps if I explained the situation." He started to come even closer.

"No!" Juliana put out a hand. "Don't get near me. I won't let you stop me from going to the constable."

"And if I want to stop you, how, pray tell, do you plan to keep me from it?" He smiled suddenly, but Juliana recognized the deadly intent beneath the charming expression on his face. "I should say you're entirely at my mercy." He took another step toward her.

Fright washed over her and, desperately, she reached out for the candlestick. Ignoring the burning candle, she swung with all her strength, landing a glancing blow to the man's forehead. With a grunt of pain and a muffled curse, he sank to the floor, his dark head in his hands.

Horrified, Juliana seized her chance for escape. She flew across the tower room and out the half-open door, flinging herself down the frail stairs without thought of danger. Her skirt caught on a jagged piece of iron railing that tore through it and the single petticoat beneath, etching a painful scratch on her bare thigh. She yanked the garment free, leaving it nearly in tatters.

At the bottom of the tower steps, she paused for a backward glance, but there was no sign of the outlaw. Breathing a quick sigh of relief, she dashed around the corner of the house and through the front door. She raced into her bedroom and slammed the door behind her, bolting it.

Leaning against the doorframe, she tried to catch her breath. Then, with shaking fingers, she began unbuttoning her dress. It was torn badly enough to be indecent, but as soon as she could throw on something else, she'd take a horse and ride into Edensfield to report the presence of the highwayman.

Juliana had slipped her dress from one shoulder when she heard a short laugh.

"As much as I enjoy seeing ladies disrobe, I feel I should warn you of my presence."

Juliana uttered a sharp cry as she whirled about to find the highwayman casually leaning against the stone wall of her bedchamber. She cursed the hold modesty and her mother's rigid training had over her. Had she not known or cared about propriety, she'd have already been on her way to the village.

In the light of day, the outlaw seemed even larger and more menacing. He was wearing a white shirt of some soft material, open nearly to the waist, and beneath his crossed arms, she could see the black hair that covered his chest. His lean hips and legs sheathed in snug black trousers and knee-high boots looked powerfully muscular.

"How did you get into this room?" she demanded, her face ashen.

"Oh, I have my ways," he assured her, "which I'll explain in due time." An ironic smile touched his lips. "Did you think I was going to oblige you by lying injured while you went for the law?"

Juliana's hand crept to her throat. "I didn't mean to hurt you. I was merely trying to defend myself."

"Defend yourself from me, my lady? I assure you, there was no need."

"Didn't you tell me I was entirely at your mercy?" she snapped. "Hardly the statement of a man without mischief in mind."

"You probably would've been quite shocked to know what was really on my mind at that moment," he said quietly. "Mischief, perhaps, but delightful mischief."

He straightened his lanky frame, as if preparing to advance upon her.

Juliana turned on her heel and darted toward the bedroom door. As her hand closed about the bolt, the man's arm caught her around the waist and lifted her till her feet dangled inches above the floor. She screamed, pounding at the door with a wildly swinging fist. The highwayman staggered and went down, pulling her with him.

"Damn, I'm weaker than I thought." He groaned, lying still upon the floor, Juliana's body trapped within the powerful circle of his arm. "Why did you have to aim so true with that candlestick?"

She was dismayed to find her cheek resting against his hard, warm chest. "I'd do it again, given the chance." She struggled against him, her breath coming in short, sharp gasps.

"Lie still," he ordered. "I have a thundering headache, thanks to you. Don't try my patience further."

Chastened by his stern tone of voice, Juliana deemed it best to obey. After a few moments of simply lying there, her normal sense of humor was restored and she couldn't prevent a small chuckle. How strange it was to be reclining on her bedroom floor, in the arms of a total stranger. Given her half-clad state, it was the most compromising situation she'd ever faced. But instead of numbing fear, she was actually experiencing a wild sort of exhilaration.

"Why do you laugh, Juliana?"

She raised her head and looked at him, but his eyes were closed, his face pale. Where his dark hair tumbled away from his forehead, she could see the wound she had inflicted. The flesh around the cut was bruised and Juliana felt a swift stab of remorse. He was the first person she had ever stricken in anger.

"How do you know my name?" she asked, her amusement gone.

"There is little I don't know about you."

"But how?"

At that moment a loud knocking sounded at the door,

and Essie's frantic voice called, "Juliana! Miss Juli, are ye all right?"

Juliana opened her mouth to answer, but heard the gypsy's voice instead. "She's fine, Essie. No need to worry."

"You *know* Essie?"

The man began to stir and, as Essie shouted "Open up!", rose to his feet, pulling Juliana with him.

He gave her a gentle push toward the door. "Let her in."

Juliana unbolted the door and threw it open to admit Essie, followed closely by an anxious Will-John. At the sight of Juliana's torn and unbuttoned gown, Essie shrieked in rage. "What have ye done to the child, Ruark? Ye heathen devil!"

The man she'd called Ruark laughed faintly. "If only you knew. 'Tisn't so much what I did to her, but what she did to me."

Juliana felt an upsurge of anger. "What's going on here? Why do you know this outlaw by name, Essie?"

Essie wrung her hands and turned a malicious look on Will-John. "Ye see? Ye see what ye have done? Now we'll all be in for it."

Will-John laid a callused hand on Juliana's shoulder. "We didn't want you to find about this, lass. But we had no other choice."

Juliana swung her gaze back to the highwayman. "How dare you use force to induce these innocent people to help you! I'll see you punished for that!"

"Now, Miss Juli," Essie said hastily, "there's no need for threats."

"Don't be afraid of him, Essie," Juliana admonished. "He's a coward! Why else would he hide behind your skirts?"

"Why, you little witch!" Ruark's growled words seemed

to spur the older woman into action. She quickly positioned her wiry body between Juliana and the advancing man.

"Ye'd best hush yer mouth, Miss Juli," she softly scolded. "The most important thing is, did the young jackanapes hurt ye?"

"Hurt me? No."

"But yer dress!" She blushed brightly, causing Juliana to glance down at the gaping bodice of her gown. She had forgotten her disheveled state. Her eyes flew quickly to those of the highwayman, and she was startled to see something that resembled admiration in the mysterious depths of his gaze. She turned her back and began fastening the buttons.

"I was going for the constable," she explained in a strained voice, "and stupidly stopped to change my dress."

"I see." Essie sounded calmer. "What are ye going to do now?"

"I still intend to ride for help." As soon as the words were out of her mouth, Juliana darted for the door again.

She'd only set one foot on the threshold when a strong hand closed over her shoulder, bringing her to an abrupt halt.

"Don't cause me any more trouble, Juliana," the outlaw said, his tone weary. "You're my prisoner now, and I'd advise you to behave yourself for a change."

She froze, tiny prickles of fright rippling over her scalp. But it wasn't the highwayman's words that caused her fear. It was the feel of his hand upon her. The fingers that had closed like an iron vise over her shoulder now relaxed and lay lightly, almost caressingly upon her, touching her with a heat that was the most terrifying sensation she'd ever experienced.

Four

Juliana shrugged off the man's hand and whirled to face him. "What are you planning to do with us?" she demanded.

"Nothing, as long as you behave yourselves."

"And how do we do that?"

"Not by going to the authorities." His grin was crooked, mocking.

"Then how? By accepting your presence here as if it meant nothing?"

"I'd appreciate that," he said lightly.

"Quarrystones has never been a haven for thieves and robbers. And it won't become one now."

"Miss Juli," Essie began. "Perhaps ye shouldn't be so hasty in condemning Ruark. Mayhap he isn't what ye think."

"He's the man I witnessed robbing the stagecoach," she declared. "I'd like to hear him explain that away."

"And you shall," Ruark promised. "But first, my head is in need of some attention. And I'm hungry. Don't forget, you interrupted my luncheon."

"Let's go down to the kitchen," Essie suggested. "I'll put some salve on that bruise, and then we can talk over a meal."

"I refuse to sit down to eat with this outlaw," Juliana announced.

"Then you'll stay in this room and be hungry," Ruark stated.

"It's what I'd prefer!"

"Very well, my lady. I'll be happy to oblige."

"But, lad," Will-John spoke up, "Miss Juli isn't accustomed to being treated this way."

"Would you have me release her so she can ride into town and spread the news of my whereabouts?"

"N-no, of course not."

"So, since Miss Lowell has refused Essie's kind invitation, I don't see that I have any other choice but to lock her in." He turned back to Juliana. "Unless you've changed your mind?"

"I have not. I won't pretend you're a welcome guest here."

"As you wish." With an arrogant smile, the tall man turned to Essie and held out a hand. "The key to this room, if you please."

For a moment, Essie looked as if she wanted to argue the point, but, casting an apologetic grimace in Juliana's direction, she took the key from the chatelaine belt she wore and surrendered it to Ruark. He promptly ushered the Cliftons from the room, then followed them, shutting the door firmly behind himself. Juliana's teeth clenched as she heard the unmistakable turn of the key in the heavy lock. Even knowing it was useless, she tried the door, which remained unyielding.

She struck the wooden panels with the flat of her hand. How dare that brigand come into her home and ruthlessly take command? There had to be something she could do!

She stood looking about the room, her mind working furiously. The windows were too high; she'd certainly break her neck if she tried to climb down to the lawn below. Knotting the bedsheets might be a possibility, but she'd have to wait until later in the day, for her descent would take her right past the front windows, making her clearly visible from the dining room.

She studied the rough stone wall opposite. The outlaw had entered the bedchamber through it, so there had to be some sort of hidden door. If she could find the turnstone that opened it, she might escape by that means. With caution and a bit of luck, she could slip over the causeway bridge and make her way to the stables without being seen.

For the next ten minutes, Juliana pushed and prodded every stone surface on the wall, finding no sign of a secret spring. It began to seem likely the door only opened from the other side, which would do her no good at all.

In frustration, she flung herself across the room and onto the bed. What on earth was she going to do? She squeezed her eyes shut, forcing herself to think. It occurred to her that she might pretend compliance and convince the gypsy to let her out, but then what? It wasn't probable that he'd conveniently turn his back long enough for her to flee Quarrystones. Her eyes flew open to resume their feverish survey of the chamber. She needed some kind of a weapon.

Her gaze fell on the bedside table and for a brief moment, she enjoyed the fantasy that her father might have concealed a flintlock pistol there. But when she pulled the drawer open, she found instead her mother's well-worn Bible. Beyond that, there was nothing but a handful of hairpins and a packet of the sleeping powder the physician had once prescribed for Eliza Lowell. Always nervous and apprehensive when spending time in the country, she habitually used the medicine to induce a sound sleep.

Juliana took out the packet and stared at it, a bold idea taking form in her mind. Her lips smoothed into a straight line as she slid off the bed to change into a fresh gown. With quiet determination, she tucked the medicine into one of the deep pockets in her skirt. The man was a crude bully, and she didn't intend to let him take over her home.

"Essie," she shouted, pounding on the door. "Essie, please come here!"

It took another round of spirited hammering before she heard movement outside the door.

"Eh?" came Essie's cautious voice. "What is it, lass?"

"I-I've decided I'm hungry after all. Would you please ask that . . . er, Ruark if I can join you for luncheon?"

Juliana couldn't believe her good fortune when she heard the immediate turning of the key in the lock. But her sudden hope that Essie had garnered enough courage to abet her escape faded the instant she saw the commanding figure of the gypsy standing in the shadows at the foot of the stairs. A gauze bandage on his forehead glowed softly in the dim light.

"Ruark says ye can come down," Essie informed her.

"Tell her the rest of it." Now the highwayman's teeth gleamed just as whitely as the bandage he wore.

"He says ye must behave yerself, Miss Juli, and promise there'll be no further ado."

Rather than lie outright, Juliana simply made no answer. Instead, she raised her chin to a haughty level and began descending the stairs, her skirts gripped in both hands. At the base of the steps, she passed so closely to the watching man that she could feel his warm breath on her face. But she refused to look at him, merely sweeping on by and into the dining room beyond.

She heard his soft, maddening chuckle as he followed her, but again, she ignored him. Giving Will-John a nod, she sank into a chair and made a conspicuous inventory of the food Essie had placed in the middle of the table. The others had already filled their plates with lamb pie and roasted potatoes, and the savory aromas made Juliana's stomach clench with hunger. Surely it couldn't hurt if she ate a bite or two before her intended ride.

Essie looked nervous as she watched Juliana fill her plate; it was obvious she knew better than to trust her young mistress's current submissive mood.

"Will ye have a cup of tea, Miss Juli?" she inquired, taking her own seat and reaching for the teapot.

"Thank you," Juliana politely murmured, well aware of the man now sitting across from her. She took the teapot from Essie and carefully filled the china cup at her place.

"I'll have a cup as well," Ruark announced, eyeing the steaming liquid. He handed her his cup and saucer, surprising Juliana with his unwitting participation in her trickery.

"Oh, dear, Essie," she said, striving for a casual tone, "the pot is nearly empty. Shall I fetch more hot water from the kitchen?"

"No," the gypsy interjected. "You're to stay where you are."

Essie got to her feet. "I'll get it. 'Tis no trouble."

Juliana gave Essie the teapot and the older woman disappeared through the door into the next room.

In an effort to create the diversion she needed, Juliana took up a platter, and said, "Will anyone have a bread roll?" She gave the plate a hearty shove in the outlaw's direction, causing it to whisk across the tablecloth and over the edge, sending the rolls flying to the far corners of the room.

"Damnation," Ruark growled. "I had my mouth set for one of those."

Juliana shrugged. "I'm sorry. I didn't mean to be so forceful. Shall I help you pick them up?"

He waved away her offer with an impatient hand. "Remain in your seat and don't move. I believe we'll all be safer that way."

The instant he and Will-John had dropped to their knees to begin collecting the scattered bread, Juliana pulled the packet of sleeping powder from her pocket and dumped a significant amount into his teacup.

"Now what has happened?" Essie asked, coming back into the room. "Oh, lud, my bread rolls!" She thumped the refilled teapot down onto the table. "All they'll be fit for is feeding the swans."

Juliana poured Ruark's tea, giving it a quick, surreptitious stir before setting it back beside his plate. When he'd resumed his seat, he paid little attention to it, merely adding two lumps of sugar and stirring it vigorously himself.

"You flung that dish at me intentionally," he accused, lifting his cup in one large hand. "Did you think to catch me off guard so that you might flee again?" His look was steady over the china rim.

"I assure you, it was an accident. I know what hard work the baking is. You can't believe I'd deliberately waste Essie's efforts."

Ruark set his cup down without taking a drink. "I don't doubt it for a moment."

Juliana's hopeful mien faded as she followed the return of the teacup to its saucer.

"Would you care for this one?" She held out the roll she had placed on her own plate.

"Don't try to placate me," he warned. Again he picked up his cup, this time using it to emphasize a point. "I can't afford to trust you, Juliana. At least, not until I've had the chance to explain my situation."

"Then go ahead and explain," she said, striving for an

agreeable demeanor. "There's nothing I'd rather hear than a good reason for this."

"All right, now seems as likely a time as any."

Ruark put down the cup a second time, making Juliana struggle to hide her wince of disappointment.

"There's no need to spoil this wonderful meal, however," she quickly conceded. "Perhaps we can talk when it's finished."

Pointedly, she took a sip of her own tea, and nearly cheered when the man across from her followed suit, swooping up his cup and draining it in one swallow. A strange look flitted across his face.

"This tea has an odd flavor, Essie. Why would that be?"

"I brewed it from hawthorn flowers. They have a calming affect, ye see. Ye're just not used to the taste."

"A calming affect?" His frown turned into a smile as he appraised Juliana. "You're a wise woman, Essie, love."

Juliana concentrated on making her expression as frosty as possible. For a few seconds, she'd almost allowed herself to forget that Ruark was a dangerous villain, a man who robbed others of their valuables, a man who forced himself on vulnerable females. She tore her glance from his and stared fixedly at the food before her. She couldn't let herself lose sight of the fact that, as handsome and charming as the rogue could be, he was still her enemy. He was an unwelcome visitor who'd taken advantage of Essie and Will-John, and the best thing she could do was continue in her efforts to outsmart him.

Deliberately she raised her eyes to his again and this time, his gaze seemed a trifle unfocused. Briefly, she wondered if it was only her imagination.

"Would you care for more tea?" she inquired.

He pushed his cup and saucer toward her, then stifled an

unexpected yawn with the back of his hand. Juliana poured the tea, bending her head to hide her face. She had only to bide her time; soon the outlaw would be as harmless as a sleeping baby.

"I assume you've been here at Quarrystones for quite some time," she commented, watching as he drained the second cup.

"A while."

"And you're the one who's been watching me."

"A most refreshing pastime for a man who has only a few books to read and a small square of garden in which to exercise. Your presence at Quarrystones has certainly made my stay more interesting." Again he yawned. "Damn, Essie, but your tea may be a bit too calming." The look he gave Juliana seemed to be filled with dawning suspicion.

Quickly, she picked up her fork and began to attack her food with ferocity. Her plan was going to work after all. She experienced a great deal of satisfaction as she watched the highwayman fork a chunk of carrot and stare at it as though he expected it to take wings and fly. Leaning forward to brace his elbows on the table, he made an attempt to put the bite into his mouth, but succeeded only in jabbing himself in the cheek. With a short, disbelieving snort, he tried again and promptly dropped the fork.

"Essie?" he muttered, then collapsed on the tabletop, his dark head only inches from the meat and gravy on his plate.

Juliana leaped to her feet, then stood poised, waiting to see if he would rouse up. When he didn't, she tossed down her napkin with a crow of delight.

"What did you do to the lad?" Will-John asked, alarmed.

"I gave him some of Mother's sleeping powder. It was the only way I could think of to incapacitate him long enough for me to go for help. You won't be afraid to stay here and guard him, will you?"

"Of course not."

She crossed to the fireplace and snatched up an iron poker. "Here, you can use this as a weapon."

"The lad's not going to hurt us, Miss Juli."

"Not while he's asleep, he won't. But if I'm delayed, you can't be certain of what he'll do."

At that moment, the dark-haired man slumped upon the table groaned. Silently, Juliana cursed herself for her hesitation in making good her escape.

"I've got to go," she said. "It's a long way to Edensfield."

"Why not ride to Quarrystones village, Miss Juli? It's much closer and the men there will be glad to come to your aid."

"Yes, that's a splendid idea. I'll return as soon as I can."

When Juliana had gone, Essie turned on her husband. "How could ye send her to the village? Ye know the danger there."

"They won't hurt Juliana. And besides, it's the best way for her to learn the truth."

Essie sniffed, her black eyes snapping. "All the same, Will-John Clifton, if those villagers harm one hair on that child's head, ye'll have me to answer to."

Riding astride with the wind streaking through her hair, Juliana decided she had been ladylike too long. Hidden somewhere not far from the surface was something within her that had missed this kind of wild freedom. She had believed the hoyden she'd once been had grown up into a sensible woman. But this mad dash through field and meadow was rapidly proving her wrong. It must have been

London that was stifling her; returning to the country had brought back all those qualities that refused to be tamed.

She couldn't spare a moment's regret over the matter. Not when her heart was pounding with such excitement, her spirit soaring as high as the larks that circled above. She was caught up in an adventure. An adventure that could end with disaster, certainly, but not if she could prevent it.

If the truth were known, she didn't really fear the highwayman all that much. Had he wanted to harm her, he'd have done so already. Perhaps that was why she'd dared to take such action. But even if he wasn't capable of hurting her or the Cliftons, he was still a man who blatantly broke the law, a man who must be handed over to the authorities. A man whose presence at Quarrystones could not be tolerated.

Juliana urged her horse to a faster pace. Ahead she could see the rooftops of the village that was her destination. The cottages of the tenant farmers were clustered around a huge barn and granary, nearly a mile from the manor house.

She felt her excitement growing as she drew nearer. As a child, she had often gone to the village to play with the farmers' children. She loved their way of life. Although they had to work hard, the entire family labored together, each with his own special task to perform. When she would return to Quarrystones sunburned and wind-blown from a day in the hayfields, or daubed with mud from an afternoon spent tending the pigs and weeding the gardens, her mother would scold and shame her, and forbid her ever to go near the tenants again. In a few days, when Eliza Lowell was preoccupied with something else, off Juliana would go again.

Now she experienced a feeling of guilt because she hadn't thought of the tenants before this. Had she not arrived at Quarrystones in such a state of distraction, she would surely have been to see them sooner, for it had been two years since she'd visited with any of her father's workers.

As she entered the village, she reined in the horse and proceeded more slowly. The cottages, with their red-tiled roofs, looked more derelict than she had ever seen them. The yards were untidy, some of them choked with weeds where once had been flowers. There were no children playing along the grassy lane, no dogs barking, and no one coming to greet her. The sly shifting of curtains in some of the front windows told her the cottages' occupants were inside, watching.

A lone man stood at the well in the center of the village, frowning as he observed her progress. Juliana guided her mount to his side.

"Do you know who I am?" she asked.

"Aye, the landlord's daughter." The man barely turned his head before spitting on the ground.

She chose to overlook the crudity. "What's happened here? Why does the village look so different?"

He shrugged and said nothing.

"Very well, I'll find someone who will talk to me. Do the Fergusons still live in that cottage with the blue door?"

"Aye."

She slid from her horse and went up the slate walk to the front door, where she knocked. Though she heard voices inside the house, there was no answer. She looked back at the man and found him still staring at her.

She knocked once again and called, "Mrs. Ferguson, open the door. It's Juliana Lowell and I need help."

The door was immediately thrown open, and Mrs. Ferguson stood there, her manner clearly hostile.

"Hello," Juliana said. "How have you been?"

"As if you'd care," snapped the other woman.

Juliana felt cold shock. "What's wrong here?" None of the tenants had ever dared exhibit such spleen before. She knew there was something dreadfully amiss.

"I have three small children and no food to give them," Mrs. Ferguson cried. "My husband and oldest son had to go to the city to look for work. And my married daughter's husband was arrested and jailed for poaching. How dare you ask me what is wrong?"

"I-I'm so sorry, but I don't understand what has happened."

"Then why don't you ask your fiancé?" came a quiet voice from behind her.

She turned to see Arthur Jacobson, another of the tenant farmers she had known since childhood. He was joined by the man from the well and several children who had appeared from nowhere.

"What does Spencer have to do with this?" Juliana asked, aware that others were slowly coming forth from their cottages, surrounding the Fergusons' house.

"Look at her, pretending to be so innocent," spoke up a woman with two children clinging to her worn skirts.

"Will you please tell me what this is all about?"

"Ye high and mighty Lowells," snarled a toothless old man. "Ye've always set yerselves above us common folk." He waved his walking stick in Juliana's face and, suddenly frightened, she stepped backward. She came up against the unyielding chest of Arthur Jacobson and whirled about to face him.

"Why'd you come here, Juliana?" he asked.

Before she could reply, one of the older children picked up a handful of mud and hurled it in her direction. It struck her skirt and rolled away, leaving dark streaks on the pale cotton. She gasped, stunned by the show of animosity.

"Maybe you made a mistake, comin' to our village," drawled the man from the well. "We don't have much to offer rich ladies."

"Here, I'll offer her this," shouted a woman with straggling hair and a face sharpened by starvation. She stooped to gather a fistful of pebbles and flung them at Juliana.

Juliana held herself stiffly, barely aware of the stinging pelt of the gravel. Never in her life had she been treated in such a manner, and she had no notion of what she should do. Her words might only inflame them further, yet physical retreat seemed improbable.

"Leave her alone," a deep voice thundered, and the crowd turned as one to see who had spoken. Juliana, too, swiveled about and saw the gypsy highwayman seated upon the same gigantic black horse he'd ridden the day he'd robbed the stagecoach. The stallion pranced and snorted, as though he'd enjoyed an exhilarating ride over the fields. Ruark himself was rather pale, his eyes dark and circled, his hair untidy. When he looked at Juliana, his countenance was anything but benevolent. Even so, he was an unexpectedly welcome sight. For whatever reason, his intention seemed to be to rescue her from the furious villagers.

"So ye've come to defend her, have ye, Ruark?" asked the old man with the blackthorn stick. "Even though she's one of *them?*"

"The Cliftons have told me that Juliana knows nothing of Hamilton's plotting."

"Plotting?" she repeated faintly.

"Your fiancé plans to take over the estate, including the village and farmland, when the two of you marry. Were you aware of that?"

"I knew my father intended to deed the estate to me after the wedding," she answered.

"And naturally, the way the law reads, your husband would actually be the landowner."

"I suppose so."

"Did you know Spencer Hamilton had been making plans about this farm?"

"He had said as much." Juliana looked from Ruark to the others. "But, of course, he would. After all, the land adjoins his own."

"Had you any idea what those plans consisted of?" Ruark asked in a quiet voice.

"Not really. We've never discussed it."

"That pompous ass walked in here and told us we'd no longer be tenants at Quarrystones," broke in Jacobson. "He's already applied for Parliamentary approval of an enclosure scheme."

"What's enclosure?" Juliana's voice was sharp, her bewilderment evident.

"It actually means that Quarrystones' individual farms and fields will be converted into one larger holding," answered Ruark. "All under the control of the richest landowner in the area. That will, of course, be Spencer Hamilton."

"He wants to take the land away from us," Mrs. Ferguson said. "This land where we've lived and worked all our lives."

"But he can't do that!" cried Juliana. "Parliament can't allow such a thing."

"The wealthy landowners who want these enclosures are usually the men who sit in Parliament and make the laws," Jacobson pointed out. "Hamilton will have no trouble getting his way."

"A private act of Parliament redistributes the land to those with power," added Ruark, "giving them the right to overrule the resistance of small tenants. These villagers will find themselves without secure homes, without a piece of ground to grow food or keep a cow. They'll be turned out, left to move into the crowded cities, where the living conditions are appalling."

"I've read of such things, of course, but . . ." Juliana shook her head. "Surely it couldn't happen at Quarrystones. There must be some mistake."

"We thought the mistake was ours, for trusting you," the woman with the small children stated, though her tone was less acid. "We reckoned you'd turned your back on us."

Staunchly, Juliana faced the crowd. "Surely you knew me better than that," she said, looking around the circle of people, meeting every eye. "I swear to you, I knew nothing of Spencer's plans. I daresay, my father knows nothing of it, either."

"Then how did that man have the nerve to come to us and tell us we'd have to leave our cottages by the first of May, when you are to marry?"

"I don't know, Mrs. Ferguson."

"He told us there was no sense in planting our vegetable gardens because we wouldn't be here to tend them. He told us to get our cows and pigs off the common ground and get rid of them. There's no more milk, no eggs. Is he trying to starve our children to death before he turns us out?"

The man speaking looked at her with a bitter frown, and Juliana swallowed deeply. No wonder these people were angry with her. They must have thought all along she had backed Spencer in his efforts to remove them from the farm.

"There's something I must tell you," she said suddenly, in a louder voice. "My marriage to Spencer Hamilton has been called off."

She was aware of the stunned silence around her, but most of all she was aware of the look on the face of the tall man standing beside her. Ruark seemed surprised, one black eyebrow quirking upward as a smile broke across his features, revealing a deep dimple in one lean cheek.

"It so happens that Spencer has discovered he'd rather marry my sister Mariette." There was a buzz of voices, and Ruark's eyebrow went up even higher.

"But I only called off the engagement on the condition my father continue with his agreement to deed Quarrystones to me. I'm not certain he'll do so, because Spencer has offered to buy the farm from him. But I promise, if I have any say in the matter, I won't let anyone put you out of your homes."

A slight cheer went up, and Mrs. Ferguson stepped closer. "I should have known you wouldn't have had any part in this scheme, Miss Juliana."

"I realize this has been terrible for you. And, as much as I wish I could be sure of what will happen, we'll just have to wait and see. I'll inform my father of Spencer's intentions the first chance I get. I'm hopeful that will change his mind about selling Quarrystones."

"I hope so, too," the woman said. "Even with Ruark's help, we can't go on this way much longer."

Juliana tossed the gypsy a curious look. Her predicament had caused her to forget her original mission. Now she surmised that the villagers not only knew Ruark, but considered him a friend. Apparently the Cliftons had been right when they'd told her he was no ordinary thief. She opened her mouth to ask the first of many questions, but he silenced her with his next words.

"I know there's much that needs to be explained, but we should return to Quarrystones first. Essie will be waiting to make sure you're unharmed."

"I have no desire to travel anywhere with you," she

stated. "Have you forgotten that you're the one I was running from?"

"And have you forgotten I was the one who rescued you from a rather tense situation?"

"Perhaps you'd care to step inside the house for some refreshment before you go, Miss Juli," interceded Mrs. Ferguson. "I can't offer you anything except a cool drink of water, but we'd be honored to have you visit a while."

Without looking at Ruark, Juliana said, "I'll gladly accept your kind invitation. A cool drink would be lovely."

The inside of the cottage was clean, but poor. Poorer even than Juliana remembered. The open shelves in the kitchen looked quite bare. Thinking of the plentiful food at Quarrystones, she said, "I'll have Will-John bring down some of the vegetables from his garden, Mrs. Ferguson. There are too many for us to eat, and there's no sense in them going to waste. You here in the village can surely use them. Also, I'll tell the cowherds to see that your children start receiving milk again at once. That may help until we see what my father intends to do."

"Bless you, Miss Juliana," the woman said tearfully. "I wish I could thank you some way."

Juliana accepted the mug of cool water she offered. "Knowing you believe and trust me once more is thanks enough. I'm not going to let you down again, I swear."

She glanced over her shoulder and saw that Ruark was engaged in conversation with a few of the village men. Leaning closer to Mrs. Ferguson, she whispered, "I came here seeking help because the highwayman had broken into the manor. I don't particularly want to return with him now."

The other woman chuckled. "Ruark is a good lad, Miss Juli. He won't hurt you."

"But who is he? Where did he come from?"

"Ask the Cliftons. They'll tell you the truth of it."

"But—"

" 'Tis time to go home, Juliana." Ruark spoke from across the room and something in his tone of voice warned her that he'd brook no argument.

"How can I know you mean me no harm?"

"Do you think these people would allow you to go with me if they thought you'd be in any danger?"

"I suppose not."

"They know I can be counted as a friend, something you're much in need of."

"What do you mean?"

"Spencer Hamilton isn't going to take your interference lightly, and we've no way of knowing what your father will decide to do. You may find I'm the only one on your side."

"I hope you're mistaken."

"At least hear me out."

"It seems I have little choice."

With a sigh, she made her farewells and left the cottage at his side.

On the stoop, she turned to him, two bright spots of color in her cheeks. "I imagine you feel I should thank you for coming to my aid. I-I believe I could have handled matters without your interference." She ignored his incredulous expression. "And frankly, after what I did to you, I'm surprised you bothered."

He grinned. "So am I. But I had no vote on the issue. Essie plied me with some foul-tasting concoction to wake me up, then told me to be about the business of rescuing you." He assisted her in mounting her horse. "The problem is, now I don't know whether to be more angry that you tricked me, or that I had to drink Essie's potion. Either way, the blame is yours."

"I was only defending my household," she protested. "And I still don't have any good reason to believe you're anything other than a low-bred outlaw."

He swung up onto the back of his huge black stallion, his face creased in a broad smile. "All in good time, my lady."

"But who are you? Where did you come from? And why are my father's tenants acquainted with you?"

"Like most women, you're full of questions. I'm sorry, but they'll have to wait."

He leaned forward and said a few words into his horse's ear, speaking in the strange tongue Juliana remembered from their first encounter. The horse whinnied and shook its head.

"What did you say to him?" Juliana asked.

"I merely said, 'Let's go, Heiden.' "

"Heiden?"

"It's his name in Romany."

"And what is Romany?"

"The language of the gypsies."

"What does Heiden mean?" she persisted, moving her horse alongside his.

"Heathen. Now cease your unending questions and let's ride for home."

Juliana tossed her head. "You're very rude," she commented. "In fact, it seems to me that the horse might have been given a name much better suited to its master."

She couldn't be sure, but she thought he laughed as he gently spurred Heiden forward to take the lead. She was left staring at his back, stricken by how massive his shoulders looked and how brightly his black hair gleamed in the afternoon sun.

Five

Hours later, when Juliana entered the dining room at Quarrystones, she was surprised to find the table laid for two. Surely she was not to dine alone with the gypsy? When they'd gotten back to the manor house, she'd gone immediately to her room and hadn't come out until she'd been summoned to supper. She'd expected the security of Essie and Will-John's presence to make her next encounter with the outlaw easier.

Essie came into the room with a bowl of salad greens and a basket of bread which she placed on the table. Juliana could sense the other woman's hesitancy.

"Are ye still upset with the husband and me?" she asked in what was for her a meek manner.

"Of course not, Essie. I can't pretend to understand everything that's happened, but at least I have a better idea of what you and Will-John were facing."

"If it hadn't been for Ruark, I don't know what the farmers would have done." Essie shook her grey head. "He has been a godsend."

Juliana was puzzled. "In what way?"

"Why, he—" Essie paused in mid-sentence as Ruark himself strode into the room. Despite herself, she smiled. "Speak of the devil!"

He smiled back, his eyes straying to Juliana's face. "Why do I get the impression I was the subject under discussion?"

"Because ye were, ye young whelp," Essie retorted.

"I must get my information from someone," Juliana told him. "Thus far you haven't been very enlightening about who you are and what you're doing at Quarrystones."

"I'm about to rectify that situation, let me assure you. During the course of what I hope is to be a bountiful meal, I plan to give you every detail of my activities."

Essie waved a hand. "Sit ye down, then, and I'll fetch the meat."

The man came around the table and pulled out a chair for Juliana, who looked uncertain. "Aren't you and Will-John going to eat with us?"

"No, we'll have supper in the kitchen and leave the two of ye to talk in private."

Juliana was at a loss for words. How could she reveal her unease at being alone with this stranger without sounding like a frightened virgin?

Essie seemed to understand her feelings. "Listen, child, if Ruark should overstep himself, call out and Will-John will be right here. Ye're safe enough."

"Indeed," said Ruark in a low voice. "I have no thought of ravishing you." He held her chair for her and, as she seated herself, whispered close to her ear, "At least, not this night."

"Ye know 'tis not proper to speak of such things in the company of a young lady, Ruark Hamilton!" scolded Essie.

Juliana forgot her indignation at his remark and her eyes widened in shock. "Hamilton?"

The man seated himself opposite her. "Yes, Hamilton. Edward Ruark Hamilton, at your service."

"Then you're Spencer's kinsman?"

"His first cousin," supplied Ruark.

"But why have we never met? And why hasn't Spencer mentioned you?"

Essie chuckled as she left the room.

"Spencer Hamilton doesn't know everything in this world," she said.

Ruark grinned. "Actually, Spencer knows nothing of my existence."

"How is that possible?"

"It's a long story, Juliana. Couldn't we have our dinner first? So far today, two meals have been spoiled, and I was rather hoping to get through this one in relative peace."

Essie Clifton had returned to the dining room and was filling their plates with slices of cold meat and vegetables.

Juliana shook her head. "I've waited as long as I'm going to. I insist you explain yourself."

Essie brought a bottle of wine and two glasses from the sideboard, then discreetly left them alone.

"All right," Ruark said. He filled a glass with dark wine and gave it to her. "It seems I might as well begin."

Juliana flinched at the warmth of his fingers and hastily withdrew her hand, spilling a little of the wine.

"There's no need to be so afraid of me, you know." The man's dark eyes sparkled in the candles' glow, and Juliana dropped her gaze quickly.

"I'm not afraid of you," she said, annoyed by the tremor in her voice. "Just get on with your story."

"It starts twenty-seven years ago." His tone grew solemn. "That's when Edward Hamilton, Duke of Hawkhurst, disowned his eldest son and sent him off into the world with a paternal curse upon his head."

"The Duke? Spencer's grandfather?"

Ruark leaned forward. "And my own grandfather as well. Though, of course, he also knows nothing of my existence."

"But how can that be?"

Ruark took a deep drink of the wine. "When my father was tossed out of the ancestral home, he went to Ireland to live, and the Hamiltons never saw him again. None of them was aware of the fact that Randolph—my father—had a son."

Juliana sensed the bitterness underlying the man's words, and felt the need to know more of the situation. "Why did your grandfather disown your father? What did he do?"

This time there was no mistaking his rancor. "He fell in love and married the wrong person. A most heinous crime, wouldn't you say?"

"I don't understand."

"The heir to a dukedom doesn't return from a trip to the family estate in Ireland and unexpectedly present his gypsy bride."

"Gypsy?" Juliana repeated. "Oh, I see."

Ruark shoved his plate aside and leaned back in the chair, bringing the wineglass to his lips once again. "No, I doubt that you do. But I think you might if you could hear my mother tell the story of their meeting." He shrugged. "It doesn't matter now, of course. The fact is, my parents were married, despite the fierce opposition of the gypsy tribe. It was unheard of for a gypsy girl to marry a *gorgio*, a non-gypsy, and when they'd overcome that obstacle, they thought their path would be smooth." His short laugh was harsh. "They hadn't reckoned on the unbending pride of my dear grandfather. He was outraged at what they'd done. He argued for an annulment and when they wouldn't agree, he sent them packing. Told them never to return to Moorlands again."

"What did they do?"

"Fortunately, Father had been left the estate in Ireland by his mother, and there was nothing the Duke could do to prevent him from taking possession of it. But he saw to it that my father never received another penny from the English property. That was to go to the younger son, Spencer's father. He became the Marquis of Edensfield in my father's place, and now that he's dead, the title has passed down to Spencer."

"What a sad story," Juliana said softly. "It seems impossible to believe a father could simply turn his son away and never see him again."

"I suppose he felt his action was justified. After all, my father hadn't exactly exhibited the most acceptable behavior. At least, not in the eyes of the great English aristocracy."

"Well, it does help explain your disguise as a gypsy highwayman. I mean, if your mother was a gypsy, it isn't entirely an act, is it?"

"Not at all. I have a very colorful heritage: half Irish gypsy and half English nobleman. Rather interesting, wouldn't you say?" His face looked more relaxed as he smiled.

Juliana couldn't resist smiling back. "As a matter of fact, it is interesting. Your childhood must have been unusual."

"You can't begin to know the truth of that. I grew up on an estate in Donegal, and spent about as much time in the gypsy encampment as in the drawing room."

"Where are your parents now?"

"My mother's in Ireland," he replied. "My father died five years ago."

"And the Duke knows nothing of his death?"

"Apparently not. You see, it was a letter written to my father that brought me here."

"After all those years, your grandfather wrote?"

Ruark pushed back his chair and left the table. He walked to the fireplace where he stood watching the small fire burn. Presently he turned to face Juliana again.

"It seems the Duke has recently had to accept a few

facts. Namely, that he's getting old and can no longer order events to his satisfaction. He's unhappy about certain circumstances at Moorlands and powerless to change them."

"What circumstances?"

"It seems the old man has started having second thoughts about naming Spencer his heir. According to his letter, he feels Spencer is responsible for a great deal of mismanagement. He wrote to ask my father to consider coming home and taking his rightful place."

"He must have been very displeased with Spencer to make contact after such a long time," Juliana ventured.

"Oh, his letter hinted at all sorts of sinister things. I suppose he thought my father would immediately forgive and forget and rush back to dear old England to put everything to rights. It's just that he left it a little late."

"Did you come in your father's place?"

"No, I came out of curiosity. I wanted to see if there was any truth to what he had written."

"And was there?"

"Juliana, you should bless the Fates your wedding to Spencer Hamilton was cancelled. The man is a selfish blackguard, with no regard for anyone or anything but himself and his money. It didn't take long to discover how bad things really are at Moorlands. The estate is in a damnable condition. The tenant farmers are barely surviving, and there are some ugly rumors about my dear cousin's future plans, concerning not only Moorlands, but also Quarrystones."

"Besides the enclosure scheme?"

"Aye. It appears Spencer is toying with the notion of building a factory, using the Quarry River as a source of power."

"My God," Juliana cried. "A factory? That would be disastrous."

"I've seen industrial areas both here and in Ireland," he

agreed. "I detest what it does to the land and to the people. Unfortunately, England seems determined to embark upon industrialization. There may be some undeniable advantages, but there will be drawbacks, too."

"It's up to the landowners to resist using their property for mills and factories," Juliana said. "As I intend to prevent it on this estate." For a long moment she was silent. "It would be horrible to see all this give way to a factory."

"Which now brings us to the reason I have chosen to masquerade as a highwayman," Ruark said. "When I saw what was happening to the tenant farmers on Moorlands, I couldn't turn around and go home to Ireland. As much as I hate to admit it, England is my country, too. What happens here is of concern to me, though God knows why it should be."

"How does that justify highway robbery?" Juliana toyed with her fork, no longer interested in her dinner.

"Think about it a moment. Just who is responsible for the misery and poverty of the local farmers?"

"Wealthy squires and landowners, as always."

"Indeed. They have more food than they need, houses with more rooms than they can use, money they can't begin to count. They've nothing more pressing to worry about than fox hunting or whiling away an evening in some club, gambling. Many of them aren't even aware of the plight of their tenants; most of them wouldn't care if they were." He came close to the table, resting his hands on the back of one of the chairs. "I decided some of these men needed to share what they had with others less fortunate." His broad grin showed perfect white teeth.

"And so you started robbing them."

"And dividing the profit among the tenants. It has helped somewhat, but their need is so great that an occasional handful of coins and jewelry can't make any vast difference. I have to be exceedingly cautious, in the bargain, because if I'm captured, they won't even have that much."

"Instead of engaging in such a dangerous and foolish venture, why didn't you simply present yourself to your grandfather?"

Ruark's eyes blazed. "You forget, my grandfather has no love for gypsies."

"Surely all that's in the past. I mean, he must have regretted his actions if he wrote to your father."

"The letter was to my father, there was no mention of my mother, or of any children they might have had. My grandfather might have decided it would be advantageous to have his son home, but he obviously wanted no part of the rest of us. So be it."

"That attitude seems a bit foolhardy," she chided. "What if you were arrested? They'd hang you."

"A chance I'm willing to take. By posing as a bandit, I can conduct my business in disguise. Being unknown by the local gentry, I'm free to wander among the tenants asking questions and seeing their living conditions for myself."

"What about your companions? Are they hiding here, too?"

He shook his head. "It might prove dangerous for you to know any more than you do now."

"As if your using my home as a hideout isn't already putting me into danger!"

"I don't believe it is."

"How reassuring."

"Put aside your sarcasm and think about it, Juliana," he parried. "No one I consider an enemy knows my whereabouts. Quarrystones is suitably isolated, which is why I chose it in the first place. And naturally, since it adjoins the Hamiltons' land, it was most convenient for my purposes. I had little difficulty persuading the Cliftons to help me because they realized the risk the villagers would be taking if they hid me." He dropped back into the chair opposite her. "If I thought my being here would put you into peril, I'd leave tomorrow."

"I'd think you'd want to leave now that I know of your presence. After all, you've no promise from me that I won't go to the authorities. Spencer is a Justice of the Peace, the highest legal authority in the area. If I went to him . . ."

"Ah, but you won't, Juliana."

"Why do you say that?"

"You have too many reasons not to. You don't really want to see him gain possession of this estate, do you? And I know you don't like the way he has treated your tenants. Besides, as a woman scorned, you'll want revenge."

"I am not a woman scorned!"

One thick eyebrow quirked upward. "Indeed? If the man threw you over for your sister, I'd say that's exactly what you are."

Juliana's blue-grey eyes smouldered. "Regardless of what you may believe, I didn't care whether or not I married Spencer. I only wanted to own Quarrystones."

"I certainly didn't expect you to admit to feeling scorned," said Ruark. "But doesn't every woman want a husband? I think I understand the workings of the female mind."

"Well, you're wrong about the way my mind works. In fact, you know nothing about me." She jumped to her feet. "Oh, damn you! I'm not going to listen to you anymore." She started pacing the floor. "And as for Spencer Hamilton, damn him, too! I'll do anything I have to to stop him. I've got to talk to my father immediately."

"You know, Juliana Lowell, I'm beginning to suspect

you're one of those females I've heard referred to as bluestockings."

She glanced up to find him watching her with a warmly amused look in his eyes. "Wh-what do you mean?"

He leaned back in his chair, arms crossed. "You are so staunchly in favor of what you think is right, and so strongly opposed to that which you consider wrong. You're fiercely outspoken, and I'd wager you'd not hesitate to take up arms, if the need arose."

He sat his chair down with a bang and got up to walk toward her.

"I'm warning you," she hissed, "stay away from me, or I *will* take up arms!"

He laughed, reaching out a hand. "I don't mind if you lack a typically feminine mind, but why don't you do something with your hair? Why do you persist in twisting it back so severely?" His quick fingers pulled one of the wire hairpins from her hair, letting one long strand drop to her shoulder.

"How dare you?" she gasped, slapping at his hand as he reached for another hairpin. "Stop it!"

She attempted to twist away and found herself pinioned in one strong arm. With his other hand, he began removing the rest of the pins.

"Let me go," she cried, struggling fiercely in his embrace. At once he turned her to face him, held tight against his muscular chest.

His words were low. "The time is coming, Juliana, when I may not be able to do as you ask."

She caught her breath as his face lowered to her own. Just as she thought he was going to kiss her, she heard a sharp intake of breath and the words, "Unhand her, ye filthy beast!"

Essie flew into the room, eyes snapping in fury. She waved one bony fist. "Ye're in for it now. I'm calling the husband and he will throw ye from the house."

Ruark released Juliana, his eyes dancing with laughter. "Please, Essie, don't call Will-John. The man's a brute. I promise to behave."

Essie put her hands on her hips. "As well ye might. I swear, ye've been acting like an untamed lout since the moment ye first saw Miss Juli. No doubt ye've frightened her out of her very wits."

Juliana could feel deep color creeping into her cheeks. Too embarrassed to face either of them, she lowered her head and escaped from the room.

Later, sitting on the hearth rug in her bedroom, knees drawn up, she recalled what she had learned of Ruark's past and his decision to become a highwayman. At least, she conceded, he had not turned to crime for personal gain. In a sense, there was a certain foolish nobility in his actions, something she hadn't seen in any other man she'd ever known. In an age when it seemed humans were rapidly developing a callous disregard for the well-being of their fellow man, he was indeed a rarity.

She put a hand to her hair, which she had hastily repinned. That was the most puzzling thing about Ruark Hamilton, she decided: his strange attitude toward her. There were times when she was positive he was mocking her, having a little sport with the shy spinster, and yet, there were moments she could almost believe he meant the provocative things he said.

Hearing a slight noise, she looked over her shoulder and was amazed to see an opening appear in the rounded stone wall. She scrambled to her feet as Ruark stepped into the room, a rather sheepish smile on his lean face.

"Tell me how you knew about the secret doorway," she demanded, at a loss as to how to greet him after the strange intimacy of the scene in the dining room.

"Will-John showed me. He's known of it since he was a child, and thought it might be useful if I should ever need to make a swift retreat from the tower."

"I knew nothing of it. And even after I saw you come through it, I couldn't find the release." Suddenly Juliana fell silent, feeling awkward.

Ruark moved forward a few steps. In one hand he held a bouquet of deeply crimson flowers. "You needn't worry, I haven't come to harm you. I only wanted to apologize for my rude behavior earlier this evening." He held out the flowers, forcing her to approach him to take them.

She buried her face in their spicy fragrance, breathing deeply. "Sweet William," she murmured, "the flower of gallantry. Did you know that was their meaning?"

"As a matter of fact, I did," he admitted. "I read it in that old dictionary of flowers."

Juliana looked up quickly. "So you did have it. No wonder Essie acted so oddly when I couldn't find it."

"I think she thought there was something odd about a man who wanted to read about flowers." Ruark grinned.

Juliana couldn't help noticing the elusive dimple had returned to his tanned cheek.

"When I found these flowers growing along the garden wall, I thought you might like them."

"That was kind of you. They always bloom early because it's so sheltered there." Again she bent her face to the bouquet. The crimson petals were ringed with a deeper red, a color so dark it looked black in the dim light. She looked up at him through her lashes. "Of course, you must never tell Essie you picked the Sweet William. It's her favorite, also, and she sets great store by them."

"Oh, Lord, what have I done?" he groaned. "She's the one woman I suspect might be more dangerous than you."

"No doubt you're right. But at this point, I don't see how either of us can be much of a threat. Essie treats you as a friend, and I seem to have wavered in my resolve to go to the law." She shrugged, as if puzzled by her own behavior. "As for the flowers, I'll put them in a vase, and tomorrow I'll paint them. Perhaps that will appease Essie."

"Then, in return, I promise to be more gentlemanly when in your presence," he said. "Now I'll bid you good night. It may be a number of days before I see you again as I have to travel up to London. There's a bit of business to attend to."

He took her hand and kissed it, bowing over it in a courtly fashion.

Juliana deliberately ignored thinking about the sort of business that would need his attention. "Good night," she murmured.

Much later, stirring from a deep sleep, Juliana heard music. Someone somewhere was strumming a guitar and singing a ballad in a deep, masculine voice. The refrain was softly haunting, even though the words seemed foreign.

Turning on her pillow, she sighed. No doubt the evening just past had reminded Ruark of his home, bringing back bittersweet memories of childhood and things that used to be.

It was a long time before sleep returned to banish the image of the gypsy from her mind.

Six

One day, nearly a week later, Juliana was awakened by a brisk knock at her door. Essie sailed into the room, wearing her best black dress.

"I thought I'd bring ye yer breakfast before I leave, Miss Juliana. The husband is anxious to be off to the fair."

"The fair?"

"Have ye forgotten? This is May Day!"

"Is it truly? I hadn't realized."

"Ye never used to forget a fair day when ye were a little girl," Essie said, fondly. "Ye always loved them."

Juliana tossed back the bedcovers. "So I did. But that was a long time ago."

"Maybe not so long as ye think, child. Why don't ye go with us now?"

"You and Will-John go ahead, Essie. I may come later." Juliana stepped up to the tall, recessed window near her bed and looked out across the front lawn.

"If ye're moping about, waiting for Ruark to return, ye might as well forget it. Ye'll learn soon enough there's no way to predict that wild gypsy's comings and goings."

Juliana frowned. "Why would I be waiting for Ruark? He's certainly no concern of mine."

"All the same, I feel ye're worrying about him," said Essie. Then, in a kinder voice, she continued, "There's no need to fret, Miss Juli. The lad can take care of himself. He'll be all right."

Juliana turned away from the window. "Do you know, today was to have been my wedding day?"

"Mercy, I'd forgotten! Oh, poor child," cried Essie. "Ye must be feeling down in the mouth."

"Not a bit of it." Juliana laughed. "It seems no one believes I really don't mind not getting married."

Essie looked doubtful. "Won't ye reconsider coming to the fair with us? It would cheer ye up."

"Essie, I don't need cheering up," she exclaimed, exasperated. "Now you and Will-John go on."

Essie drew herself up, obviously miffed. "Very well, but if ye should decide to honor us with yer presence, for goodness sake, put on something pretty, not one of those drab gowns ye usually wear."

"I didn't mean to make you angry," Juliana said. "And as for my clothes, what would you advise me to wear?"

"None of the things ye brought with ye from London," the old woman snapped. "If ye'd like, I'll fetch one of the dresses I made."

"Oh, Essie, the dresses," Juliana cried. "I'm sorry. You must have thought I was ungrateful not to have mentioned them again." She put her arms around the frailer woman. "It's just that everything has been so confused lately."

"And well I know it," Essie said, a smile finding its way to her wrinkled face. "The gowns are in yer old bedroom, Miss Juli. I'm certain ye can find something among them to wear to the fair."

"All right. But you go along and don't keep Will-John waiting."

* * *

After carrying her breakfast tray down to the kitchen and washing up the few dishes, Juliana wandered through the empty house. Drawn by the bright sunshine, she strolled along the garden path and though she briefly entertained ideas of getting out her paints, somehow she didn't feel in the mood.

It was amazingly quiet at Quarrystones. At odd moments, she found herself wondering if it was because the outlaw had left, taking with him the excitement that had colored her days for a short time.

She paused near a yew hedge, thinking of the noise and gaiety she would find at the May Day fair. She decided to walk down to the meadow near the farming village and watch the fun.

Remembering Essie's words, she climbed the stairs to her former bedroom. There in the oak clothespress she found the gowns the other woman had made for her. She felt a thrill of pleasure seeing their deep, gemlike colors glow against the dark interior of the cupboard. They were like nothing she had ever seen before; the golds, greens, roses, and blues subtly reflected the hues of nature.

As she drew out a gown of blue, the exact color of the delphiniums that filled the garden in mid-summer, she imagined Essie's delight in being able to create such lovely colors. She must have spent many long hours working on the elaborate surprise: there were at least eight new gowns in the clothespress.

Juliana shrugged out of the solemn grey dress she was wearing. She could hardly wait to find Essie and thank her. Not for the first time, she realized she had always been favored by the Cliftons. No matter how handsome and charming the other two Lowell children were, it had been evident that Essie and Will-John's loyalty lay with her.

They'll have a home with me for as long as they want, she vowed silently. *And I'll persuade them not to work so hard. They aren't getting any younger and they've certainly earned a rest.*

She turned to look in the full-length mirror and her thoughts halted abruptly. The dress was clearly the most attractive garment she'd ever worn, despite the fact it was merely a summer frock of plain cotton. The sleeves were elbow-length, puffed and tied with blue-violet ribbons. The neckline was modestly low, the waist tight and the flaring skirt of the popular shorter length that showed a flash of slender ankle as she moved in front of the mirror. But it was the color that made the gown so appealing; the vibrant blue fairly shimmered. It repeated itself in Juliana's eyes as she went closer to the mirror.

In addition to the dress, she seemed to have donned an unexpected feeling of festivity. Suddenly she couldn't wait to get to the fair. She was filled with the same excitement she'd once known as a child on May Day.

She picked up a hairbrush from the dresser and began to brush her hair. Just as she started to sweep it back into the usual knot, she glanced up and caught sight of her reflection again. Unbidden, Ruark's words came to her. *Why do you persist in twisting your hair back so severely?*

Critically, she studied the waves that fell around her shoulders. The color, a deep shining brown, was dramatic against the blue of the dress, reminding her that her mother had always preached that unbound hair indicated wantonness. Juliana smiled at the thought, recalling how many of Eliza Lowell's standards she had ignored lately. Feeling light-hearted, she decided she might as well disregard one more. Something told her the carefree days she had been enjoying would soon end, and she was determined to savor this one to the fullest.

Knowing the morning dew would ruin her good slippers and, not wanting to wear her battered walking shoes, she decided to simply go barefoot. As she left the room, she took a handful of blue and violet ribbons from a dresser drawer.

Walking across the meadow, she indulged in one of her favorite childhood pastimes, picking the delicate wild hyacinths that grew along the river and weaving them into a flower garland. Using the ribbons she'd brought, she tied each little "trumpet" separately, alternating the flowerets from a stalk of mauve hyacinth with those from a pale blue one. When she had finished the garland, she placed it on her head and let the trailing ends of ribbon stream out behind.

Before she reached the actual site, Juliana could hear the music and noise of the May fair, which was held in a large grove of trees at the edge of the meadow.

When she entered the grove, she was immediately surrounded by the activities of the country fair. Children were running and shouting; the crowd of villagers drifted about among the peddlers and craftsmen, talking and laughing. Juliana spied a few of her own tenant farmers, and this time they greeted her in the usual friendly manner. Even in their present state of poverty, a fair was something they could enjoy. A few pennies would buy hot beef pies and a mug of ale, and if that price was too steep, at least they could view the exhibits and wander about in the early summer sunshine in the company of the other merrymakers. For a time, she hoped, they might be able to forget some of the grave problems with which they were faced.

Essie and Will-John were chatting with a broad-faced

lady who was weaving corn-dollies from stalks of wheat as she talked. When Juliana approached them, Essie began to smile.

"Oh, lud, isn't she a pretty thing?" she asked Will-John.

The old countryman whipped the bedraggled straw hat off his head and grinned slowly. "I can't recall ever seeing a finer lass," he replied. "Miss Juli, you look like a bride."

Essie glared and jabbed him in the ribs with a sharp elbow. "Ye big oaf! What are ye thinking of?"

Will-John seemed lost. "But what did I say, woman?"

Juliana had to laugh. "Don't be angry, Essie. He didn't mean anything by it."

Will-John looked from one to the other of them. "But, what did I say?"

"As if ye didn't know, ye great lump!" railed Essie.

"Will-John, this was supposed to be my wedding day. I think Essie believes I might fall into a decline at the mention of brides."

"Oh. I'm a fool, lass," he mumbled.

"No, you're not," she assured him. "Please don't worry about it. I thought your compliment was lovely, and I don't feel in the least like going into a decline." She turned to Essie. "The gowns are beautiful. I can never thank you enough."

The small woman glowed with pride. "Just let me see ye wearing them, child, and that will be thanks a-plenty. Ye truly look pretty in that blue."

Juliana smiled. "This wonderful color would look nice on anyone."

The corn-dolly lady beamed at her. "Here ye be, lass, a good-luck charm for the lady of the manor." She held out a small square of intricately woven wheat.

"It's very pretty," Juliana told her, "but I've just realized, I came to the fair with no money."

"Oh, there be no charge fer ye, my lady. 'Tis a gift."

"That's very nice of you." She took the charm and slipped it into one of the pockets of her gown.

"May it bring ye all the luck in the world."

"Thank you."

At that moment they heard the sound of approaching music, and presently a man playing a flute came along the main path, followed by a crowd of young people, laughing and calling out to one another.

"Oh, 'tis time to dance the May pole," exclaimed Essie. "Come on, let's go to the meadow and watch."

The three of them joined the throng following the piper, and in a few minutes arrived at the meadow where the gaily beribboned May pole stood, its long pink, green, and yellow streamers billowing in the breeze.

A short, wiry man dressed as a jester in a brilliant scarlet and gold costume stood in front of the May pole, gesturing for silence. This was the May Gosling, a character similar to the fool at April Fools' Day fetes.

"Attention!" he shouted. "Good folk, give me your attention!"

Slowly, the crowd fell silent and gathered around him.

"Before we have the dancing of the May pole, we must choose a new May Queen." As he talked, he nodded and smiled, making the bells on his tall, horned hat jingle gaily. "Who have you decided shall be May King?"

There was a buzz of voices and, with a great deal of laughter, some of the older men in the crowd carried a youth forward on their shoulders. As they set him on his feet a round of applause greeted the May King, and he blushed and bowed.

"It's young Fred Ferguson," announced Essie in a low voice. "Do ye remember him, Miss Juli?"

"Of course, I do. I played with the Ferguson children for years."

The man was stockily built, with bulging arm muscles. A thick mat of dark brown hair tumbled over his broad forehead and, as his laughing brown eyes swept the crowd, he was a handsome sight. Juliana could hear a trio of young girls near her tittering in excitement.

It was indeed an honor to be chosen Queen of the May, and many a friendship had been destroyed in the fierce competition. The king was chosen by the other men in the village, who usually selected a personable, hard-working lad. Since it then fell to him to name his own May Queen, each prospective king enjoyed a few days of extreme popularity. Pies and cakes often appeared mysteriously in his cottage, and the attention he received whenever he went out among the village females was both daunting and exhilarating.

Fred Ferguson began walking through the crowd, pausing to study each of the anxious young ladies who caught his eye. He stopped before Juliana and favored her with a gleaming smile.

"Hello, Miss Juliana," he said. "It's nice to see you back at Quarrystones. My ma told me what you're doing for the tenants."

Juliana returned his smile, but didn't speak. She knew a prolonged conversation would only further agitate those awaiting his decision.

A squeal of mingled delight and disappointment went up when he made his choice. He took the hand of a delicate blond girl standing near the back of the crowd and drew her forward.

"Why, that's Rosemary Jacobson," whispered Essie.

"Their mothers have been trying to get them together for years."

"Perhaps they've succeeded at last," Juliana commented. "They do make a handsome couple."

Young Rosemary was shy and undeniably pretty. When Fred placed a crown upon her fair head and kissed her, the crowd cheered with pleasure. The couple was then seated on their thrones, two woven-birch chairs decorated with flowers and ribbons, to watch the dancing of the May pole.

A group of four musicians readied their instruments, while the dancers found their places around the pole. Each dancer grasped a streamer, and when the music began, moved around the pole, weaving the ribbons in and out. Sometimes someone would go astray and the others would laughingly undo the damage.

Juliana smiled and clapped her hands, delighted by the beauty of the folk dance. Suddenly one of the dancers, a brawny fellow with burnished red hair, reached out and grasped her hand, pulling her into the dance beside him.

"Oh, no," she cried, laughing, "I can't do this."

He put the streamer into her hand and, clasping her about the waist, guided her along in time to the music. "Nonsense, my lady, 'tis simple."

To her amazement, it was easy, and in only a few moments, she'd mastered the trick of weaving the ribbon, though her partner did not relinquish his firm grip on her.

The dance drew to a close when all the streamers were wrapped around the pole in a pretty pattern. Still flushed with pleasure, Juliana didn't notice the tall figure that stood at the back of the crowd watching her, a faint smile on his lips.

* * *

Later, Juliana parted company with the Cliftons when they decided to sit and rest over mugs of ale. She wandered back through the grove of trees, stopping now and then to talk to old acquaintances or to watch one of the craftsmen at work. Soon the banging of a drum claimed her attention and she followed the gathering crowd to see what new entertainment was about to start.

A tow-headed boy, nine or ten years old, was noisily beating on a battered drum. "Come see Doctor Edwin Arthur perform. Doctor Arthur is the strongest tooth-puller in all of Kent. No rotten tooth is a match for his strength!"

At this point in his spiel, the boy indicated a thin man standing behind him, flexing his right arm. Considering the bony look of the rest of the man's physique, Juliana strongly suspected his muscles were a matter of strategic padding. Her eyes widened as she caught sight of the pair of long metal pliers he held in his hand.

"Now, step right up, ladies and gentlemen. Surely there is some brave soul among you who needs a tooth pulled. How about you, sir? Doctor Arthur is the most painless tooth-puller in the south of England. What do you say? I can see you are in pain."

The man to whom the boy was speaking did, indeed, look pained, but whether from the aching tooth he was obviously nursing or from the sight of Doctor Arthur's pliers, Juliana couldn't tell. The farmer turned to his wife and held a whispered conversation, during which one beefy hand kept straying to his swollen jaw. Finally, with a look of resignation, he reached into his pocket and drew out a coin which he handed to the child.

At the sight of the farmer's money, the good doctor stepped forward and greeted his would-be patient. Juliana watched in fascinated horror as the tooth-puller seated the man in a straight wooden chair and instructed him to open his mouth. Placing one sharp knee across the man's lap, the physician leaned forward and stuck the pliers into the man's mouth, positioning them around the diseased tooth. With a grunt, he yanked and the farmer stiffened in pain, a muffled scream torn from his throat. The young boy began pounding on the drum again, louder than ever. Wiping the perspiration from his forehead, the tooth-puller got a firmer grip and tried again. This time, with a shout of triumph, he waved the pliers aloft, a bloody tooth clamped between the pincers. The farmer stopped screaming and slumped in the chair, clutching his jaw.

With a shudder, Juliana closed her eyes and turned away, only to find herself clasped in two strong arms. Her eyes flew open and she was looking up into Ruark Hamilton's laughing face.

"Not a pleasant sight, was it?" he queried.

"What? You or the tooth-puller?" She felt almost giddy and tried not to analyze her sudden happiness.

Delighted with her saucy answer, Ruark flung back his head and laughed. The sunlight sparkled on the small gold hoop in his ear.

"Believe it or not, Juliana, I've missed you."

Not knowing how to respond, she posed a hesitant question. "Did everything go as planned?"

"Things went very well."

Realizing he still had his arms around her, Juliana moved away and he released her.

"Where did you go?" she asked, as they began to walk on through the crowd.

"To the outskirts of London. There were certain men's clubs whose members felt inclined to make donations to our worthy cause."

Juliana looked up at him, smiling.

"How generous of them."

Her attention was taken by the colors of a gaudy silk tent and, as she watched, an aged crone, obviously a gypsy, stepped to the opening and beckoned to her. "Would the lady like her fortune told?"

The gypsy's wrinkled face was dominated by a pair of agelessly beautiful eyes. As their gaze fell upon Ruark, the woman smiled and greeted him in Romany. He nodded, replying in the same language. Again, the woman looked at Juliana. "Come." She turned and went back inside, clearly expecting them to follow.

Without discussion, Ruark took Juliana's elbow and escorted her into the tent.

"Sit there and let me see your palm," the gypsy instructed, pointing to a low stool at one side of a table. There was a long fringed cloth with a round lump of crystal set in the center.

Juliana seated herself, aware that Ruark was standing close behind her. The woman, a kerchief on her head and worn shawl around her shoulders, dropped into the other chair and took Juliana's hand, turning it palm-upward.

After a few moments of concentration, she looked up, but her gaze went to Ruark's face and she cackled happily. Again they conversed in their strange tongue, but Juliana had no doubt she was the topic of discussion.

The gypsy, as if sensing her anxiety, turned a sharp glance on Juliana's face. "You have a lucky palm, my girl. All good things in life will be yours: wealth and happiness and a handsome man to share them with."

Juliana's mouth twitched with amusement. Surely she didn't appear such a fool as to believe just anything the gypsy told her.

"Your destiny is entwined with that of a tall, dark man. A man strong enough to protect you from the danger which lurks all about. But you must listen to him, obeying him in all things." She paused to cackle again, and Juliana shot Ruark a wicked look.

"You'll have to be strong, however, for there will be a time when you must protect your man. When danger threatens him, you're his salvation. Do you understand?" Her words were so fierce that Juliana nodded. "You alone can save him."

She studied the palm for a moment longer. "Everything you want is within your grasp, child. You only have to be strong enough to reach out and take it."

Ruark dropped a handful of coins on the table over the old woman's protest. Again they spoke in Romany and finally, with a chuckle, she scooped up the money and tucked it into her pocket.

As they left, Juliana asked, "Why did she refuse the coins at first? I thought fortune-tellers wanted their palms crossed with silver."

"Not always. There's an unwritten rule that gypsies don't profit from their own kind."

"What did you say to change her mind?"

"I told her the last two days had been very lucrative for me, and that I wanted to share my good fortune. She said it might be bad luck for both of us if she scorned an offering from the Kentish Gypsy."

"Does everyone know about your masquerade as the highwayman?" asked Juliana.

"It would seem so."

She frowned. "How long, then, do you think to keep your identity hidden from the authorities?"

"I don't fear those pompous bigots. They'd have to look

farther than the ends of their noses before they could possibly see the facts. And I don't fear betrayal by the villagers, either."

"Do you think I could somehow endanger you?"

He stopped walking and gazed into her face. "Aye, girl dear, you very well might." His sudden smile flashed. "But, oh, what delightful danger."

He lifted a hand to brush back wayward curls from her forehead, letting one finger trace a line along her cheekbone and down to her chin. He gently raised her face. "You should have been the Queen of the May, you know. If I'd been king, I'd have chosen you."

For the first time, she really looked into his eyes and was astonished at how dark they were, nearly black beneath the raven brows and lashes. But, dark as they were, small glints of warm light seemed to dwell within their depths.

Before she could think of a reply, the spell was broken by the shouts of the pieman and, laughing a bit shakily, she turned away and said, "I just realized I'm famished. I haven't eaten since early this morning."

"Nor have I." He fished more coins from his pocket and purchased two meat pies from the peddlar.

Taking Juliana's hand, he led her through the crowd to a quiet spot a little way into the forest. They seated themselves on the trunk of a huge fallen tree, Ruark lifting Juliana and then climbing up beside her.

Juliana was puzzled by her lack of animosity toward the man she knew to be a thief and outlaw. When had she lost all fear of danger at his hands? And when had she abandoned her anger with him?

As they finished their food, a crowd of young men wandered past, pausing to drink wine from a goatskin. Spying Ruark and Juliana, one of them offered the goatskin.

"It's fair day," he shouted, "so drink up. Let the wine flow." He staggered clumsily and his comrades laughed.

He came closer to Juliana, holding out the goatskin. With a quick glance at Ruark, she reached out to take it, but as her fingers closed on the soft leather, the man pulled back, causing her to lose her balance and tumble from the tree trunk. He cast the goatskin aside and wrapped his arms about her, pulling her close against him. His fellow revelers hooted and cheered.

"Whoops, milady!" He grinned broadly. "You could have done yourself harm. 'Tis lucky I was here to catch you."

Juliana placed her hands against his chest and tried to push him away. "Let me go," she said calmly.

"Ah, surely you won't deny me a reward for saving you from a nasty fall?" He bent his head, intent upon kissing her, and did not hear the gypsy drop lightly to the ground beside him.

Ruark uttered a short, sharp Romany curse and lifted the man from his feet, causing Juliana to shrink back against the log. His face was a mask of fury as he tossed her attacker bodily into the underbrush, where he lay unmoving.

His companions grew silent, their merry mood destroyed. Ruark faced them, feet apart and fists clenched, but none of them accepted his unspoken challenge. Instead, two or three of them hoisted up the fallen man and quietly dragged him away, darting quick glances back over their shoulders to make certain the infuriated gypsy was not following them. The rest of the group moved slowly away, one or two of them muttering brief apologies.

Ruark turned to Juliana. "I know what you're going to say," he stated. "You're about to tell me what a bully I am, and how uncouth I was to attack that man. And that you could have taken care of yourself."

Her blue-grey eyes danced with laughter. "Not at all," she said. "I'm grateful for your intervention."

He looked surprised. "You are?"

"Of course. I would've done the same thing to him, had I been able."

He bent to pick up the goatskin. "You're the most unusual female I've ever known, Juliana. You don't react in a normal way to anything." His dark gaze glowed. "Sometimes I wonder . . ."

"Well, don't," she warned.

"Aye, you're right. There's no point in speculating about something I intend to find out for myself anyway."

Night fell, but the May Day celebration continued. As in ancient times, bonfires were lighted across the hillsides.

As they stood watching the great fires flare in the distant darkness, Ruark said, " 'Tis a custom the church tries hard to discourage."

"Because it was started by the Druids?" asked Juliana.

"Yes, and because of the cruelties associated with the bonfires."

"What sort of cruelties?"

"To insure a good harvest, the Druids made sacrifices to the fires. Sometimes even human sacrifices."

"That does sound horrible." Juliana shivered in the cool night air. This hillside seemed very far removed from her life in London.

"Now, of course," Ruark went on, "dancing around the fires is only an excuse for the village lads and lasses to have a bit of fun."

Even as he spoke the dancers moved toward them, wending their way in and around each bonfire. They were led by the King and Queen of the May, and their steps were accompanied by the band of musicians that had played earlier in the afternoon.

Ruark took Juliana's hands and pulled her into the line of dancers with him. She followed willingly, swaying in time to the strains of the strange music. Perhaps it was the wine she had drunk, or perhaps it was the heady atmosphere, but somehow, she felt happier and more carefree than she ever had before. She found herself wishing this night, this mood, could go on and on.

But eventually the music ended and when she turned to face Ruark, she had to stifle a yawn behind her hand. He smiled.

"I think it's time for you to go home, Juliana."

She nodded. "I know. I was wishing the night would never end, but suddenly I realize how tired I am."

"Come along, I'll walk you back to Quarrystones."

"That's not necessary. Don't you want to stay and dance?"

"I doubt it would be safe for you to walk through the meadows alone. If some mere mortal crossed your path, he'd swear you were a Druid and try to capture you. With that garland on your head and those dirty feet, you do look like a pagan."

"I do?" Juliana was shocked back to reality. "Oh, heavens, I must look awful."

He chuckled. "Not to me; I like pagans. Now, come on." He took her hand again and led her away from the crowd. As they started along the path they could hear the noisy music and the laughter of the dancers once more.

They walked quickly and soon left the revelry behind. The only sound they heard in the still night was the chirp of crickets. Overhead, in the black velvet sky, millions of stars scattered pinpoints of light. The moon was new and surrounded by a soft haze of silver.

"Did you believe the things the gypsy lady told me?" Juliana asked, tilting her head to look up at Ruark.

"Of course, didn't you?"

"I don't know. It was rather confusing. All that about danger and salvation." She yawned again, putting the back of her hand against her mouth. "I suppose they have to try to make it sound exciting, because they always end by telling everyone the same thing: that their's is a lucky hand, that they'll be rich and happy."

"So you think she was a fraud?"

"I do."

They had reached a wooden stile in the fence, and instead of walking up and over it, Ruark turned and seated himself on the middle step. "Don't you think it's possible your palm actually did reveal good fortune?"

Juliana paused in front of him. "I don't know," she answered honestly, "but I'm afraid I believe that gypsy woman about as capable of really telling my fortune as *you* would be!"

"What makes you think I can't look into the future? I happen to be rather adept at reading palms. Shall I prove it?"

Without waiting to hear her reply, he took her hand and drew her closer to him. "Romanies always read the left hand, and much of what they tell you is based on its shape. See, yours is tapered, with long, slim fingers. That means you're creative and artistic. It also shows that you're idealistic, perhaps even unworldly." He paused and smiled at her, his face alight with deviltry. "You like intellectual pursuits, but there must also be music and beauty in your surroundings. I suspect you're the kind of person who can be happy one moment, then utterly miserable the next."

"How could you possibly tell all that from the shape of a hand?"

"It takes years of study, little skeptic." He turned her palm upward. Cradling her hand in his larger one, he used his other forefinger to trace a curving line.

"This is your life line, Juliana. See how lengthy and deep it is? That means you'll have a long and healthy life. And here, see how the line is forked toward the end, with this little tendril curving round the thumb?" She nodded, leaning closer to see better in the shadowy light. "That shows you'll have an active, vigorous old age." He looked up. "You have a double life line, also. That means there's a second line, or shadow, along the life line. Someone in your life will have great influence over you."

"Oh?"

"Aye, and whether you believe it or not, it's another lucky sign. Now, this line that curves downward is the head line. It shows you to be an intelligent woman and, because it separates from the life line here at the start, you're adventurous, daring, and quite independent." His eyes teased her.

"What you're saying is interesting, but even you have to admit the qualities you've mentioned could either be accurate guesses or things you've already learned about me."

"Still not convinced, eh? I see I'll just have to delve deeper to find some trait that can be proven. Ah, here's something. This is your heart line. It's very defined." He rubbed a thumb along the crease in her palm, causing her to flinch and try to pull away. He kept her hand within his grip, and slid warm fingers around her wrist. "Do you know what that means?"

Silently, she shook her head, refusing to meet his eyes.

"It means, sweetheart, that you have a passionate nature. And that your love life will be very exciting."

She didn't speak, and when she finally forced herself to look up, he was smiling with amusement. Slowly his smile died. "And I can prove that." He moved from his seat on the wooden stile to stand against her. Putting his hands at her waist he pulled her into the curve of his lean body and before she could protest, began kissing her.

His lips were warm and deliberate, tasting of the wine they had drunk earlier. After the first shock at his audacity faded, Juliana relaxed against him and enjoyed the sensation of his ardent mouth against her own. His hands spread across her back, pressing her ever closer, and, fearing she would lose her balance, she slipped her arms around his waist.

Lips against her ear, he murmured, "You smell of sunshine and hyacinths, Juliana." He pulled back to look into her face. "Juliana is a damnably long name when a man is in a hurry," he said. "From now on, I'm going to call you 'Liana—a shorter name I can just manage to say,"—he began lowering his face to hers—"before I kiss you."

Once again she was lost in his embrace, only vaguely aware of the crescent moon glowing somewhere over his shoulder.

She shut her eyes and stood on tiptoe to return his kiss. When finally his mouth left hers, she kept her eyes closed and laid her head against his chest. His hand caressed her hair.

"This has been a long day," he whispered. "I think it's time we went home."

Juliana opened her eyes reluctantly. "Yes, Essie will be worrying about me."

Ruark climbed over the stile, then put up a hand to assist

her. As she reached the top step, he lifted his arms and set her on the ground beside him. For an instant, she sagged wearily against him. Before she realized what he intended, he'd scooped her back into his arms.

"Close your eyes and let me carry you, 'Liana. I'll take you safely home."

She sighed and nestled her head against his chest. "I don't know why I'm so tired. Must have been the wine."

He smiled to himself as he started off down the grassy path.

Left behind, lying upon the wooden steps in the pale moonlight, was a garland of wilted hyacinths, its sweet scent wafting out on the still night air.

Seven

When Juliana awoke the next morning, she was lying on her own bed, still dressed in the rumpled blue gown. She had a vague memory of Ruark putting her there and then pulling a quilt over her. She sat up, feeling her face grow warm as her mind was flooded with disturbing memories of the night before.

She had never acted in such a way. What must Ruark think of her? For a moment she nurtured the hope that the whole thing had been a dream. But no, there was the woven wheat charm in her pocket, and when she stood up, her dusty, grass-stained feet presented further undeniable evidence.

A light rapping sounded at the door and Essie came into the room, carrying two pails of steaming water. "Ye've nearly slept the morning away," she scolded. "I thought ye might be in need of a bath." She looked pointedly at Juliana's feet.

She took one of the pails and followed Essie into the adjoining bathing chamber. Pouring the hot water into the copper bathtub, she said, "I'm sorry I was so late last night, but I did have a wonderful time at the fair."

"So I gather." Essie's lips pursed into a thin line. "Coming home in the middle of the night in a stranger's arms. Hmmph!"

Juliana had to laugh. "Ruark is no stranger. I feel I've begun to know him very well."

"Not as well as he'd have liked, obviously." The woman stood, hands on hips, a stern expression on her face.

"You needn't think he tried to take advantage of me, because he didn't."

"No, but only because I met ye at the front door and stayed close on his heels while he carried ye to yer bed. I shudder to think what might have happened had I not been here."

Juliana turned away to hide the expression on her face. She, too, wondered what might have happened. No doubt it was a blessing her guardian angel, in the wiry form of Essie Clifton, had been present, for something told her that no matter what Ruark Hamilton had asked of her last night, she wouldn't have denied him.

"I'm sure there was nothing to worry about," she murmured, though she felt she might be telling a lie. She began to unfasten her dress.

"Hmmph," Essie repeated. "I'll leave ye now, but don't be long. 'Tis nearly time for yer lunch."

When she'd gone, Juliana stepped into the bath.

What, she wondered, had become of her resolve to report the highwayman to the authorities? She'd been raised to be a law-abiding citizen, but somehow, in this instance, she couldn't help but think the laws were wrong. Wealth shouldn't bring unlimited power; it shouldn't bestow the right to cruelly alter the lives of others less fortunate. Ruark was only acting in defiance of a condition that should never have been allowed to exist. She couldn't fault the man for that.

Twenty minutes later, as she got out of the tub and reached for her dressing gown, she was still arguing the point with herself. What was the real reason she hadn't been more indignant at the presence of an outlaw in her home?

Was she so bemused by the nearness of a handsome, charming man that she forgot the scruples of which she'd always been so proud?

She entered her bedroom again and went to the dresser where, lost in thought, she began brushing her hair. When she looked into the mirror, she was shocked to see Ruark's reflection. He was across the room, sitting on her bed. She whirled to face him.

"What are you doing here? If Essie should find you, she'd skin you alive."

Slowly, he stood up and came close to her. He was dressed in the same clothes he'd worn the first time she had seen him: a white, open-necked shirt and black trousers, with the red cummerbund at his waist and tall, dust-covered black boots. Suddenly she was aware of the thin robe she wore and of his intense ebony gaze. His eyes moved very deliberately from her face down the slim length of her body, to stop at the hem of the dressing gown. White teeth flashed in a quick smile.

"I see the pagan has washed her feet."

Despite her best efforts to remain stern, Juliana felt a small laugh bubbling forth.

He took two steps and put his hands on her shoulders. They felt strong and warm through the thin fabric. " 'Liana, I must confess I dreamed about you all night long."

Before she could think of a reply, there was a commotion in the yard below. Startled, she backed away from him and ran to the open window to look down at the front lawn.

A familiar carriage had crossed the causeway, coming to a halt before the main door of the house. A heavy-set man was alighting.

Juliana spun about. "It's my father," she exclaimed.

"Hurry, you've got to hide. He mustn't know you're in the house."

Ruark grasped one of her hands and pressed it hard. "Don't worry, 'Liana, everything is going to be all right. I promise."

Juliana and her father met in the dining room over lunch, and his first words had an ominous ring.

"I'll warn you right now, Daughter, I'm not in the best of moods. It's bad enough when a man has to inconvenience himself because of a thoughtless child, but to make matters worse, I was accosted by some damned highwayman this morning."

Juliana's head snapped up. "A highwayman?"

"Yes, someone the groom referred to as the Kentish Gypsy. Seems the fellow has been making quite a nuisance of himself lately."

"I think Essie and Will-John have spoken of the man," Juliana faltered. "You weren't hurt, were you?"

"No," he growled, "he didn't hurt anyone. But the insolent rogue took every penny I had on me, and grinned all the time he was doing it. It made my blood boil, but there was little I could do about it. He and his men were armed."

"Oh."

"Now do you understand my objection to you living in the country alone? It's a wonder the man didn't stop the stagecoach you traveled down here in. I'm inclined to think it would have served you right." He sawed at the meat on his plate as if venting his anger on it. "What were you thinking of, running away like that?"

"I'm sorry if I worried you," she replied, noticing that her father was yet able to indulge his usual hearty appetite despite the ordeal he'd suffered. Her own food was untasted. "It seemed the thing to do at the moment."

"You don't realize how much it upset your mother, miss. She had enough on her mind what with the wedding and all. The last thing she needed was one of your temper tantrums."

"It wasn't a tantrum."

"She was most distressed that you weren't there for Spencer and Mariette's wedding yesterday."

Juliana looked surprised. "Yesterday? Do you mean they kept the original wedding date? I thought they might have changed it."

"They saw no need. After all, as soon as it was publicly announced he was marrying your sister instead of you and the furor had died down, it was rather late to start changing things. The scheduled date was at hand and everything had been ordered. Unlike you, Mariette did not choose to inconvenience anyone."

Juliana's mouth tightened. "I regret having missed the wedding."

"I would've come for you sooner but the general opinion seemed to be that you'd fled to the country to avoid embarrassment. We decided it might be better if you didn't make an appearance."

"I'd like to have been there for Mariette's sake. As for what everyone else thinks, it really doesn't matter to me."

"You've proven that, I should say. However, those things matter very much to your mother and she insists you come home with me immediately. As soon as Mariette and Spencer return from their honeymoon trip, she expects you to help give a welcome-home party to show there are no harsh feelings between you and your sister."

"But if I'm to live at Quarrystones, I won't want to be traveling back and forth to London."

Dodsworth Lowell looked rather uncomfortable. "No one has agreed to your living here, Juliana. I thought we'd decided you would have a townhouse."

"Father, I don't want a townhouse."

"I'm afraid your mother and I find Quarrystones an unsuitable place for a young woman to live alone." He waved an impatient hand. "And don't tell me the Cliftons will be here. I'm well aware of that, and I still think you need more protection. The incident this morning made that all the more evident. The city is unsafe enough; the country is out of the question."

Juliana looked stricken. "I've been here all this time and I've been perfectly safe. I can take care of myself. I'm not an infant."

"Then stop acting like one," he snapped. "You created a minor scandal by running off down here on your own, and we won't allow you to further damage your reputation, or ours, by any more scatterbrained actions. It's time for you to act your age."

"How can I, when you and Mother continually coddle me? There's really no good reason I can't live here."

"No reason except that I promised to sell the estate to Spencer, and there's no place for you in your sister's home."

"Home?"

"It seems Mariette has decided she'd like to stay here for a time." He chuckled slightly. "I think she and Spencer have been reminiscing about their childhoods, and suddenly, Quarrystones sounds very appealing to her."

"Are you certain that's what made this place so appealing? Mariette has never been the sentimental type, after all."

"What other reason could there be?"

"I can think of several, but I have a feeling the most

important one is that she wants this estate because Spencer has convinced her it could be profitable."

"Profitable?"

"Yes. Father, you don't know what Spencer has been up to behind your back. Did you know he has already petitioned Parliament for rights of enclosure at Quarrystones?"

Lowell's thick eyebrows rose in surprise. "He what?"

"And not only that, he's so certain he'll be granted his petition that he's ordered all your tenant farmers off the property. He's forbidden them to plant gardens or keep animals, trying to starve them out."

"Can you back up these accusations, Daughter?"

"Of course, I can. I've seen the cottages and talked to the farmers. Oh, it's true, all right. And that isn't the end of it. Spencer also has plans to build some sort of factory here on the Quarry River."

Lowell leaned back in his chair, rubbing his broad jaw thoughtfully. "Well, I have to admit, I'm rather surprised at Spencer. I thought the man too dandified to be interested in the land."

"He isn't interested in the land, only the money it can make him. And, Father, if he's allowed to take possession of Quarrystones, he'll destroy it. All of his profit will come from the misery of people who've always lived and worked here."

"Perhaps I should go down and talk to the farmers myself. I can trust Jacobson to tell me the truth of it."

"Please do that. I think you'll learn a great deal about your new son-in-law."

"Well, be that as it may, it doesn't change your circumstance. However, I can promise you I won't let Spencer turn the tenants off the land. I can have a clause written into the sales contract."

"You can't still mean to let them have this estate?" she cried, stunned.

"There's no reason not to."

"Spencer will never agree to your terms."

"Oh, he'll come around. Or, if not, I'll sell to someone else. I shouldn't have any difficulty finding another buyer."

"Why must you sell it?"

Lowell sighed heavily. "Juliana, we've had this conversation before and I'm growing weary of it. There's no sense in my keeping a property that has become a financial burden. It would be different if I were free to spend more time down here, attending to the business of agriculture. But with all I have to do in London, I can't. There have been expenses: Mariette's trip abroad, the wedding. Quarrystones can help pay for those things."

Juliana struck the table a sharp blow with her clenched fist. "You can't do this. You promised me the estate as a wedding gift."

"It was your own fault that you weren't Spencer's bride. Why should I honor an agreement that you didn't see fit to honor yourself?"

"At least give me the opportunity to buy Quarrystones from you myself."

His laugh was harsh. "And just where would you get that kind of money?"

"I don't know, but perhaps Auntie Lowell would make me a loan. I could find employment and repay her."

"Good lord, Juliana, listen to yourself," he roared. "You're beginning to sound more and more like one of those unnatural women who publicly campaign for equal rights. Now, I won't have it. The matter is closed."

"But . . ."

"The only way I'd allow you to settle here at Quarrystones is if you were married. If I thought you'd find a suitable husband anywhere in the near future, I'd reconsider. But that hardly seems likely since you'll never put forth any effort to be attractive."

"Why do men persist in thinking a woman must have a husband to be happy?" cried Juliana.

"Because it seems to be true. Ask any married woman you know."

"Of course a married woman would claim to be happy. She'd hardly be fool enough to admit she made a mistake and ruined her life. I fail to see why a woman needs a man before she can be considered a real person."

Lowell frowned. "Juliana, if you continue with this stubborn attitude, you can forget my offer to purchase you a townhouse. For all I care, you can live out the rest of your days in your bedroom at home."

She opened her mouth to speak, but realized the utter futility of it. There was no way to reason with him when they were both so angry.

"Get your things packed and be ready to leave for London first thing in the morning."

She bit back all the harsh words she would have spoken and forced herself merely to nod before walking out of the room and up the stairs to her bedchamber.

Juliana spent the afternoon in her bedroom, alternately pacing the floor, muttering unladylike phrases, and sitting in the window seat, staring unseeingly at the river.

Where was Ruark? she wondered. She couldn't help but think his untimely attack on her father's coach had further damaged her chances of remaining in the country. Still, he might have a solution. Hadn't he promised everything would be all right? For some inexplicable reason, she'd begun to trust Ruark to be able to accomplish nearly anything.

She spent an hour searching diligently for the spring that would trigger the opening of the secret door, but to no avail. She even tried calling his name through the wall, but there was no answer and she dared not call louder, for fear of alerting her father to his presence.

At dusk Essie came to summon her to supper.

"I'm not hungry," Juliana said impatiently. "Essie, have you seen Ruark?"

"No, I haven't. But he's no fool and most likely he's laying low until yer father has gone. Speaking of yer father, Miss Juli, he says he's in no mood for more of yer pouting. Ye'd better go down and try to behave yerself."

"Do you know what he intends?"

The old lady laid a sympathetic hand on her arm. "Yes, child, I know. But there's little ye can do to change his mind. For yer own sake, try not to anger him further."

When Juliana entered the dining room a short time later, she was determined to do as Essie had suggested. There was no need to continue annoying her father when she might yet come up with a solution that would suit everyone.

During the meal Dodsworth Lowell, apparently satisfied Juliana had come around to his way of thinking, attempted to entertain her with bits of news about the wedding and those friends and relatives who had attended. Though she tried to smile occasionally, it was an ordeal she hoped would soon be over. She felt hypocritical trying to hide her seething anger beneath a veneer of enforced pleasantness. Essie had cleared away the dishes and was pouring glasses of homemade wine when someone knocked loudly at the front door. Lowell looked irritated.

"Who could that be? I'd hoped no one knew I was at Quarrystones so I could make an early night of it."

When Essie returned, she was followed by a tall man. As he stepped out of the shadows and into the lighted dining room, Juliana gasped. It was Ruark.

Before she could utter a word, he crossed the room to her and, taking her hand, bowed over it and said, "Good evening, my dear. You're looking lovely, as usual."

Lowell's expression was one of total astonishment. Ruark turned to him, saying, "Forgive my intrusion, but as soon as I learned Juliana's esteemed father was down from London, I wanted to present myself forthwith. I hope you'll overlook my unannounced arrival."

"Indeed, but might I ask who you are?"

"Allow me to introduce myself. I'm Edward Ruark, Duke of Kilcairn." He extended a gloved hand which was immediately gripped by Lowell.

"Duke?" He seemed properly impressed. "Hmm, Kilcairn, you say? Don't believe I've heard of the title."

"I'm from Ireland, sir," Ruark informed him. "I'm here in the country visiting friends. Er, that's how I made the acquaintance of your charming daughter." He favored Juliana with a gentle smile, and her mouth went dry.

What game was Ruark playing? She closed her eyes tightly, but when she opened them again, he was still there, presenting an elegant figure quite unlike the dusty outlaw she'd last seen.

He was dressed in the latest fashion: a bottle-green frock coat over an ivory linen shirt with ruffled jabot and immaculate fawn trousers. His black hair was neatly dressed, and the gold earring was missing. He was without doubt the most handsome man Juliana had ever seen.

"My daughter failed to mention she'd made the acquaintance of a duke, your Grace."

"Ah, yes. Well, dear Juliana seems to have scant regard for the aristocracy." Ruark's expression was suitably ironic. "I've done my best to impress her, but neither my money nor my acreage in Ireland has made any inroads on her affections."

Dodsworth Lowell cast a disapproving look at his daughter, who merely stood and stared at first one man, then the other. She was truly at a loss for words. "Permit me to apologize for her lack of respect. I fear I've been far too indulgent a father where Juliana is concerned."

"Oh, no need for apologies, sir. I greatly admire Juliana just the way she is." He sighed. "Actually, it's quite refreshing to meet someone who'll speak up to me and not cower in fear of distressing me over some triviality."

Lowell looked surprised, then pleased. "Oh, quite. Quite." He briskly rubbed his hands together. "Well, it would seem I am remiss in my duties as host. Why don't we go into the parlor? I'll instruct my servant to bring us some brandy."

"Smashing idea. I'd relish the chance to get to know you better. I have a great favor to ask of you."

Lowell's broad face beamed and his shaggy eyebrows inched upward. "Indeed, your Grace?"

Ruark again bowed over Juliana's hand. "Please allow me some time with your father, dear heart, and then I must speak with you on a matter of importance." He pressed her hand firmly and his dark eyes seemed to convey a message, but she was too upset to care. Her own eyes had gone grey and stormy.

"If you care to wait in your room, Juliana, I'll send Essie for you directly." Her father turned and, with a smiling bow, ushered Ruark through the doorway. Before he followed his guest, he scuttled back to his daughter's side. "A matter of importance," he hissed in glee. "Juliana, you sly minx!"

"I don't know what you mean, Father," she said, although a blush had already begun coloring her face. She moved away. "I won't be in my room. I'm going to help Essie in the kitchen. And she is not a *servant!*"

Eight

"What is Ruark trying to do?" Juliana cried, drying a dinner plate with swift, angry motions.

Essie looked at her with sympathy. "He's only trying to help ye, child."

"I can't believe his audacity." Juliana placed the plate in the rack on the dresser with a crash. "How is his masquerading as some foppish duke going to help anything? And what on earth could he be speaking to Father about?" She snatched up another dish and began drying it.

"Be patient and ye'll soon find out," Essie advised. "Ruark is no simpleton. He'll have come up with some good plan."

Juliana put down the dish with another resounding crash. "I don't trust him," she cried. "Why couldn't he have told me what he was going to do?"

"Lass, if ye keep throwing the dishes about like that, there'll be none left. Why don't ye let me finish up here and ye go outside and wait in the garden? It might help to cool ye down a bit."

Juliana paced up and down along the causeway for three-quarters of an hour before there was any sign of Ruark and her father.

When she saw them emerging from the house, it was evident her father was beside himself with joy. She'd been seated on the low wall around the moat, idly dropping pebbles into the water, but now she got to her feet.

"You're a good one for keeping secrets, Juliana," Lowell said heartily. "You never said a word about your little affair of the heart."

"My what?"

"But, rest assured, I have given my permission," he continued, apparently oblivious to the shocked look on her face.

"Permission?" she echoed faintly.

"Yes, I've agreed that you shall marry the Duke."

"Me marry *him?*"

Before she could protest further, Ruark quickly enfolded her in a somewhat stiff embrace. "Shh, 'Liana," he whispered into her ear. "Don't say anything." Aloud, he said, "Isn't that wonderful, sweetheart? Your father's such a reasonable man."

"Once I'd gotten past my astonishment, I could see the advantage of an alliance between you. It will do you good to have a husband, Juli. Besides, no businessman would refuse the generous offer the Duke has made to buy Quarrystones. My only stipulation is that the wedding take place immediately so I can be on my way back to London."

"Immediately?" Juliana choked.

"Oh, I quite agree," Ruark said hastily. "There's no reason to delay. I myself must return to Ireland in a few days on business, and I can think of nothing I'd like better than to take my new bride with me." He beamed down at Juliana, who scowled back.

"We'll have to drive into town first thing in the morning to get a special license, your Grace, but with our combined influences, there shouldn't be any difficulty. Then the wedding can take place in the early afternoon and I'll be on my way home." Lowell wagged a thick forefinger in Juliana's face. "After all, I dare not delay in letting your mother know what mischief you've been up to this time."

He was so pleased with himself that Juliana could gladly have strangled him. "I couldn't possibly get married on such short notice," she said firmly.

"Nonsense," scoffed her father. "There's no valid reason to wait now. Not when the courtship has been so rapid. Besides, I have business to attend to, and I refuse to leave you here unless you're finally settled."

"And you must know how impatient I've been to marry you," broke in Ruark. His smug smile belied the way she glared at him.

"No, Daughter, I won't allow you to delay the matter. The wedding will be tomorrow or not at all." He winked broadly at Ruark. "That should bring her around. Well, I think I'll retire and leave you lovebirds alone for a while. Good night, your Grace."

He started off, then turned back to Juliana. "I believe you have the deed to the estate. I'll need to take it back to London with me so my solicitor can transfer it to the Duke's name." The stocky man waited until he had her assent, then walked with springing steps across the lawn to the front door. Juliana thought she could hear him humming as he went. She gritted her teeth and, as soon as he was gone, whirled on Ruark.

"How dare you?" Her fury broke around her. "What gives you the right to interfere in my life this way?"

Ruark leaned against the stone pillar at one end of the causeway. "Would you rather see Quarrystones go to your sister and her husband?" he asked quietly.

"I'd have thought of something. Something besides bonding myself in marriage to an outlaw."

"Perhaps marriage won't be as nasty as you seem to think."

"Ruark, this whole scheme is impossible. Besides, what's the point to it?"

"The point, my dear, is that we'll each get something we want badly. You'll gain control of the house and land you love so much, and I'll gain security. You'd never risk the scandal of handing your own husband over to the authorities. And that will enable me to continue my disguise as a highwayman and provide aid for the people at Moorlands. In addition, I can live here freely, able to come and go in all the best houses. Think of the information I can gather."

She walked away from him, hands clenched at her sides.

" 'Liana, what's wrong?" He hurried to catch up with her. "You don't seem very pleased with my solution. Tell me what's going through your mind."

She confronted him. "You've made an arrangement that's entirely advantageous as far as you're concerned. But what about the others involved? What about my father?"

"What about him?"

"He's bound to find out you deceived him by pretending to be a wealthy duke. Do you think he'll be pleased to learn his son-in-law is a highwayman? Or that you're paying for this estate with stolen money?"

Ruark put out his hand, but she backed away from him. "And what about me? How do you think I feel? Or do you even care? You're like all other men, thinking it's your duty to make sense of a woman's life."

Ruark looked concerned. " 'Liana, I didn't expect you to be so upset."

"I'm not upset, I'm infuriated. I hate the idea of you and

my father deciding my future without so much as a word to me." She raised her chin, fighting to keep tears from her eyes. "Shouldn't I have had a say in the matter?"

"You know as well as I do that your choices are limited at best." He took her by the arms and gave her a gentle shake. " 'Liana, I overheard the conversation you had with your father this afternoon. He made it perfectly clear that Quarrystones was to go to Spencer, despite all your pleas. He refused to consider your buying the place, didn't he?"

She nodded.

"And, didn't he tell you the *only* way you'd ever gain possession of the estate was if you were to marry?"

She pulled away. "Adding the charge of eavesdropping to your other crimes does nothing to improve your character."

He chuckled. "That particular crime gave me an idea for solving our problems, however."

"It gave you the opportunity to commit even further outrages, you mean. Impersonation is against the law. So is enforced marriage."

"If nothing else, think how much fun it will be to prove to your father that you're not an 'unnatural' woman, after all."

The dimple appeared in his cheek, but this time it only made her want to slap him. She clasped her hands together tightly. "I suppose you think this is amusing."

His smile faded. "Not really. I happen to believe getting married is very serious. Regardless of what you think, I've given this a great deal of thought. There's no better solution to our problems." He took her arm and began walking, forcing her to keep pace. "I didn't have the time to discuss anything with you beforehand, 'Liana, and obviously, I presumed too much by expecting you to go along with me.

I'm sorry for that, but it doesn't change anything. There's no other way to handle this."

"Have you considered that I might like to decide that for myself? That I don't relish being *told* what to do?"

"What does it matter who decides it? There's only one answer." Agitated, he ran a hand through his thick dark hair as Juliana heaved an angry sigh and turned away.

" 'Liana, someday you may come to agree with me on this. In the meantime, why not think of it as a bargain between the two of us? Admit it's all we can do and make the best of it."

He indicated a small rosebush by the wall. It was covered with flowers, some of which were red, some white, some a mottled combination of the two colors, growing side by side. "We'll be like that York-and-Lancaster rose. We'll blend our differences and be stronger for it."

The closed expression on her face both amused and exasperated him. "It may seem strange to you right now," he went on, "but in time, you'll come to accept it. The variegated rose is a symbol of unity, the very thing we must have for either of us to survive."

Juliana knelt then, putting her face close to the sweetness of the flowers. Events had moved too quickly, leaving her uncertain. "All right," she finally conceded. "I'll think about it. But if there's any other way, we call off the bargain. I don't want to be married."

"Why not?"

"I'm neither blind nor stupid. And I've yet to see a marriage where anyone but the husband benefitted."

"What of your own parents?"

"Precisely what I had in mind." She rose to face him, defiance in every line of her body. "I suppose most people would think my mother a fortunate woman, but I find it very sad that she has only her children and the running of her household to occupy her mind. She knows nothing of world events, because my father thinks it's unladylike for a female to read the newspapers. She can't go out of the house alone because it isn't safe; he doles out what money he deems necessary. He chooses her gowns for her, tells her how to style her hair. I've spent my entire life battling his restrictions. Why should I willingly surrender what freedom I've won?"

"You were willing to marry Spencer," he reminded her.

"For two reasons only. It was a way to gain Quarrystones, the thing I want above all else. And it seemed fairly obvious that Spencer was mild-mannered enough—"

"That you could bully him instead of the other way around?"

She blushed, but refused to look away. "I was under the impression he might be more manageable than most men."

"So your plan was to marry the poor fool, then insist you live down here in the country?"

"If you must know, I was rather hoping I could live at Quarrystones and persuade him to remain in London."

Ruark gave a brief snort of disbelief. "And what was he supposed to do in London?"

"Whatever he pleased."

"Gambling?"

"If he liked."

"What about other women? Wouldn't you have worried about that?"

She shrugged. "Not especially."

Understanding quickly dawned. "Why, bless your devious soul. You were hoping he'd find someone else, weren't you? That was your intention all along. But why?"

"That's none of your concern."

"Why?" he persisted. "What were you planning?"

"Not a thing."

"I already know you better than that, 'Liana. Let me think, I can probably figure it out without too much trouble. No doubt you wanted him to become involved with another woman so you could use his own guilt against him."

"That's not true."

"I can see it now. The rejected wife bravely stepping aside so her husband might pursue his own happiness. You were counting on him giving you Quarrystones in exchange for a divorce, weren't you?"

"It might have worked," she defended herself.

"Maybe, though something tells me you wouldn't have found Spencer all that malleable."

She sighed, her defiance fading. "No, perhaps not."

"Well, despite my discovery of your scheming nature, my offer stands. And unlike you, at least I'm straightforward."

"I still don't like being forced."

"I'm sorry about that, but you've little time to come up with any alternative."

"I know."

A sudden, malicious thought drifted into her mind, and even though she realized it was prompted by her feelings of helpless frustration, she found herself acting upon it.

"Give me an hour to think it over," she said. "Then, as soon as the household has retired for the night, come to my room and I'll tell you what I've decided."

"Ah, reason at last."

"In that amount of time, I may devise some other means of swaying my father without your help."

"Just remember, 'Liana," Ruark said quietly, "there's a

point where independence becomes foolish stubbornness." He stalked off across the lawn.

Watching him go, Juliana's mouth quirked in a tiny half-smile. Soon his arrogance would be dashed, she promised herself. Upon his return to Quarrystones, Dodsworth Lowell had reclaimed his former bedroom, and she laughed silently to think of Ruark slipping into the chamber, only to find his midnight rendezvous was with the father instead of the daughter!

She felt the first pang of remorse as soon as she entered the house. Its very stillness seemed to rebuke her. How could she cast aside what might be her only opportunity to save the estate for a bit of petty revenge?

And, revenge for what? she asked herself as she climbed the stairs to her old room on the third floor. After all, Ruark was trying to help her keep her home from falling into Spencer Hamilton's hands. Surely she stood to gain more from their alliance than he did.

She undressed slowly, letting her mind dwell on Quarrystones. So much of her life was bound up in the estate. It was her security, her life. Everything she had known of happiness had been found within its boundaries.

Loving memories were deeply ingrained on her mind. How could she forget the smell of bread baking in Essie's kitchen? The sight of afternoon sunlight striking a bowl of nasturtiums on the dresser in the hallway? The pocket-sized garden with its crumbling statue of Venus where she went when troubled because it brought her peace?

No, there was no way she could give it up. She couldn't survive anywhere else.

She pulled a nightgown over her head and fastened the

long line of buttons that began at the waist and ended at the throat.

It had been a vile trick to tell Ruark to go to the tower bedroom. She couldn't understand her own reasoning. If Ruark should awaken her father, everything would be lost. Not only would her chance to own Quarrystones be forfeited, but Ruark himself would be in serious jeopardy. Finding the Irish duke so familiar with his house, not to mention his daughter's bedroom, Lowell was bound to demand a further explanation of his identity. It would never do for him to discover he was face to face with the highwayman who had so angered him earlier in the day. Nor would it serve any good purpose for him to know Ruark was Spencer's cousin, and, she thought of it for the first time, as the survivor of Edward Hamilton's eldest son, the *legal* heir to Moorlands.

Juliana thrust her feet into a pair of slippers and flung a shawl around her shoulders. She had to stop Ruark before it was too late. She prayed she could reach him before he entered her father's bedroom and exposed the entire scheme.

The house was dark and quiet as she hurried down the stairs and let herself out the front door. She was glad of the watery moonlight, for it allowed her to move more quickly. She pulled herself up onto the weakened staircase leading to the tower, flinching as cold, damp fingers of vine trailed across her ankles. At the top of the stairs she knocked softly on the wooden door, waiting impatiently for an answer. When there was none, she pushed the door open. She was horrified to see Ruark stepping through the secret passage into the bedchamber.

Without further thought, she darted across the candlelit tower room and flung herself at his back, throwing her arms about his waist.

"What the—?"

"Shh," she whispered, against his back. "Ruark, it's me."

" 'Liana?" He turned in her embrace, a questioning look on his face.

She released him, then put a cautious finger to her lips and indicated he should close the door. When he had done so, he faced her again, hands on hips, eyes twinkling.

"Does this mean you've changed your mind about marrying me?" he asked.

She dropped her head and stared at the stone floor. Finally she gathered her courage and met his eyes. "I came to warn you. I was playing a trick on you."

"What sort of trick?"

She turned and walked away, straightening the shawl about her shoulders. Her reply was deliberately muffled.

Ruark followed her. "I didn't hear that," he said. "I think you'd better repeat it."

He grasped her shoulders and spun her about.

"I said, my father is asleep in that bedchamber. I don't know why, but for some reason, I thought it would be amusing if you sneaked in there and found him instead of me."

"Amusing, you say?" He looked stern. "You have a very odd sense of humor, my dear."

"I realize that now," she confessed. "I was angry before. But I've calmed down somewhat, and I see the foolishness of such a prank. I could've ruined everything."

"So you admit the advantage of my plan?"

"I suppose I do," she said in a resigned tone. She was filled with chagrin at the prospect and looked everywhere but at Ruark.

As her eyes moved around the room, she noticed there was a black curtain hung across the window to hide the light of the candle from anyone outside. At once she began to realize what his existence had actually been.

"You can't have been very comfortable in this tower," she commented. "It's so small and dark." She shivered uncontrollably. "And cold! It must have been awful for you, not being able to come and go as you pleased."

"I moved about rather freely," he replied, "until you came down from London. Then my activities were severely curtailed."

"Because of me?"

"In a roundabout way. You see, Essie Clifton has had the notion from the start that I entertained thoughts of ravishing you. I think she appointed herself your bodyguard."

"How ridiculous." Abruptly she turned her back again, pulling the shawl more tightly about her.

His voice was close to her ear, causing her to jump nervously. "What's ridiculous? My ravishing you, or Essie preventing it?"

She moved a bit farther away. "You needn't think you'll intimidate me with all this talk of ravishing, Ruark Hamilton. I'm well aware it's only a crude jest on your part."

He came close to her. "Is it now?" The Irish lilt was back in his voice, along with a curious huskiness that added intent to his words and made her heart start to hammer in apprehension.

He put a hand on her shoulder and she couldn't suppress a tremor.

"Why are you shivering, 'Liana?"

"Because it's as icy as a tomb in this tower," she snapped. "I'm freezing to death."

"Is that all?" he asked with a deep laugh. "I can remedy that very quickly." He swung her up into his arms and carried her across the room. "This, my lady, is by far the warmest spot in the chamber." He gently deposited her on his bed, reaching for a blanket to wrap around her.

Juliana recoiled. "Let me up," she exclaimed, struggling to free herself from the folds of the blanket.

"Sit still," he said, firmly. "There are a few things yet to be discussed and this is the most comfortable place for you. No need to catch a chill and delay the wedding." His grin was raffish.

Her protests stifled, Juliana huddled in the blanket and swallowed deeply. "This marriage," she said in a low voice, "that is to so benefit the two of us. Am I correct in assuming it's to be strictly a business agreement?"

His grin widened. "Not entirely."

"What do you mean?"

"A marriage is usually a bit different from business," he told her. "Would you like me to explain those differences?"

She put up a quick hand, causing the shawl to slide from her shoulders. Fumbling to retrieve it, she said, "No, that shouldn't be necessary."

"Good."

"But, those differences, as you refer to them, needn't have anything to do with us. I mean, we're two mature people. Don't you think it should be possible for us to live in the same house without . . . without . . . ?"

He moved closer to her, resting one knee on the edge of the bed. She scrambled away from him until her back was against the cold wall. "In answer to your question, no, I don't." His black eyes seemed to burn into her own. "I'm not Spencer Hamilton."

"I didn't think you were."

"Even so, you obviously don't know much about me. If you did, you'd never have come to my room in the middle of the night, dressed as you are, to discuss the *practical* terms of our marriage."

Her eyes were huge in her pale face. "I don't know what you mean."

"Do I look like the sort of man who would allow his marriage to be a business arrangement?"

To her horror, his lean fingers flashed out to undo the top button of her nightgown. "Surely you must recognize in me the kind of man who would insist upon his rights?" The fingers moved downward, undoing the second button. This time Juliana pushed his hand away.

"I'm leaving," she announced. "I won't stay here and be insulted."

He laughed easily. "Love, it's definitely not an insult when a man tries to remove your nightgown."

"Ohh," she stormed, swatting at his hand. "You're horrible."

Undeterred, his fingers closed on the third button, which, as she flung herself away from him, came loose in his grasp.

Juliana got to her knees, and crossed her arms over her bosom. "Ruark Hamilton, stop it! It's not too late for me to call my father and have you thrown into prison. If you make one more move toward me, that's exactly what I'll do."

He reached out, his steely fingers grasping her wrist. He pulled her to him, crushing her in his embrace. His hot mouth covered hers in a searing, demanding kiss, sending her senses staggering. She was so faint she let herself sag against him. When she discovered his body's aroused state, she began to struggle.

Ruark brushed his lips over her mouth and down her throat, to the open neck of the gown. He could feel her rapid, erratic pulse and gloried in the knowledge he could so excite her. He was confident that she was excited because, though she struggled in his arms, her mouth was actively answering his, opening in innocent invitation, even against her will.

Drawing a deep, ragged breath, he leaned away to look into her eyes. "See what happens to bold females who make threats?" he asked. His voice was a low growl. "Now, 'Liana, listen to me. This is to be a real marriage, in every sense of the word. I won't have you entertaining notions of keeping me out of your bed, do you understand? You're free to refuse my offer, of course, but at least you know my terms."

When she didn't answer, he continued, "You'd better go along to your own room and think it over. In the morning, I'll be the Duke of Kilcairn, arriving in a borrowed carriage for our nuptial ceremony. If you should change your mind, you'll have to let me know then."

He kissed her good night, this time a slow, sweet kiss. Juliana closed her eyes, overwhelmed by the sensation of his nearness. Tomorrow this man, this maddening, exciting, passionate man, was going to become her *husband*. The thought of what that might entail was more than she could deal with, and when he released her at last, she simply averted her eyes and scurried obediently from the tower room.

Ruark watched her go, an admiring smile on his face. He'd frightened her badly, he knew, and yet, there had been an answering spark in her. When her fears had calmed somewhat, they could share a glorious passion. Until she discovered that, he'd let the little hoyden worry a bit. It would serve her right for the way she'd tried to trick him. He shook his head at the thought of how things might have gone had she not warned him.

Unexpectedly, Juliana was back at the door, meek and mild no longer. "By the way," she said tartly, "I hope you realize that if I do decide to marry you, it's only because there's no other solution. I'm not fond of the idea in any way. And another thing—I found the York-and-Lancaster rose in the flower dictionary and you seem to have overlooked its secondary meaning. It's also a symbol of war."

With those words and an insolent toss of the head, she disappeared from sight down the dark stairway.

Ruark stared at the empty doorframe. It occurred to him that she had just issued a challenge. He smiled broadly.

By God, he thought, *life with a woman like 'Liana might have its trials, but it could prove to be a damnably interesting adventure.*

Nine

Juliana faced her new husband across the wide table in the dining room and tried to force a smile to her stiff lips. It had been a long day, and she was tired. A meal was just one more ordeal to be gotten through. She sighed and picked up her fork, but instead of concentrating on the food before her, she let her mind drift back to this morning, the dawning of her wedding day.

She'd been awakened from a sound sleep by a highly agitated Essie Clifton.

"Oh, lud, tell me it isn't so!" she had cried. "I went to bed last night thinking Ruark was going to put things to rights, and woke this morning to find I have a wedding on my hands!"

Juliana sat up in bed. "I should have told you. I guess I still don't believe it myself."

The other woman was busily sorting through the clothespress. "Ye haven't got a decent wedding dress and no cake! Yer mother and brother won't even be here. If I didn't know better, I'd swear your father was anxious to be rid of ye."

"He's anxious to gain another rich son-in-law," Juliana replied. "Can you believe Ruark told him he's a duke?"

Essie opened her mouth to speak, but clamped it shut as a knock sounded at the door. Dodsworth Lowell stepped into the room, looking heavier than ever in a burgundy brocade dressing gown.

"Good morning, ladies. You're up at an early hour, Juliana."

"If ye intend to persist with this foolishness, there's more to do than we'll have the time for," Essie snapped.

"Nonsense," he argued. "What has to be done besides traveling to town for the license and having the ceremony performed?"

Essie put her hands on her hips and favored him with a baleful glare. "Surely ye cannot expect yer own daughter to be married on such short notice? No banns have been proclaimed, she doesn't have a proper silk gown or flowers. The rest of the family isn't even here."

"Listen to me, woman. Juliana has already passed up the opportunity to have a big church wedding. She claims to have no interest in clothes, so why should she care what she wears? As for flowers, there's a garden full out there." His jowls quivered as he shook his head emphatically. "No, the wedding takes place today. No excuses."

"But why?" Essie persisted.

"It won't be like last time. I refuse to risk her changing her mind or growing tired of her fiancé. I don't for the life of me know how she ever caught the eye of such a man as the Duke, but I won't allow her to back out of this marriage."

"What about Mother?" Juliana asked. "Won't she be angry at your haste?"

"While she may be somewhat put out at first, when she knows the why of it, she'll agree with me. Besides, she's just gotten through one big wedding. She wouldn't have enjoyed another so quickly."

"Nevertheless," Essie stated, "there are things we must

do, and if we don't get them done, there'll be no wedding today."

Dodsworth Lowell looked taken aback at her vehemence. Ordinarily, Essie would never have spoken to him in such a manner.

"What things are so important to you, Essie?" he queried.

"Ye've got to give us time to fix a wedding dress, and I intend to bake a cake and prepare a decent meal. And the wedding will take place here at Quarrystones." She folded her freckled hands and gave one deliberate nod, as though she had issued an order not to be challenged.

"Here? Now, Essie, it would be much more convenient for us to go into town and have the ceremony there."

"Surely ye wouldn't deny yer oldest daughter that one small favor?" Essie cried. "She's asking for very little else."

Lowell turned to face Juliana. "Is this true? You prefer to be married here at the house?"

"I hadn't thought about it, Father, but yes, that would be nicer. Perhaps we could have the wedding in the Venus garden."

Lowell sighed. "Oh, all right. When Kilcairn arrives, he and I will drive into Edensfield and get the license. When we return, we'll bring the parish priest with us and the wedding can take place immediately. What doesn't get done while we are gone, doesn't get done at all. Is that understood, Essie?" The elderly woman nodded, though her expression was still rebellious. Lowell then turned back to his daughter. "Juliana, you do see the necessity for this haste, do you not?"

Her chin rose. "I understand your reasons very well."

"You disapprove of them?"

"I dislike the way in which this marriage has come about, but I have to realize that it's my most intelligent choice."

"Good girl." Her father beamed. "I'm glad you're going to be sensible about this."

"Still and all, 'tis a shameful haste," moaned Essie, backing away from the cupboard with an armload of petticoats. "I don't know what folks will say."

"When a man is as rich as the Duke," Lowell laughed, "he can do as he pleases and gossip be damned. Well, I'd best be getting dressed. Kilcairn is such an impetuous bridegroom, he'll be chomping at the bit."

He left the room chuckling, and they could hear his cheerful whistling as he bounded down the stairs.

Essie looked at Juliana for a long moment, then shook her head sadly. "I feel for ye, child. I can't imagine what either of those two butter-brains is thinking. Yer father can't think past the money. And Ruark, that devil, is doing his thinking with his—"

"Essie," Juliana warned. "I've spent the night turning this over in my mind. No matter what, I want to own this estate and be free to live my life here. If being married to Ruark is the only way to accomplish that, then I have no alternative."

"Pardon me for saying it," Essie muttered, "but damn yer father for a greedy man. And damn Ruark for a rutting stag."

Juliana smiled momentarily, then said, "We've certainly done a great deal of damning men lately."

"And with good cause."

Juliana pulled at a thread on the bedspread. "Essie, do you think Ruark is what you called him? A rutting stag?"

Essie looked shocked. "I should never have said that. It's not fit language for a young girl's ears."

"I'm about to become a married woman, don't forget. Surely such a discussion is in order." She shrugged. "I realize I'm terribly ignorant for my age, but to tell you the truth, I'd never given the matter much thought before."

"Hmmph, ye should be talking to yer mother about such things."

"I don't think she'd be much help. I once overheard her telling Auntie Lowell that she considered her marital duties quite unpleasant. When I asked her what she meant, she nearly swooned."

Bright crimson coloring crept along Essie's scrawny neck. "I take it ye didn't have any such qualms when ye were marrying Spencer Hamilton?"

Juliana's smile was wry. "Spencer wasn't exactly a rutting stag. I never spent much time worrying about that part of the marriage."

"And ye shouldn't worry about it now. Pay no heed to a foolish old woman's careless words."

"Why do you think Ruark is really marrying me?"

Essie frowned. "I believe he has a high regard for you, Miss Juli."

"That can't be it," Juliana mused, as if talking to herself. "Surely he doesn't know me well enough to have formed any opinion of my character. And it's not that he's desperate for a wife. If that was the case, he's the sort of man who'd have any number of women to choose from."

"I don't know the entire truth of it, child. All we can do is trust him. He's the only hope we have at the moment."

"I guess you're right." Juliana eyed the first shaft of sunlight coming through the window and tossed back the bedcovers. "Time is passing, Essie. We've got to get busy. I'll get dressed and help you in the kitchen. Then, while the cake is baking, we can find a gown for the wedding."

"I'll send Will-John out to gather a bouquet of those early

roses," Essie said, scurrying out of the room. "And I'd best set a hen to stew."

Now, hours later, as Juliana sat in the small, candlelit dining room, she looked up to find Ruark quietly studying her. His eyes were as black as onyx in the dim light, but even from this distance, she could feel the warmth in them. She recalled their first meeting that morning.

She had left Essie in the kitchen putting the last layer of wedding cake on the hearth plate to bake when she heard the sound of a carriage pulling up in front of the house.

"Ah, the bridegroom," boomed Dodsworth Lowell, flinging open the door. "Come in, your Grace."

Through the open doorway Juliana could see a fine coach and pair and wondered how on earth Ruark had managed to gain possession of them. Not by honorable means, she was willing to wager.

A young gypsy man Ruark addressed as Chavo was at the reins, handsomely dressed in dark green livery. Even though he looked straight ahead, impassive in the role of a well-trained servant, she was almost certain he was one of the men who'd been with Ruark the day he'd robbed the stagecoach.

Ruark stepped into the room, blocking her view of the carriage. He was dressed in an expertly tailored charcoal-grey frock coat worn over close-fitting silver-grey breeches. A single deep pink rosebud was pinned to his lapel. He looked like a man dressed for a wedding, and Juliana suddenly felt drab and insignificant in the presence of his magnificence. Shyness overcame her and she could think of nothing to say to this incredibly good-looking man.

Ruark tossed a perfunctory greeting to her father, crossing the room to take her hands. "Good morning, 'Liana." His smile was warm. " 'Tis a lovely day for a wedding."

She smiled back uncertainly, and still no words came.

"Speaking of weddings," Lowell put in, "if we're going to have one here today, we'd better get cracking. Essie informs me the ceremony is to be in the garden, so we'll have to induce the priest to return to Quarrystones with us. I expect we should be on our way to obtain the license, eh, Kilcairn?"

Not taking his eyes from Juliana's face, Ruark nodded. "I see no need for further delay. We'll take the carriage I've borrowed." It was clear he expected the older man to precede him to the vehicle, and with an indulgent chuckle, Lowell took up his hat and gloves and left the house.

When he had gone, Ruark said, "We won't be long, 'Liana. And in a few short hours you'll find yourself the owner of both a house and a husband." His black eyes almost seemed to caress her. "May the possession of both bring you good fortune."

He bent his head as if to kiss her when Essie's voice rang out. "None of that, ye young ape! Don't ye know the bride and groom are not to meet before the ceremony? Now, out with ye. We've got a world of things to do, thanks to this harebrained scheme of yers."

Ruark laughed good-naturedly, and, after pressing Juliana's hands firmly between his own, released her. "I'll be back soon," he promised, starting toward the door. He took three steps, stopped and walked back to her. "By the way, I believe this is yours, my dear." He dropped a small object onto her open palm, then, with a slight bow, went out the door to the waiting carriage.

Juliana watched his retreating back for a long moment before glancing down at her hand. Lying on the outstretched palm was the button he'd pulled from her nightgown the night before. Cheeks flaming, she fled up the stairs, ignoring Essie's questioning look.

The wedding took place at mid-morning in the smallest of Quarrystones's gardens.

The parish priest who had arrived at the estate with Ruark and Juliana's father was rather elderly, but he showed a lively interest in the unusual circumstances of the wedding. When he entered the garden, he clearly disapproved of the weather-worn statue of the Goddess of Love, and carefully positioned himself with his back to her bare-breasted image. Fancifully, Juliana imagined that the goddess's upraised hands were blessing the union between herself and Ruark, a blessing they desperately needed.

Juliana's wedding dress was a pale-yellow silk gown belonging to her mother. Essie had found it in one of the spare bedrooms along with some other clothing Eliza Lowell hadn't taken to London with her. Two seams to tighten the waist were all that was needed to make it fit Juliana.

Though the dress was out-of-date, its old-fashioned style flattered her. Her throat and shoulders were left bare by a low neckline, so she wore a simple gold locket and the filigree earrings that matched it. The skirt had a bell-shaped fullness that emphasized her slender height and the smallness of her waist. The gown's pastel hue enhanced the creamy flawlessness of her complexion and brought out the stormy-sky color of her eyes. Her dark hair was coiled on top of her head, adorned with pink and yellow rosebuds and ivy leaves. She carried the bouquet Will-John had fashioned for her, yellow roses surrounded by a thick cascade of dark green ivy.

Even as the priest began the solemn ceremony, Juliana was filled with misgivings. There had to be some other way to save the estate, if only she'd had the time to think of it.

"Don't fret, 'Liana," Ruark whispered, capturing her hand in his. "You won't be sorry, I swear."

At his fervent words, she raised her gaze to his face. He smiled reassuringly, that elusive dimple scoring his cheek. He pressed her hand tightly. "After all, our goddess is overseeing the wedding. How could we ask for a more favorable sign?"

For the first time all day, she spoke to him, and her voice came out in a harsh whisper. "What do you mean, *our* goddess?"

"Venus," he replied. "She rules both our birth signs, Libra and Taurus. 'Tis a good omen."

She smiled faintly, but his words actually held very little meaning for her. She was mesmerized by the dark fire in his eyes as they touched her face. The priest, her father, and the Cliftons seemed to fade away, leaving the two of them standing alone. Juliana Lowell, self-proclaimed spinster, was mindlessly murmuring the words of assent that would legally place her in the keeping of a man she knew to be an outlaw. Even though it appeared she had abandoned good sense, that she was probably making the most monumental mistake of her life, she suddenly couldn't imagine doing anything else. Fate had dealt her this hand, and all she could do was play it out and see what happened.

The ceremony droned on, then was over. Ruark bent his dark head and placed a kiss at her temple, leaving her grateful that he had acted with propriety. Though they were officially man and wife, she still had an unreasoning fear that her father would see through the masquerade. Apparently, their actions satisfied him, however, for he kissed Juliana's cheek and shook Ruark's hand with bluff heartiness. The bridal pair was hugged and congratulated by a tearful Essie, dressed in her best black gown, and a beaming Will-John, the comb marks still showing on his thin white hair.

Soon afterwards the little party moved inside for an early luncheon, and Dodsworth Lowell announced his intention of getting started on the tedious journey back to London.

As soon as the wedding cake had been cut and served, he made his farewells and departed, offering to return the well-paid priest to Edensfield.

When they had gone, Essie took one look at Juliana's pale, strained face and ordered her upstairs to take a nap. "No argument from ye, girl," she fussed. "Ye're so weary ye can barely stand. And no argument from ye either, Ruark."

Juliana let Essie lead her away, up the stairs and into the master bedroom, now vacated by Dodsworth Lowell. Helping her remove the gown, Essie said, "Ye were the prettiest bride I've ever seen, Miss Juli, and I say it honestly."

"Thank you, Essie. You know I could never have made it through this day without you, don't you?"

Essie looked pleased, but demurred, "Of course ye could have." Instantly her eyes snapped and sparked. "Though it fair makes me boil to think of the way they've treated ye, child. Do ye think the pampered Mariette would have pitched in and helped bake her own cake? Or worn a secondhand dress? Or settled for anything less than the grandest cathedral for her wedding?" She turned to spread the yellow dress over the back of a chair as Juliana slipped on her dressing gown. "But I'll tell ye one thing, for sure and certain. If there was any way in God's world, I'd wager she'd trade bridegrooms with ye in a minute."

An unexpected knot of misery formed in the pit of

Juliana's stomach, and she crawled onto the bed, closing her eyes.

"See, I knew ye were tired, poor thing." Essie pulled the coverlet over her and tiptoed from the room, shutting the door behind her.

Juliana's eyes opened slowly and she stared unseeingly at the ceiling. In a few careless, well-meaning words Essie had sliced right to the heart of her deepest fear. Ruark Hamilton *should* have had a beautiful bride, someone to match his own physical handsomeness.

She threw back the quilt and crossed the room to the oak-framed mirror. Now, without the flattery of the wedding dress, her skin seemed plain and dark once again. Her elaborate hair-do was coming down untidily. Her eyes were somber pools of painful self-doubt. A vision of Mariette's lovely, piquant face floated before her, and she tried to imagine what it must be like to be so beautiful. Mariette must know that every blond curl upon her head was perfect, and that one saucy glance from sapphire eyes was the only invitation a man would need to fall in love with her.

Juliana opened the robe she wore and studied the reflection of her slender chemise-clad body. Mariette was dainty and delicately rounded; by contrast, she seemed tall and angular. Mariette had softly curved breasts and full hips; Juliana hated the high-breasted, long-legged look of her own figure. Dejection rode heavily upon her shoulders as she turned away from the looking glass.

She brushed a hand over her eyes. What was wrong with her? She'd never been particularly affected by Mariette's superior beauty before. Why had it suddenly become so devastatingly important to her? She retied her robe and settled herself in the window seat, looking out at the breeze-rippled river. She sighed and rested her head against the window frame. She was probably experiencing the customary bridal jitters, she told herself.

For so long, she'd thought her objections to marriage were based on the fear of losing her identity and independence; now she realized there had been another underlying concern. She was afraid of the mysterious physical side of the marital relationship. All she knew of it was what she'd seen in her own home, and those examples were widely divergent and confusing. Her Aunt Lowell had always avoided men altogether and her mother admittedly looked upon such matters as a distasteful duty. On the other hand, Mariette lived for flirtation with any male who happened into her life. She'd hinted at clandestine meetings with a variety of men, and now Juliana wished she'd had the foresight to listen. Her sister's accounts might have provided her some insight into her current situation. In her heart, Juliana feared she was more like her aunt and mother than Mariette, and yet, when Ruark had kissed her, she hadn't been the least repelled. That thought gave her a small amount of hope.

Just as his image filled her mind, Ruark's voice sounded through the bedroom door. " 'Liana, it's me. Let me in."

One hand crept to her throat and she nervously chewed at her lower lip. She hadn't wanted to face him again until she'd managed to subdue her anxieties, so she didn't know whether to let him in or ask him to go away. The decision was taken out of her hands when she heard the strident sounds of another voice beyond the door.

"Ruark Hamilton, shame on ye!" cried Essie. "The child is exhausted. Ye can't be bothering her."

"I only wanted to see if she was all right," Ruark objected.

"Ha!"

"Essie, you seem to have some fantastic notion that I'm going to force my evil attentions upon 'Liana without her consent."

"Don't tell me ye haven't thought of it."

"I shouldn't have to explain myself to you, dear lady." His tone was gentle. "Even you can't fault a new husband seeking admittance to his bride's chamber."

The sound of Essie's disgusted snort carried easily through the wooden door. "There'll be plenty of time for that later, Ruark, and naught I can do to prevent it, more's the pity. But for now, can't ye leave the child to her rest?"

"You persist in thinking the worst of me, don't you?"

"Indeed, I do, especially after this last prank ye've pulled. I don't like ye forcing Miss Juli to marry ye, and neither does the husband. If ye mistreat her, we'll see that ye're punished."

Juliana leaned against the door. It was strange to listen to them arguing about her.

"You and Will-John have nothing to fear, and neither does 'Liana. I'm not some kind of monster."

"Well, we'll see about that." Essie's words were clearly doubtful, and Juliana could hear Ruark's short laugh.

"All right, I'll prove it by going away for now. But, Essie, my love, I wish you'd abandon your role as watch dog. Whether you like it or not, I've married the lass and sooner or later, she'll have to admit me to *our* bedchamber."

"What are you thinking about, 'Liana?"

Ruark's unexpected question brought her back to the present.

"Nothing, really," she replied. "Just musing on the events of the day."

"It has been a long, eventful one, I'll agree. Are you still tired?" He noticed the faint purple shadows beneath her eyes, the strained look around her mouth.

She nodded. "A bit."

He rose from his chair and came around to stand beside her. Taking her hands, he pulled her to her feet. "Perhaps you need time to adjust to being a married woman," he said. "It must be quite a change for the spirited Miss Lowell to find herself with a husband."

She turned her face away quickly, oddly stung by the teasing quality of his voice.

"Don't turn away from me," he urged, pulling her into an embrace. "What did I say?"

"It's not what you said, but the way you said it," she murmured. "It seems you're making fun of me."

"It does?" he asked, surprised. "I was only trying to coax you into a better mood. After all, sweetheart, this is our wedding night, and it isn't very flattering to see my bride with such a long face."

She couldn't answer his smile; she knew her countenance must be frozen into an unpleasant grimace. Gently, she disentangled herself from his arms.

"I think I'll go upstairs now," she said in a low voice. "Do you mind?"

He flashed another rapid smile. "Not at all."

As she left the dining room she thought she heard him say, "I'll be up in a short while," but she wasn't certain.

Juliana lit the candle on the nightstand and turned back the bedcovers. Moving to the dresser she spied the lacy nightgown Essie had laid out for her. With an inward trembling, she held it up. No, she couldn't bring herself to wear such a flimsy garment. She was convinced she'd feel ridiculous in it, like an old maid trying to look enticing. On the other hand, she told herself, she was about to share a bed with the handsomest man she'd ever met. What could be more ridiculous than that? How could she possibly hope to deal with a husband like Ruark? She could never please him in the way that someone like Mariette could. Why humiliate herself by trying?

For whatever reasons Ruark had married her, she had no illusion that it was because he was head-over-heels in love with her. No doubt she'd soon learn the real motive behind his actions, but in the meantime, she couldn't allow herself to be deluded into thinking he cared anything for her. She'd not make herself look foolish by wearing seductive gowns or acting in some false, flirtatious manner.

She took one of her everyday nightgowns out of the drawer and pulled it over her head, buttoning every last button, right up to her chin. Then she brushed her hair and scraped it back into a tight knot. She had slipped on her spectacles and headed to the bookshelf to find a book to read when she heard his footsteps on the stairs. She grabbed the first book she could reach and dashed back across the floor, throwing herself into bed.

When Ruark entered the room, he found her propped against several pillows, the book resting on her bent knees, and the expression in her eyes well-hidden by the light reflecting on her eyeglasses.

Ruark took in her altered appearance with a look of amused surprise, but before he could make a comment, the bedroom door opened and in sailed Essie Clifton, carrying a tray with two cups of tea on it.

"I thought I'd bring ye some nice red clover tea," she

explained, setting the tray on the nightstand. "It might relax ye for a good night's sleep, Miss Juli."

Ruark put his hands on his hips and leaned over the woman somewhat menacingly. "I have thought of several ways to relax Miss Juli for her night's sleep, Essie," he said pointedly.

Essie gasped in shock and leaped away from him, hand over her heart. "Ruark Hamilton, ye fiendish devil! Shame on ye, *shame!*"

"Essie, don't be upset," Juliana pleaded. "Everything will be all right."

"How can I leave ye with him?" wailed Essie. "Ye're too innocent to know anything of a man like him."

"What's so wrong with a husband wanting to spend his wedding night with his wife?" demanded Ruark. "It doesn't make me some kind of fiend."

"Ye're wicked, and well ye know it," Essie shouted back. "Juliana is a chaste lass, mind ye. Something *ye'd* know nothing about."

"Essie, I warn you, I've had enough of your interference."

"I wish the two of you wouldn't argue," Juliana stated.

"I can't entrust her to ye until ye swear ye'll be gentle with her."

"Essie!" Juliana's voice was shocked.

"Might I remind you that I don't have to answer to you?" Ruark ground out between clenched teeth. "From now on I will be the master in this house."

"See what sort of a man he is, Miss Juli?" Essie cried. "Selfish, unfeeling—oh!"

Ruark grasped the old woman by the upper arms and lifted her off her feet, still voicing her complaints. He carried her to a spot in the hallway beyond the door and, setting her down, said, "Good night, Essie." Gently, he shut the door in her face and shot the bolt.

There was a muffled flurry of words, but eventually they could hear her retreating footsteps. Ruark turned to face Juliana with a wry smile.

"I hope you don't disapprove of my methods too much, but I couldn't think of another way to get rid of her."

"She's worried about me," Juliana said in a small voice. "Otherwise, she'd never have acted like that."

He crossed to the bed. "I know, and I'm glad she's so devoted. But I wish she wouldn't always think the worst of me."

"She'll get over it, given a little time."

He sat down on the edge of the bed. When she attempted to move away, he placed his hands on either side of her hips and leaned close.

"What's going on here, 'Liana?"

She swallowed deeply. "I don't know what you mean."

"I think you do. Why have you buttoned yourself up in that prudish nightgown? Why is your hair like that?" The dimple flashed swiftly. "Wife, dear, I believe you're trying to make yourself unattractive to me in the hope of discouraging my amorous advances. I feel I should warn you, it's not going to work."

He carefully removed her spectacles and, folding them, placed them on the nightstand beside the bed. He then took the book out of her hands, saying with a low laugh, "I really can't believe you were all that interested in reading *Twelve Beautiful Designs for Farmhouses* anyway."

Juliana was at a loss for words, as she so often seemed to be in his presence.

"Now, tell me what's wrong."

He leaned forward, putting his face so close to hers she

could feel the warmth of his skin. She closed her eyes tightly and her heart began to hammer. Ruark brushed her mouth with his, not really kissing her, but rubbing her lips very softly with his own. She could hear his deeply indrawn breath.

"Mmm, you smell good, 'Liana. Like roses and honey."

The pressure of his lips deepened, became more possessive. His hands closed around her shoulders, pulling her against his chest. Instinctively, her hands crept between them, holding their bodies apart. Ruark moved one of his own hands downward to capture hers, and she felt a sharp thrill at the feel of his hard knuckles against her breast.

He leaned away from her and studied the hand he now held. On the ring finger was her opal birthstone, a substitute for the wedding ring there'd been no time to buy. He turned it absently with his thumb.

"You aren't afraid of me, are you?"

"Should I be?" she asked in a choked voice.

"Never. I mean you no harm. But, 'Liana, if you aren't afraid of me, what's wrong? Why are you holding yourself back?"

An unreasoning anger filled her and she pulled her hand away. "Do you think that because we're legally married, I should throw myself at you?"

One eyebrow shot upward. "What?"

She moved out of his grasp, to the other side of the bed.

"I don't know you, Ruark Hamilton. How can you possibly expect me to have any sort of . . . ?" She flung out her hands and gazed wildly around the room, as if searching for the words she wanted to use.

"Romantic feelings?" he supplied.

"Exactly!"

"I didn't expect you to have them initially, sweetheart. I'd looked forward to, shall we say, engendering them?"

"Shouldn't it be something we both look forward to?"

"Oh, I see." He nodded. "It's not something you foresee as pleasurable."

"I hadn't thought about it."

"I think you're lying. I believe you've given it a great deal of thought."

Her cheeks colored guiltily. "I have not."

"Well, I have." His fingers closed over her arm and he tugged her toward him. "I've pictured myself doing this." He removed the hairpins from her hair, letting it cascade to her shoulders. "And I've thought about kissing you like this." His mouth swooped down upon hers, hungrily, fiercely. The weight of his body pressed her into the soft feather mattress. "And you don't know how often I've imagined myself doing this." One brown hand swiftly unbuttoned the nightgown, despite her protests. When half the long line of buttons was undone, his hand slipped inside the bodice of the gown, closing over one breast. Juliana gasped, and, with a moan, Ruark's mouth found hers again, moving urgently against her pliant lips.

"Ruark, please don't," she whispered frantically, as his mouth moved to her ear, then along the side of her neck. She could feel his triumphant chuckle.

"Shh," he whispered. "It'll be all right."

She began to struggle. "Let me up. We have to stop this."

The mood broken, Ruark released her. "Why, in God's name?"

Juliana edged away, swinging her legs over the side of the bed and getting to her feet. "There are too many things we have to settle before we can continue with this marriage."

"What sort of things?"

"Well, what happens if we discover we don't like each other?"

His look was incredulous. "Like each other? 'Liana, what in hell are you getting at? What a *stupid* notion."

Her eyes blazed dangerously. "See? That's precisely what I meant. You think I'm stupid. What other distasteful things do you think we'll find out about each other? And yet, here we are, bound together forever by this farce of a marriage. What have we done?"

"I intend to see that this marriage is no farce," he promised.

"But how? The odds are very much against it ever being normal."

"Why?"

"For one thing, you should've married someone more suited to you."

"More suited? What do you mean?"

"You yourself called me a bluestocking."

"What about me? I'm an outlaw."

"But I'm so plain and bookish."

"And I'm half-gypsy. So what? Those things don't have to be weaknesses, 'Liana. We can use those differences to bind ourselves together, separate from the rest of the world. In that way, they become strengths."

"I'm so afraid we've made a terrible mistake."

He rose from the bed and took her in his arms again. He could feel the tremors coursing through her body, and his earlier desire was replaced by compassion. Unexpectedly, he wanted nothing more than to reassure her.

"Get into bed and warm yourself. I've no wish to force matters. I'll wait until you've resolved this issue in your mind."

He pulled the bedcovers up around her shoulders. "I'm inclined to think we can make our marriage successful, but I'll be patient and let you decide for yourself."

He walked to the other side of the bed and blew out the candle. She lay in the dark half-expecting to hear him leave the room. Instead, she detected the rustling sounds of his undressing, and in another moment, felt him crawl into the bed beside her. She tensed, but soon realized he didn't intend to touch her. Flooded with relief, she sighed heavily. Hopefully there'd be time enough to sort the whole thing through.

As it turned out, Juliana was given more than a few days to address her anxieties. When she awoke the morning following the wedding, there was a single pink rose laying on Ruark's pillow. Beside it was a note.

Juliana reached for her spectacles and unfolded the paper with trembling fingers.

"My dear 'Liana," she read, "I am leaving for Ireland today. I'd planned to take you with me, but now I believe you need this time alone to discover your true feelings about our marriage. I can only hope that you'll have resolved everything by the time I return. Ruark."

Ten

Juliana read the note a hundred times in the following days and with each reading found herself more confused.

Had Ruark been angry when he'd written it? Or merely disgusted by her immature fears. Was he already regretting the rash impulse that made him marry her?

The most significant thing about the note was that he hadn't told her precisely when he'd be back. Perhaps he'd think it over and decide not to return at all. Juliana couldn't help but consider that possibility. At first she believed she really didn't care; after all, she was now in legal possession of Quarrystones. Then she reluctantly admitted she had no wish to declare their marriage a failure so quickly. A fierce pride she hadn't reckoned on rebelled at the thought of announcing to her family that her marriage was over, almost as soon as it began.

Finally, she decided to tell everyone Ruark had gone away on urgent business. When and if he returned, she'd force herself to calmly discuss the problems they faced. They'd have to reach an agreement that would be suitable to both of them. It was the only way.

She knew Essie and Will-John hadn't totally accepted her story about Ruark's need to travel to Ireland, but they asked no questions. Sometimes she'd look up to find Essie watching her, seamed face sad, as though she wanted to cry over

Juliana's plight. When that happened, Juliana became even more determinedly cheerful, throwing herself into the household chores.

As the days passed, she began to spend more and more time in the woods painting, for it seemed the best way to avoid the pity she saw in the Cliftons' eyes.

Unexpectedly, the real desolation came at night. Despite her pride, she realized she missed Ruark. In the short time she'd been back at Quarrystones, it had somehow become commonplace to see his wide-shouldered frame dwarfing a room whenever he entered, to meet his slow smile across the dinner table or hear his booted feet on the stairs. Now there was only the silent shadow of his memory lurking in the dark corners or haunting the deathly silence of her room each night. She chided herself for being overly imaginative, even maudlin, but every time she crawled into the wide bed, she was beset with vivid recollections of their wedding night.

Sometimes, lying with her eyes closed, she could even feel his ardent mouth brushing her own or his strong hand against her breast. Those were the times when she would fling back the covers and leap out of bed to pace the bedroom floor, her mind a whirl of agitated thoughts. She'd try to think about the activities planned for the following day, or the next picture she intended to paint, but sooner or later, her undisciplined thoughts would return to Ruark. Incredibly, she'd begun imagining what it would be like to really become his wife, in every sense of the word. She knew he would be a demanding and sensual lover, but something told her there would be warmth and tenderness also. Tiny chills of excitement traced their way down her spine as she wondered whether she'd ever be brave enough to take the steps necessary to end her virginal state.

* * *

Days later, mind weary from such disturbing thoughts, Juliana packed a basket containing her paints and a lunch, promising herself a change of scene. She remembered the long meadow between Quarrystones and Moorlands and knew it would provide a flower-filled haven away from the daily reminders of Ruark.

She started off on the path that bordered the lily moat. When she passed the stables, she was startled to see the gypsy man who'd driven Ruark's carriage standing in the shadowed doorway. He watched her with a closed, guarded expression.

"Good morning . . . Chavo, isn't it?" Even though she smiled and nodded, his face didn't change. "I'm surprised to find you here," she ventured on. "I thought you'd gone with Ruark."

"He left me to look after things." There was something almost malevolent in his attitude, making it clear that he considered the duty distasteful.

"I see," she murmured, not knowing how else to respond to his rudeness. When he made no answer, she turned away to resume her walk, all the while feeling his sharp gaze like a knife between her shoulder blades.

The path wound upward along the other side of the moat before branching off into the woods at the north end. Walking through the forest, she was able to shake off the feeling of unease the encounter with the gypsy had given her. She paused once to sketch a circle of toadstools and again to examine a nest containing three newly hatched birds. She could hear their mother's frantic scolding from the thick foliage above and, since she didn't want to cause further alarm, Juliana hurried on her way.

She burst into a small clearing before she saw the man sitting there. Her sharp gasp of surprise made his head snap upward. He was seated on a low boulder and had been cradling his head in two gnarled hands, shoulders hunched beneath the coarse jacket he wore. Now she found herself looking into the most desolate eyes she'd ever seen. Thinking he must be ill, she rushed to his side.

"Is something wrong?" she asked, setting the basket aside.

He smiled faintly. "No, lass. Just an old man lost in his thoughts."

"I was afraid you were ill," she explained. She studied the man's face: the lean, leathery cheeks, thick shock of white hair, and faded hazel eyes. There was something familiar about him, something elusive.

"I'm sorry if I frightened you," he said. "I hadn't expected to see another soul in these woods."

"I know I'm trespassing," Juliana said hastily, "but I didn't think anyone would mind. I was on my way to the long meadow to paint wildflowers."

Mild interest flickered in his eyes. "Paint, you say? You're an artist?"

"Very much an amateur," she assured him. "I really should introduce myself. I'm Juliana Lowell, from Quarrystones."

Now there was no mistaking the interest he showed. "Ah, the young woman my grandson was supposed to marry."

"Your grandson?" Understanding began to dawn. No wonder this old man looked familiar. Not only was he Spencer's grandfather, he was also Ruark's. And that was why she felt such a sense of recognition. With his lean, large-boned body, sculpted facial features, and the wide, intelligent set of his eyes, he looked very much like his youngest grandson.

"So," he said in a flat voice, "you're the girl Spencer jilted."

"And you're the Duke of Hawkhurst," she murmured. "I don't believe we've ever met, your Grace."

"If you're one of Dodsworth Lowell's children, I used to see you occasionally, although the last time you were probably no more than ten or eleven years old. No surprise that you don't remember me. What was the real story behind your engagement to my grandson?" He waved one large hand. "Not that you didn't get the best end of the bargain. Your life would have been hell with Spencer as your husband."

Juliana was astonished to hear the man speak of his own flesh and blood in such a way. "It's simple, really. I have a very pretty sister who caught Spencer's attention."

"The much touted Mariette, I assume."

"Yes. During the course of my engagement to Spencer, she'd been on a tour of Europe with our aunt. When she got home, she and Spencer met and, as I'm sure you know, fell in love and decided to marry."

"And how did you feel about that, Juliana?"

She looked at him quickly, but he didn't appear to be asking the question spitefully. Rather, he seemed genuinely concerned with her answer.

She smiled and sat down on the boulder beside him. Maybe it was because he was so much like Ruark, but unexpectedly, she began to feel comfortable with him.

"To be honest," she replied, "the only thing about the broken engagement that bothered me was the fact that I stood to lose Quarrystones. You see, I've always loved it and my father had promised it as my wedding settlement."

"No remorse over losing your bridegroom?" His eyes held the same amused expression she'd seen so often in Ruark's.

"None whatsoever. I've never thought I needed a husband to survive."

"Lord, no, I can tell that already. You're a strong, independent sort with enough brains to get along very well by yourself. So, do you intend to remain a spinster now that you've escaped Spencer's clutches?"

Juliana knew there must be a very odd expression on her face. Just as she'd been about to render a cheerfully affirmative answer, her eyes fell on the opal ring she wore and she remembered she was a married woman.

"Yes, that's what I'd intended," she answered with a wry smile. "But events conspired against me and I find I'm already married to another man."

Edward Hamilton's bushy eyebrows quivered, then shot upward. He gave a short laugh. "Not one to nurse wounded pride, eh?"

"I didn't plan it that way, but my father had reached a decision about Quarrystones. He'd only give it to me if I married. I decided to do as he wished because I couldn't face losing the estate. I suppose not many people would understand such blind devotion to a piece of property."

He laid a firm hand on her shoulder. "Not many. However, I know exactly what you mean. Sometimes there's a love of the land, a pride in ownership, that goes beyond all reason."

"That's exactly how I feel." She glanced up at him, and once again saw his face fill with pain.

"But it's wrong, Juliana. Very wrong."

"Why do you say that?"

"When a man puts places before people, he's doomed to sorrow."

"I don't know why," she said slowly. "You can love a house, a farm, and it will never betray you. It won't lie to you or take advantage of you. It won't leave you."

"Yes, all that's true enough. And if you're content to exist rather than truly *live,* perhaps that's enough. But to lead the life we humans were meant to lead, we must take some risks."

"Risks?"

"Of course. If a man dares to love people instead of places, he risks being hurt. It takes courage to place trust in another, knowing the power human beings have to wound."

"It seems to me the sensible way to live would be to avoid such risks," Juliana said crisply. "What happens if one takes the chance and gets hurt?"

"I'm not certain, but I suppose it's possible to survive. Maybe even learn to trust again in time. But what of your own risk?"

"What do you mean?"

"You've just told me you recently married. Isn't that putting your trust in another human?" His faded eyes watched her shrewdly.

"I guess it is."

"This husband of yours, does he realize he must compete with an estate for your affection?"

She glanced up quickly, to find the sting of his question was tempered with a faint smile.

"He knows I'm very fond of Quarrystones, if that's what you mean."

He gave a short laugh. "You'll have to forgive my rudeness in questioning you. Old men tend to forget their manners. What's your husband's name?"

"Edward Ruark," she said slowly, watching his face for any sign of recognition. There was none.

"Not a name I know," he commented. "I assume he's not a local lad."

"No, he's not." Words seemed to crowd her lips and she had difficulty refraining from blurting out the truth about Ruark's identity. Only the knowledge of how angry he would be kept her silent.

"I've asked enough personal questions for one day." Edward Hamilton chuckled. "I didn't mean to detain you so long. You say you're on your way to the meadow?"

"Yes, I wanted to find some red campion to paint. That's one of the few places it grows around here."

"Do you mind if I walk with you? I'd enjoy watching an artist at work. That is, if you're not the temperamental type and don't mind having someone peer over your shoulder."

Juliana felt a tiny stab of vexation. She'd gone into the woods to escape reminders of Ruark, and now found herself face to face with a man whose every gesture brought him to mind. Still, the duke seemed eager for company, and she couldn't deny there'd been an instant fellowship between them. What harm could it do?

"I'm not artistic enough to be temperamental," she said. "Please come along if you like."

The afternoon proved to be extremely entertaining. Not only was Ruark's grandfather lavish in his praise of her talent, he was also eager to accept her suggestion that he try his own hand at painting. Not at all interested in the red campions she was drawing, he turned out a very creditable portrait of Juliana sitting on the grass with her paints spread out about her.

As they shared the bread and cheese she'd brought for lunch, Juliana complimented his efforts. "I'd like to have your painting, if you don't mind."

"Not this one." He laughed. "Next time I'll do better, and one of these days, I promise, I'll do something I like well enough to let you have. Though," he went on, beaming with pride, "this isn't bad for a first try."

Juliana liked Edward Hamilton a great deal. Obviously, he had mellowed since that unhappy day he'd quarreled with his son. When Ruark returned, perhaps she could initiate a meeting between the two of them.

As the afternoon drew to a close, the Duke and Juliana made plans to meet again in a week's time. Then he said, "Now, hurry on home to your husband and remember what I told you: people, not places."

Somehow, the enjoyment she had found in spending a day with Ruark's grandfather catapulted Juliana out of her worried, introspective mood. Suddenly, two things became quite apparent to her.

First, it was doing no good whatsoever to wonder about Ruark's intentions. She'd never been one to shape her life to the whims of a man, and there was no sense in starting now. When he actually made his reappearance at Quarrystones, they could begin sorting through their difficulties.

Secondly, she had longed for ownership of the estate, but now that it was hers, she'd done nothing to prove she deserved the responsibility. Not only was it up to her to provide for her tenants, she also had to learn something of agriculture. Quarrystones must continue to be a working farm, and in the absence of her husband, it fell to her to see that it did so.

The following day Juliana met with her tenant farmers and announced her plans. The most important task at hand, she told them, was to plant the cottage gardens. True, it was late, but not too late. Since the men and boys would soon be in the hayfields, it was imperative the planting begin immediately.

Armed with bags of seed which she'd purchased from a dealer in Edensfield, spades, rakes, and hoes, the tenants began at one end of the village and worked their way to the other end, leaving neatly planted garden rows at each residence. Essie, Will-John, and Juliana worked side by side with the villagers, digging furrows in the soil, sowing the seeds, or carrying endless pails of water. In the evenings, they trudged wearily back to Quarrystones, ate a bit of supper and fell into bed, exhausted from their labors.

But Juliana had never before experienced such pleasure. Words could not express her utter contentment when, kneeling to gather handfuls of sun-warmed soil, she'd look up to see the quietly approving gazes of her farmers upon her. When the water bottle was passed and she took her turn at drinking with no show of fastidiousness, she knew they noticed and were pleased. Her father hadn't been a bad landlord, just a disinterested one. He only cared that the farming operations were carried out; not once had he ever dirtied his own hands to see that they were.

Juliana felt a fierce pride in knowing the farmers' children were once again receiving milk and eggs. Cartloads of vegetables from Will-John's garden were brought to the village at least once a week, and such staples as flour, sugar, and tea were being distributed. Juliana soon found herself without adequate funds to make further purchases, but the shopkeepers had allowed her credit until her husband returned to settle her debts. Guiltily, she wondered what

Ruark would think of her reckless spending, and hoped he would see the necessity for it. If he didn't have any means of paying her bills, she'd have to approach her father for a loan, though that was something she'd rather not do.

Meat for the tenants was not such a problem. Sheep and hogs were available for slaughter, and later, in the autumn, there would be beef. Though Juliana did not enjoy it as she had the planting, she was on hand to help with the slaughtering. She worked alongside the women, cutting the meat and packing it in salt, or carrying the bacon and hams to the smokehouse.

Lastly, the cottages themselves received some much-needed attention. The yards were weeded and trimmed, and the wooden doors given fresh coats of bright paint. One morning when Juliana walked the path to the village, she was thrilled to see the return of something she'd always loved as a child. Hanging outside each cottage door was a woven-willow birdcage containing pairs of linnets. The songbirds filled the air with their sweet warbling melodies, and to her, they were a symbol of the peace and contentment that had returned to Quarrystones.

Edward Hamilton was waiting impatiently in the designated meeting place in the woods beside the river.

"My lord, girl, but you've gotten brown," he said in his forthright way. "What have you been up to?"

As she set about putting out her paints and brushes, Juliana replied, "I've been working with my tenant farmers, and I didn't always take time to put on a hat. My mother would be horrified to see what I've done to my complexion."

"Nonsense," he countered. "A good healthy tan is far

more attractive than the pasty, milk-white skin most women strive for. I think it becomes you."

"Thank you," she murmured, smiling. "Even though my mother would never agree."

"What kind of work were you doing?"

"Just about everything," she confessed. "I don't remember ever being so tired. We planted gardens and slaughtered animals for meat and painted cottages."

He looked surprised. "You had a hand in all that?"

"There was a great deal to be done, and time was short. I felt responsible for their problems in the first place, and by helping them work, I exorcised some of my guilt."

"How were you responsible?"

She hesitated.

"I'll wager you had nothing to do with it. Spencer was the culprit, if I'm not mistaken."

Slowly she nodded. A shadow seemed to cross his face.

"I'm not surprised. I knew he'd had dealings with the Quarrystones farmers, and I've learned that where Spencer is involved, things are usually unpleasant for someone." He sighed heavily. "The situation with my own tenant farmers is a disgrace. I only wish I could put it to rights with a few days of hard labor on my part. Unfortunately, things have gone beyond the point where that would help."

He seated himself on a log and stared at the river. Juliana paused in her activities.

"Why is that?"

"Spencer has so undermined my authority that I have no way to turn. He's spread such rumors of my senility about that no one will even listen to me anymore. I have no credit, and my own grandson has taken it upon himself to convince the banker not to give me funds without his approval." He spread his hands helplessly.

"He doesn't approve of putting any money back into the farm or the land. He overworks his tenants shamefully, and allows them a mere pittance to live on. He knows employment is very scarce these days, and most of them are forced to stay at Moorlands even though they detest the life there."

"Spencer does have a great deal of power," Juliana agreed. "And he commands respect throughout the county."

"Which is why everyone is willing to believe I'm a useless, worn-out old fool, babbling over my porridge."

"But when people meet you, can't they see how you really are?"

"No one meets me. I'm virtually a prisoner at the estate. Spencer hired a housekeeper and a collection of London thugs to do her bidding. I'm not allowed off the premises alone. If they ever suspected I'd met someone in the woods, my walks would quickly become a thing of the past. I have to be careful they don't follow me. Now that I have a friend, I don't want to jeopardize my chances of seeing you."

"Come to Quarrystones with me," she cried impulsively. "I'll help you expose Spencer and regain possession of your home."

He shook his white head sadly. "There's no way we can do that as long as Spencer is a Justice of the Peace. He has every public official in the district right in the palm of his greedy hand. He could overrule any plan we'd devise."

"There has to be something we can do, your Grace."

He smiled gently. "I'd like for you to call me Edward, if you don't mind. No sense standing on formality."

"No, I suppose not, especially if we're going to find a way to get you out of Spencer's grasp."

Juliana couldn't help but wish Ruark would come back. Surely his grandfather's plight would soften his resolve.

"My dear, I don't believe we can overcome my grandson's influence. He seems to have blocked every means of escape. I think he plans to keep me silent until I die of old age. Even now, if I could get to the king, I might persuade him that I'm still deserving of my title and property. But Spencer won't let that happen."

"I can help you get to London," Juliana offered. "I know I can."

He laid a hand on hers. "Thanks, but I don't want you involved that deeply. All I ask is your friendship. That'll keep me buoyed up until I concoct a plan that won't endanger anyone else."

Juliana said no more of assisting him, but in her mind she was already formulating the argument she would use to persuade Ruark to rally to his grandsire's aid.

"I've already put one plan into action," Edward Hamilton went on. "I only hope it will soon bear fruit."

With a sinking heart, she asked, "What sort of plan?"

"I had another son besides Spencer's father. He would've been the heir to Moorlands, except for my own damned stubbornness. I sent him away and haven't seen him in twenty-seven years."

Juliana looked at the man beside her with great compassion. His private pain etched deep lines along either side of his mouth and furrowed the broad brow.

"I secretly wrote a letter to my son and bribed the kitchen boy to post it for me. He hates the housekeeper as much as I do, so he was glad for the opportunity to put one over on her." He chuckled briefly.

"How did you know where to send the letter?"

"I didn't for certain. But he owned an estate in Ireland that my wife left to him. I've always imagined him living there, and that's where I sent the letter."

"But you don't know if he received it or not?"

"No. I just keep hoping. God knows, even if he did get my letter, he might refuse to come back after what I did. Can't say that I'd blame him."

He was silent for a time, then went on. "I disowned my son for a reason that now seems ridiculous. I'm afraid I was a pretty cold-hearted man in my younger days. Thought too damned much about power and prestige. When my boy came back from Ireland with a bride I considered less than suitable, I flew into a rage and tried to force them to dissolve the marriage. Randolph's new wife meant more to him than I did and he refused. I retaliated in the only way I knew, the way I thought would hurt him most. I took away his inheritance. However, as it turns out, the joke was on me. Titles and money didn't mean all that much to him. He walked away without a backward glance, and I haven't seen him since."

Juliana swallowed around the lump that had formed in her throat. Edward Hamilton had suffered through the years, and now she longed to ease that suffering. But how could she? To tell him that his son was dead and that the grandson he didn't even know existed hated him would hardly ease his mind. It galled her to remain silent, but she had no choice.

Later, as they painted together, Edward Hamilton spoke of his daughter-in-law.

"Randolph met a young gypsy girl when he was in Ireland. For years the gypsies had been allowed to camp on one corner of the estate when they traveled through, and as fate would have it, they were there when Randolph went for his visit. It seems they overcame the objections of her people, mainly because Randolph bribed them by promising help or hospitality whenever they needed it. In Ireland the gypsies are very poor, and that must have meant a great deal to them, for they eventually accepted the marriage." He met Juliana's eyes. "That was something I couldn't do."

"The English aristocracy has always been strict," she said softly. "Perhaps you were only a victim of the times."

"I'm afraid I was a victim of my own pride and arrogance," he said harshly. "Unfortunately, I wasn't the only victim. Randolph must have suffered, not being able to return home. And now I realize, Sara, his wife, must have suffered most of all."

"Why do you say that?"

"I did my best to humiliate her." He studied the brush he held. "Oddly enough, she never made a stand against me. She waited quietly and listened to the arguments going on around her. Even then, in the midst of my unreasoning anger, I knew exactly why Randolph was so smitten by her. She was worthy of being a duchess. Why did I let fear of what my peers would think destroy all our lives?"

"You shouldn't blame yourself this way."

"Over the years, my dear, I've had to face the fact that there is no one else to blame. The one good thing about it all was that my wife wasn't alive to see the way I treated our son. I've thanked Fate for that many times."

After a few moments, he said, "I pray that Randolph will forgive me and come back to Moorlands. If he doesn't return soon, it will be ruined. He's my only hope, Juliana."

That evening as she strolled through the gardens, Juliana thought of Edward Hamilton and the bitter lesson life had taught him. It seemed to her he'd suffered enough for his mistake, and she vowed to find some way to force Ruark to see that. Edward could never make peace with his son now, but there was still time for him to know his grandson and heir.

A mass of purple lilacs crowded an old stone wall in the garden and as she approached, their fragrance was heady. For a moment, she experienced an overwhelming longing for Ruark. She was astonished to realize how badly she missed him.

What a comfort it would be to glance up and see his rangy form crossing the lawn toward her. What a relief to run to him and pour out her troubled thoughts, to put herself in his hands, as she had the night of the May Fair, and be confident he'd see her safely through.

She gathered enough lilac branches for a bouquet. They symbolized the first emotions of love, she knew, and somehow their sweet fragrance was a solace. And even though there was no real love between them, she already had unshakable faith in the man she'd married. She knew he was strong and reliable. And perhaps trust would ultimately prove more valuable than love.

Eleven

May drifted slowly toward June and the days grew warmer and longer. Still Ruark did not come home, and Juliana's moods switched from worry about his safety to fury over his prolonged absence, and then back to anxiety again.

Late one afternoon she was pulling weeds in the flower garden when she heard the sound of a galloping horse.

Straightening, she muttered, "Ruark," and hurried down the path and across the lawn toward the causeway. She stopped short, shading her eyes against the bright sun.

In the stable yard she saw not Ruark, but her sister, who, with the assistance of Chavo, was alighting from a handsome chestnut stallion. She was filled with curious disappointment and unease. Mariette tapped the young gypsy lightly on the shoulder with her riding crop, tilting her head to say something that brought color to his face and a flash of fire to his dark eyes. Juliana noticed that when her sister turned to walk away, Chavo stared after her for a long moment before leading the horse away. It was the same effect Etta had on every man she met.

"Well, Juliana," Mariette said in a clear, carrying tone, "marriage doesn't seem to have changed you."

Her amused, rather pitying inspection raked Juliana from untidy head to dusty toes. Aware she was not exactly dressed to receive guests, Juliana pulled off her soiled gloves and quickly smoothed her rumpled skirt.

"I was working in the garden."

"So you still act like a servant," Mariette mused, shaking her head. "And look what you have done to your skin! You're as brown as a native. Mother would have apoplexy if she could see you now."

"Yes, I know," Juliana said, with a sigh. "But never mind that, tell me about you. When did you come down to the country?"

"We arrived this afternoon. Our honeymoon trip was so tiring that Spencer thought we needed a rest before returning to London to stay. We did make a stop there to call on Mother and Father. I couldn't believe it when I heard you'd gotten married."

"It was rather sudden."

"Sudden is hardly the word for it," exclaimed Mariette. "I'm positively dying to hear all about it. And to meet the bridegroom, of course."

"Unfortunately, Ruark isn't here right now." Juliana volunteered the information reluctantly.

"Not here? Where on earth is he?"

"He was called away on business, I'm afraid."

"What a shame." Mariette allowed a frown to mar her face, but only for a moment. Standing there in her sapphire-blue riding habit and matching hat, she was quite lovely. Juliana tried in vain to stifle the ungracious and decidedly petty thought that, had Mariette been his bride, Ruark would never have left Quarrystones without her.

"Shall we go inside?" she asked quickly. "I'll see if Essie will bring us tea."

"Very well," Mariette agreed, "I am a bit thirsty. I left Spencer pouting at Moorlands because he was going to have to take tea alone." As they entered the house, she laughed gaily. "I told him we'd been together night and day for too long, and I needed a change of scene. Besides, his grandfather was there, and I don't think I could bear to spend more than a few minutes in his company. Horrid, rude old man."

Juliana bit her tongue to keep from defending Edward Hamilton. She knew she couldn't reveal her acquaintance with him or Spencer would take steps to prevent them meeting again. Instead of saying what she wanted, she merely called out for Essie and invited Mariette to sit down.

Essie appeared in the doorway at once, her face set in a scowl. "Good afternoon, Miss Mariette."

Dropping gracefully onto the couch, Mariette removed her leather gloves and the small veiled hat which had been perched high on her golden curls. "Hello, Essie. So it's still to be 'Miss Mariette,' is it? I suppose I can expect no further respect from you even though I am a marchioness now."

Essie drew her scrawny self upright. "I still call your sister Miss Juliana, and *she's* a duchess."

Embarrassed at the mention of her husband's supposed duchy, Juliana hastily interjected, "Oh, Essie, would you mind bringing us some tea?"

"Anything you say, Miss Juli." With a somewhat malicious look at Mariette, the woman swept from the room.

"Lord, that old hag disapproves of me," Mariette observed. "You always were her favorite. But never mind that, tell me about your husband. How did you meet him? What does he look like?"

Juliana sat down in the chair opposite her sister, taking a few seconds to arrange her skirts. Finally, she said, "We met at a neighbor's house. At a dinner party." She didn't like lying, but if she didn't tell Mariette something, she'd only keep prying.

"And I gather it was love at first sight?" There was a slight edge to Mariette's voice, a hint of sarcasm.

"Well, we liked each other right from the start. I mean, we managed to get on well together."

Mariette gave a short laugh. "I suppose that means he's an intellectual and the two of you could discuss books and politics. A perfect type for you, sister dear."

"Yes," Juliana murmured, her mind filled with a sudden, delicious image of the real Ruark. He was far from the sort of man Mariette had in mind.

"Father says his name is Edward Ruark, Duke of Kilcairn. Very impressive."

"Hmmm." Juliana was relieved when Essie came back into the room with the tea tray. She busied herself filling the cups and passing a plate of cakes to Mariette.

"Was your husband's business in Edensfield, Juli?"

"No. Actually, he was called back to Ireland."

Mariette was astonished. "Ireland? Do you mean to tell me he went all the way to Ireland and you didn't accompany him?"

"He was going to be occupied with business dealings, so I didn't see any point in it," Juliana replied, taking refuge in a sip of tea.

"No point?" Mariette's tone was incredulous. "Oh, Juliana, this is too much, even for you! I don't know of another woman who would be content to let her new husband leave on a trip and not insist on being taken along." Her expression sharpened. "Unless, of course, he's either old or ugly."

Juliana shook her head. "No, he's neither of those things."

"Did you manage any sort of honeymoon before he left?" Mariette asked boldly.

Juliana lowered her gaze. "No, there was no honeymoon." The literal truth of that statement brought a flush to her cheeks.

Mariette's avid glance moved over her sister's face, assessing her discomfiture. "There's something odd about this marriage, Juli. I wonder what it is." When no answer was forthcoming, she went on, "When did your husband leave for Ireland?"

Juliana debated lying again, but decided against it. One lie only led to another and then another. It would be best to get the truth into the open, and let Mariette draw whatever conclusions she wished.

"He left the day after the wedding."

"What? Oh, lord, it's worse than I thought." Mariette took a drink of tea, then set her cup and saucer aside. "Don't tell me you drove him away."

"What do you mean?" Juliana asked stiffly.

"Surely you weren't so horrified by his attentions that you created a scene?"

"I told you, he was called away on business. We plan to take a real honeymoon as soon as possible."

Mariette looked doubtful, but when she spoke, she merely said, "May I recommend Paris? It's an absolutely wonderful place for a honeymoon. So romantic." She went on then to describe the quaint hotel where they'd stayed, a moonlight cruise on the River Seine, and Spencer's endearing habit of showering her with expensive gifts. By the time the afternoon had drawn to a close, Juliana was suffering from a pounding headache. All she could think about was lying down in the blessed quiet of her bedchamber, away from Mariette and her questions and knowing looks.

As her sister prepared to depart, she favored Juliana with one last, intense scrutiny. "It must be terribly lonely for you with your husband away. Why don't Spencer and I come to dinner one of these evenings? I'm certain you could use the company."

"I really don't mind being alone. You shouldn't put yourselves out on my behalf. I know you're still on your own honeymoon."

"Believe me, I would welcome the change." Mariette toyed with the lace at her cuff. "Spencer's constant attentions are getting a bit wearying." She sighed. "At least, if we're in public, he'll have to behave himself. You know what I mean—well, no, perhaps you don't."

Juliana's mouth tightened, but she said nothing. She was aware of Mariette's avid study of her face. "You're not afraid to see Spencer again, are you?" she asked. "You aren't still hurt about his breaking off your engagement?"

"Nonsense," Juliana snapped.

"I thought that might be why you're reluctant to invite us over."

"Not at all," Juliana assured her. "I was only thinking of you, that you might prefer your privacy. By all means, come to dinner anytime you like."

"How about this Friday evening, then?"

Juliana could see that Mariette didn't intend to let her delay her first meeting with Spencer since the wedding. No doubt she thought it would be amusing, something to alleviate the boredom she always experienced when in the country. It might be best to go along with Etta's plan and prove she had no qualms about facing Spencer again.

"Friday will be fine. Why don't you come about eight o'clock?"

When Mariette had gone, she leaned against the doorframe wearily, fingers massaging her aching forehead.

She knew that if she could manage to get through Friday evening, the ordeal would soon be over. Spencer and Mariette wouldn't linger at Moorlands, for Mariette could never bear to be away from London more than a few days at a time.

Juliana heaved a sigh of relief, knowing how much better she would feel once they were gone.

On Thursday Juliana was to have met Edward Hamilton for their weekly sojourn in the woods, but early that morning the kitchen boy from Moorlands appeared at her door with a note. Edward sent the message that he dared not risk meeting her, for, if his grandson became suspicious, his walks would be eliminated at once. It was a chance he was unwilling to take.

Juliana fumed at the old gentleman's circumstances, but realized there was little she could do about it just yet.

Later in the day she had a thought that sent her hurrying down to the stables. To her dismay, Chavo seemed to be the only stableman about, but she took a deep breath and approached him.

"Excuse me, Chavo."

The man mumbled a curt reply, propping the pitchfork he was using against the stable wall and turning to face her. His dark good looks were spoiled by the brooding expression he wore.

"I need someone to ride over to Moorlands with a message. Would you mind doing it?"

Instead of answering her question, he simply asked, "What is the message?"

"Please inform Mr. Hamilton that my dinner invitation also includes his grandfather. Tell him I should very much like to meet the duke."

Without a word, Chavo started into the stable. Juliana felt a quick surge of anger.

"Chavo," she rasped, "why are you so rude to me? What have I done to make you dislike me?"

He whipped about and she could sense the war of emotions going on within him. His expression was cold. "It's not that I dislike you, your ladyship. 'Tis only that my loyalty lies with Ruark. I don't like seeing you put him in danger."

"But how do I endanger Ruark?"

"He has enough battles of his own to fight. He didn't need to take on yours as well."

"Do you think I married him just so he could fight my battles?" she asked, feeling guilty because she realized how close to the truth that statement actually was.

The man seemed to look right through her. "It doesn't matter what I think," he said. "I'm only concerned with my friend. Perhaps you should be, also."

With that, he turned and walked away, leaving Juliana staring after him, feeling as though he had issued a dire warning.

Friday arrived, bringing weather that matched Juliana's mood. All day long thunder sounded in the distance and evil-looking clouds began to mass. As she helped Essie with the baking and housecleaning, Juliana was aware of the intense heat, a sure sign a storm was building.

Early in the evening as she went up to her room to bathe and dress, she noticed the wind had begun to stir and that the darkening sky was marred by occasional streaks of lightning.

Juliana sprinkled a handful of dried meadowsweet into her bath, then eased her body into the hot water, breathing deeply of its sweet almond fragrance. She remembered reading that in Tudor days, meadowsweet was known by the country name of bridewort because its creamy flowers were used to make garlands and posies for brides. The blooms were even strewn along pathways and throughout churches where weddings were to take place.

The very thought filled her with trepidation. Spencer and Mariette would expect her to act like a bride, and she really hadn't the faintest notion of what that involved. She certainly couldn't wax poetic about a man who'd lived at Quarrystones less than twenty-four hours as her husband. But undoubtedly, they'd find it strange if she didn't mention him at all.

Pride was a damnable thing that rose up to taunt her at the most inconvenient moments. It wouldn't let her admit she had a bridegroom who neither loved nor cherished her, and it certainly wouldn't countenance letting her sister know greed was her only reason for marrying.

She rubbed her forehead in an effort to clear away the ugly thoughts. Why did the prospect of spending an evening in the company of her sister always lead to this depression of her mind?

Aware that the hour was growing late, she took a cake of soap and began to lather her long hair. She didn't have any more time to ponder the whys and wherefores of her married state.

She finished her bath and put a dressing gown on over her undergarments. She was brushing out her damp hair when someone knocked at the bedroom door.

"Come in, Essie," she called, crossing the room to open the door. "I think I—Ruark!"

Standing before her was a smiling Ruark Hamilton, his dark cape swirling about him. He stepped forward and caught her by the shoulders. Juliana was filled with such conflicting emotions that she didn't know whether to cling to him or kick him in the shins.

"I wasn't expecting you," she half-whispered. "It's been so long, I thought you weren't coming."

He bent his head as if to kiss her and his assumption she would gladly receive his touch tipped the balance toward anger. She pushed away from him and, to her own horrified amazement, pummeled his wide chest with clenched fists. "Where have you been for the past month?" she cried. "What have you been doing?"

His surprised amusement showed in his deep laugh. "Make up your mind, woman," he growled in mock anger. "Are you glad to see me or not?"

"Oh, I don't know!" She spun away from him.

He closed the short distance between them and pulled her into an embrace. "Well, I'm glad to see you," he said firmly, resting his chin on the top of her head. The almond scent of her damp, tangled hair invaded his senses and he murmured, "Lord, but you smell good. I've missed you, 'Liana."

Slowly, he turned her in his arms and kissed her mouth. At the salty taste of tears on her lips, he raised his head and looked at her in alarm. "Why are you crying?"

She shook her head. "I'm not."

"Little liar," he said softly. "Tell me what's wrong."

"Nothing, only that I'm not sure if I missed you terribly or if you just make me furious. Damn it, Ruark, where have you been?"

"In Ireland. I left you a note, remember?"

She moved away from him, struggling for composure. "Yes, of course. But it was rather vague."

"Did you think I wasn't coming back?" he asked gently. "If so, you don't know me very well."

"I don't know you at all."

"You didn't think I'd miss the opportunity to collect on the wedding night you owe me, did you?"

A faint blush stained her cheeks as she looked away from his intent gaze. But, in spite of herself, she laughed. "You really are the most terrible rogue."

He grinned. "Be that as it may, I'm still sorry to have caused you worry or confusion. Remember that I wrote that note under duress."

"What sort of duress?" she challenged.

"Come here and I'll tell you." He unfastened his cape and tossed it across the bed. Then, taking her hand, he seated himself in an armchair and drew her down across his lap. His arm encircled her waist and eased her close against his chest. Juliana stiffened, but didn't pull away.

"Things got very complicated after the wedding," he muttered. "That night I came to our chamber expecting my wife to be sweet and compliant. Instead, a prickly female determined to disguise herself as a testy old maid was waiting for me. Then, when I challenged the disguise, I found a very vulnerable young woman underneath. Now, tell me, how could I have my evil way with someone like that?" He answered for her. "I couldn't. Therefore, I spent a sleepless night tossing and turning beside you, instead of doing what I most wanted to do." His breath was hot against her ear. "Do you know what that was?"

Her grey eyes widened as she stared silently into his face, now so close to her own.

Wish You Were Here?

You can be, every month, with Zebra Historical Romance Novels.

AND TO GET YOU STARTED, ALLOW US TO SEND YOU

4 Historical Romances Free

AN $18.00 VALUE!
With absolutely no obligation to buy anything.

YOU ARE CORDIALLY INVITED TO GET SWEPT AWAY INTO NEW WORLDS OF PASSION AND ADVENTURE.

AND IT WON'T COST YOU A PENNY!

Receive 4 Zebra Historical Romances, Absolutely _Free_!

(An $18.00 value)

Now you can have your pick of handsome, noble adventurers with romance in their hearts and you on their minds. Zebra publishes Historical Romances That Burn With The Fire Of History by the world's finest romance authors.

This very special FREE offer entitles you to 4 Zebra novels at absolutely no cost, with no obligation to buy anything, ever. It's an offer designed to excite your most vivid dreams and desires...and save you $18!

And that's not all you get...

Your Home Subscription Saves You Money Every Month.

After you've enjoyed your initial FREE package of 4 books, you'll begin to receive monthly shipments of new Zebra titles. These novels are delivered direct to your home as soon as they are published...sometimes even before the bookstores get them! Each monthly shipment of 4 books will be yours to examine for 10 days. Then if you decide to keep the books, you'll pay the preferred subscriber's price of just $3.75 per title. That's $15 for all 4 books...a savings of $3 off the publisher's price! What's more, $15 is your total price...there is no additional charge for the convenience of home delivery.

There Is No Minimum Purchase. And Your Continued Satisfaction Is Guaranteed.

We're so sure that you'll appreciate the money-saving convenience of home delivery that we guarantee your complete satisfaction. You may return any shipment...for any reason...within 10 days and pay nothing that month. And if you want us to stop sending books, just say the word. There is no minimum number of books you must buy.

It's a no-lose proposition, so send for your 4 FREE books today!

YOU'RE GOING TO LOVE GETTING
4 FREE BOOKS

These books worth $18, are yours without cost or obligation when you fill out and mail this certificate.
(If the certificate is missing below, write to: Zebra Home Subscription Service, Inc., 120 Brighton Road, P.O. Box 5214, Clifton, New Jersey 07015-5214

Complete and mail this card to receive 4 Free books!

Yes! Please send me 4 Zebra Historical Romances without cost or obligation. I understand that each month thereafter I will be able to preview 4 new Zebra Historical Romances FREE for 10 days. Then, if I should decide to keep them, I will pay the money-saving preferred publisher's price of just $3.75 each...a total of $15. That's $3 less than the publisher's price, and there is no additional charge for shipping and handling. I may return any shipment within 10 days and owe nothing, and I may cancel this subscription at any time. The 4 FREE books will be mine to keep in any case.

Name _____

Address _____ Apt. _____

City _____ State _____ Zip _____

Telephone ( ) _____

Signature _____
(If under 18, parent or guardian must sign.)

LF1094

Terms, offer and prices subject to change without notice. Subscription subject to acceptance by Zebra Books. Zebra Books reserves the right to reject any order or cancel any subscription.

An $18 value. FREE!

No obligation to buy anything, ever.

TREAT YOURSELF TO 4 FREE BOOKS.

ZEBRA HOME SUBSCRIPTION SERVICE, INC.
120 BRIGHTON ROAD
P.O. BOX 5214
CLIFTON, NEW JERSEY 07015-5214

AFFIX STAMP HERE

"Do you want me to explain?"

She summoned a hint of her old defensiveness as she said, "I don't believe it will be necessary. I think you're only trying to embarrass me."

"If I am, it's because you deserve it, sweetheart."

"I what?"

"You heard me right." He chuckled ruefully. "Maybe you don't realize what torture it was for me to share the same bed with you, yet have to resist the urge to make love to you. I knew if I rushed you, you'd never forgive me." He placed a feather-light kiss on her brow. "You're too damned stubborn for that. But I also knew that if I gave you time to make up your own mind, I was going to have to put a considerable distance between us to be sure I could keep my hands off you until you were ready."

Her heart began to thump within her breast, making breathing difficult.

"Do you understand why I had to go?" he asked in a low voice. "Why I had to force myself to stay away so long?"

"I suppose so," she conceded.

"And did you use the time to think about our marriage?"

"I've thought about it," she managed to say.

"Have you become reconciled to it?"

He seemed so earnest, so sincere. If only she could be certain. "Ruark, there are so many questions I need to ask."

"Can you ask them later?" He gave her a crooked smile. "What I want to know now is, are we going to be married or not?"

"You're still willing, I take it," she said with resignation.

"I've no objection to being your husband. And I've already sent your father payment for Quarrystones."

"Did you pay him with stolen money?"

"Don't be so inquisitive. All you need to know is that I've held up my end of our bargain."

"Then I'm forced to accept my responsibility as well. You've left me no alternative."

"Thank you so much for that bit of flattery."

"Sorry."

"Don't be meek, 'Liana. I don't trust it," he teased. "Now, if all serious discussion is at an end, I have a gift for you."

"A gift?"

"Yes," he replied, taking a small box from the pocket of his jacket. "Since we're to remain man and wife, I want you to have a proper wedding ring."

He put the box into her hands, and when she opened it, she gasped in pleasure at the sight of the delicate gold ring inside.

"It's beautiful," she breathed. "And so unusual."

Ruark picked it up, holding it for her inspection. "It's a *claddagh,* an Irish betrothal ring."

The main body of the ring was formed by two hands holding a heart, atop which was a finely wrought crown.

"The hands stand for friendship," he told her. "The crown for loyalty, and the heart for love. The romantic Irish believe it takes all three of those things to make a successful marriage."

He removed the opal ring she was wearing and slipped it on the smallest finger of his own left hand. Then, he placed the *claddagh* ring on her finger.

"It's exquisite, Ruark," she whispered. "Thank you."

"You're more than welcome." He leaned forward and laid his mouth across hers, gently caressing her lips with his.

There was a tapping at the door. "Miss Juli," came Essie's anxious voice. "Miss Juli?"

Ruark groaned. "Not again. 'Tis like a bad dream that keeps recurring."

"Did ye know it's nearly eight o'clock?" Essie continued. "Yer sister will be here any moment."

"Oh, no," cried Juliana. "I forgot Mariette and Spencer are coming for dinner. I'll never be ready on time."

Ruark stood, easily setting her on her feet. "We can continue this discussion later. Now, what needs doing?"

"My hair's damp," she fretted. "I'll never be able to manage it."

"Don't fly into a panic. It's only your sister, after all. Here, sit on the floor in front of me and I'll braid it for you."

At her stunned expression, he said, "Don't look so shocked. I'm a man of many talents, and someday you're going to learn the truth of that." He turned toward the door. "Essie? Are you still there?"

"Yes," came the clipped reply. Obviously, she wasn't entirely ready to resume their former bantering relationship.

"Can you bring your mistress something to wear? Does she have something green? A nice, dark green?"

"Hmmph, what would ye know about colors?" the old woman snapped. "I'll see what I can find."

Fifteen minutes later, as the Hamilton carriage swept into the front drive, Juliana was standing in front of the mirror, surprised at her own reflection. The deep forest-green of the gown Essie had brought made her eyes look dark and mysterious. Her hair was burnished chestnut, the thick braid twisted and pinned high on the crown of her head, a few frivolous tendrils escaping to curl about her ears. Best of all, she told herself, was the gold ring now shining on her finger, its soft glow promising all sorts of things about which she dared not think just yet.

"You go on down and greet your sister and her husband," Ruark suggested, holding the bedroom door for her. "I'll have a bath and change clothes, and join you as quickly as possible."

Juliana's new-found confidence waned rapidly as soon as she saw Mariette. Her sister was so beautiful it took her breath away. She came down the stairs in time to see Spencer helping his wife remove her cape. As Mariette stepped forward into the light, her pink satin skirts swirled gracefully. She carried a sheaf of golden roses.

"Here," she said, handing them to the waiting Essie, "I brought these for the dinner table. They're from the hothouse at Moorlands."

"They're lovely," Juliana said. "Thank you."

"I've always preferred yellow roses," Mariette continued. "Of course, you've told me they represent jealousy in the language of flowers, but that doesn't lessen their appeal for me. And since there's no envy between us, what difference could it possibly make?"

"None whatsoever," Juliana said briskly.

"I'll put these into water," Essie announced, casting a wicked look at Mariette. "Dinner will be ready in a short while."

Juliana turned to the man beside her sister. "Spencer, how nice to see you again. I'm sorry your grandfather didn't come with you this evening. I was looking forward to meeting him."

Spencer straightened his shoulders, smoothing the sleeves of his dark brown jacket. "It was kind of you to invite him, Juli, but unfortunately, my grandfather rarely goes out into public these days. He's become something of a hermit, and to tell the truth, it's for the best. His mind, you know."

He didn't quite meet her eye, and Juliana longed to tell him she knew he was lying. Instead, she suggested they go into the parlor and sit down.

"What's this?" asked Mariette. She indicated a traveling case left at the foot of the stairs. Propped against it was a guitar. "Does this mean the errant husband has returned?" She exuded mischievous curiosity. "You didn't tell me he was a musician, Juli."

"Ruark arrived home a short time ago," Juliana replied. "He'll join us for dinner and you can meet him then."

"I must say," spoke up Spencer, "I was surprised, to say the least, when I heard you'd married. A bit sudden, wasn't it?"

"I suppose it was." Juliana hoped she didn't sound as uneasy as she felt. "But you yourself know these things sometimes happen."

Now it was Spencer's turn to look uncomfortable. Mariette giggled.

"She has a valid point, Spence. You can't deny our own courtship was rather rapid."

"That's true, but your family knew and approved of me," Spencer retorted. "What do we know about this man Juliana chose to wed? He could be some opportunist drawn by your father's money."

"Nonsense," said Juliana. "My husband is a duke, after all. He has money of his own."

Mariette's voice had a slight edge to it. "And I'm certain my sister's far too prudent to take up with any sort of opportunist. No, I can easily envision the man she'd choose. He'd be older than her, very proper and scrupulous. An intellectual, naturally, with interests in art and literature to match her own. No doubt a rather moral soul and not too *physical."* Her clear laugh rang out. "Am I correct, Juli?"

Juliana smiled faintly. "Judge for yourself," she said. "Here's Ruark now."

Ruark's tall frame filled the doorway, and as she looked up at him, Juliana's heart leaped into her throat. Dressed in casual clothes, his hair still damp from the bath, he'd never looked more handsome. He was wearing a white linen shirt, and form-fitting black breeches.

Juliana stole a swift look at her sister and was pleased to see an expression of utter amazement on her face.

Ruark approached Juliana and, taking her hand, pulled her into his embrace. He placed a light kiss on her brow and, keeping one arm about her waist, turned to the others. "Sorry to have kept you waiting. Unfortunately, my arrival this evening was a trifle late. The coach in which I was traveling was accosted by a highwayman. Some gypsy fellow."

"Hmm, yes. I understand he's been making a damned nuisance of himself," mumbled Spencer.

Juliana's mouth twitched with laughter at her husband's audacity. Quickly she said, "Spencer, Mariette, this is my husband, Ruark. Ruark, this is my sister Mariette, and her husband, Spencer Hamilton."

"How do you do?" Spencer said, presenting his hand for a vigorous handshake.

"I'm so very pleased to meet you, your Grace," Mariette uttered, lowering her lashes prettily.

"Please, call me Ruark. There's no need for such formality between a brother and sister." Ruark's smile brought the dimple to his cheek, and as Mariette raised her eyes to his face, they seemed to linger on his mouth with fascination.

At that moment, Essie announced dinner, and the four of

them went into the candlelit dining room. The vase of roses in the center of the table made a spot of softly glowing color.

Outside, foreboding clouds masked the last of the daylight, and the occasional streak of lightning stood out in bold relief against the darkness.

Essie served rack of lamb and bowls of garden vegetables, moving silently about the room.

When she had gone, Mariette said, "Essie may be a sour old thing, but she's an excellent cook. You're lucky to have her, Juli."

"Yes, I don't know what I'd have done without her and Will-John. They've kept this place going."

Mariette looked about the room and grimaced. "I'd forgotten what a funny, old-fashioned house this is. And to think, I almost ended up living here." She gave a small shudder of distaste.

"I don't mind telling you, I'm still rather put out because you bested me in acquiring Quarrystones," Spencer admitted to Ruark. "I'd made plans to combine this estate with my own."

"So I heard," Ruark said smoothly. "However, you've quite a large property already, so surely the acquisition of Quarrystones wasn't all that important to you."

Spencer took a sip of wine. "In this day and age, a man should be snapping up any and all available farm land. With new methods of farming being developed, bigger fields are going to be a necessity. Since the invention of Tull's grain drill, planting is much simpler. A few men can sow an acreage that once would've required the work of twenty or thirty men."

Ruark's dark look was level. "But, if the work is done

by a machine and a handful of men, how do the others manage to make a living?"

"That's not my worry, man. Time's are changing, and I intend to ride the crest of the wave. I'm lucky enough to be a landowner, and I plan to take advantage of that. Some of the small farmers may suffer a bit, but they can migrate into the cities and find plenty of work."

"Do you have any idea how dreadful the city would be for people who've always lived in the country?" exclaimed Juliana. "I doubt if they could ever adjust."

"Isn't it a matter of adjust or die?" Spencer asked casually, leaning back in his chair. "No sense in molly-coddling these people."

"You call it molly-coddling?" Juliana's voice rose.

Ruark broke into the exchange. "Progress is a wonderful thing, to be sure. But I've always been of the opinion that it's a landowner's duty to protect his tenants."

Boldly, Mariette scanned Ruark's chest and broad shoulders. "Tell me," she said, "what does being under your protection entail?"

"It means my tenants can expect a fair wage for the work they do. In addition to that, they'll have an allotment of ground to grow their own gardens or keep a few animals." He reached for his wineglass. "The tenants have made money for me and my family for generations. How could I justify turning them off the land so I could make more profit using machinery and new agricultural methods? I owe them more loyalty than that."

"Come now, Ruark," spluttered Spencer. "Are you seriously expecting us to believe you'd limit your own income to pamper your tenant farmers? A ridiculous notion!"

Juliana observed a dangerous stillness in her husband as he sipped his wine, then carefully set the goblet down. She glanced from him to Spencer, then back again, conscious of how badly her sister's husband suffered by comparison.

Spencer, though somewhere near Ruark's age, looked at least ten years older. His hair was a pale, sandy color, already tending to thinness. His features were regular and undistinguished, and his bright brown eyes gave him the look of a terrier, as she had once confided to her brother. He wasn't as tall as Ruark, and his body was stocky and ungainly.

Juliana knew her sister also realized the differences between the two men. With a sinking heart, she recognized the greedy look on Mariette's face. She'd seen it too many times before not to understand what it meant. As children, the look had surfaced every time Mariette decided Juliana's doll was prettier or her new dress nicer. Through the years, it had usually been easier to give in than to deny her. Now, it seemed Mariette was discovering she wanted another of Juliana's possessions: her husband.

Fortunately, the arrival of Essie with syllabub for dessert broke the tension of the moment. During the remainder of the meal, Mariette kept them entertained with stories about her travels abroad. Most often her focus was Ruark's face, and he favored her with grave attention.

Juliana wished time would pass more quickly and bring the evening to an end. As Mariette's vivacious charm became more and more evident, she felt herself growing more silent and withdrawn. Suddenly she was once again the plain, dull spinster. Not even the sight of the shining gold ring on her finger could revive her earlier feeling of happiness.

She was filled with foreboding. When had she ever been allowed to own something Etta wanted? Why should she think a husband would be any different?

Mariette finished a rather naughty tale which brought a flattering blush of color to her face. One hand fluttered at her throat, drawing attention to her bared shoulders and bosom. With a surge of anger, Juliana noticed that Ruark's eyes obediently followed where Mariette led them. She glanced at Spencer, only to see he, too, was completely entranced by his wife's beauty.

Men are such fools, she thought. *A pretty smile can render them witless.*

She laid aside the napkin she'd been twisting in nervous fingers. "Shall we go into the parlor?" Her voice sounded harsh even to her own ears.

"No, wait," cried Mariette gaily. "Before we do, I want to hear Ruark play something on the guitar I saw in the hallway. Wouldn't that be fun, Spencer?" She turned her attention on her husband, who indulgently patted her hand.

"Mariette is quite a little music-lover." He beamed. "I'm afraid you'll have to give a command performance, Ruark. She'll never take no for an answer."

Ruark dipped his dark head graciously. "As you wish, madam. If it won't inconvenience your plans, 'Liana."

"No, not at all." Juliana sank back into her chair, moodily aware of the way her sister watched Ruark as he strode from the room to get the guitar.

When he returned, Mariette gracefully rose from her chair and rounded the table to stand at his side. She put out one dainty hand to stroke the satiny wood of the instrument he held.

"What kind of wood is this?" she asked, leaning closer to inspect it.

"Rosemary," he answered. "Guitars made of the wood are said to make sweeter music."

"Are they?" Mariette smiled up at him. "Then you must

play something and let us judge for ourselves." She dropped into the chair next to him.

"Very well."

The guitar looked incongruous in Ruark's large hands as he strummed it, but the sounds were soothing and melodious. He played easily, filling the room with the strains of a well-known love ballad.

"Oh, I know this song," cried Mariette, clasping her hands together. "Do you mind if I sing?"

"Please do," replied Ruark. "What about you, 'Liana? Would you like to join Mariette?"

"I'm afraid I don't sing very well." Though she told herself she was only being sensible by admitting the truth, the admission caused her an overwhelming feeling of inadequacy. She pulled one of the long-stemmed roses from the vase in front of her and put it to her nose, breathing deeply of its scent. She hoped it concealed the tight expression she knew must be stealing over her face.

Mariette's clear soprano voice complemented the notes Ruark played, producing a very pleasant rendition of the old country song. As it ended, she laid a hand on his arm and said, "Now you sing with me."

Their voices blended together so perfectly on the intimate words of the song that Juliana felt completely shaken by her jealousy.

"Oh, that was fun!" Mariette laid her head against Ruark's shoulder for an instant. "Do you know 'Love's Sweet Dream?' It's one of my favorites."

"Then, by all means, we must sing it," said Ruark, his hands moving to the guitar strings once more.

Juliana's head began to pound, and she was frightened by the depth of her emotions. If she remained in Mariette's presence much longer, she wouldn't be responsible for her actions. In all the years she'd had to deal with her sister, this was the first time she'd ever envisioned doing anything vengeful to her. And she didn't exactly care to explore the reasons why.

Also, she didn't want Ruark to know she felt betrayed by him. He knew nothing of the silly rivalry between her and Etta, and even if he did, she had no right to expect loyalty from a man who was virtually a make-believe husband.

She chewed her lip as she cast one more agitated look at him. How could he be so charmingly sincere when they were alone, then exhibit such interest in another's wife? Obviously, he was as human as the next man, a willing victim of a beautiful woman's wiles.

Mariette's laugh trilled out and an innocent hand fluttered, coming to rest on Ruark's muscular thigh. Juliana stifled hasty words as she looked at Spencer. He was smiling fatuously, not noticing his wife's bold gesture.

Juliana leaned toward him and whispered, "I have a miserable headache, Spencer. I don't want to spoil everyone else's fun, so I think I'll go on up to bed. Please feel free to stay as long as you like. Good night."

She rose quickly from her chair and left the room. Outside, the storm broke with a blinding flash of lightning that seemed to highlight the long-stemmed yellow rose she still held in her hand.

Twelve

There was a resounding crash of thunder and through the open window, Ruark could hear the rain begin to fall.

"Where has 'Liana gone?" he asked, laying aside the guitar.

"It seems she developed a particularly nasty headache," replied Spencer. "She went on up to bed."

"I want to go see about her." Ruark got to his feet. "Will you excuse me?"

"Certainly. From the sounds of the storm, we'd better start for Moorlands anyway."

"But we haven't finished our song." Mariette framed a pretty pout with her full lips. "Once again, Juliana has managed to spoil everyone's fun."

Ruark cast a quick look in her direction, but said nothing.

Spencer smiled indulgently. "Come now, darling, don't be tiresome. Your sister can't help it if she has a headache."

"Don't you think it's terribly convenient?" Mariette appealed to Ruark. "Perhaps we shouldn't have sung together. I'd forgotten Juli resents the fact I can sing and she can't."

"Don't worry about upsetting her." Ruark's smile was deliberately roguish. "Since our marriage, she's discovered many fascinating abilities. No doubt being unable to sing has faded in significance."

Mariette drew in a quick breath and her eyes narrowed

speculatively. Spencer continued to smile in his obtuse way, unaware of the innuendoes in the conversation.

"But I do hate to see the evening end so early."

"Etta, Ruark must see to Juliana," Spencer reminded her. "And we should be on our way before the road becomes impassable. We'll have other evenings together, my dear." He turned to his host. "If you wouldn't mind, you might ring for Essie before you go up. I suspect my coachman is sitting in the kitchen over a mug of Will-John's beer."

Having summoned Essie and leaving his guests in her care, Ruark climbed the stairs two at a time. He entered the candlelit bedchamber without knocking. Juliana was standing in front of the dresser, taking the pins out of her hair. She didn't look up as he approached.

"Perhaps your hair was braided too tightly," he said, laying his hands on her shoulders. "Sometimes that can bring on a headache, I'm told." He placed a light kiss on the nape of her neck, then began unplaiting her hair.

"Did you know that unbraiding the bride's hair is an old gypsy custom?" he asked, running his fingers through her now unbound tresses. "After the wedding feast, her family bids her farewell and then unbraids her hair as a symbol of her new marital status."

Juliana picked up her hairbrush and moved slightly away from him. Their glances met in the mirror, and as Ruark reached out to gently take the brush from her, he asked, "What's the real reason you left our little dinner party, 'Liana? Somehow, I don't think it was a headache."

He began to brush her hair with long, soothing strokes and she sighed wearily. After a few moments, he put down the brush and turned her to face him. His arms went around her, pulling her against his chest.

"What's wrong, love?"

Juliana had removed her dress and now wore a robe over her petticoats. Through the thinness of the material, he could feel a slight tremor ripple through her body.

She took a deep breath. "I'm afraid this evening proved I've made a terrible mistake by marrying."

"Why do you say that?"

"It's not important. What matters is that I've realized my mistake while there's still time to do something about it."

"What are you suggesting?"

"Since our marriage hasn't been consummated, it'd be simple to arrange for an annulment."

"Not so simple as you might think," he warned.

"Why not?"

"Because our marriage won't just be in name only by the time the night is done."

Juliana pushed him away with sudden anger. "Is that a threat?"

His onyx eyes narrowed. "Threat or promise, whichever you like."

"I don't like either. Please go away and we'll discuss it in the morning."

"We'll discuss it now." He undid the buttons at his wrists and with a swift movement, pulled the shirt he wore over his head. Dropping into the nearby chair he began removing his boots.

"Stop it," she ordered. "You can't spend the night here."

"But, my love," he drawled, "have you forgotten the conversation we had earlier this evening? When you accepted the *claddagh* ring, you agreed we were to be man and wife."

"Your behavior tonight changed that," she retorted.

"My behavior? What in hell are you talking about?"

Her spine stiffened. "You know exactly what I mean."

He leaped to his feet and stood close in front of her. "I think you'd better explain yourself."

"All right, if I have to say it aloud," she muttered. "You gave me that fine talk of love and friendship and sincerity, and then barely managed to keep your hands off my sister tonight."

"What!"

"And, may I point out, she *didn't* manage to keep hers off you!"

He looked thunderstruck. "For God's sake, I thought you were an intelligent woman."

"I'm intelligent enough to realize when someone is making a fool of me. I know when I've been lied to."

"I did not lie to you."

"You did. If you really felt the way you said, how could you have fallen all over Mariette that way?"

"How did I fall all over your sister?"

"You didn't take your eyes off her all evening, for one thing. And you hung on her every word."

"She's your sister, damn it. I was trying to be polite. God knows I had nothing to say to Spencer, and you were unusually quiet. What was I supposed to do?"

"Don't you dare try to make this my fault. Just because I was quiet you didn't have to ogle Mariette's chest all night!"

To her outraged astonishment, he laughed heartily. " 'Liana, I believe you're jealous."

"I am not," she flared.

"Why else would you be so angry?"

"Because it's quite evident that Essie was right. You *are* a rutting stag!"

He gaped. "Essie said that? Lord, her opinion of me is even lower than I thought. A rutting stag, eh?"

"Precisely. You claim you spent that month in Ireland because you didn't trust yourself around me. Well, who knows how you passed your time there? And on your first evening home, you act as if you'd never seen a woman before. I'm surprised Spencer took it so well."

"Did you ever stop to think that he took it so well because there was nothing to be upset about? Perhaps it was your imagination that conjured up this wealth of misdeeds on my part."

"The way you looked at Mariette was not my imagination."

"I won't deny that your sister's a beautiful woman. And when such a woman flaunts herself, a man would have to be a monk, and a truly dedicated one, at that, not to look. But, dear wife, looking does not constitute the sins you imply."

"Your honesty is commendable. So tell me, would you rather it was Mariette standing here in front of you?" Her voice was challenging, but her eyes, dark and enormous in her pale face, exposed her dread of the answer he might give.

"Except for my mother," Ruark said solemnly, "every woman I've ever known was like Mariette. Pretty to look at, but shallow, vain, and selfish in the bargain. That was before I met you."

With a smile that dispelled some of the tension of the moment, he untied the belt of her robe and, holding the ends of it in his hands, used it to pull her closer. "In answer to your question, no, I much prefer you."

"I can't believe that," she said in a small voice. "Why would you?"

"When I first came to Quarrystones to hide out, all Essie or Will-John could talk about was you. It was perfectly clear they hoped someday you'd come back to the estate to live. They told me I was welcome here until I became a threat to you or your reputation. And what a reputation! I was certain no one could be such a paragon." He chuckled. " 'Brilliant mind,' they said. 'Artistic talent.' 'Miss Juli,' " he gently mimicked, " 'is a down-to-earth lass with a tender heart.' I didn't think anyone could be so perfect. I soon learned everything the Cliftons said was true. That and more, for they hadn't told me you were beautiful."

"Because I'm . . ." He laid a finger across her lips, silencing her denial.

"That day I robbed the coach, I suspected who you were right away. Then, when you flew into such a rage because I dared to look through your books and painting things, I was certain. I'll never forget how you looked sitting there among the gorse, your hair blowing in the wind. Don't tell me you're not beautiful. I know better."

Before she could voice further protest, he bent his head and kissed her, his arms sliding tightly around her waist. Her mind still reeling from his unexpected words, Juliana could only cling to him. She couldn't even find the will to make him stop when he raised his hands to brush the robe from her shoulders and let it drop to the floor at her feet. His hands were warm against her bared flesh.

The room around them faded away as his kiss deepened and she allowed her arms to reach upward, embracing his broad shoulders. She was no longer aware of the mellow candlelight, the flickering fire on the grate, or the rain-washed breeze coming through the open window. She was only cognizant of the man in her arms, of his sweetly insistent mouth moving against her own.

She was shocked to hear herself moan slightly as the kiss ended.

"Now do you doubt my feelings?" Ruark murmured, lips grazing her hair.

"I want to believe you," she whispered. "It's just that when I saw you and Mariette together, I lost all confidence in myself."

With firm hands on her shoulders, he turned her to face the mirror, holding her body against his own. "Look in the glass, 'Liana, and see what I see."

He lifted a strand of her hair, letting the candle's light play on its burnished length. "Your hair is wondrous. I love the way it swirls about your shoulders as you walk, the way it curls around my fingers anytime you let me close enough to touch it." His gaze was wicked as it met hers in the mirror. "The color is like one of those deep, mysterious dyes Essie makes from her forest plants: dark, yet alive with highlights, sometimes red, sometimes gold."

Hesitantly, Juliana put up a hand to touch her hair, as if she had never really looked at it before. Ruark's lips brushed her wrist.

"Your skin is as smooth as marble, but so much warmer to touch. Your mouth makes me ache just to look at it. And when we're together, merely looking isn't enough." One warm hand cradled her face, turning it toward him so he could place a kiss upon her softly parted lips. As she rested her head against his shoulder, his deep voice with its Irish lilt went on.

"No one could look into your eyes and not see beauty there. That day you sat in the gorse so furious with me, they were the same stormy grey color as the sky above you. Right now, they're as blue as the heart of a sapphire."

Juliana leaned closer to the mirror, studying her image as though it was that of a stranger. In all honesty, she had never seen her face glow as it now did. Never before had her eyes shone with such feeling, as if they hid delicious secrets behind the fringe of thick, black lashes. Her mouth, soft and slightly swollen from Ruark's kisses, turned up at the corners and she was surprised at how happy she looked.

She twisted in his arms to face him, a question on her lips. Without a word being spoken, somehow he sensed her query and answered it truthfully.

"Your sister's beautiful, there's no doubt. Tonight, in that pink gown she wore, she was an exotic hothouse flower. But standing beside her in your simple green dress, you were like a fern deep in the cool forest. Tall and graceful, elegant. Given my choice, I'd trade the stifling atmosphere of the greenhouse for the splendor of the woods anytime."

He caught her up into his arms and she put a hand against his cheek, bringing her face close to his. "Thank you," she whispered.

She experimented with a kiss that made his breath quicken and his soul flame with desire. He crossed the room to the wide bed and, his mouth still clinging to hers, sank down onto its softness. One hand had moved from her waist upward, lingering to untie the ribbon at the top of her chemise when a sudden noise claimed his attention.

"Juliana, Ruark. It's me, Mariette."

"What the hell?" Ruark released Juliana and, with a reluctant smile, left their bed to open the door.

Mariette was standing in the hallway. "Oh, please, can we spend the night?" she gasped, one hand pressed against her breasts. "I'm so afraid of storms, I can't bear the thought of going out in this weather."

Ruark threw a quick look over his shoulder at Juliana, then shrugged. "Of course, you're welcome to stay. Let me get Essie to find you a place to sleep."

As he started through the door, there was another loud

clap of thunder and, with a shriek, Mariette threw herself against him. Startled, his arms closed around her and he patted her back in a distracted, yet comforting way.

To Ruark, Mariette's blue gaze was more calculating than frightened as it sought out her sister. Juliana sat in the midst of the rumpled bedcovers, an indisputably arresting vision. Her dark hair tumbled about her shoulders, spilling down over the loosened top of her chemise. Her cheeks were glowing with color, her eyes passion-dark. Even from this distance her lips looked sweetly bruised from his kisses. It would be obvious to the most casual observer that they'd been engaged in love-play. And Mariette was anything but a casual observer.

She tipped back her head to look into Ruark's face. As she did so, she pressed closer to his body in unmistakable invitation. "I've always been scared witless by storms," she said meekly.

" 'Tis only rain now," Ruark pointed out, setting her away from him. "A little thunder and lightning, but the worst is over."

Boldly, she appraised him. "I expect you think I'm an awful fool. Juliana is as brave as a man, and I'm such a ninny."

"Ye're certainly acting like a ninny now." As Essie bustled down the hallway, arms full of blankets, her voice fairly vibrated with disapproval. "I told ye I'd prepare yer old room. There was no need to bother Ruark and Juliana."

Mariette looked at the woman with something akin to hatred and Ruark speculated that, had he not been watching, she'd have slapped Essie's face.

"Oh, darling, there you are," called out Spencer, reaching the landing, puffing slightly from his rapid climb. "I went to talk to the coachman and my wife disappeared," he explained to Ruark. "Don't want to lose track of my new bride on a cold, stormy night like this." He laughed, laying a possessive hand on Mariette's arm.

"For God's sake, Spencer, stop pawing me," Mariette snapped, turning abruptly to follow Essie down the darkened hallway.

Spencer stared after her an instant, then turned back to Ruark. "She's only put off by the storm. They seem to frighten her rather badly. Look, we appreciate your hospitality for the night. Sorry to be such a nuisance."

"No trouble at all," Ruark assured him, stepping back inside his bedchamber and firmly closing the door.

He approached the bed warily. Juliana's expression confirmed that his caution wasn't unfounded.

"Surely you aren't going to be upset by that brazen display, are you?" he asked. "Mariette was being dramatic."

"If that's what you thought, why did you indulge her?"

"Would you rather I'd have thrown her out? Remember, she's the one who hurled herself at me."

Juliana slid to the edge of the bed. "It doesn't matter," she said dully. "Mariette will keep managing to come between us until she gets what she wants."

"How is she coming between us now? Essie's taken her off to her own room."

"After all these years, my sister's methods are no secret. For the moment, she's content because she knows you'll be coming to my bed straight from her arms. It pleased her to stage that scene in front of me."

"Not even Mariette could be that devious." He reached out to grasp her wrist, pulling her roughly against his bare chest. "You're letting your imagination run wild."

"It makes me furious that you think that," she cried. "And furthermore, I don't want to be touched by a man who smells like another woman's perfume!" She struck out blindly with her free hand, but, angered by her words, he pushed her away and her blow fell short of its mark.

They stood glaring at each other for several seconds before she wheeled about and flounced across the room. She stopped at the open window to speak, her words muffled by the pouring rain. "I forgot that you don't know my sister as well as I do." Her shoulders lifted slightly. "How could you?"

"What do you want me to do?" He shortened the distance between them. "Do you want me to tell her and Spencer to leave?"

She turned around to face him. "No, that would be silly. Of course they must stay. I wasn't thinking logically."

"Then you'll come to bed?" He held out a hand and Mariette's perfume drifted on the air again.

"No." Juliana crossed her arms, hugging herself. "I'm sorry I can't make you understand, Ruark."

"Try again," he demanded.

"I don't think my marriage should be something I sacrifice to Etta just to keep peace in the family."

"No one's asking you to sacrifice anything."

"I can't be certain of that. Tonight I've seen that Mariette will do everything in her power to destroy our relationship. I simply don't know how to fight her. Maybe it's better if I don't try."

With those words, she twisted the gold ring off her finger and pressed it into his hand. "Here, I'd like you to take this and go ahead with an annulment."

"I don't want the damned thing," he roared. "I gave it to you in good faith, remember? You keep it."

"I don't want it."

"Neither do I." With a muttered oath, Ruark flung the ring through the open window.

As soon as it disappeared into the night, Juliana clamped both hands over her mouth and blinked back tears. Then she rounded on him. "My God, how could you have done that?"

Ruark started toward her. "You said you didn't want it."

"I didn't mean it!" She pushed past him, saying, "I've got to find my ring. I'll never forgive you if it's lost."

"Wait," he rasped, but she was already gone, running down the stairs. Ruark followed her out through the kitchen door, flinching as the icy rain struck his naked skin.

Oblivious to the cold water sluicing from the heavens, Juliana was on her hands and knees, searching frantically through the grass directly below her bedroom window. Ruark dropped down beside her, knowing the task could be hopeless.

"What was I thinking?" she moaned. "How could I have done such a thing?"

"I'm the one who threw it out the window, remember."

"But it was my fault. I shouldn't have said what I did."

Her words ended in a sob, and she paused to dash away rain and tears before continuing the search. Out in front of them the river moved along swiftly, swollen by the torrential downpour. Ruark edged closer to the bank, knowing that if the ring had somehow reached the water, they'd never recover it.

" 'Liana, you're soaked. Come back inside and we'll find it tomorrow when the rain has stopped."

"I can't leave it out here."

She looked at him with such a forlorn expression he couldn't bear it. He got to his feet and pulled her up into his arms. "Don't worry about it, sweetheart, I'll get you another ring. We'll go to Ireland and buy it together."

"I want this one, Ruark. It's the one you brought me."

A strand of wet hair lay across her pale cheek, and he raised a gentle hand to smooth it away. "Come back inside. The ring will be here in the morning, I promise."

She cast another despairing look around the shadowed grass at her feet, just as Essie appeared at the back door, holding a lantern aloft.

"What in the name of all that's holy are ye two doing out here in a blinding rainstorm?" she yelled, holding her woolen robe tightly about herself. "Ye'll catch yer death, half-dressed like that."

"There!" cried Juliana. "I see it." She dropped to her knees to retrieve the ring. The lantern light shining down across the lawn had picked out the subtle golden glow, bringing it to her attention. "Oh, thank you, Essie."

Essie looked completely confused. "What's the child blithering about?"

Ruark smiled broadly. "It's nothing. I'll explain tomorrow. You go on to bed; we're coming in out of the storm now."

"Hmmph. It's about time." She shook her head. "This has been a strange night." With that she turned and went into the kitchen, taking the lantern with her.

Juliana stared at the ring she held until Ruark reached out and took it from her. He slid it back onto her finger.

"Now, Mrs. Hamilton, please see that you leave it where it belongs," he scolded, holding her rain-soaked body against his. "No more foolishness?"

"No more foolishness." She pressed closer to his warmth.

Ruark slanted his mouth over hers and they stood, locked together, oblivious to the rain streaming down around them. Her hands moved upwards along his powerful arms, coming to rest at the back of his wet hair. She pressed her face against the strong arch of his neck.

"Ruark," she whispered, "I'm sorry."

"So am I, love. Perhaps we've both learned a valuable lesson."

"I regret that I spoiled the night."

He put his lips close to her ear. "The night's not over yet."

The look he gave her warmed her as he bent and lifted her into his arms. He carried her through the back door of Quarrystones and up the stairs to their private chamber, her sodden petticoats leaving rivulets of summer rain to mark their path.

Ruark set her down on the hearth rug, then hurried to stoke up the fire. "You'd better get out of those clothes before you catch a chill," he said.

At the sight of her standing there in the nearly transparent chemise and petticoats the rain had molded to her slender form, he halted. A tiny flame began to burn deep within his eyes, and the dimple leaped to his cheek.

Suddenly overcome by timidity, Juliana said, "I'll go into the bathing chamber and put on dry clothing."

He couldn't keep from grinning, even as he recognized her need to forestall the events to come. Thinking to give her more time, he said, "I'll find us something warming to drink. I won't be gone long."

By the time he returned, Juliana was dressed in a modest white nightgown, sitting in a chair drawn up to the fire, drying her hair. He set a bottle of wine and two pewter goblets on the floor near her chair. Then, striding across the room, he gathered an armload of covers from the bed, including the feather tick, blankets and pillows. These he dropped onto the hearth rug before the fire.

As he moved about the room, she watched him. The rain

had plastered the breeches he wore to his obviously masculine body, accentuating the strength of his thighs and the leanness of his hips. He noticed her interest and teased, "Best look away if you don't want to be embarrassed. I'm getting out of these wet clothes."

Quickly, she turned her face toward the fire and concentrated on the flames leaping on the grate.

"Now, come here," he invited after a few moments. He was sitting cross-legged on the pile of bedding, a linen sheet drawn casually over his lap. He put out one brown hand and when she laid hers within it, pulled her down next to him.

"Are you warmer now?"

The firelight played over the breadth of his naked chest, gilding the black hair with gold. The flames were repeated in his gypsy eyes. Juliana could answer his question with an affirmative nod, for suddenly she felt very warm indeed.

He reached for the bottle of wine, deftly removing the wax seal and the cork. "I found this in Will-John's secret cache in the still room. Hopefully, he'll think the occasion special enough for his best blackberry cordial."

He filled the goblets, handing one to Juliana.

"Ruark," she cried in delight, "there are flowers floating in the wine."

Delicate white blossoms starred the dark liquid in the goblet, giving off a faint minty aroma.

"I know." His glance teased hers over the rim of his wineglass. " 'Tis white dittany. It grows by the back door, so I risked another soaking to pick a few flowers."

Juliana took a sip of the wine, the blossoms tickling her nose. "But why?"

Ruark took the goblet from her hand and set it aside, with his own. "Dittany is the flower of passion, my love, and that's what you've been promising me all night."

He drew her close, one hand dropping to the buttons on her nightgown. She lowered her gaze, but when it fell on his long, muscled legs stretched out beside her, she rapidly raised it to his face again. The intent look on it frightened her, and she put a restraining hand on his.

"There's something I have to say, Ruark."

"What is it?"

She looked back down, this time at her own tightly clenched hands. "I overheard Spencer tell my father he thought I was cold and unfeeling. What if he was right?"

He was stricken by her anxiety. He separated her hands and brought the left one to his lips. "Have you forgotten your palm reading so quickly, then?" The corners of his mouth turned up. "Remember what I told you about your heart line?" He traced the line in her palm with the tip of his tongue, causing a delicious tremor to move down her spine. "You'll find you're a passionate woman, I promise."

"I'm so afraid I can't please you." At the admission, she was unable to meet his eyes any longer.

"Look at me, 'Liana," he said sternly. When she did, she was instantly lost in ebony depths. "You already please me more than any woman I've ever known, and I haven't even made love to you yet."

He kissed her deeply, moving against her mouth until her lips parted beneath his. Her body arched closer; his urgent mouth moved downward to her throat, placing burning kisses from her ear to the pulse beating wildly in the hollow of her neck.

One large hand cupped her breast, and Juliana gasped in pleasure at the sensation. Without realizing, she moved her own hand to the row of buttons, opening her gown to his searching touch.

"I've waited for this moment a long time," he whispered.

Juliana gave a soft, throaty laugh. "Do you keep expecting to hear Essie at the door?" she asked.

He groaned. "God forbid. If she appears at this moment, I swear I'll have no patience with her." He slid the nightgown from her shoulders, baring her breasts to his avid attention.

Juliana kissed him lightly on the lips, then raised to her knees to remove the gown, sliding it down over her hips and legs. She was surprised at her own daring, but Ruark's response soon made her forget everything but the desire to be close to him. He placed his hands on her hips, pulling her over on top of him as he lay back upon the pillows.

"You're so lovely," he murmured, as the curtain of her hair veiled them.

She was stretched out along the full, hard length of him, fitting and molding her softer curves to his granite ones. A soft groan issued from his throat, and he suddenly shifted his weight, cradling her in his arms and pulling her body beneath his.

"I'm afraid I'll hurt you, love," he began, but she put her slender fingers against his lips.

"Shh, don't waste time talking. I'm not afraid." He pulled her close into the most intimate embrace.

And so, she thought, closing her mind against the expected pain, *the gypsy highwayman steals again. First my heart and now my innocence.*

She looked at the beloved face above her, and a new thought pierced her consciousness. The truth was that those things hadn't been stolen, but given freely.

Her body began to respond to her husband's and the momentary pain she'd felt was gone. She tightened her hold on him, completely lost in the rise and fall of their passion. She reveled in his powerful masculinity, relished the pleasure of his arms wrapped about her like bands of steel. She returned his probing, searching kisses with an ardor that stunned them both. For the first time in her life, Juliana Lowell Hamilton, spinster no more, abandoned her independence, letting him guide her to a shattering ecstasy she had never anticipated.

She lay quiet for a long moment, and when she opened her eyes she saw him leaning over her with a questioning expression.

"Does this change your mind about our marriage?"

She smiled. "I'm beginning to think it may be pleasant enough. I have much to learn, but something tells me the lessons won't be too tedious."

He threw back his head and laughed. "No more lessons tonight, however. This has been an exhausting day and we both need some rest."

He lay back on the pillows and after she drew the blankets over them, Juliana snuggled beside him, within the circle of his arms. He kissed her softly and she breathed a small sigh.

Suddenly, her dull life had altered completely. Without her quite knowing how it had happened, she possessed the home she loved so much and a husband whose very touch promised a wealth of happiness she hadn't even known existed.

Thirteen

Juliana sighed in her sleep and turned, throwing out a careless hand. She was startled into wakefulness as her outstretched fingers encountered warm flesh.

A soft pink suffused her face as she found herself looking into Ruark's amused eyes.

"Good morning," he murmured, kissing her ear. "I trust you slept well?"

"Mmm." She stretched, then blushed again as she realized she was completely naked beneath the concealing sheet. She caught sight of her carelessly discarded nightgown at the foot of their makeshift bed before the fireplace. "I slept quite well, thank you."

Clutching the sheet to her breasts, she sat up and quickly reached for the nightgown. Ruark laid a restraining hand on her arm. "You're not thinking of running away, are you?"

"I'm afraid it's late. I really should go help Essie in the kitchen."

He pulled her down into his arms and put his face against her neck. "No need for haste, love." His lips grazed her skin.

"But we have guests, remember?" Juliana turned her face to meet his questing mouth.

"At this moment, it's difficult for me to remember anything but you."

As the kiss ended, she sighed. "I should help Essie with breakfast."

"I expect that would be the decent thing to do." He nibbled at her bare shoulder. "But somehow I doubt our guests are as hungry as I find myself."

She had to laugh as she gently disentangled herself from his embrace. "Behave yourself, Ruark. Your hunger can wait until later."

His dark brows went up. "I'll take that as a promise," he warned.

"It was meant as such." She gave him a swift kiss, then sat up, hurriedly pulling the nightgown over her head.

At the brief glimpse of her nudity, Ruark smiled broadly and said, "Let's hope our guests don't linger."

"Feel free to stay here if you'd rather not come down for breakfast," she said, scrambling to her feet.

"No, I'll play the host. Besides, this is one day I definitely want to keep you in sight."

As the two of them entered the kitchen, they came face to face with Essie Clifton, who was preparing to take a platter of sliced ham into the dining room. Ruark lifted it from her hands, saying, "Good morning, Essie. You're looking fine today."

The old woman favored him with doubtful scrutiny. "Ye're in unusually high spirits, I should think."

"And why not?" he countered.

"Why not, indeed," Essie sniffed. "All that carrying on last night."

Juliana felt it was time to change the subject. "Shall I take in the bowl of fruit?" she inquired.

"Yes, ye do that. I'll get the muffins and that'll be everything. Spencer and Mariette are already in the dining room."

When Ruark left the room, Essie laid a hand on Juliana's arm. "Psst, child," she whispered. "Are ye all right? Did ye work out yer differences?"

Juliana's cheeks were rosy, but she smiled at the other's concern. "I'm fine. Ruark was very patient and kind. I must admit, he convinced me he's actually not too unhappy being married to me."

"No doubt the lad has his methods. I only hope ye didn't find them too bothersome."

Juliana suppressed a laugh. "Essie, I can assure you I didn't find Ruark or his methods the least bit bothersome. Quite the opposite, in fact. My husband is a very complicated and unique man."

Essie tossed a disdainful head toward the dining room. "That spoiled sister of yers knows it, too. She's so eaten up with envy she can barely stand it." The slight woman chuckled heartily. "Does my heart good, I tell ye."

When they entered the dining room, the first thing Juliana saw was her sister talking to Ruark with a bright smile and animated gestures. Before she could manage to quell the feeling, she was stricken by a pang of jealousy. However, as soon as he looked up and saw her, Ruark came to her side, unceremoniously leaving Mariette standing alone. He bent to kiss her as though they had been parted for hours instead of minutes, and as she raised her mouth to his, she glimpsed the vexation on her sister's face.

As the meal progressed and Ruark continued to display his affection, Mariette grew more and more moody. Spencer, on the other hand, seemed oblivious to the undercurrents in the room and ate a large breakfast.

"Ruark, you and Juliana will have to come to Moorlands to visit us," he said. "We must repay your hospitality."

"Do you plan to stay in the country long?" Ruark asked casually.

"It all depends on Mariette. I've a few business matters to clear up, but that shouldn't take long. By the time they're taken care of, I expect she'll be ready to return to London. She already misses her busy social life."

"Quite true," Mariette agreed. "Ruark, why don't you and Juli travel up to London with us? You could visit Mother and Father, and join us for some of the parties."

Ruark placed his hand over Juliana's. " 'Liana and I are perfectly content to stay in the country, Mariette. The heat and noise of the city have no appeal for us."

Mariette tossed down the linen napkin she held. "Don't you miss making the rounds of the parties and soirees? Or gaming at the clubs?"

"We don't have much interest in society. Actually, we have everything we need right here at Quarrystones." Ruark favored Juliana with a look that was an intimate caress. The warmth of his onyx eyes as they moved over her face made her feel weak. Even though she knew he might have spoken simply to irritate Mariette, his words had a profound effect on her.

"Lord, you two country bumpkins are well-suited to each other," Mariette snapped, with a sulky expression.

"Oh, come now, darling. You of all people should know how newlyweds feel." Spencer patted her shoulder, but she twisted away from him.

"Can we return to Moorlands now?" she asked peevishly. "I want to get out of this dress. I hate wearing the same thing twice." She shuddered. "I suppose I could borrow something from Juliana, but her clothes are so much larger than mine, I'd look like a waif."

Stung by her sister's cruel words, Juliana glanced up quickly. Ruark met her gaze with a half-smile, and then deliberately closed one eye in a conspiratorial wink. With that simple gesture he rendered Mariette's barb harmless, and Juliana found herself amazed at his ability to sway her emotions so easily.

As soon as the Hamiltons had gone, Ruark turned to Juliana, saying, "Let's go down to the stables, love. I have something to show you."

"At the stables? What is it?"

"A surprise, something I brought you from Ireland."

They walked hand in hand to the stable where, at Ruark's request, one of the stablehands disappeared inside the brick building, to return with a wriggling puppy which he placed in Juliana's arms.

"A dog," she exclaimed. "He's so pretty, but I've never seen one like him before." The puppy lapped her chin with its eager tongue and she laughed in delight.

Ruark patted the animal's head. " 'Tis a Brittany spaniel, a very old breed that originated in France. They say the Irish chieftains who invaded Gaul took their hunting dogs with them, and they mated with French spaniels."

The puppy Juliana held was mainly white, but there were several dark reddish-brown splotches along his back. The top of his head and the graceful ears were also red, and his forehead was starred with an irregular white spot. His short muzzle was covered with tiny burnt sienna freckles, as were his legs. Juliana stroked the animal, calming him with her quiet voice, and he looked up at her through large golden brown eyes.

"He's beautiful, Ruark. Thank you."

"When I arrived home, there was a new litter of pups. As soon as I saw them, I wanted one for you. Even though they were bred to be hunting dogs, they're small and affectionate enough to make good pets, as well."

"Can he stay in the house with us?" she asked, setting the dog on the grass and watching him dash away after a yellow butterfly.

Ruark draped an arm about her shoulders and hugged her to him. "My dear, you're the lady of the manor. It's up to you whether we keep the dog inside or not."

She looked surprised. "I keep forgetting," she admitted. "I'm so used to doing as my mother says."

"And what would she say about a pet in the house?"

"Oh, she'd never allow it. When I was six years old, the Cliftons gave me a puppy for my birthday, but he had to stay outdoors because he frightened Mariette and made her ill." Juliana watched as the Brittany poked his nose into a clump of flowers. "It was only recently that Father permitted Jeremy to own a dog. Etta finally outgrew her unfortunate reaction to animals, I expect."

Ruark thought it more likely that Mariette had suffered from childish resentment over Juliana's gift from the Cliftons, but decided against pointing out such a possibility. Instead, he queried, "What about the dauntless Essie? She's not likely to welcome this little beggar."

"I'll convince her it will be all right. And once he's housebroken, what objection could she possibly have?"

"If I know Essie, we'll soon find out." They exchanged a smile.

"What's the dog's name, Ruark?"

"That, too, is up to you. All the way back from Ireland, I called him 'Boy,' so I think it's time he had a proper name."

She savored the thought of Ruark making the effort to bring the puppy to her. It couldn't have been easy managing him on the boat, or during the several days he'd have spent on the road. She was touched knowing he'd gone to such lengths to please her.

"I'll have to give it some thought," she announced. "But I'll come up with something appropriate before too long."

For a time they watched the dog romping through the tall grass along the banks of the moat. He chased various insects, then stopped to tilt his head in curiosity at the sudden splash of a striped frog leaping into the water.

Juliana laughed merrily. "I think he's going to be an amusing companion."

"I hope so, 'Liana." They watched the puppy's antics for a few more minutes and then he spoke again. "How would you like to accompany me to the village and show me the changes you've made? Since my return, Will-John hasn't stopped praising your efforts. I'd like to see for myself."

"I'd enjoy showing you the improvements, but what about the dog?"

"He's probably ready for a nap," Ruark told her. "I'll put him in the stable, and we can collect him on our return to the house."

When he emerged again, he was leading his black stallion. "I thought we could ride over to the village. It still looks rainy, and neither of us needs to be caught out in another storm."

Juliana refused to meet his teasing gaze. "Shall I get my mare?"

Ruark swung up into the saddle and reached down a hand for her. "No, it'll be more fun to ride together."

Effortlessly, he pulled her up in front of him. His arms

went around her as he grasped the reins, and she settled back against his chest.

As they started along the path that followed the river, the air was filled with the fragrance of the rhododendrons and azaleas now blooming. Ruark rode close to one of the tall rhododendron shrubs and picked a bright blossom which he tucked behind her ear.

"You look more like a gypsy lass all the time, love. I'm anxious for my mother to meet you. I think the two of you will get on well together."

"Was she upset when you informed her of our marriage?"

"Surprised, but not upset. Don't forget, she has reason to be tolerant of such a situation."

"Yes, I suppose so. She'd take care not to respond to your marriage in the same way your grandfather did to hers."

"Exactly."

"Well, I'd like to meet her soon. She must be an extraordinary woman."

"She is that."

They rode in silence for a while, and finally she said, "Ruark, do you ever wonder about your grandfather? I mean, do you think about what his life must be like?"

"Not often," he said in clipped tones. "I'm no more concerned with him than he was my father."

"Isn't that awfully harsh? He may have regretted the past many times."

" 'Liana, what prompted you to bring up my grandfather?"

"Oh, I don't know. Perhaps because I feel it's a shame you've never known him. You might like him very much if you were to meet."

"Possible, but not probable. I know his type: pompous,

self-satisfied, overbearing. The very sort of man Spencer is quickly becoming." His eyes fastened on the rooftops of the village as they came into view. "Why make his acquaintance when it's sure to be a matter of mutual dislike from the start? We'd only hold the past against each other."

Juliana sighed. "Maybe it isn't your place to seek revenge for something that happened so long ago. The quarrel was between your father and grandfather, it had nothing to do with you."

"It had everything to do with me," he countered. "Why do you think the old man objected so to a gypsy daughter-in-law? Because his prejudices led him to believe her children would be unfit to inherit his property and titles. That, and of course, the social stigma of having a person of inferior blood bearing his name."

She shook her head in despair. "If only I could prove to you how wrong it is to feel such bitterness."

"You've no reason to prove anything to me. You're not responsible for my bitterness in any way."

"But now that I've discovered what a gentle man you are, I wish I could persuade you to abandon this one last hatred. You won't ever be entirely happy until you do."

He reined in the stallion and slid from its back, lifting her down after him. "I'll tie Heiden at this gate while we're in the village. He can have a meal of fresh clover."

Juliana watched him with worried eyes. "Will you please just think about what I've said?" she asked.

He knelt swiftly and plucked a handful of the plant growing at his feet. " 'Liana, this three-leaved clover is the symbol of Ireland," he said, extending his hand. "Because of my grandfather, I've taken the shamrock as my insignia. It stands for revenge, and I intend to have the satisfaction of seeing that old man suffer for what he did to my parents."

His fist clenched tightly, crushing the tender green leaves within it. "Now please, let the matter lie."

Juliana turned away, filled with a numbing dread. In one rapid movement, he was at her side, his hands on her shoulders. "I'm sorry to cause you distress, but, sweetheart, this shouldn't concern you. It happened long before you were born, and there isn't any way you can understand the destructiveness of human greed and false pride."

She looked up into his face, and though she said nothing further, in her heart she realized pride might someday be the cause of his own destruction. She had to find a way to deter him from the vengeful path he had chosen.

Ruark was greatly impressed with the appearance of the village. He talked with the farmers, moving from cottage to cottage to admire the changes that had been made in the time he was gone. While he conferred with the men, Juliana paid a call on Mrs. Ferguson and her married daughter. It wasn't until they proudly offered her a cup of tea that she suddenly remembered she hadn't yet told Ruark about the debts she had acquired in his name. That was something, she decided, she must do without further delay.

Seeing the men coming back to the cottage, Juliana rose to her feet and thanked her hostess warmly. As she stepped through the door of the cottage, her eyes met and clung to those of her husband. A silent message passed between them, and just as surely as if Ruark had whispered the words into her ear, she knew he was ready to leave.

"We'd best be on our way," he announced. "It looks like it's going to rain again."

The day had, indeed, grown grey and overcast, the wind sighing through the treetops. But somehow, Juliana knew his impatience to be on their way had nothing to do with the weather.

Bidding the friendly tenants farewell, they mounted Heiden and commenced the journey back toward Quarrystones.

"You did a wonderful job in the village, 'Liana," he said as they rode along. "Maybe now the Gypsy Highwayman can concentrate his efforts on Moorlands exclusively."

"Speaking of that, how could you have been so bold as to tell Spencer and Mariette the coach in which you were riding was robbed?"

His deep laugh rang out. "It was worth the risk to see the look on your lovely face. Besides, I thought they might think it odd if mine was one of the few to escape the fellow."

"Still, you took an unnecessary chance."

"No need to worry. Let's talk about the Quarrystones tenants instead. The men tell me you worked right alongside them planting the gardens and putting up the meat. How I'd like to have seen that."

"We all worked hard. We had to, there was so much to be done. But I'll always remember how the tenants greeted me that first time I went back to the village." She shuddered slightly. "I never want that to happen again. So it was time I became a responsible landowner."

"I'm proud of you," he said, close to her ear.

"You may not be when I confess something I've done." She twisted to look back into his face. "It may have been dreadfully stupid."

He grinned. "What was it?"

She faced forward again. "We needed supplies for the planting, for one thing. For another, the villagers had to have food. I spent what money I had, then received permission from the shopkeepers to charge the rest." She turned again to look at him. "I told them you'd pay for it."

"I'll go into town tomorrow and settle our debts," he said. " 'Tis a small price to pay to see such contentment among the tenants. And to see you looking so happy."

"Actually it may be rather a large sum," she said hesitantly, shifting about in the saddle again. "We needed so many items."

"Don't worry, I can manage it. The Duke of Kilcairn isn't exactly destitute, you know." He placed a kiss on her neck.

"You're not?" She turned back toward him, her soft body brushing against him once again, eliciting a soft groan.

"Well, not for money, at any rate. Love, you'll have to sit still and stop tormenting me or we'll be very late getting back to Quarrystones."

She couldn't pretend to misunderstand him, so she faced forward and was careful to sit very quietly. "I'm sorry," she said, and felt his laughter. Ignoring it, she went on, "What do you mean, the Duke of Kilcairn?"

"Just that. I actually am a duke, with some money at my disposal."

"I thought you were lying when you told my father that story."

"I seldom lie, especially when the truth often works so nicely."

"But if you are a duke and rich, why do you need to masquerade as a highwayman?"

"I said I was a duke, I didn't say I was rich."

"You said you had some money."

"My estate brings in good revenues, but as long as my mother is alive, I consider that income hers. Times are always hard in Ireland, and there are many people she tries to help. I can't bleed the estate for my own purposes, when hers are so worthwhile."

"I see."

A few drops of rain began to fall, and Ruark urged the horse into a trot.

"You're the legal heir to Moorlands, remember. Why not simply claim your rights?"

"Even if my claim was believed, the old man still controls the purse strings. Can you imagine him giving me money to clean up the filthy pig sties in which his tenants are forced to live? If he'd wanted them cleaned up, he'd do it himself."

Knowing it would be useless to refute his words until he had met his grandfather and found out for himself, she merely said, "Well, I'm sorry to have burdened you with these debts. I'll be careful that it doesn't happen again."

"It is nothing to worry about, 'Liana. We're not penniless, by any means. It'll be no hardship to pay for your purchases, and you need not ask permission before spending money for whatever you need."

As the raindrops increased, they rode into the stable yard. No one came to meet them as they dismounted, and when he led Heiden into his stall, Ruark found the stable empty. "The men must have taken advantage of the bad weather to return to their cottages. Come on inside, love, and you can play with the puppy while I curry Heiden."

Juliana found the spaniel curled into a ball, nestled deep in the fresh hay in the last stall. She knelt beside him and he was instantly alert, bobbed tail wagging furiously with joy at finding himself no longer alone.

"Hello, Boy," she said, scratching his ears. He leaped at her in a frenzy of happiness and she laughed as she sat back in the hay. "All right, all right. We won't leave you again. From now on, you'll go everywhere we go."

The dog bounded onto her lap, his salmon-colored nose bumping her hand until she began petting him.

"He's a spoiled little ruffian already," said Ruark, coming to stand in the doorway to the stall.

Just then the dog was distracted by a tiny rustling noise. Looking in the direction from which it came, he tilted his head to first one side, then the other. Suddenly a mouse went scurrying along the far side of the aisle between the stalls, and with a high yipping bark, the puppy gave chase.

Ruark and Juliana laughed heartily, but when their eyes met, they grew serious at once.

"No doubt that mouse will keep him occupied for a while," Ruark said, dropping into the clean, dry hay beside her, "and we really shouldn't go out in the rain." He paused to nibble at her ear, causing her to shiver in delight. "Conveniently, we're all alone." His mouth moved downward to her neck, continuing the softly biting kisses. "And all I've been able to think about this morning was last night." He placed a teasing kiss at the corner of her mouth and another on each eyelid. "Shall we . . . ?"

"In the stable?" she asked breathlessly.

Ruark put a hand on each shoulder, bearing her down onto the loose hay. He rained light kisses all over her face, each time avoiding her lips.

"Why not?" he murmured.

"We could go up to our bedchamber."

"Too far."

Finally, his warm mouth closed over hers, and her lips parted and softened, bringing him sweet, intense pleasure. Her answering kiss was so fervent it filled him with an excitement that wouldn't be denied.

Continuing his assault on her mouth, he allowed one hand to unfasten her gown, slipping inside to caress her bare skin. She gasped as his searching fingers gently closed over one breast, teasing and arousing.

"Ruark," she whispered faintly, making one last weak attempt to forestall him. "What if someone should come in here?"

"Shh, love. We can discuss it later."

He was deftly removing her gown from her shoulders, then pushing it and the chemise she wore downward.

"Damn these things," he cursed, hampered from further removing her clothing by the cumbersome petticoats she wore. "Why do women wear so many clothes?"

His irritation broke the spell she seemed to be under. She laughed and tried to scramble away from him. "Obviously, to protect our virtue."

He caught her around the waist with one strong arm, then got to his feet swinging her around in front of him. With his free hand, he succeeded in pulling off her dress and tossing it aside. Lean fingers fumbled with the hooks at the waists of her petticoats and when she protested, he clamped her to his chest and covered her mouth with impassioned kisses. Intending to fend him off, she put up her hands, and instead, found them traitorously stroking his heavily corded shoulders, sliding upwards to encircle his neck.

One by one the petticoats dropped onto the hay, to be followed finally by her beribboned chemise. He lowered her onto the pile of garments and began struggling with the fastening of the pantalettes she wore.

"No," she cried, laughing and thrashing her feet. At the sight of her lying among the petticoats, slim hips moving so invitingly, rounded breasts only partially hidden by her dark hair cascading down around her shoulders, Ruark's smile faded, to be replaced by a look of sensual determination.

" 'Liana, my love," he said huskily, covering her body with his.

Impatient now, he stripped the undergarment from her, ignoring the protesting rip of the fabric. His own clothing was removed just as swiftly, discarded and forgotten.

He poised himself above her and she looked up into his midnight eyes. Lost in their velvet depths, she opened her arms to him, giving herself up to the delightful mastery of his virility. There was no pain this time, except for the exquisite torture of a blinding ecstasy that built to an incredible height before plunging them downward into a tranquil after-bliss.

Spent, they lay together silently. As the fresh sunshiny scent of the hay rose around them, they could hear the rain striking the tiled roof overhead.

After a time, Ruark turned on his side to study her. "I'm beginning to understand why the gypsies think bachelorhood is an unnatural state," he said. "It would seem there's much to recommend married life."

"Yes, it would seem so."

"Ouch!" Ruark shot upright, grimacing in pain.

"What's wrong?"

"That devil bit me," he complained, rubbing an ankle.

Tired of pursuing the elusive rodent, the Brittany pup had returned to the stall and was now making a bid for their attention.

"Poor thing," cried Juliana, "he doesn't like being so neglected."

Ruark's black brows rose. "Poor thing? That dog? What about me? I'm injured, I tell you."

She examined the barely discernible red mark on his ankle, then dropped a quick kiss onto it. "Better?"

"Mmm, much," he replied, reaching out to draw her back

into his embrace. Just as he bent his head to her, the growling puppy pounced, backside high in the air, tail wagging.

Juliana began to laugh. "He wants to play, Ruark. Isn't he darling?"

The pup made another lunge at them, but this time, as he darted away, he grabbed an article of clothing and made for the door of the stall. He stopped and turned to look back at them expectantly, hoping they would follow. It was obvious he anticipated a merry chase.

"Ruark, he took my chemise!"

The dog's stubby tail wagged happily. As Ruark leaped to his feet, the dog shook the cotton chemise and growled fiercely.

Juliana hadn't even a moment to enjoy the sight of Ruark in his naked splendor before the puppy ran out of the stall, dragging the undergarment with him.

"Oh, lord, stop him before someone sees what he has." Juliana started snatching up her clothes, getting into them as hastily as possible.

"Damn the mongrel," Ruark panted, pulling on his breeches and boots. "Finish dressing and I'll catch him."

Juliana slipped her dress over her head and, gathering up Ruark's shirt, ran out of the stable to join the chase. She could see her husband in pursuit of the dog who was dashing across the causeway, the chemise flying out behind him.

"Stop, you miserable thief!" Ruark shouted in exasperation. "Damn your hide!"

The dog paused long enough to allow his pursuer to gain ground, then he was off again. Despite herself, Juliana had to laugh, as she gathered up her skirts and hurried to catch up with them.

Only a light rain was falling now, but the grass was still slippery and, as Ruark rounded the corner of the house, he lost his footing and fell. Juliana rushed to his side, dropping to her knees.

"Are you all right?" she panted. "Did you hurt yourself?"

"No, I'm all right. But if I ever get my hands on that dog, I won't be responsible for my actions."

At that moment Will-John Clifton came around the corner, clad in oil cloth and whistling merrily. He stopped short and, as he surveyed them, his eyes began to twinkle. "Anything wrong?" he asked in a droll tone.

"No," Ruark said between clenched teeth. "We're just playing with the dog. The blasted cur stole something from us."

"This couldn't be what you were looking for, could it?" Will-John asked, bringing forth the bedraggled chemise from the pocket of his rain cape. "I saw the little feller with it and thought I ought to make a rescue."

Juliana wondered afterwards how Will-John could have kept such a straight face. They must have made a ludicrous pair, she in her wrinkled dress, hair snarled and full of hay, Ruark only half-dressed and fuming, as he sprawled on the lawn in the rain. Peeking around the hem of the old man's cape she could see the puppy, tongue lolling, eyes regarding them with interest.

Since she could think of no plausible explanation, Juliana merely muttered, "Thank you," and took the garment from him. Then, chin in the air, she marched into the house, leaving the two men and the dog staring after her.

Fourteen

Supper was an uncomfortable affair that night. Essie and Will-John joined them, as they usually did, and Juliana was certain each look that passed between the couple was significant. Her face flamed every time she thought of Will-John rescuing her chemise from the dog and then encountering them on the lawn. The man would have to be a simpleton not to realize what had gone on. With an inward groan, she rested her head on one hand. Curse Ruark and his impetuous ideas!

Glancing at her husband, she saw that he was watching her with concern and something inside her seemed to melt. No, it hadn't been entirely his fault, she knew. She could have insisted they retire to the privacy of their room; she should never have let her newly stirred emotions rule her natural practicality. She'd have to learn to control her own impulsiveness if she wanted to avoid such compromising situations.

And yet, she realized, despite her embarrassment, it was all she could do at this moment to keep from crossing to the other side of the table to lay a caressing hand against her husband's lean cheek. She knew her eyes must reveal her innermost thoughts as they roved slowly over his face as if stroking each strong feature. She knew exactly how his firm, tanned skin would feel beneath her touch, how his crisp black hair would spring away as she laced her fingers through it. She sought his gaze again, wondering if he had any idea at all in which direction her thoughts lay.

"Ye're too quiet this evening, Miss Juli," Essie said. "I shouldn't wonder if ye're coming down with a fever, running about in the rain, half-dressed."

Juliana gave a guilty start. Before she could stop herself, she threw a quick look at Will-John.

"I'm fine," she protested. "Just a bit tired."

"Hmmph."

Ignoring Essie's rude snort, Ruark said, "Why don't we retire early tonight, sweetheart? It'd probably be best for you to get some extra rest."

Juliana nodded agreement, unable to meet anyone else's eyes. Her lowered gaze fell upon the Brittany puppy, asleep on the floor beside her chair.

"Yes, and when ye go up, take that bothersome cur with ye," Essie grumbled. "All evening long he's been underfoot in the kitchen, begging. And when I resist his begging, he simply steals what he wants."

Will-John laughed. "Seems to me the poor fellow only craves attention from folks who're too busy with other things to pay him any heed."

Ruark and Juliana exchanged an agonized look, but fortunately, Essie failed to find any relevance in her husband's comment. She gathered a stack of plates and whisked from the room, her skirts rustling starchly.

Juliana turned to Will-John. "Did you mention what happened to Essie?" she forced herself to ask.

He chuckled heartily. "No, lass. I saw no need. But even if I had, the old girl would've had nothing to say about it. She wouldn't dare."

"What do you mean, she wouldn't dare?" Juliana smiled uncertainly as she noticed his eyes crinkling with amusement.

"Don't you think Essie ever misplaced a chemise?"

"Essie?" Juliana gasped the name. "You can't mean it!"

"I won't give you the particulars, but had she known about your little mishap, she'd not have been able to speak a word of reproach." He winked. "Now, don't fret about it anymore. I shouldn't have teased you so."

She watched in wordless amazement as Will-John shuffled from the room, tamping tobacco into the battered pipe he smoked.

Ruark linked his arm in hers as they climbed the stairs together, followed by the puppy.

"I thought dinner would never end," Juliana breathed, as he shut the door to their chamber behind them. "I was so mortified, knowing what Will-John must have been thinking."

"You didn't look mortified to me, love." Ruark kissed her lightly. "When I met your eyes across the table a short while ago, I could've sworn something else was on your mind."

"Well," she said saucily, "you'll never know for certain, will you?"

"You're refusing to tell me what was going on behind those devilish eyes?" His mobile lips formed a lopsided smile.

"I do."

His hands slid around her waist. "Then I'll have to force the information from you." He began tickling her, and she twisted away with a laughing objection, darting across the room. Relentlessly, he pursued her and with a flying leap, caught her around the middle and flung her to the bed, throwing himself down beside her. Though she kicked and struggled, he resumed the tickling, murmuring, "Are you prepared to give in, sweetheart? Tell me what you were thinking."

"Never," she panted, trying to elude his hands.

At that moment, the puppy, who had been watching their antics, bared his sharp little teeth and joined the melee. He landed on the bed, wriggling in between the two of them. Ruark laughed at the sound of his high-pitched growl, but the laughter quickly turned to a yowl of pain as the dog nipped him on the arm and again on one leg.

"Damn, he's not playing," he cried, attempting to fend off the angered animal.

"Of course not. He's protecting his mistress." Juliana patted the dog, suppressing a smile.

"His mistress doesn't need protection from her own husband. Put him off the bed, 'Liana."

"Do you promise to behave yourself?"

"Aye, I promise."

Juliana set the puppy on the floor beside the bed. "Stay there, Boy," she gently admonished.

The dog tilted its head to one side, watching them intently.

"I'm afraid he's in need of some serious training," Ruark said. "We'll have to teach him discipline."

"You're a fine one to talk of discipline."

He leaned over her, a menacing look on his face. "And what is that supposed to mean?"

"How do you propose to teach him something you know nothing of yourself?"

"Wench, you're trying my patience," he muttered, wrapping his arms about her. Just as she thought he was going to kiss her, he started tickling her again and her small, surprised scream rang out. She twisted beneath him.

"Ruark, stop it."

"Not until you apologize for that remark. *Ouch!*"

The puppy hurled himself onto Ruark's back, teeth snapping. There was an ominous rending sound as the sleeve of his shirt was caught and ripped away from the shoulder seam.

"You win! Call him off. I promise to leave you alone."

Juliana scooped up the puppy, soothing it in a quiet voice. "Shhh, Boy, it's all right."

Ruark got off the bed, keeping a wary eye on the dog in her arms. "Bringing him here may have been the biggest mistake of my life," he mumbled, examining the torn sleeve. "How was I to know he'd turn into a damned watch dog?"

Juliana slid off the bed. "As long as you behave yourself, I'm sure you won't have any trouble with him. Now, I'm going to put on my nightgown and go to bed."

She disappeared into the bathing chamber, taking the animal with her. When she returned, Ruark was already in bed, arms propped behind his head. A look of relief passed over his features as he saw the dog settle himself on the hearth rug.

When Juliana approached the bed, he held the bedcovers back for her. As she slipped beneath them, he turned to put his arm around her.

"It has been quite a day, hasn't it?"

"Indeed it has." She snuggled deeper into his embrace and lifted her lips for his kiss. A warning growl caused them to spring apart.

Ruark groaned. "By God, I won't have this," he declared. "Can't we shut him in the bathing chamber? It's unnerving to hear him growl every time I touch you."

Juliana was entertained by his pained expression. "He may not like it in there, but I suppose we can try."

No sooner had she put the dog into the adjoining room than he began to bark and scratch at the door.

"Do you think he'll wake Essie and Will-John?" she asked anxiously.

The sharp barks turned into resounding howls which echoed through the room and bounced from the rafters. Juliana clapped her hands over her ears. "Oh, heavens!"

"That miserable, wretched little beast," swore Ruark. "Why didn't I leave him in Ireland?"

A second series of howls reverberated through the chamber.

"I've got to quiet him," Juliana stated firmly.

She opened the door and out shot the puppy, to jump against her legs, his tail wagging furiously. She patted him on the head. "Lay down and go to sleep, puppy. Everything is all right now."

She came back to the bed, but just as she laid her head on the pillow, the dog scrambled up after her, flopping at her feet.

Ruark tested him by putting a hand on Juliana's arm. The pup growled fiercely and edged closer, putting his body between the two of them. Lying against Juliana's side, he seemed to study Ruark with defiant golden brown eyes.

"Maybe he'll go off to sleep," Juliana suggested. "Let's be still for a while and see what happens."

There was a look of grim longing on Ruark's face as he lay facing her. "I should turn him out and be done with it."

"If we put him in the hall, he'll keep everyone awake."

"I was thinking of the stables."

"We can't do that. He wouldn't understand why he's being punished."

Ruark grimaced. "I don't understand why I'm being punished either," he groused.

She laughed softly. "Look, he's already asleep."

As silently as she could, she shifted toward her husband, but the moment his hand moved to her shoulder, the dog stirred and growled, showing his pointed teeth.

Ruark dropped back onto his pillow. "I give up. I'm going to go to sleep."

Testily, he turned his back and pulled the covers up around his neck. His final words were muffled, but vehement. "I'm glad I didn't bring you an Irish wolfhound."

Throughout the night, the dog kept his vigilant watch. Every time Ruark changed positions or encroached on Juliana's side of the bed, the animal growled loudly, the hair on his back bristling. Ruark muttered in his sleep; Juliana smiled in hers.

That state of affairs lasted two nights. On the third morning, Ruark strode into the kitchen and requested Essie pack a picnic lunch. With an intent look at Juliana, he announced, " 'Liana and I are going someplace where we can be alone. Without the company of that mongrel."

Essie looked up from the bread dough she was kneading. "I don't know where that will be. The rascal goes almost everywhere."

"Don't worry, I've thought it out carefully. Fix us a lunch and 'Liana, you be ready to leave in an hour."

When he had gone, Essie chuckled. "My, my, Miss Juli. Yer bridegroom seems disgruntled."

Juliana smiled faintly. "He does, doesn't he? But as soon as we set this bread to raise, I'd better go change my gown. I wouldn't want to keep him waiting."

An hour later, Ruark came for her. At the sight of her in a summery white dress sprigged with yellow flowers, he broke into a broad smile, the first anyone had seen in awhile.

"You look pretty, sweetheart. It'll be a pleasure to have you to myself for a change."

Collecting the wicker hamper Essie had packed, they

went out the back door and down to the river. The wooden row boat the Lowell children had played in every summer was tied at the bank.

Ruark set the lunch basket among the cushions with which he had covered the bottom of the boat. Then, turning to Juliana, he lifted her in his arms and carefully stepped into the boat, settling her in the bow, more cushions at her back.

Deftly, he untied the tether rope that held the craft and used an oar to push them away from the bank. As he fitted the oars into the oarlocks and took his seat, a streak of white along the shore caught his eye.

The Brittany darted out of the garden where he had been chasing butterflies and ran along the bank, barking querulously. It was quite evident he thought they should return for him, and, at his forlorn look, Juliana started to suggest perhaps they should allow him to accompany them. However, a quick survey of Ruark's determined jaw made her bite back the words.

As they moved upriver, away from the house, the dog ran after them, until he came to the end of the lawn. He put one paw into the water, gingerly, but drew it back. Since swimming didn't appeal to him, all he could do was watch and bark as they glided swiftly out of sight.

It was a warm, sunny day filled with all the scents of summer: the fragrance of flowering shrubs massed along the riverbanks, the resiny smell of the tall pines, the fresh grassy perfume of the high meadows baking dry in the heat. Rowing with smooth, powerful motions, Ruark guided the boat into the deep shade along the far bank which was overhung with trees trailing in the clear water.

"We're going to the pool where the river meets the channel," he informed her. "It's cool and quiet there, and out of sight of the house."

Juliana smiled and nodded, overcome with peaceful lethargy. She let one hand drift through the water, sometimes catching at the lily pads as they brushed by. Their cupped white blossoms were just beginning to unfold to reveal golden centers.

When they came to the pool, Ruark edged the boat inland, tying it up at a young willow tree. He dropped down beside her on the cushions.

"Do you know how wonderful it feels to be able to touch you again and not have that dog attack me?" He laid one warm hand at the side of her neck and leaned forward to cover her mouth with his. As his kiss grew more insistent, Juliana pulled away. She knew where his attentions were leading, but it was broad daylight and she was still embarrassed by the outcome of their interlude in the stable.

"Don't you think we'd better see what Essie has sent us for lunch?" she hedged softly.

"Mmm, I do find myself with a considerable appetite," he admitted, allowing his lips to trail kisses from her hairline to the point of her jaw.

Juliana reached for the hamper, opening it to reveal cold ham, watercress sandwiches, currant turnovers, and a bottle of cool wine.

"Doesn't this look delicious?" she asked, unfolding two linen napkins.

Ruark grinned at her. "All right, sweetheart, we'll have lunch. Perhaps later I can show you my real reason for bringing you here. This time there'll be no pampered cur to come between us."

Ruark opened the wine, filling one stemmed glass. He held it for Juliana to take a sip, then put his lips where hers had been and took a drink himself.

As she fed him a sandwich, she observed, "The puppy will outgrow all this nonsense, I believe."

"Let's hope he does," Ruark replied, taking the piece of ham she offered. "I don't especially enjoy being thwarted."

She smiled into his eyes. "So I've noticed."

"Don't look at me that way if you want to finish your lunch," he warned.

"Sorry." With a shy laugh, she dropped her gaze and concentrated on the food before her.

Presently, she said, "That day you held up the stagecoach, I never dreamed we'd ever see each other again. And I certainly never thought we'd be together like this."

"You should have asked me. I knew the moment you alighted from the coach. When my man offered to help you down and you were so defiant, you immediately took my attention. And when your hood slipped away so I could really see you, I was lost."

She gave a small, self-conscious shrug as she unwrapped the currant-filled pastries and handed one to Ruark. "I think you're exaggerating. There was nothing very attractive about me that day."

"Don't forget, I was already intrigued by the description the Cliftons had given me. To meet the real Saint Juliana in person was very thrilling." Laughter danced in his eyes. "And I think I'm a fair judge of feminine beauty."

"As I recall, Chavo certainly didn't agree with you. I couldn't understand his words, but his tone made it very evident."

Ruark finished the turnover and drained his wineglass, putting it back into the hamper. "Some men are fools when it comes to women. They see what's before them and nothing else. With me, it was different from the start."

"In what way?"

"I saw beyond the loveliness of your face to the beauty of your mind and soul. While Chavo thought you looked like a schoolteacher, I didn't at all. And my instincts have been proven correct. Do you want to know how I see you?"

Juliana crumbled the rest of her turnover and tossed the pieces to some ducks swimming by on the river. "Yes."

Ruark settled back on the cushions beside her. "You remind me of one of the great courtesans of the past."

"A courtesan?" She was shocked by his choice of words. "Is that what you think of me?"

"Don't be upset. I meant it as a compliment."

"I fail to see how it could be complimentary," she said stiffly.

He grinned and reached out a hand to turn her face toward him. "I meant that, not only are you beautiful, but you have an intelligence and spirit which make you very special. Look at the women who've been the mistresses of kings through the ages. Most of them were pretty enough, but the ones whose names are remembered today were those with something besides beauty. Do you see what I mean?"

"I think so."

"Good looks might attract in the beginning, but it takes more than that. You, for instance. Your mind is refreshingly original and creative, and your spirit is dauntless. You'd be nearly the perfect mistress." He brushed her lips with his.

"Why did you marry me then?" she asked tartly.

"You lack the proper cold-hearted promiscuity necessary. That lack is what makes you the perfect wife."

"I'm afraid perfect is hardly the word," she said in a low voice. "There's so much I don't know."

"But that *is* perfect. It gives me the opportunity to teach you."

"I only hope you do better at training a wife than you

do at training dogs," she said with a sudden giggle, burying her face in his shoulder.

She could feel the laughter rumble in his chest. "Let's hope my wife is a more willing student."

She raised her eyes to his, and he was stirred by their smoky look.

"Sweetheart, I've missed you these last two nights," he said huskily. His mouth coupled with hers in a kiss that burned and left them both breathless.

Juliana felt shaken by the depth of her own passion. How could it be she had learned desire so quickly? Before meeting Ruark, she'd never given such things much thought, and now, just the touch of his hand or a meaningful look from his daring eyes and she was eager to be in his embrace again. It was, she knew, a far cry from her old independence. But with Ruark's sensual mouth coaxing hers into willing submission, she didn't mind in the least.

Ruark slipped the gown she wore from her shoulders and, pulling her onto his chest, began unfastening the row of hooks down the back. She kissed the side of his neck, breathing in the exciting masculine scent of him. Mischievously, she traced the outer rim of his ear with her tongue, and felt his start of surprise.

" 'Liana," he murmured, capturing her mouth again. "Help me with these petticoats, will you? I'm of a mind to be impatient, and I don't think you'd appreciate the damage to your clothing."

She laughed softly and, with his assistance, stood. Poised above him, she struggled out of her dress, letting it fall to the floor of the boat. She unfastened and stepped out of the several petticoats she wore.

Ruark watched her unlace the chemise with admiring eyes. He put out a hand to caress her bare calf, letting his fingers slide up her cotton-clad leg to her waist, coming to rest at the fastening to her pantalettes. Though she smiled, her first reaction was to move away from him, and when she did, she lost her balance and swayed dangerously.

" 'Liana," he shouted, grabbing for her.

With a shriek, she toppled backwards and into the river. Ruark rapidly tossed his boots aside, but before he could dive over the side of the boat, she surfaced, splashing and spluttering.

"Are you all right?" he asked.

"Yes. At least the water's fairly warm."

"Here, let me help you out."

Juliana made an impish face. "Since I'm already wet, I may as well enjoy a swim while I'm at it." She began swimming away from him with strong, sure strokes. "Come on in."

He watched her, a bemused expression on his face. With sudden, purposeful action, he stripped off his shirt and breeches and dived into the river. He towed the boat to the bank, securing it to a slender willow. Then, plucking one of the yellow irises growing along the shore, he placed the stem between his teeth and swam lazily after her.

For a time he was content to merely keep pace with her, but after a few moments he tired of the chase. He closed the stretch of water between them and encircled her waist with one muscular arm, pulling her back against his body.

Taking the iris from his mouth, he brushed it against her lips. She reached up a hand to take it from him.

"Did you know, my little scholar," he whispered, "that the fleur-de-lis symbolizes flame? It means 'I burn for you,' and at this moment I'm well and truly ablaze."

He brought his mouth down on hers. The iris dropped

from her grasp and fell onto the water, to be caught and whirled dreamily away by the current.

Juliana entangled her legs with his and he moved closer, taking her mouth in a fiercely demanding kiss. He kissed the hollow of her throat, letting his lips slide slowly downward to breasts that seemed to beg for his immediate attention. Juliana sighed in stunned pleasure as his mouth pillaged them through the wet cotton of her chemise. Her fingers clutched at his shoulders as she strained closer to him.

When Ruark unfastened the waistband of her pantalettes, she obligingly kicked them away. His hands cupped her buttocks, bringing her to him and there could be no mistaking his intention. Caught up in the fever of the moment, she embraced him with her legs, even knowing how her boldness might shame her later.

They drifted in the lily-filled water for a few moments, but then, driven by their mutual need, Ruark found the pebbled floor of the river with his feet and braced himself to support her weight. He eased into her body, muffling her cry of ecstasy with a long, languorous kiss.

Juliana clung to her husband, lost in the exquisite sensations that rushed through her. She abandoned herself to his demanding mouth, his seeking hands, his fierce masculine strength. She found herself unable to do more than writhe against him, kissing his face mindlessly and murmuring vague promises in his ear. She'd devise some means of making it up to him later, she vowed; she'd manage some way to repay him for the wondrously passionate feelings he'd stoked to life within her.

For now, it was all she could do to survive the sharp thrill of elation that tore through her, that hurled her higher and higher. She felt as though the blue water surrounding them had turned to sky and she was soaring, higher, faster, and with more freedom than she'd ever imagined. Ruark's cry of release was harsh in her ear, and she knew he'd joined her in the wild, exhilarating journey.

They floated aimlessly for a time, but the fall of the sun in the late afternoon sky finally drove them back to the boat to get warm and dry. As they donned their clothes, Juliana discovered her pantalettes were missing. She found it difficult to meet her husband's eyes while announcing the fact because, now that reality had reasserted itself, she felt shy and somewhat shamed by the impatient haste she had shown. Sensing her uneasiness, Ruark was gracious in his effort to locate the missing item. However, a diligent search of the riverbank turned up no sign of the undergarment and they were forced to admit defeat.

Admonishing her not to worry, Ruark sat back among the cushions and pulled Juliana to him.

"While that wasn't exactly the way I had planned for things to go, 'Liana, it was wonderful."

She snuggled closer to the heat of his body. "I never knew I could act like that," she confided in a whisper.

"You were magnificent." He reached out to untie the cord tethering the boat to the willow. Immediately the current caught it and sent it moving downstream.

Ruark settled more deeply into the cushions, his arms folding protectively about Juliana. He rested his head on the top of her damp, tangled hair and sighed contentedly.

"The heart line in your palm doesn't lie, love. You're filled with splendid passion. I'm just glad I'm the one you've chosen to share it with."

The boat drifted slowly, lulling them into a dreamless sleep. They lay clasped in each other's arms, not even waking when the rowboat reached the far end of the lake and rode on the water, gently bobbing, its bow nudging the grassy bank.

An hour later, Ruark rowed them back to the house.

Will-John was sitting outside the kitchen door and came forward to tie up their boat. He then stood observing them with an amused grin.

"What's on your mind?" Ruark asked suspiciously.

"I've been fishing," the older man stated, patting the woven-reed creel hung over his shoulder. "Thought you might like to see my catch."

"Will-John, have you finally caught that huge speckled trout you've been after for years?" exclaimed Juliana. "Are we having it for dinner tonight?"

He chuckled and opened the creel. "Essie'd have to cook up her best sauce to make this fish palatable." He lifted a strip of sodden cloth, his black eyes nearly obscured by the grin that covered his face. "I snagged this in the main channel of the river."

Juliana felt the color drain from her cheeks as she recognized her missing pantalettes. She thought that Ruark, standing behind her, had begun to laugh, but the blood pounded in her ears with such fury that she couldn't be certain. This following so closely on the heels of her humiliation in the stable was simply too much.

She stepped from the boat and snatched the pantalettes from Will-John's hand. "Thank you," she said through clenched teeth. "I must have thrown them out with the wash water when I did the laundry."

Then, with as much dignity as she could muster, she marched across the grass to the back door. Once through it, she ran headlong up the stairs and into her bedchamber.

Slamming the door shut behind her, she vowed never to set foot outside the room again!

The warm sunshiny days passed, filled with a relaxed contentment Juliana had never before experienced. Sometimes, passing a mirror she had to stop and marvel at her own reflection. She looked so different to herself. There was no strained expression on her face, no tenseness in the way she held her body. She seemed to be smiling all the time, and her eyes sparkled with a new awareness of the joy to be found in sharing her life with Ruark.

One afternoon she took her paints into the garden to do a picture of the brilliant blue delphiniums that lined the pathways. She had neglected her painting lately, nearly forgetting how enjoyable it was to sit amid the various delights of the garden, challenged by the difficulty of relegating the intricate details of a flower to paper.

With the sun striking her back and the air filled with the lazy hum of bees from the herb garden, she completed two studies of the delphiniums.

Satisfied at last by her second portrait of the stately bell-shaped flowers, she set the paintings on the easel to dry and was gathering up her brushes and paint pots when there was a sudden flurry of short, yipping barks. She looked up to see the puppy romping merrily through a bed of daisies, followed more discreetly by Ruark.

"We came to see if you're finished with your painting. Essie says tea will be ready in thirty minutes and I thought we could teach the dog some obedience while we wait. I'm going to try to get him to retrieve this leather ball."

As she got to her feet, he came up behind her and wrapped his arms around her. Looking over her shoulder at the paintings, he said, "You're wonderfully talented, 'Liana. I'm proud of you." He placed a kiss on her neck.

She leaned back against him, murmuring, "Thank you, even though I suspect your compliments are meant to overcome my reluctance to help you train Jakel." Just recently they had given the Brittany the name Jakel, which meant *dog* in Romany.

"He's behaving better all the time," Ruark pointed out, watching the pup select one of Juliana's paintbrushes to chew on. With a grin, he bent down to remove it from Jakel's teeth and hand it to his wife. "He does permit me to sleep in my own bed now, and only growls a little when I make amorous advances to you."

He removed the spectacles she wore and folded them carefully, tucking them into her painting case. "Surely you'll spare us a few moments? You can't want to impede his progress."

"Oh, all right, I'll help."

In the end, it wasn't simple to teach the dog to fetch the ball. Ruark gave it a toss, but Jakel only sat and looked at it, his head tilted sideways. Finally, Ruark discovered the one way to get the animal to go after the ball was if he held it aloft and ran with it. Juliana watched their ridiculous antics, laughing until her sides hurt. When Ruark collided with the sundial and sprawled among the day lilies, she clamped one hand over her mouth to stifle her merriment and ran to his side. As she dropped to one knee, he caught her around the waist and rolled her onto her back in the grass.

"Aha," he cried, "now you'll pay for laughing at me. I'm going to rub your nose in this dirt."

She protested and squirmed, her hands pushing against his chest while Jakel jumped at them, barking in glee. Suddenly, catching sight of the new look of seriousness in

Ruark's caressing eyes, Juliana ceased to struggle and put her arms around his neck. His mouth softened against hers.

"This is a pretty scene, I must say."

They sprang apart to see Mariette standing nearby. Chavo was leading her horse away across the causeway bridge.

"I called out," she said. "Didn't you hear me?"

Ruark got to his feet, pulling Juliana up after him. "Sorry, we were busy . . . ah, training the dog," he said, grinning at the expression on Mariette's face.

To his amazement, his wife smiled at her sister, seemingly unconcerned by her mussed hair or wrinkled skirts. "What brings you to Quarrystones, Mariette?"

"I thought I'd come over to take tea with you," she replied, fastening a petulant gaze on Juliana. Ruark knew that she, too, saw the changes. "It does get boring at Moorlands."

"Well, let's go inside. I expect Essie is about to call us for tea anyway." Juliana glanced up at the tall man beside her. "We'll resume Jakel's lessons some other time."

He put an arm around her waist as they walked toward the house, aware that Mariette's narrowed eyes missed no detail of their intimacy.

Essie had laid tea in the living room before the open windows. She gave Mariette a perfunctory greeting, not bothering to disguise her disapproval of the younger woman's unannounced arrival.

Mariette sank onto the couch, arranging the skirts of her riding habit around her. She stripped off the gloves she wore and leaned forward to reach for the teapot. "I'll pour, shall I?"

"No need to bother yourself," Juliana said smoothly, taking up the teapot and filling the three cups before her.

"I was only trying to be helpful."

"I'm sure you were, but there's no need for you to exert yourself. After all, you're a guest in our home."

Mariette took the cup and saucer Ruark held out to her. "Speaking of guests," she said, "it seems we're about to have some at Moorlands. Actually, they're Spencer's friends, but it should be a change to have someone to entertain."

"It'll be nice for you to meet some of your husband's acquaintances," Ruark said casually. "Where are they coming from?"

"London." Mariette took a tea cake from the tray. "Spencer used to play cards with them at the various clubs in the city, and they claim to have missed his company. He says it's more likely they want to get a better look at me. I don't know whether to be flattered or annoyed."

"Annoyed?" Juliana murmured, over the rim of her cup.

"Yes. I'll be the only woman in the house except for the servants. Think how tedious it will be for me while they're busy with their silly card-playing. I suppose I'll find myself seeing to their comfort and having an altogether tiresome time."

"Perhaps it won't be as bad as you think," suggested Juliana.

Mariette ignored the words and turned her aqua gaze on Ruark. "By the way, dear brother, Spencer asked me to issue you a special invitation to the card party he's giving this Saturday night. He thought you might find it amusing to meet some of his friends."

"How considerate of him," Ruark said. "Tell him I'll be happy to attend." He reached out to capture Juliana's free hand. "That is, if my wife can spare me."

Juliana blushed faintly. "By all means, go to the card party. It has been quite some time since you've had the pleasure of an evening in the company of others."

He turned her hand and pressed his lips to her palm, his

eyes shining roguishly. "While that's true, my evenings with you leave no room for complaint."

Mariette set her teacup down with such force that it rattled noisily in the saucer. "I really must go," she said, picking up her gloves and rising to her feet.

"But you've just arrived," Juliana protested.

"I shouldn't tarry or Spencer will miss me. I only came to extend the invitation."

They stood in the doorway and watched her hurry back across the causeway to the stables. When she had ridden away, Ruark turned to Juliana and enfolded her in his arms again.

"Now, where were we?" he asked.

Fifteen

The good weather held and soon the men were laboring in the hayfields. On one of the days Ruark had gone to help, Juliana received a message from Edward Hamilton and slipped away to meet him in the woods north of Quarrystones.

When she first saw the old man, she was stricken by the look of unhappiness about him. Somehow he seemed more stooped, his face more lined.

"Lord, but it's good to see you," he said, taking her arm. "I'm growing weary of long, gloomy faces and of being watched as though I were a child. I keep thinking Spencer will tire of the country and go back to London, but he stays on."

"Perhaps he and Mariette will leave after their guests have come and gone," Juliana suggested.

"I hope so. I can hardly bear the restrictions when my grandson is at Moorlands. You can't imagine how I've missed my meetings with you. Or how much I've longed to sit down with paints and paper."

"I'm sorry things are terrible for you." She gazed at the man who looked so much like her husband. "But at least we have this afternoon to talk and paint, and wish Spencer and Mariette gone."

The elderly man gave a shudder of distaste. "Mariette!

I refuse to believe the two of you are blood related. I don't think I've ever seen a more selfish, grasping woman."

"Mariette was spoiled from the beginning," Juliana explained. "Her health was quite fragile when she was a baby, so I'm afraid she was simply indulged too much. With special care and treatment, she got stronger, but by then, she was accustomed to having her own way."

"Her health improved, but her disposition didn't, eh?" A faint smile eased his frown. "I can't think it was very pleasant for you growing up in her shadow."

"I always thought Mother and Father loved her more than they did my brother or me, and that used to cause me unhappiness. But as I got older, I realized there are different ways of loving people, and different ways to demonstrate that love. Mariette needs more attention than either Jeremy or I do, and my parents seem to understand that."

"Perhaps you're right. She'll never be as strong as you. Never as self-reliant or capable."

"But she's a married woman now and has Spencer to look after her."

The elderly man snorted. "God help us all. My grandson needs someone to take care of him. Of the two of them, it seems to me she's the stronger."

"Then maybe Mariette's new responsibilities will mature her."

"We can only hope, but I fear she won't outgrow her greediness. It's deeply ingrained."

"Yes, it is."

"Another thing, my dear. I want to caution you to be extremely cautious around her. Somehow I don't believe she harbors any feelings of sisterly love."

Juliana smiled at his concern. "Mariette will soon be back in the city. Then she'll pose no threat to anyone."

They walked for a while, talking, until Edward expressed a desire to begin painting. "I don't have much time before they'll begin to wonder where I've gone. And I've a notion that I want to try painting you again."

"As you wish," she said. "Have you thought of taking paints back to Moorlands with you? Then you could work any time you please."

He shook his head. "I've already broached the subject of purchasing a few paints, and Spencer found the idea quaintly amusing. Thinks I'm too old to be taking up a new and expensive hobby. So, if I should suddenly acquire paints, he'd create a scene, thinking I'd spent his money foolishly."

"But it's your money," Juliana cried angrily. "How can he be so cruel?"

"I suppose, at some point, I've wounded Spencer unknowingly, and this is the form his revenge takes. Perhaps it's nothing more than the fact his father was the second son, and therefore, in the eyes of society, a trifle inferior. Who knows?"

"I'm certain I don't. Spencer never seemed that hardhearted, so his motive must be a powerful one."

"I'm sure it is. And I'm equally positive that he'd frown on our friendship, if he knew of it. I've been so afraid he'd get suspicious of our meetings that I haven't even taken the few paintings I've done home. I hide them in that old woodcutter's hut near the river. Do you know of it?"

"We played there when we were children. It must be nearly overgrown by now, but I think I could still find it."

"It's the one place Spencer would never go, and so far, his hired men know nothing of it."

Juliana touched his arm. "Edward, I wish you'd come home with me and allow my husband to help you."

She held her breath, hoping he'd agree, yet worried about

what might happen if he did. She could imagine what kind of scene there'd be if she introduced Ruark to the grandfather he'd hated all his life. And yet, she felt it was wrong to let the situation continue as it was.

Edward Hamilton shook his shaggy head. "Not yet, Juliana. There's still hope Randolph will return. I know the chances of that happening are dwindling, but I can't give up now. Not yet."

That was also the day the Gypsies came to Quarrystones. When Ruark returned from the fields, he told her of their presence.

"The old grandfather of the tribe approached me to ask if they could camp on that ground below the farm village. I granted permission for them to stay a few days, but told him the final decision would rest with you."

They were in their bedchamber, talking while Ruark got ready to go to Spencer's card party. She was laying out his clothes while he shaved and prepared to bathe.

"Why are they here?" she asked.

"They usually travel about during the warmer months, looking for work on the farms. Then, after harvest, they find a suitable place and settle in for the winter. These Gypsies worked in the hop fields and are now cutting hay. Quarrystones seems to be a fairly central location for them."

"I certainly don't mind if they stay," she said. "We've never had Gypsies on the estate before."

"No, I don't imagine so. Most Englishmen view them as beggars and thieves. Or as evil-doers who cast spells to cause disease and bad luck."

She gave him a wry smile. "If I hadn't met you, I might have felt that way about them. All I knew was what I'd been told, and until you came into my life, there was no need to question that."

"An open mind is the surest sign of intelligence, 'Liana. I wish everyone possessed such a quality."

"Yourself included?" she softly asked.

"What?"

"Your grandfather, Ruark. You may meet him when you go to Moorlands tonight. Don't you think you should tell him who you are?"

He held up a hand. "Please don't start that again, love. I have no reason to make myself known to him yet, and I don't have time to argue the point right now. Can we discuss it later?"

"If you'll agree to keep an open mind."

"I'll try." He began stripping off his dusty clothes as he moved toward the bathing chamber. "But I can't promise to come around to your way of thinking."

She followed him, picking up the discarded articles of clothing. "I think I can convince you, if you'll only listen to my arguments."

He stopped in the doorway, his naked back to her. "Damn. Wives aren't supposed to be so reasonable, did you know that?"

She laughed, though her mind wasn't really on his words. She let her admiring eyes take in the glorious nudity of the man before her. His skin had a healthy golden glow that was so uniform it clearly came from his heritage and not the sun. Her gaze traveled across his wide shoulders, down the sinewy back to the narrow waist and beyond, to the tightly muscled buttocks that gave way to long, lean legs. With an uncharacteristic boldness, she stepped close to him and let one daring hand stroke the smoothness of his lower back. Startled, he turned to face her, a wide grin bringing his dimple into evidence.

"Why didn't you get this idea fifteen minutes ago?" he asked.

Aware of his immediate arousal, she backed away, laughing. "I meant nothing by it. I was only thinking what a handsome man you are."

He put his hands on her shoulders. "You know, I really don't want to go to this card party anyway. Perhaps I should stay here with you."

She placed a light kiss on his mouth and moved out of his grasp. "No, I think you should go. I'll be waiting when you come home."

Hours later, Ruark sat at the card table remembering her words. It seemed the evening had dragged on forever. He found Spencer's friends foppish and self-centered, prone to stupid, prejudicial remarks and bad jokes. He couldn't even lose himself in the cards, for they had chosen to play whist, a game he particularly disliked, and his partner was a rash player who lost points on nearly every trick.

At ten o'clock Ruark pushed back his chair and announced, "I'm going to call it a night, gentlemen. I've lost enough for one evening."

"Oh, come now, Ruark," chided Spencer. "Surely a duke can't be so pressed for money he has to worry about the expense of one night at cards?"

Ruark forced a smile. "Perhaps not, but the hour grows late. As you know, I have a bride awaiting my return home. I don't want to disappoint her."

Spencer didn't smile back. "Then I suppose we'd best not detain you."

Mariette swept into the room carrying a large tray filled with sandwiches and cakes. "Perhaps I can tempt you," she said. "You can't leave without refreshment."

"No, I don't care for anything, Mariette, though I do appreciate the offer." He turned and spoke to the room at large. "Good evening, gentlemen. So nice to have met all of you."

There were a few replies, but the other men in the room were crowding around Mariette, vying for her attention as they helped themselves to the sandwiches. With an amused nod to Spencer, Ruark strode from the room, stopping in the hallway to get his cloak.

Just as he reached his stallion he heard his name called.

"Ruark, wait." Mariette was breathless and laughing when she reached his side. "I couldn't let you go without a proper farewell," she said.

"There was no need. You have guests to attend to."

"I left those mincing fools to fend for themselves." She turned her face up to his. "Truly, must you go? It's early yet."

"I don't want Juliana to worry," he replied.

"Why should she worry? You're a grown man, after all." She measured the breadth of his shoulders with her bold gaze.

"Yes, a grown man who chooses to go home to his wife."

Mariette whirled away, lips curling. "I never dreamed Juliana would be so shrewish," she muttered. "She must think her best chance to hold you is by denying you the company of others."

"I believe you've misjudged your sister, Mariette." Ruark swung up onto his horse. "And, just so you'll know, Juliana denies me nothing."

Mariette stepped close to Heiden. "You only say such shocking things because you delight in teasing me. Well, enjoy your little game. I'm a patient woman who's willing to wait. As a matter of fact, it's my opinion that anticipation often adds spice."

She laid her hand on his knee, moving it upwards along his thigh. He could see her eyes glittering in the moonlight, their invitation blatant.

"Mariette, does your husband condone this kind of behavior?"

"What do you mean?"

"I mean he's standing by the front window watching us. You might find it difficult to explain your hand on my leg, unless, of course, this is a common occurrence."

She snatched her hand away. "Don't be ridiculous. I don't see what objection Spencer could possibly have to my saying farewell to my brother."

"No, since you put it that way, he couldn't object. Now I must be on my way back to Quarrystones. Good night, *Sister*."

He rode off into the darkness leaving Mariette standing on the lawn, hands clenched at her sides.

Nearly an hour later, Ruark slipped into the shadows that shrouded Moorlands manor. Peering through a window, he could see that the card players were still very much involved in their game. His departure had left an uneven number at the whist table, so the odd man, a good-looking fellow named Farnsworth, had engaged Mariette in a game of piquet. They sat together at one end of a long oak table, shielded from the others by a vase of hothouse tuberoses.

As he watched, Ruark could see that Spencer was distracted by the couple. He glanced their way often, apparently unable to concentrate on his own game. His forehead was creased in a tight frown, his mouth grimly set.

Judging the time excellent for a dramatic entrance, Ruark

signaled to the two other men waiting by their horses. They burst through the front doors, their footsteps clattering on the marble floor. As they brandished the pistols they carried, several of the players gasped in shock and Mariette gave a frightened scream.

Spencer started forward in protest, but Ruark waved the flintlock he held and warned, "Stay back. Do as I say and no one will be injured. Cause me trouble and I won't hesitate to kill you all." He kept his voice guttural and heavily accented.

"Spence, is this some jest?" the man named Farnsworth asked. "Something you dreamed up to frighten the little city mice?"

"I wish it were," Spencer began.

"This is no jest, I assure you." Beyond the card table, Ruark could see his own reflection in a mirrored wall. He was dressed as the gypsy highwayman, with mask, brimmed hat, black cape, and boots. He'd taken the extra precaution of using the red bandanna to conceal the lower half of his face. Lamplight highlighted the gleam of gold in his ear and danced on the barrel of the gun he held.

"I want all your money and jewelry," he announced. "Put everything on the tables to be collected."

He turned and spoke to one of the men behind him in Romany. The fellow came forward and almost immediately, Spencer's guests began bringing forth rings, watches, and wallets. The gypsy scooped the money and jewelry into a canvas bag. There was an angry mutter or two, but no one made a move to stop him.

"Are you just going to stand there and let these thieves rob us of our valuables?" Mariette cried, casting a disdainful look at Spencer.

"And what do you suggest I do, dear wife?"

"Act like a man for once," she snapped. "I daresay I fear this outlaw less than you do."

"Then why don't *you* stop him?"

Mariette tossed her head. She came close to Ruark and said in a low voice, "Perhaps there *is* some way I might dissuade you from taking our belongings." She swayed toward him, raising her blue eyes to his and favoring him with a practiced smile.

"What do you propose?" Ruark asked, thankful for the bandanna hiding his face from her.

"I'll do anything you'd care to suggest," she half-whispered.

"I can't hear you, Etta," Spencer complained. "What are you saying to him?"

Ruark put out a hand, but instead of caressing her as she obviously expected, he broke the chain of the necklace she wore and tossed it toward his cohort. "Now give me that bracelet and your rings," he commanded.

"How dare you?" she hissed, eyes blazing in anger.

He laid the cold barrel of the pistol alongside her neck and she shrank from its touch. "Take care," she pleaded, her fury replaced by real fear. "That weapon is dangerous."

"Not as dangerous as what you were suggesting, my lady. Now, your jewelry, please."

Eyes burning with tearful fury, she complied, placing the requested items on his outstretched hand. "Take them and be damned."

He dumped the rings and bracelet into the bag his companion held out to him. "We want to thank you for your generosity," he said, bowing deeply. "You may be certain your contributions will be used in a worthwhile way. We bid you good night, gentlemen."

He and the other masked bandits began backing from the

room, weapons raised. As he passed the vase standing on the oak table, Ruark pulled a long-stemmed tuberose from it and tossed it toward Mariette. Startled, she caught the white flower and her eyes met those gleaming behind the mask.

"You'd best beware of what you offer to strange men, madam," he said. "The tuberose stands for dangerous pleasures."

With those words, he followed the others from the room and into the darkness of night.

Behind him, he could hear Mariette crying out in a shrill voice, "I'll have my revenge on you, Gypsy. I'll never rest until I do."

Juliana had been asleep for quite some time when she was awakened by a strange noise in the darkened bedchamber. She sat up, reaching for the flint and a candle.

When the resulting light invaded the shadowed corners of the room, she was surprised to see her husband just closing the secret door to the old tower.

"Ruark, you startled me."

He crossed the room and sat on the edge of the bed, taking her hands. "I'm sorry. I didn't mean to wake you."

"Why did you come from the tower?" she asked. "Has something happened?"

He looked serious for a moment, then smiled slightly. "I hadn't meant to involve you, 'Liana, but I suppose you'll hear about it soon anyway."

Concerned, she searched his face with anxious eyes. "Hear about what?"

"The Gypsy Highwayman made an unexpected appearance at Moorlands tonight."

"How is that possible?"

"It's possible because I left around ten o'clock, saying I was coming home to you."

"And, instead, returned to rob them."

He nodded. "Chavo and my other man, Pulika, were waiting in the woods. I changed clothes and then we paid our call on the card players. It was a very successful venture indeed."

"Ruark, how could you do such a thing?" she cried. "It was too dangerous. What if someone recognized you?"

"None of them got a good look at me. Don't worry, love, they'll never suspect me. And even if they do, you'll be my alibi. I can count on you for that, can't I?"

"Of course." Her words were prompt, although a frown flickered across her face.

"What is it? Regretting the bargain we made?"

"No, but I hadn't expected you to take up the role of the highwayman again so soon."

"I refrained from staging these little hold-ups as long as I could, but unfortunately, the farmers still need money."

"Isn't the situation here at Quarrystones much better?"

"Aye, but the tenants at Moorlands are in worse straits than ever. This is the only way I can help them right now."

She shook her head. "But it isn't! You can go to your grandfather and tell him the truth. He'll support you, I know."

"Don't ask it of me, 'Liana." He put his hands on her shoulders. "I've spent a lifetime hating that old man for what he did. I'm just not ready to trust him yet."

She rested her head against his chest. "I won't argue with you, but I'm worried. This is too dangerous, and I couldn't bear it if anything happened to you."

"Is that so?" he asked, leaning away to look into her face.

She smiled shakily. "Yes, it's so. I've gotten used to having you around. I can't imagine what life would be like without you."

"You'll never be without me, love. I swear it."

His lips warmed her cold ones, and she clung to him, weakened by her apprehension. She welcomed the heat of his hands as they unfastened her nightdress. When he joined her in the wide bed, she met his advances eagerly, hopeful that the pleasures of their love would erase her nagging fears for his safety.

Sixteen

The following morning Spencer made an early appearance as Ruark and Juliana were finishing breakfast. When Essie showed him into the dining room, it was obvious he was agitated.

"Good morning, Juliana, Ruark," he said briskly. "I don't suppose you've heard about the robbery at Moorlands last night?"

"A robbery?" Juliana echoed. "Good heavens!"

"Some insolent rogue and his men broke into my home and held us up. Using pistols, I might add. We were powerless to stop him."

Ruark looked concerned. "What time did this occur?"

"Oh, perhaps an hour after you left. Did you see anyone on your way back to Quarrystones?"

"No, I can't say that I did. Can you describe the men?"

Spencer shook his head. "They were in some sort of disguise. Gypsy clothes, masks. I couldn't tell you more than that, except their leader was a tall fellow, about your size."

Juliana swallowed with difficulty, but Ruark's demeanor never changed. "Hmm, not much to go on, is it?"

"Won't you sit down and take a cup of coffee, Spencer?" she quickly interceded.

"No, thanks. I'm on my way into Edensfield to report this to the constable. It's his duty to track these men down."

"It'll be difficult with no clues," Ruark observed. "I don't suppose anyone happened to see their horses?"

"No, I'm afraid not. But my hired men tell me this gypsy highwayman has been a problem in the area for quite a while. You yourself were robbed by him, weren't you?"

Ruark nodded. "A nasty scoundrel, to my way of thinking."

"Surely someone around here knows something about him. He's likely to be a local man. I doubt he's really a gypsy."

"Who knows? It could merely be a clever disguise," Ruark commented. "Though of course there are some gypsies in the vicinity. My own man, Chavo, is one, though, naturally, I can vouch for his integrity."

Spencer coughed lightly. "I've heard you have a gypsy encampment here on your land."

"Yes, that's so, but it seems improbable your outlaws would be among them."

"Would you object to my sending the constable there to ask questions? Perhaps a bribe in the right place can turn up some information. You know these gypsy beggars, they'll do anything for money."

Juliana saw her husband's jaw tighten, but his words showed no sign of his irritation. "Certainly, ask all the questions you want. If those men are hiding out on my land, I want to know it."

"Well, thanks for your cooperation." Spencer pulled out his watch and glanced at it. "I'd better be going before it gets any later. The scoundrels took Mariette's diamond engagement ring and she's furious. If I don't do something to get it back for her, I'll never hear the end of it." He started for the door, then hesitated. "You're lucky to have left early, Ruark. The rogues picked us clean, damn their eyes."

When he had gone, Ruark turned to Juliana and said, "Since Spencer will be occupied by his trip into town, this is the perfect time for me to show you the conditions at Moorlands. I think it will help you understand my resolve to continue as a highwayman."

Juliana could smell the village long before they arrived at it. They were riding through the countryside, enjoying the capricious breezes that stirred the elderberry shrubs lining the lanes, listening to the jaunty call of the cuckoo. Suddenly, there was an overpowering stench.

"Oh, my lord, what is that?" cried Juliana, clamping one hand over her nose.

"That, sweetheart, is the tenants' village at Moorlands. Not exactly a pleasant place to live."

As soon as they entered the village, which was actually only a stretch of rutted road between two rows of dismal cottages, it was possible to see where the horrible odors came from. On either side of the road were shallow ditches filled with sewage. As they rode along the street, their horses disturbed black clouds of flies which buzzed furiously before settling back upon anything in their path.

The cottages were bordered in the back by large pig pens, where grunting swine stood in deep mire.

"Why do they keep them so close to the cottages?" Juliana asked.

"They're not allowed to have animals of their own. Spencer thinks it takes too much valuable land that could be put to better use. These pigs belong to him, and in order to preserve space, his tenants give up backyards or gardens."

"How awful," she murmured, appalled at the smell and the look of the place.

The cottages themselves were shabby, most in need of new roofs, a few even missing outside doors. Nowhere was there any evidence of grass; the yards in front of the houses were nothing more than packed earth.

At the end of the street was the community well, an open hole surrounded by mud. A few dirty children played there, accompanied by the skinniest dog Juliana had ever seen. Thinking of Jakel and how plump he was becoming due to Essie's generosity, she felt ill. Looking at the children only increased the feeling. They were dressed in rags, their bare feet and legs encrusted with filth. Unwashed, tangled hair fell over pasty, thin-cheeked faces, and there wasn't a smile among them. Juliana felt such a tightening in her chest she could hardly breathe. How could Spencer have let this happen?

The worst part of it was, he probably wouldn't even understand what they were talking about should they corner him with accusations about the condition of his tenants. He most likely hadn't been down to the village for years. Thoughtlessly unconcerned for those under his care, he'd issue orders and expect them to be carried out by an overseer. An overseer with no more interest in the welfare of these people than Spencer. Even if he was concerned, he wouldn't risk a good-paying position by criticizing his employer's methods.

Ruark had filled his pockets with the peppermint candies Essie liked to make, and now he handed these around to the children, who seized them greedily. They stood in a silent circle, chewing and staring up at Ruark and Juliana. The bleak look in their eyes broke Juliana's heart and filled her with an unrelenting desire to do something to better their situation.

"Let's stop here, 'Liana," Ruark said, dismounting and

tying his horse to a wobbly fence. "This is where Jed Morecombe and his wife live. Jed is an unofficial spokesman for the tenants."

The Morecombe cottage was no better than the others in the miserable community, one of the worst hovels Juliana had ever seen. Even at their most derelict, the tenants' cottages at Quarrystones had never looked like this.

Jed Morecombe could not have been more than fifty years old, but he looked seventy. He was stooped, and walked with an odd, stumbling gait. His face was lined and leathery, with little more life in the eyes than in those of the children. His hand when he held it out to shake Juliana's was gnarled and knobby, the joints thick and swollen.

"The men and I made quite a good showing last night, Jed," Ruark declared. "Chavo and Pulika have taken the jewelry into Canterbury to sell, so by tomorrow or the next day, there should be some supplies for your village."

The man nodded. "Bless you, Ruark. We haven't even had our wages, such as they are, this week. Hamilton's overseer is withholding them until the men finish the haying. Seems he thinks it should have been done by now."

"Have you appealed to Mr. Hamilton?" Juliana inquired. "I can't believe he'd allow these things to happen, if he knew about them."

"Damned fine gentleman, is our Mr. Hamilton, beggin' your pardon, ma'am. I went up to the house to try and talk to him but that lady wife of his was in the yard and when she saw me, she took to screamin'. Thought I was a beggar or something, and that I was going to attack her."

"What happened then?"

"She carried on so that her husband and all his men came runnin'. I was given a hasty farewell and told never to show my face around the manor again." He shook his head angrily. "Can you imagine?"

Juliana and Ruark exchanged looks. "I'm sorry," she said softly. "But you can count on us to help. We'll keep bringing what money and supplies we can, and somehow, we're going to change this village into a better place to live."

Jed's wife hadn't spoken until now, and as she came forward, there was a shy smile on her face. "It used to be a decent place, your ladyship, with grass and flowers and fresh water. That was in the days when the old Duke's two sons were young. Times were better then."

"Why did it change?" Juliana asked.

"Oh, the boys grew up and Randolph went away. The master just lost interest after that. When Spencer's father took over the estate, he let first one overseer and then another handle everything for him. By the time Spencer was old enough to take over, the damage was done."

"And, of course, his greed and indifference haven't helped at all," Ruark stated.

"I'm afraid you're right," Juliana agreed. "Spencer is the worst kind of villain, the kind who doesn't even know the harm he does. And probably wouldn't care if he did."

"Nay, his time is occupied with trying to keep that wife of his content," Jed surmised. "Though, if rumor be true, she's not the sort to be happy about anything for long."

Juliana could tell that Ruark felt he should inform the Morecombes she and Mariette were related, but she gave a small shake of her head and he kept silent.

"Why do you stay here when conditions are so bad?" she asked the couple.

"Where else could we go?" Jed questioned in turn. "The only other place for us is the workhouse. God help us if we ever come to that."

"Yes," his wife joined in. "It's true we don't have much, but at least there's the beauty of the countryside around us for consolation. Our children may never own any property, but they can enjoy the meadows and streams. If we left here, we'd be forced to live in the city slums. We couldn't survive that."

"I see what you mean," Juliana said slowly. "It would be even worse than this, if that's possible."

Later, as they rode away from the village, Ruark asked, "You understand why I have to masquerade as the highwayman, don't you?"

"Yes, you really have no choice. But that doesn't keep me from being afraid. So many things could happen to you."

He stopped Heiden beside her horse and, encircling her waist with his arm, pulled her onto his lap. Holding her close against him, he murmured, "I promise to be as cautious as it's possible to be. I have too much to lose to take any reckless chances."

She wrapped her arms around him and laid her head upon his shoulder, trying to deny the icy terror she felt within. Ruark took the reins to the other horse and it followed obediently as they made their slow way back to Quarrystones.

The next afternoon Juliana and Essie took the carriage into Edensfield to do some shopping. Anxious to purchase gardening supplies, Will-John volunteered to be their driver, thus leaving Ruark free to do as he pleased.

Calling to Jakel, he went to the stables to help Chavo shoe two of the horses. As they worked, the day grew still and sultry, causing them to shed their shirts and wipe rivulets of sweat from their eyes.

As they finished with the second horse and Chavo was

leading it away, Ruark heard a rider approaching. He was surprised to see Mariette galloping along the lane toward him.

"Good afternoon," she called gaily.

He returned her greeting, then added, "I'm sorry, Juliana isn't here right now. She and Essie have gone into town to do some shopping."

"Why, I just came from town myself. I didn't see them on the road." She heaved a big sigh. "It's a pity I missed her, but perhaps you'd offer me a cold drink before I go on to Moorlands? The road is terribly dusty today."

"I can give you a glass of Will-John's wine if you'd care to walk to the house. I was about to go up myself. As you can see, I'm in need of a bath."

As she gathered her skirts to dismount, Ruark offered a helping hand. He set her on the ground, but with her first step, she stumbled, crying out in pain. "Oh, my ankle!"

Ruark steadied her. "Have you hurt yourself?" he asked, a sudden wariness coiling in his chest.

She tilted her heart-shaped face to look up at him, and he could see the tears welling in her clear blue eyes. There was no guile in her expression.

"I seem to have twisted something when I stepped down. The pain is very sharp." She sagged against him and he had no choice but to lift her into his arms.

"I'll take you into the house and we can evaluate the damage," he said grimly, starting down the path. "Chavo, see to Mrs. Hamilton's horse, will you?"

Mariette put her arms around Ruark's neck, making him uncomfortably aware of his bare chest. "I apologize for my griminess," he said in an attempt at lightness. "Chavo and I have been working with horses."

"I don't mind," she murmured. "It's a relief not to have to walk all this way by myself."

When they entered the parlor, Ruark set her down on the couch, but her arms clung a moment longer than necessary. She raised the hem of her riding skirt and held out one slim leg for his perusal. He kept his touch impersonal as he examined the ankle.

"I don't see any swelling, Mariette. It's probably nothing too serious."

"Well, perhaps it will soon feel better, if I rest here for a time."

"I'm positive it will," Ruark said. "Shall I fetch you that glass of wine now?"

"Oh, please," she replied, laying back against the cushions. "That's exactly what I need."

When Ruark came back with the wine, Mariette asked, "Aren't you going to join me?"

"Do you mind if I excuse myself long enough for a quick bath? You can lie here and rest, and maybe 'Liana will be back from Edensfield before I return."

"Oh, all right." She made a pretty face at him. "Go take your silly bath."

As Ruark bathed, he wondered what Mariette's arrival at Quarrystones really meant. She was plainly a woman with a purpose, and it made him uneasy not knowing what that purpose was. He hoped Juliana and the Cliftons would be back from town before he was forced to return to the parlor to entertain her.

As he toweled himself dry, he thought about the injury to Mariette's ankle. He could swear there was nothing wrong with it, that the whole business was just a ruse. But why?

Fastening the towel about his waist, he walked into the bedroom.

"You certainly took long enough." Mariette was sitting on the edge of the bed, dressed only in her petticoats. Her riding habit was laying in a heap on the carpet.

Ruark stopped abruptly, silently cursing his stupidity in trusting her. "For God's sake, Mariette! Have you lost your mind?"

"No, sweet, just my clothing." She smiled wickedly and raised one hand to toy with the ribbon on her chemise. The artfully sensuous gesture irritated Ruark and he crossed the room in quick, angry steps.

"I don't know what sort of game you're playing," he said between clenched teeth, "but I'm not interested." He bent and seized a handful of her clothing, tossing it into her lap. "I suggest you get dressed and get out of here."

Her coquettish facade crumbled. "Ruark, don't be mean," she whimpered, her aquamarine eyes huge. "If I wait for you to make the first move, I'll wait forever."

"That's right." He glared at her, hands on his hips. In his mind he was picturing the scene that might ensue should Juliana walk into the room at that moment.

Mariette flung the clothing aside and rose gracefully to stand close to him. "Why won't you admit you find me beautiful? I've seen it in your eyes."

"When we first met, I did think you were beautiful," he said in a tight voice. "I wasn't displeased to have a beautiful sister."

She stamped one bare foot. "Sister? Is that how you think of me?" Her eyes sparked dangerously. "Well, I'm not your sister and I never will be. You can pretend all you want, but you can't deny the attraction between us." She took a step closer. "I'll prove it."

Swiftly, Mariette grasped the towel he was wearing and, with a sharp pull, tore it from his body. Then, her arms snaking upwards around his neck, she dragged his face down to hers. She pressed her body as tightly to his as she could, and crushed her lips against his mouth.

Embarrassed and disgusted, Ruark didn't push her away as he longed to do. He knew instinctively that complete indifference would discourage her far more readily than heated protest. He forced himself to stand there, enduring her assault until, disbelieving, she backed away a step and looked into his eyes.

"Damn you, Ruark, why are you being so cold? You're going to spoil our chance to be alone together."

Her eyes dropped, moving over him with barely concealed hunger. "My God, but you're a beautiful man," she breathed. "I've never known anyone who looked like you." Her laugh was harsh, self-pitying. "Certainly not my soft, paunchy husband."

Ruark stooped to retrieve the towel at his feet and fastened it about his waist once more. As he did so, Mariette put out a hand to caress him, but he caught it around the wrist and held it in a painful grip.

"I want you to leave. Now."

"Please don't make me go." The easy tears were back in her eyes. "All I'm asking is for you to stop denying what's between us."

"Mariette, there is not, nor will there ever be, anything between us."

"But I need you," she cried. "You don't know what it's like to be married to Spencer. Either he's too interested in business or playing cards to make love to me, or he's too dull and clumsy. He doesn't know the first thing about pleasing me." She caught her breath. "I have dreams of how it would be with you."

"Don't say anything more," he warned.

"I've never begged a man in my life, but if that's what you want, I'll do it."

"You amaze me, Mariette. It's difficult to remember how young you are, and what a short time you've been married. You talk and act like a well-used strumpet."

"How can you call me a strumpet? Just because I see love as a pleasure and not a duty. Unlike your precious Juliana, no doubt."

Ruark's jaw tightened. "Again, you misjudge your sister. Juliana's a very passionate woman."

"A stick like her? I don't believe it. And it sickens me to think of the two of you together, when I know I have so much more to offer." With trembling fingers, she yanked at the loosened chemise, pulling it low over the voluptuous swell of her breasts.

Ruark couldn't hide his scorn as his eyes moved quickly over her eagerly displayed contours. "I'm sorry, but I've always preferred the elegant lily to the overblown rose."

Mariette gave a shriek of anger. "What do you mean?"

"I'm only telling you I'm more than content with the wife I have. I don't need or want another man's."

"You're a fool, Ruark."

"Perhaps, but not enough of one to get involved with you."

"You'll regret this, you know. You'll always wonder what you missed."

"I'll take that chance," he said drily. "Now, I'm going to get dressed. Why don't you do the same and then go home?"

"You can't dismiss me like this," she said haughtily. "I'm not accustomed to being put out like the cat."

Ruark crossed the room to the clothespress and, after selecting a shirt and trousers, began to dress.

"What if I don't go?" she challenged. "Aren't you worried that Juliana might come home and find me in her bed?"

He tucked the tail of a linen shirt into his breeches. "So that's what this is all about," he remarked. "You're so envious of 'Liana that you're doing the one thing you think would hurt her the most. You came here hoping to be discovered by her, didn't you?"

Mariette's pointed chin went up. "Haven't you got things backwards? I'm not jealous of Juliana. All her life she's been the one who envied me. She suffers by comparison and she knows it."

Ruark pulled on his boots, then came to face her. "You're mistaken, Mariette. The truth is, you're so eaten up by jealousy that you need to strike out and injure Juliana any way you can. But I warn you, I won't let you hurt her."

"Just what do you think you can do?"

"I hope 'Liana never knows what you really are, but if it becomes necessary, I'll say or do whatever it takes to stop you. A talk with Spencer could work wonders. He's already growing suspicious of you where other men are concerned. If I were to confirm his suspicions, he might decide to curtail your spending or social activities. He's your legal husband, and it's his right to do those things."

"Threaten all you like," she snapped. "I have nothing to fear from Spencer. Even if he did try to punish me in some way, there are plenty of wealthy men who'd want a beautiful mistress."

"A splendid idea, but are you sure the illustrious Lowell family would approve?"

"You're hateful," she cried, at last bending to pick up her

clothing. "I humble myself and you make me feel like a cheap whore."

"You're only half right, Mariette. You *are* a whore, but I doubt you'd ever be cheap."

"You'll never know."

"No, nor am I interested. A few hours of your company isn't worth all I'd stand to lose."

He paused at the door. "I'll wait downstairs. Remove yourself from this room as quickly as possible, because if Juliana comes home and finds you here, I'll tell her everything. With me dressed and downstairs in the parlor, I doubt she'd believe any story you'd tell her."

Ten minutes later a fuming, but completely dressed Mariette stalked down the stairs and out the front door. With an amused and relieved grin, Ruark followed her.

"Next time, please plan your visit when my wife is home."

She whirled on him. "I'd love to claw your eyes out!"

Ruark leaned against the vine-covered wall of the causeway, his arms crossed over his chest. "I wouldn't try it."

"Oh, no, I have a better means of getting even with you." Her voice was breathy with anger. "I'll find a man who doesn't scorn what I offer. And I'll flaunt our relationship in front of you, making you regret the day you refused me."

With that she hurried away without a backward look. When she met Chavo at the door of the stable, her limp suddenly returned. Ruark watched from a safe distance, slightly amused at the way she leaned against the young gypsy. Chavo helped her to a seat on a low stone wall, then disappeared inside the stable once again. When he returned, he was leading two horses, Mariette's mare and one he'd saddled for himself. Gently, he lifted her up onto the mare's back, then mounted his own horse. In the instant Chavo's back was turned, Mariette threw Ruark a triumphant look.

Tossing her head, she began riding slowly out of the stableyard, the gypsy following close behind.

Just that easily, she had chosen her confederate in revenge.

Ruark was still waiting on the causeway when Juliana returned. Seeing him there, she climbed out of the carriage and ran to meet him. In two long strides, he closed the distance between them and swung her high into the air, gathering her to him with a rough fierceness. Lips against her hair, he murmured, "Lord, I'm glad you're home, 'Liana. I've missed you."

Puzzled by his relief at seeing her, she studied his face. "I haven't been gone long. Has something happened?"

He gave her a slow, searching kiss, and when he lifted his head, she leaned against the wall, too weak to stand alone.

"No, love, but I was lonely without you." Tenderly, he brushed a strand of hair from her face. "Do you know how beautiful you look today? Your eyes are as blue as that clematis growing on the wall."

Juliana turned to look at one of the flowers. "Impossible," she scoffed. "No one could have eyes that blue."

He pressed a kiss on the tip of her nose. "You do."

She reached out to pluck one of the starry blossoms and hold it to her nose. "What does the clematis stand for? Do you remember?"

"Oddly enough, it represents trickery."

"A strange meaning for such a pretty flower."

"They say the juice of the clematis is very acrid, that if it's applied to the skin, it can cause ulceration. I've heard that gypsy beggars use it to cover themselves with sores in order to look doubly pitiful and elicit more coins from their victims."

"Is that true?" she questioned.

Ruark grinned broadly. "I wouldn't put it past some I've known."

She brushed the flower across the width of his chest. "Thank heavens you're more honorable than that."

He caught her hand and tugged her into his arms, slanting his mouth across hers. When he raised his head again, he said, "The world is full of scheming and trickery, sweetheart. May it never affect us."

There was an uncertainty about Ruark that she had never before witnessed. She realized that something unusual must have occurred to make her normally strong, sure husband act so shaken.

"What causes you to say such a thing?"

He forced a laugh. "I'm feeling pensive, I guess. Maybe I've become one of those men who can't tolerate being separated from his wife for more than an hour at a time."

"You? Never."

"I'm not so certain." He released her, keeping an arm about her waist. "Here come Essie and Will-John. We'd better help them with the parcels. It looks as if you've bought everything Edensfield had to offer."

She smiled up at him. "Wait until you see what I've purchased for the children at Moorlands."

As they walked, she chattered gaily and it seemed to her that Ruark hung on her every word. Still, beneath her happiness, she felt a tiny, niggling fear. What had happened that made him turn to her with such desperate devotion? What was it that he thought threatened them?

Seventeen

More than a week later the kitchen boy from Moorlands arrived with a message for Juliana. Edward Hamilton wanted her to meet him at the woodcutter's hut and, since Ruark had ridden into Edensfield, she was free to spend the afternoon as she chose.

Calling Jakel, she informed Essie she was going for a walk, and set out, the Brittany pup running along the path ahead of her.

It was good to be away from the house for a while, and she fervently hoped Edward could distract her. Her mind had been in turmoil ever since her return from the village the day Ruark had been so relieved to see her. Even though puzzled by his attitude, she'd thought little of it until later in the evening when she'd gone upstairs to their bedchamber.

The instant she stepped inside the room, she knew. The scent of the exotic perfume Mariette always wore hung heavily in the air, making it a certainty that she had been there. Juliana was filled with a dreadful jealousy thinking of her sister and Ruark alone together in such an intimate setting. No wonder he'd been so perturbed.

Her first reaction was anger, and it was all she could do to keep from flinging her knowledge of Mariette's presence in his face. She remembered the words he'd spoken as he'd clasped her in his arms. *The world is full of scheming and trickery.* She hadn't speculated that he might be referring to an act of treachery on his own part.

She dismissed the thought almost as soon as it occurred. If she'd learned one thing during her association with Ruark, it was that she could trust him. She knew, too, that if she let herself be swayed by old doubts and fears, she'd be the one betraying him.

Common sense urged her to give the matter calm, logical thought. Perhaps the seduction she envisioned had been the result of Mariette's actions. Maybe Ruark was innocent. It was possible he hadn't told her the truth because he didn't want to hurt her by making accusations against her sister. And it wasn't difficult to believe Mariette would seize an opportunity to seduce Ruark. She'd made it clear she found him attractive; the fact that he was married to Juliana would only make it more challenging.

That night when Ruark came into the bedroom, she'd looked into his eyes and discerned no guilt or deceit within their clear depths. She decided not to mention her suspicions. It suddenly seemed very important to her that she trust him. She could not and would not believe him capable of doing anything to deliberately jeopardize the marriage he'd worked so hard to arrange.

The woodcutter's hut came into sight, and Jakel scampered on ahead, throwing his small body against the door, scratching and whining for admittance. As Juliana walked into the clearing, the door to the hut opened and Chavo stood there.

When he saw her, a guarded expression came over his face.

"Oh, you startled me," Juliana stammered. "I didn't expect anyone to be here."

Before the gypsy could say anything, a feminine voice called out, "Chavo, who's there?"

Juliana caught a glimpse of Mariette in the shadowy interior of the hut. She was sitting on a cot, her ivory shoulders and bare breasts gleaming in the dim light. Juliana knew her sister's question had been deliberate, that she wanted to be sure she was seen.

She took a quick pace backward as Chavo stepped outside the hut and pulled the door shut. He stood silently, as though daring her to make a comment.

To her dismay she felt acute embarrassment. "I'm sorry to have disturbed you," she said stiffly, turning to walk away. "Come, Jakel." She could feel the gypsy's unwavering stare as she turned and left the clearing.

Only a few yards down the path someone called her name in a harsh whisper. "Psst, Juliana." It was Edward Hamilton, beckoning to her from a grove of young oaks. As she joined him, he said, "I'm sorry I couldn't keep you from stumbling onto that little scene."

"The lovers' tryst, you mean?" Her tone was bitter. "What can Mariette be thinking?"

Edward looked about to make certain she hadn't been followed. Then, taking her arm, he led her deeper into the forest, away from the hut. "Don't fret about it, my dear. There's nothing you can do to change the situation."

"But I can't believe Mariette would behave like this. Adultery is far more serious than anything she's ever done before."

"I knew someone had been using the hut, but even I was surprised this afternoon when I saw Mariette and the gypsy lad together."

"Do you think their affair has been going on for some time?"

"More than likely. Your sister has spent a considerable

amount of time away from home of late. Even Spencer has begun to question her absences."

"Will you tell him about seeing her with Chavo?"

"No, I won't interfere. The less you or I meddle in it, the better off we'll be. I've no doubt Spencer will find out soon enough, one way or another."

"Why would Mariette risk her marriage for a dalliance with another man?"

"Who knows?" Edward Hamilton said. "I daresay she couldn't even answer that question."

Later, on her way back to Quarrystones, Juliana pondered another puzzling aspect of the matter. If, as Edward suggested, the affair with Chavo had been underway for some time, what had her sister been doing in Ruark's bedchamber? What flaw in Mariette's character made her desire every attractive man she met?

Ruark burst through the bedroom door, a parcel under his arm and a smile on his face. He seized Juliana in an exuberant hug, saying, "We've been invited to a *pakiv* at the gypsy encampment."

Juliana laughed. "What's a *pakiv?*"

"That, my love, is a party given for special visitors. And we're the guests of honor."

"Why are we being honored?"

"A new band of gypsies has arrived at Quarrystones and among them are kinsmen I haven't seen for quite some time. They want to meet my wife and celebrate our wedding. But more importantly, there's someone with them I want you to meet."

Juliana's eyes began to shine. "Your mother, Ruark? Is she here?"

"Indeed she is."

"Then, I shall look forward to this *pakiv.*"

He placed the parcel in her hands. "She sent you a gift."

With a pleased smile, Juliana quickly opened the package. "Oh, look," she cried, holding up the skirt and blouse she found inside. "This must be to wear to the feast. There's even a shawl. And gold earrings!"

"Go put them on," urged Ruark. "I'll dress as a gypsy, too."

She studied his face with anxious eyes. "Isn't that dangerous? What if someone should see you?"

"We'll be on our own land, among other gypsies. There'll be no one to see us. Now, stop worrying and go get dressed."

Twenty minutes later when Juliana emerged from the bathing chamber, Ruark was leaning casually against the doorframe waiting for her. He was dressed in the highwayman's clothing, but without the outlaw's mask or brimmed hat. His white shirt was open halfway to the waist and there was a red kerchief knotted about his neck. Once more he wore the gold ring in his ear.

When he saw Juliana, he broke into a broad grin. "I've often imagined you this way," he told her, "but you're even more bewitching than I'd envisioned."

She wore a white peasant-style blouse whose deep, flounced neckline left her shoulders bare. A long skirt of dark red paisley fell in soft folds from the tightly fitted waist to her slippered feet. Around her shoulders was draped a heavily fringed shawl of soft wool in shades of dark red and dull gold. Large hoop earrings gleamed in her ears and in one hand she carried several gold chains.

She turned about for his inspection before asking, "Will you fasten these necklaces for me?"

"With pleasure, love." He pulled her to him, and as she

lifted her heavy hair, placed the chains about her neck, one by one. As he closed the clasp of the last one, he rested his warm hands on her shoulders and pressed a kiss close behind one ear.

She sighed and leaned back against him. "I hope your mother likes me."

"She'll love you," he vowed, shifting her to face him. "Why wouldn't she?"

"I might not be exactly what she'd have expected."

"I've told her all about you, 'Liana. She's anxious to meet you."

"Did you know she was coming to Quarrystones?"

"Aye, though I didn't know when. Most of her time is spent at Kilcairn, acting the part of a lady. But once in a while, she puts that aside and goes to live as a gypsy again."

"It sounds as though she's an interesting and unusual woman."

"She is. She enjoys the company of her friends and family, and thinks theirs is a much freer life."

"It must be wonderful to live like a gypsy," Juliana mused. "They go where they please, do what they want."

"In theory it sounds pleasant," Ruark said, "but the reality can be altogether different. Most people don't trust gypsies because they have a reputation for being thieves and tramps. At this moment, there's a bounty on gypsies captured in France."

Juliana looked stricken. "Why should they be treated like wild animals?"

"It's how many people think of them. Life has always been difficult for the wanderers, even though they only want to live in peace, keeping their own traditions and beliefs. You'll see for yourself."

"I can't wait."

"Good. Let's be on our way. We don't want to delay the feast." He took her arm and his smile flashed brightly. "I'll wager you'll be dancing around the campfire before this night is through."

As they walked to the gypsy encampment, Ruark explained to her how the different gypsy *familia* knew where and when to gather.

"They use an ancient system of communication called *vurma*," he said. "It's a trail of messages left along roadsides traveled by the different bands. The messages are formed by twigs or bones, or scraps of cloth and colored glass. Gypsies know where to look for these signs and how to interpret them."

"And that's how one band knows where the others are gathering?"

"Aye. *Vurma* is also a means of passing on word of deaths or marriages. Or feasts like the one we're attending this evening. That's why there are more caravans at Quarrystones than there were a few days ago. Gypsies love any excuse for festivities."

As they neared the encampment, they could hear music and laughter and see the glow of several campfires in the twilight. The last slanting rays of the sun picked out the brilliant colors of the caravans that ringed the large clearing. The painted wooden wagons were mostly red or green, with fanciful gold trim and etched glass windows. These caravans, Ruark told her, were called *vardos*, and contained everything the wandering families needed for life on the road.

At one end of the encampment was a corral constructed of saplings lashed together. Inside were the sleek horses used to pull the caravans.

"Gypsies pride themselves on their ability to breed and train horses," Ruark said. "Few things are more important to them than a close relationship with their animals. They're the best horse-traders in the world, and it's said they can cure nearly all equine ailments or injuries."

Juliana was admiring the milling horses when she glanced up to see a slim figure detach itself from the group standing about one of the fires and start toward them. She knew immediately it was Sara Hamilton, Ruark's mother.

The woman walking toward them was tall. Though slender, she gave the impression of strength, and there was an aura of calm self-assurance about her. She was dressed in a long black dress that swayed gracefully as she walked; about her shoulders was a black and gold lace shawl, reaching nearly to the ground. Her ears, neck and wrists were hung with the usual abundance of gold jewelry, and she wore several rings on her fingers.

Her face was a perfect oval, with high cheekbones and dark eyes that tilted slightly at the ends. Black hair attractively threaded with silver was braided and coiled about the crown of her head, giving her a regal look. When she smiled, the smile reached all the way into her eyes and lighted her face with warmth. Juliana thought she was one of the loveliest women she'd ever seen.

"Hello," Sara said, reaching for Juliana's hands. Her voice was low and musical. "I welcome you to our family."

"Thank you," murmured Juliana. "I'm very happy to meet you at last."

"And I'm pleased to see the young woman my son has told me so much about. I believe his praise was justified."

Juliana colored faintly. "Thank you for the gifts you sent. The clothes and jewelry are wonderful."

"I regretted not being at your wedding, my dear," Sara

said. "My gift is a small way of saying I'm glad Ruark has finally found someone to make him happy. He told me that the first time the two of you met, you reminded him of a gypsy girl. I thought he might enjoy seeing you in the traditional dress."

"And I do," Ruark assured her, putting an arm around each of them. "I'm so proud of 'Liana that I can't wait for the rest of the family to meet her."

For the next hour they moved from campfire to campfire, stopping to speak with the men and women gathered there. Juliana was gratified by the friendly way she was greeted and welcomed into the tribe's midst.

All about them was gaiety and laughter. Glasses were raised as the bridal couple was toasted again and again. The rich red wine sparkled in the firelight and Juliana soon lost count of the glasses pressed into her hand. When it was time for the meal to commence, they seated themselves on the ground near one of the fires and Juliana leaned against her husband.

"Ruark," she whispered.

When he bent his head to catch her words, she lifted her face and gave him a softly clinging kiss. "I fear I'm slightly drunk."

He smiled and placed an arm about her, hugging her closer. "No matter, this is a celebration. Just enjoy yourself. I'll be here to take care of you."

Ruark's mother handed them plates heaped with food. Juliana looked at hers in dismay. "I couldn't possibly eat this much," she demurred. "Though it does smell good. Mmm, what's this?" She took a bite of succulent roasted meat.

"Perhaps it's *hotchi-witchi*," Ruark said, with a wicked grin.

"What's that?"

"One of the gypsies' favorite delicacies. I believe you *gorgios* call it hedgehog."

Juliana looked horrified. "Hedgehog? Ruark Hamilton! You let me eat hedgehog?"

He threw back his head and laughed. "No, sweetheart, what you're eating is actually roast pork. I only suggested it could have been hedgehog."

Gingerly, she poked the meat on her plate with one finger. "Are you certain it's pork?"

Sara Hamilton, overhearing the exchange, leaned close and said, "It is indeed. Stop teasing, Son."

"Why would anyone want to eat hedgehog?" Juliana shuddered.

"They say it's quite delicious," Sara replied. "I've seen it prepared, but I must confess I've never tried it. It's flavored with garlic and wrapped, skin and all, in clay. Then it's placed on burning hot stones so it can bake in its own fat. When the clay is removed, all the prickles come away with it."

"I can't imagine such a thing." Juliana's wide eyes met her husband's amused ones. "Suddenly I don't feel very hungry."

She set her plate aside, but before Ruark could protest her action, the sound of music began to fill the night, bringing a welcome diversion.

Several men strolled into the circle of light around the campfire, playing stringed instruments and singing. As they entertained, the feast continued, with the participants consuming vast amounts of food and drink.

When their song ended, the rhythmic beating of a drum began emanating from the shadows. It throbbed sensually, drawing everyone's attention.

A striking gypsy girl moved into the firelight, shoulders moving sinuously above the low-cut red satin blouse she wore. Her hips, swathed in a tight black skirt that flared out into a froth of red ruffles, undulated in time to the provocative beat of the drums. Graceful arms reached upward, twining together while she skillfully manipulated the finger cymbals she wore. Each metallic ring of the cymbals emphasized the movement of her hips.

She danced with eyes closed, a sensual smile on her face. As the music began to quicken, she tossed her head from side to side, and a curtain of jet-black hair flew out about her, first concealing, and then revealing her features. Suddenly, as though sensing her whereabouts, she paused and opened kohl-darkened eyes which fastened on Ruark.

The music slowed again and she danced in front of him with an exaggerated writhing motion. Kneeling, she allowed her torso to sway toward him, bringing her half-bare breasts to within inches of his face. One hand reached out to brazenly stroke his jaw, fingers trailing downward to brush his lips. Casting a quick sideways look at Juliana, Ruark broke into a wide smile.

The dancer slowly straightened and backed away, beckoning him to join her in the dance. With another glance at Juliana, he shrugged and, accompanied by a din of shouting and hand-clapping, rose to his feet and followed the girl into the ring of firelight.

At first Ruark merely stood, arms crossed over his chest, as the dancer whirled about him, wantonly brushing his body with her own. Then, as she placed one hand on his shoulder and the other on his hip, he began to move with her in time to the tempestuous music. With her eyes half-closed and her head thrown back, the gypsy woman offered an invitation as old as time, and Ruark did not appear reluctant.

As she watched the bold display before her, Juliana experienced a hot tide of anger. She turned to her new mother-in-law and saw similar disapproval on her face. Leaning close to Sara, she whispered, "Who is that girl? Obviously Ruark knows her well."

Sara nodded. "They've known each other since childhood. For a time, it was thought they would marry. Of course, that was before my son met you. Tshaya was only supposed to dance tonight, not indulge herself this way."

"Ruark doesn't seem to mind," Juliana observed dryly.

"Perhaps he's only trying to inspire a little jealousy," Sara suggested. "He keeps looking your way."

"What does he expect me to do? I can't create a scene by demanding their dance be stopped."

Sara smiled. "On the other hand, it might be advisable for you to remind everyone just who the bride is. This feast is supposed to be in your honor. You shouldn't let Tshaya have all the glory."

Juliana solemnly studied the older woman for a long moment, then turned back to stare at the couple limned by the leaping flames.

"No, I shouldn't," she murmured, getting to her feet.

As she stood, a strange lightheadedness made her recall all the wine she had drunk. Its effect spiraled through her body, charging her with unaccustomed courage. She experienced a new awareness of her surroundings, but even that didn't slow her footsteps as she moved into the firelight. She smelled the tangy scent of wood smoke, heard the sharp intake of Tshaya's breath and sensed the crowd's suppressed excitement as her intention became clear.

She raised her head and looked directly into Ruark's astonished eyes. A half-smile appeared on his lips, and one black eyebrow arched upward. An expression of interest came over his lean face as he waited to see what she would do next.

Without a look in Tshaya's direction, Juliana stepped between the dancer and Ruark. The rhythm of the drum seemed to beat within her body, causing the blood to sing in her veins. Her limbs took on a wayward will of their own, and, amazed at her temerity, she began to move in time to the music, giving herself up to the overpowering sensuality of the dance.

Tshaya stood a moment watching, then with a disgusted toss of her head, stalked away into the shadows, muttering malevolent Romany curses.

Neither Ruark nor Juliana noticed her departure, for they were conscious only of each other. Their eyes met and held, hers challenging, his hot with burgeoning desire.

She moved close in front of him, turning so her shoulder barely touched his chest and her skirts brushed his legs. He put out a possessive hand to take her arm.

"Come here," he commanded softly.

Deftly she twisted out of his grasp.

"I think not," she said, a faint smile lifting her mouth. As she whirled away, he followed, matching his motion to the tempestuous music so it would seem the dance continued.

"'Liana," he murmured, fitting an arm about her waist and drawing her close to him. "Are you teasing me?"

"Ha! How can you ask that after the way you danced with Tshaya? Weren't you teasing me?"

He nuzzled her neck. "I was testing your reaction."

"And now I'm testing yours," she said, again twirling out of his reach.

With a slightly puzzled look, he advanced again, but she turned her back and with an arrogant hand, tossed her long hair, causing it to strike him in the face like a fragrant cloud. A round of laughter went up from the gypsies sitting in a ring about the fire, and a few of the men called out advice. It was clearly evident they were enjoying Ruark's quandary.

Juliana began to stamp her feet, lifting her skirts to show a flash of bare leg. With a muttered curse, Ruark started after her but she darted away. As she danced past the crowd, a smiling gypsy grandmother offered her a glass brimming with wine and Juliana seized it, raising it high to drink. The ruby liquid spilled over the side of the glass, coursing down the slender length of her neck to stain the front of her embroidered blouse. She threw back her head and laughed exultantly. Before she could elude him, Ruark grasped her wrists and, standing close in front of her, began to kiss the wine from her neck. She gasped as she felt his warm lips and exploring tongue move over her sensitive skin.

"Ruark, stop it," she cried, her command edged with laughter.

"I think not," he mocked her. He dipped his head to seek the hollow between her breasts. With a cry she wrenched away and began dancing about the fire. Those watching clapped their hands in time to the music, as Ruark, too, began to execute the same steps. He advanced, she withdrew, always managing to keep a safe distance between them.

"Don't run away now," Ruark entreated.

"And why not?"

He grinned. "You've stirred my gypsy blood, sweetheart."

"Me? Are you certain it wasn't Tshaya?"

"I'm certain." He came dangerously close and the music seemed to build to a climax. "Come now, 'Liana, let the dance end."

She shook her head. "You must think I'm a very meek wife."

His white teeth flashed. "No, I wouldn't say you were meek at all."

"What would you say of me?"

"That you're nothing less than brazen."

"Brazen?"

"Aye, very."

"I've done nothing brazen yet," she declared, "but if that's what you think, I'll be happy to." She swayed gracefully as Ruark's face began to spin before her eyes with dizzying speed. Even the pale silver stars overhead seemed to be whirling about. As the music crashed to an abrupt halt, Ruark caught her in his arms and easily tossed her over his shoulder.

She struggled momentarily, to the delight of the onlookers, but then, with a heavy sigh, she settled against him and was still. Raising a hand to bid the others good night, Ruark strode out of the circle of light and into the deepening shadows beyond.

When he'd walked some distance from the gypsy encampment, he stopped and shifted Juliana's body so that he was cradling her in his arms. She put her hand against his chest and murmured, "Do you really think I'm brazen?"

"Delightfully so," he replied, his arms tightening. "And I wouldn't want you any other way." His breath was warm against her ear.

Juliana placed a small kiss beneath his chin and sighed. "Where are we going?"

"Where gypsy lovers always go when the dancing is finished. To their caravan."

Just then he stepped through an opening in the trees. Bathed in moonlight, the clearing was empty except for a small campfire and a painted *vardo* pulled to one side. Beyond, the river flowed serenely, its silver-tipped wavelets gently lapping at the grassy shore.

Overhead floated a full moon whose pearly brilliance was

mirrored in the water below. All around them was the silence of the forest, broken only occasionally by the distant sounds of merriment from the encampment.

"Ruark, what a lovely caravan. Whose is it?"

"It's ours, a gift from my mother. Do you like it?"

"It's wonderful, but what will we do with a gypsy caravan?"

He set her on her feet and put his hands on her shoulders, turning her toward him. His lean fingers caressed her neck, moving upward to cup her face. "I have something very definite in mind." His lips grazed hers. "Tonight we'll stay here." His voice grew husky. "It'll be our gypsy wedding night."

She looked up at him with wide eyes. "Ruark," she whispered, "your mother said everyone thought you and Tshaya would marry."

In answer, he lowered his head and once more claimed her mouth in a demanding kiss. "Don't ask if I'd prefer her," he warned. "You're the only one I want."

Ardently, his lips moved against hers, causing them to part beneath his loving assault. She moaned, putting her arms about his neck and pressing her body against the full, hard length of his.

"I want you, too," she breathed.

His response was immediate, intense. His strong hands closed about her waist, lifting her onto the step of the *vardo*. He leaped up beside her and held the door so she might enter the caravan.

Inside, there was enough moonlight streaming through the window to illuminate wooden cupboards and benches, but her eyes were drawn to the bed strewn with satin pillows. She didn't resist as Ruark drew her down among the cushions to lay at his side.

Swiftly, he removed her shawl, tossing it away. With unerring surety his fingers moved to the lacing of her blouse. As the fabric gave way beneath his invading touch, baring her flesh, he placed fiery kisses along her collarbone, causing her to shiver with delight.

He pulled her into a sitting position and she willingly abetted him in stripping away her blouse. She unfastened her skirt for him and, with deft motions, he slipped it and her petticoats off, letting them slide unheeded to the floor.

One at a time he took off her slippers, and then his hands played slowly up her naked legs to grasp her hips and pull her beneath him. For a long moment he remained poised above her, his weight resting on his forearms.

His eyes were obsidian as they caressed her shoulders and bosom, tantalizingly draped by fragile strands of golden chains. He scattered kisses along her throat before allowing his hungry mouth to seek the sweetness of firm breasts and tightly budded nipples.

Juliana moaned with pleasure, eventually drawing his attention back to her mouth. The kiss they shared created wildly compelling desires that thrummed within her like the wanton gypsy music. She clutched at his shoulders and writhed beneath him, her breathing growing distracted, ragged.

"Ruark, aren't you going to get undressed?" she whispered into his ear. She could feel the frantic beat of his heart all through her body in the moment before he pulled back to begin unbuttoning his shirt. He bent to take off his boots and then her fingers moved to the fastening of his tight black trousers. With quick, eager movements, she peeled the garment away, letting her hands rove freely over his heated flesh.

He muttered a Romany phrase in barely audible tones as he settled over her, possessing her body with a slow, deliberate thrust.

"Oh, Ruark." Her breath sobbed in her throat, and he soothed her with quiet murmurings.

Soon he grew impatient and began moving with an urgency that transported both of them to a fever-pitch of passion. Juliana met him thrust for thrust, reveling in the glorious, thrilling intimacy they shared.

From the distant campfire came the sound of gypsy music, and once again Juliana and Ruark found themselves caught up in the erotic rhythms. They clung together while the music lifted them, finally flinging them headlong into shattering culmination.

Shaken by the powerful release, Juliana cried out; Ruark quenched her cries with his mouth as he chanted endearments. He shifted his position to enfold her tenderly within the protection of his arms.

As they lay together in replete and restful silence, their individual thoughts roamed along separate pathways, through the confusing maze of their life together and the events of the past weeks. Incredibly, those thoughts merged into a single understanding of their own hearts and minds. Juliana was spurred by an undeniable need to speak and reveal her feelings. She turned to her husband and, gently tracing his jawline with her fingers, she murmured, "Ruark, I have a confession to make. I've fallen in love with you."

"Don't make it sound like a crime," he remonstrated, amusement gleaming in his eyes.

"The crime is that I've loved you for a long time and didn't tell you."

"I've never told you that I love you, either, yet I do. Maybe neither of us was ready to accept that until tonight."

"There was something very special about tonight, wasn't there?" Her gaze turned smoky. "I'll never forget it."

"Nor will I." He nestled his face against her neck. "How long have you loved me?"

For a moment, she looked startled, and then she laughed softly. "I've felt this way for a long time, I think. I just didn't recognize my feelings for what they were."

"I've loved you since our first meeting, but I was never certain how you felt." He toyed with a strand of her hair. "I thought you might still resent the fact that our marriage was one of necessity."

"I did resent it at first," she admitted, "but not anymore. You've been wonderful to me in the time we've been together."

"You make it easy, you know."

"I didn't always." She changed positions so she could look more closely into his face. "In the beginning, I considered marriage my only means of keeping Quarrystones. But right from the first, you've said the most intimate and audacious things. It confused me. I didn't know if you were merely teasing me or if, by some miracle, you meant what you said."

He pressed a lingering kiss on her lips. "Tell me, do you still doubt my seriousness?"

"No." She chuckled softly. "You've found ways to be more than convincing."

"From the start, I've only had one purpose: to win the most splendid woman I'd ever met. And when Fate allowed me that privilege, I found happiness I never expected."

"Me, too, Ruark."

"You've forgiven me for forcing you into marriage?"

"How could I not? I thought it would be worse than prison, but you're not like other husbands I've heard about. You've given me more freedom than I've ever had."

"But now that I know how you feel, I'll never let you go. Doesn't that frighten you?"

"Not at all. By indulging my independence, somehow you've bound me to you for a lifetime."

They shared a kiss that was both solemn and reverent, a promise of the trust and devotion each pledged the other. When he raised his head, Ruark spoke again.

"We've talked often about the meanings of flowers. I wonder if you know the significance of the name 'Liana?'"

"It has a meaning? I thought it was just something you'd made up for me."

"The word *liana* actually means any green vine that roots in the ground and twines itself around the trunk of a tree."

She poked him gently in the chest. "Is that how you think of me, as a clinging vine?"

He laughed. "Far from it. Vines don't necessarily cling. For instance, see those grapevines along the edge of the clearing?" He held back the curtain as she leaned forward to peer out into the moon-silvered night.

Just beyond the caravan was the dark wall of the forest. One large and imposing oak stood out from the rest. At its base and spiraling upward along the tree trunk was a thickly luxuriant grapevine, its leaves seemingly molded of pewter.

"Though the grapevine could grow independently, it chooses to entwine itself with the oak, thus strengthening them both," said Ruark. "That's how I see the two of us."

She smiled at him. "You are like an oak, you know. Tall, strong, and steadfast."

"And you're like the vine, independent, yet drawing strength from other sources about you." He hugged her to him. "That's how it'll be when we're old. We'll have been together so long, we won't know whether the oak supports the vine, or the vine supports the oak."

"Or if either could exist without the other." Juliana lowered her face for his kiss.

Wrapped within each other's arms, they lay back among the soft cushions and Ruark drew a silk coverlet over them. From out of the night came the haunting strains of a gypsy violin. The eerily beautiful melody lulled them into a deep and peaceful sleep.

Eighteen

The next morning Ruark and Juliana departed the sleeping gypsy encampment to walk home through dew-misted meadows. Before leaving, they spoke with Sara Hamilton a few moments, Juliana feeling vaguely mortified as she recalled the hazy events of the evening just past. Ruark's mother seemed determined to ignore her discomfiture as she again welcomed her into the family.

Juliana invited the older woman to dinner the next night, and, after Ruark had kissed his mother goodbye, they set out for home.

"Did you enjoy the *pakiv?*" he asked with a smile.

"It was wonderful. I liked the food and the dancing." She glanced up at him wickedly. "And what followed."

"To think you questioned our need for a caravan. Didn't I tell you I had a definite purpose in mind for the *vardo?*"

"Indeed you did, though I can't think of a single other reason we'd need one. You don't intend to adopt the wandering life of the gypsy, do you?"

"It might have its advantages. Besides, we can leave the caravan in the clearing and slip away to it whenever the mood strikes us."

"We could do that," she agreed.

"And someday, our children might want to use the wagon as a play house."

"Our children?" she echoed, as though the idea was completely new to her.

"It's not impossible, you know," he said, white teeth flashing in a broad smile.

Faint color came into her face. "No, of course not. But I can't imagine myself as the mother of a child."

"Maybe several children," he ventured. "Two or three boys, perhaps. And as many daughters." He looked at her with one eyebrow lifted, as though gauging her reaction.

"What would we do with so many children?"

"Have a boisterous time of it, I expect."

She had to laugh. "Essie wasn't overjoyed with our one small dog. What would she say to a houseful of children?"

"She and Will-John would love them, and you know it."

"Yes, I'm sure they would."

"We'd have to decide whether or not to observe the gypsy way of naming a child."

"How do they do it?"

"Their children are given three names," he explained, "but the first is always kept secret. The babe's mother is the only one who knows it. She whispers it at the moment of birth, and then it's never used again."

Juliana looked puzzled. "Why does the baby need a secret name?"

"Gypsies believe that keeping the child's true identity a mystery will confuse the demons they fear."

"Oh, demons." Her eyes twinkled. "Of course."

"The second name is Romany, the one used by the members of the tribe. The third is given at a baptism that takes place according to the laws of the country where the child is born. This is considered the least important since it's used mainly in dealing with *gorgios*."

"If you were named according to tradition, Edward must be your gypsy name."

"*Eduardo,* actually. Chosen by my father who, for some odd reason, thought to honor his own sire."

"Not so odd," she said. "No doubt he loved his father and hoped someday their quarrel would be resolved."

"I suppose so."

"Then Ruark is your non-gypsy name?"

"Aye. Would you like to use it for our firstborn son?"

Juliana batted playfully at him. "Even if we did, we'd still be hard pressed to come up with enough names for all the children you plan on fathering."

They laughed together as they crossed the causeway bridge.

Later in the morning, after Juliana had bathed and dressed in a plum-colored gown, Essie summoned her to the living room.

"Yer sister is here, Miss Juli," she announced as they went down the stairs. "Said she had something important to talk to ye about." The woman sniffed audibly. "Though I doubt the girl ever had an important thought in her life."

Juliana tried not to frown, though she was filled with foreboding at seeing Mariette.

Seated on the couch, Mariette was looking out the tall, leaded glass windows. With her skirts spread out about her and a wistful smile on her face, she made a charming picture. It was nearly impossible for Juliana to realize she was the same woman who'd been in the woodcutters' hut with Chavo. Or indeed, in her own bedroom with Ruark.

"Hello, Mariette."

Her sister turned and stared at Juliana for a long moment.

Finally she said, "I suppose you thought I'd come to offer some explanation about being with Chavo?"

"No, I didn't."

"That's good, because I don't have to account to you."

"Nor do I expect it. I'm only concerned about Spencer."

"You're worried about Spencer? Even after the way he treated you? Juli, you're such an innocent. He wouldn't hesitate to have an affair if the opportunity arose. These things are perfectly acceptable in today's society."

"You know much more about social behavior than I do. And how you conduct yourself is none of my business."

"Then don't look so disapproving."

"I'm sorry. I didn't mean to."

"No, I realize that." Mariette sighed. "Doing the right thing comes easy for you, doesn't it?"

Juliana was startled. "What do you mean?"

"When we were children, you were always so perfect. You never muddled up your schoolwork or infuriated the governess. You were never sick or dirty or cross. I used to despise you because you were Mother and Father's favorite."

Juliana dropped onto the couch, her mouth agape in astonishment. She managed a short, half-laugh. "What are you talking about? You were their pampered darling, Etta."

"I was sickly, that's the only reason. They spent so much time with me because my medications and therapy took hours. And all that while I'd have to listen to them chortle about your latest scholastic achievement, or your artistic talents. If Mother needed something from the shops, Father would suggest she send you because you were so practical. And trustworthy."

"You were the one they dressed in beautiful clothes," Juliana reminded her sister. "The one they showed off to their friends. If guests came for the evening, Mother could barely wait for the meal to end so she could usher them into the parlor to hear you sing."

"Did you ever think how I felt about that? I hated being dressed up like a brainless mannequin and expected to perform and be charming."

"I didn't consider it from your point of view. I'm sure I was sitting in a corner somewhere, feeling dull and plain."

"At least you didn't have to throw temper tantrums to get Mother and Father's attention. Their true attention, I mean." Mariette's expression was one of wry amusement. "It seems they were too busy taking my pulse or watching for fevers to realize I had any other needs. I wanted to be like you, Juli. Someone they could count on, not just poor, sickly Mariette who had to have everything done for her."

Impulsively, Juliana reached out to take Mariette's hand. "I never knew how you felt. I'm sorry."

"It wasn't your fault, as much as I tried to believe it was."

"Still, I shouldn't have thought only of myself." She glanced down at their clasped hands. "Think of all the years we've wasted, when we might have been friends. But it's not too late, Etta."

Mariette bowed her head and when she spoke, her voice was bleak. "I've done something I'm ashamed of," she admitted. "Something horrid."

Juliana studied the top of Mariette's golden head, picturing it against Ruark's chest. She dredged up the hateful memory of her sister and her husband singing together, of Mariette's hand upon his thigh. She waited for the customary pang of envy to strike, but instead, she felt sympathy. She'd assumed Mariette was everything any woman in the world could want to be. Never once had she guessed that her sister might have experienced a lack of any kind. Or that she, too, was sometimes insecure or unfulfilled. Knowing Mariette's life had never been the blissful idyll that she'd imagined made it easier to be forgiving.

"I know, Etta," she murmured. "You don't have to explain."

"But I tried to take something that belonged to you. I—"

"Please don't go on," Juliana entreated. "It doesn't matter now."

Mariette bit her lower lip. "All our lives, it has seemed that everything truly good and solid and worthwhile has come to you."

Visions of Ruark, the Cliftons, and Quarrystones drifted through Juliana's mind, and she smiled. "Yes, I believe you're right. I must have been a fool to ever doubt my good fortune."

"I've tried so hard to make you jealous of me." Mariette drew in a deep, shuddering breath. "The truth is, you've got everything and I have nothing. I want someone to love me for me, Juli. Someone who really needs me. I don't think that's asking for too much, do you?"

"Of course not." She put her arms around her sister and gave her a quick, hard hug. "If you try harder, maybe Spencer could be that person. He seems to love you a great deal."

Mariette pulled away. "But I don't love him. He was just something you had that I coveted. As terrible as it sounds, I only wanted to hurt you."

"I don't mind now. As it turned out, I found Ruark and I'm happier than I've ever been."

"I'll never have that same happiness with Spencer."

"Or with Chavo," Juliana said gently.

"Don't lecture me," Mariette responded, with a show of her usual asperity. "I know what I'm doing."

"Very well, I won't interfere."

Mariette jumped to her feet and paced the length of the room, satin skirts swishing in the sudden silence. "Let's not argue again," she said after a moment. "Besides, none of this is what I came to discuss with you."

"Why did you come?"

"To issue an invitation to a ball Spencer and I are giving next week. All our friends from London have agreed to attend; even Mother and Father will be here."

"Oh, really? I'd like to see them," Juliana said. "But I'll need to talk to Ruark about it."

"Talk to me about what?" Ruark asked, coming into the room. He leaned over the back of the couch to drop a kiss on Juliana's hair.

"Spencer and Mariette have invited us to a ball they're giving. Mother and Father will be down for it."

"If you'd like to go, 'Liana, it would be my pleasure to escort you."

She looked up at him. "You're certain you don't mind?"

"I'm sure you'd like an opportunity to visit with your parents. And I'll look forward to dancing with you again."

Juliana basked in the warm glance he gave her, though at the same time, she was aware of Mariette shifting uncomfortably at the other end of the room. "Tell Spencer we'll be pleased to come to the ball."

"Wonderful. Our other guests will be arriving around nine o'clock." She smoothed her skirts, as if anxious to avoid Ruark's direct gaze. "Well, I really must be on my way. I have to go into Edensfield to deliver a few more invitations."

Juliana walked Mariette to the door where she said, "I'm glad we had the chance to talk, Etta."

"Me, too." Mariette gave her a somber smile, then hurried off to her waiting carriage.

When she had gone, Juliana returned to Ruark. "I hope you really don't mind attending Mariette's party."

"If it's something you want to do, I don't mind in the least."

She went into his arms. "I'd like to see Mother and Father. I only wish they were bringing Jeremy with them." She smiled fondly. "I've missed the little scamp. Besides, I want you to meet him. I know you'd get on well together."

"Why don't we ask your parents' permission to have him down for a stay at Quarrystones? I'd like to meet the lad, since he's such a favorite of yours."

"That's a wonderful idea," she exclaimed. She threw her arms about his neck, drawing his face down to be thoroughly kissed.

"I must have these ideas more often," he teased.

She let her fingers slide upward to ruffle his black hair. As she traced the curve of his ear, she gasped, "Oh, no! I hope Mariette didn't notice this." She gently tugged at the single gold hoop he had neglected to remove the night before.

"Your sister never even looked my direction, 'Liana. Don't worry."

"I can't help it."

He bent his face to hers. "Then I'll have to come up with another good idea to distract you."

"What kind of idea?"

"We could go for a walk in the woods. And maybe stop to see our *vardo* again."

"For what purpose?" she queried, her eyes dancing.

He gathered her closer to whisper into her ear.

"Mmm," she approved. "Very enterprising."

Early the morning of Mariette's ball, Juliana went into the garden to pick several armloads of lavender, which was to be dried and used to scent the linens. As she worked, she was interrupted by the kitchen boy from Moorlands, bringing her a note from Edward.

He needed to talk to her about something important and asked if she could meet him that afternoon at the forest hut. She presumed it would be easier than usual for him to slip away due to the confusion of preparations for the festivities that night.

Juliana sighed. The time was coming when she would have to tell Ruark about her secret meetings with his grandfather. To say nothing was the same as lying, and she felt more and more compelled to have it out in the open. She decided to meet Edward one last time and then, somehow, she'd have to find a way to tell Ruark everything.

Hearing the front door close, she looked up in time to see Chavo striding away across the lawn. She couldn't help wondering what business he'd had with her husband at such an early hour.

Her arms filled with the fragrant lavender, she entered the house and left the flowers on the bench in the still-room. Taking only a handful with which to scent her bedchamber, she went up the stairs.

As she stepped into her bedroom, she saw Ruark standing near the window with his back turned.

"I noticed Chavo leaving," she said. "Is anything wrong?"

Her husband whirled about, and she was stricken by the look of fury on his face.

"I'm glad you're here, 'Liana," he said in clipped tones. "Would you mind explaining this to me?"

For the first time she observed the scroll of parchment he was holding. He thrust it at her.

Still clutching the lavender, she took the scroll and unrolled it. "It's a painting," she said, her eyes flying to his.

"Surely you aren't thinking of pretending you don't recognize the subject?"

Juliana was filled with sudden dread. The painting was a portrait of a young woman in a blue gown. Her sun-warmed face was lighted by laughing grey eyes and surrounded by wildly blowing strands of long dark hair. "No, it's me."

Ruark's laugh was short. "Most definitely, love. A very good likeness, I might add."

"It hardly seems like me at all," she said, studying the parchment.

"It's a very intimate portrait to my way of thinking," he said. "Would you care to tell me who the artist might be?"

"I don't know what you're implying," she said, lifting uncertain eyes to his face.

"I wonder if it's possible you're more like your sister than I knew."

Stung, Juliana cried out, "What have I done to make you even think such a thing?"

"I suggest that you tell me," he replied evenly.

"You believe I have sins to confess?"

He nodded grimly. "It seems these sins have been being committed for some weeks now."

"Who told you something like that?"

"Chavo told me. It appears I've been more the besotted husband than I realized. He says you've been secretly meeting someone in the woods." He came closer, putting his hands on her shoulders in an iron grip. "Did he tell me the truth?"

"Is that all the faith you have in me, Ruark?"

"I'm beginning to think there's nothing to be gained in trusting any woman," he growled. "Instead of trying to put me on the defensive, I'd rather you told me who painted this picture and when."

Juliana's chin rose stubbornly. "Even if I tried to explain, would you believe me? Or would you prefer to listen to the imaginings of others?"

"Chavo didn't bring me this portrait simply for the purpose of creating trouble between us. He was very hesitant, in fact. But he's my friend and felt he should inform me of what's happening behind my back. It takes courage to tell a man he's being betrayed by the wife he thinks is so virtuous."

"You've assumed I'm guilty," she exclaimed angrily. "Did you never think Chavo might have been mistaken? Or that you might be jumping to ridiculous conclusions?"

" 'Liana, I'd love to think that," he said in a dull voice. "But even you must agree, the situation looks bad."

"Only because you don't know the entire story."

"Then tell me."

Ignoring his command, she went on. "I thought we could solve any problem with calm reason. But because you think a terrible transgression has been committed, you immediately place the blame on me."

"What am I supposed to think?" he asked. "A friend I've known all my life tells me he's seen my wife slipping away into the woods on a number of occasions. That he once caught a glimpse of her in the company of another man."

"Why does that mean he's my lover?"

"Look at this painting. Up until now, I thought I was the only man who'd seen you this way." His hands dropped away from her shoulders and he half-turned from her. "The artist is obviously someone who knows you well."

"Your jealousy is entirely unfounded," Juliana said quietly. "In fact, it's more preposterous than you know."

"I'd like to hear the truth from your own lips," he stated, raking his hand through his hair.

"You should know instinctively that I wouldn't do anything to hurt you. If you trust me so little, I'd be wasting my time trying to make excuses or explanations."

She turned and started out of the room. Ruark's voice boomed out. "Wait. I want to know who it is you meet in the woods. Who painted this picture and hid it in the woodcutters' hut?"

She paused, but didn't speak.

"Well? Have you nothing to say?" Ruark stalked across the floor to stand behind her. She turned to face him, her eyes darkening dangerously.

"I won't defend myself against such a senseless charge," she declared, meeting his fierce scowl defiantly. "You can believe what you want."

Ruark put out a restraining hand, but she shrugged it away impatiently. Seeing the tangle of lavender she still held, she thrust it against his chest. "Here," she said in a chilly tone. "Take these. They're the flower of distrust, so appropriate for the occasion."

Before he could reply, she wrenched open the door and ran down the hall, leaving him staring after her in angry frustration.

Calling to Jakel, Juliana escaped to the Venus garden. She huddled against the base of the goddess's statue and tried to calm her wildly beating heart. She couldn't believe the scene that had just taken place between Ruark and herself. How could anyone be so loving and devoted one moment, and so unreasonably accusing the next?

The Brittany pup seemed to sense her unhappiness, for he snuggled close against her and watched with sorrowful eyes.

"Oh, Jakel," she moaned, "if Ruark hadn't been so condemning, I would've told him the truth."

The dog tilted his head sideways as though considering her words and Juliana had to laugh despite her misery. "All right, I'm too stubborn for my own good. But he should know me better than that."

Juliana avoided her husband at the midday meal by packing a lunch and her painting supplies, telling Essie to inform him she would be back later. She was very careful to cross the causeway bridge and start off in the direction of the tenant farms in case he was watching from an upstairs window. She waited until she was safely in the woods before doubling back and following the path along the river to the old hut deep in the forest.

Knowing she was early, she went inside to wait. She nibbled at the lunch she'd brought, but thoughts of her confrontation with Ruark destroyed any appetite she might have had, and she ended up tossing the food to the birds and squirrels.

When Edward Hamilton appeared, Juliana opened the door so he could step inside. He looked decidedly worried.

"Juliana, someone has taken my painting of you," he said abruptly. "I shudder to think who might have found it."

She patted his shoulder. "I know who took the painting. It was Chavo, our stablehand."

"Mariette's gypsy? But why would he—?"

"He gave it to Ruark," she said quietly.

Edward groaned. "And what did your husband make of it?"

"That doesn't really matter. Edward, I want to tell you something I should've admitted a long time ago."

"That your husband is my grandson?"

Juliana gasped. "How did you know?"

Edward shook his head. "It occurred to me gradually. You were a bit secretive about him, but when I found out he was Irish, that he was named Edward, and that he'd ap peared at Quarrystones under somewhat mysterious circumstances, it struck me. As I believe you hoped it would." He smiled faintly. "I think I've known for a long time, just as I've known that Randolph is dead." He raised bleak eyes to hers. "He *is* dead, isn't he?"

Juliana moved to put her arms around him. "Edward, I'm so sorry."

"I suppose he never forgave me then," Edward said brokenly. "He must have gone to his grave cursing my very existence."

"No, I'm certain he didn't," Juliana soothed. "If he'd hated you, he wouldn't have named his son after you."

New light came into the old man's deeply set hazel eyes. "Yes, you may be right."

At that moment the door to the hut flew open and a large masculine frame filled the doorway. Startled, Juliana stepped away from Edward and spun about. "Ruark!"

His face was mocking. "Uninvited and unwelcome, I'm sure." His tone was scathing, his eyes blackly furious. "Didn't you think I might follow you?"

Two bright spots of color burned in her cheeks and her eyes smoldered with wrath. "Ruark," she said in a deceptively cool tone, "let me introduce my friend." She stepped aside so the two men could see each other. "This is Edward Hamilton, Duke of Hawkhurst. Your grandfather."

Ruark's face registered shock, but there was a curious mixture of pride and trepidation on Edward's lined one.

"Hello, Ruark," he said hesitantly.

The younger man stared at first his grandfather, and then his wife. "Juliana, what have you been up to?"

"I haven't been up to anything," she replied patiently. "I made Edward's acquaintance quite by accident while you were away in Ireland."

"I should have known he was the man you met in the woods."

"Yes, you should've. Our outings had to be kept secret because Spencer would forbid Edward to talk to me if he knew. And I couldn't tell you because of your attitude toward your father's family. I knew you'd be angry."

"Angry doesn't begin to describe what I'm feeling," he rasped. "Knowing what this man did to my parents, you sneaked around behind my back and befriended him. How could you do such a thing and blithely expect me to understand?"

"I didn't set out to meet your grandfather, Ruark, but it happened. After I heard his side of the story, I thought you should meet him, too. Remember the times I brought up the subject? Remember the times you so flatly refused to give an inch in your stubbornness? I knew it was wrong not to tell you, but how could I? I didn't want to hurt either of you."

"She's right, lad. This isn't her argument and we've no right to involve her in it."

Ruark rounded on the older man. "You stay out of this," he roared. "I have nothing to say to you."

"Stop it," Juliana cried. "How can you be so horrid? Don't you think it's time to forget something that happened twenty-six years ago?"

"That quarrel ruined several lives."

"Including my own, Ruark," Edward said solemnly. "But we can't let it continue to take a toll."

"I want it continued until you've paid for the wrong you did my mother or until you are dead."

Juliana stepped close to Edward Hamilton, linking her arm with his. "I can't believe you're saying these things, Ruark. I didn't think you could be so prejudiced and narrow-minded

At least your grandfather is man enough to admit his mistakes."

"Fine. If you think so much of him, stay here with him. Move into Moorlands with him. The two of you can sneak and connive all you please, so long as you leave me alone. I want nothing to do with either of you."

Ruark turned on his heel and stomped out the door, slamming it with a mighty crash. Juliana could feel Edward shaking, and she put a comforting arm around his shoulders.

"Don't feel too badly. He was bound to react this way at first. He'll calm down after he's had a chance to think about it."

The man shook his head sadly. "I knew that if something had happened to Randolph it'd be too late to salvage anything. What I didn't know was how very much I had to lose."

Nineteen

Juliana and Ruark dressed for the ball in silence, the atmosphere heavy with unspoken thoughts.

There was much she wanted to say to her husband, but a sudden reserve seemed to have put a lock on her tongue. Each time she summoned courage to begin a statement of explanation and apology, she'd recall his fury and fall silent. She didn't know how to deal with his disappointment and anger.

Behind the stoic expression on his face, Ruark was filled with confused emotions. He felt shame at having accused Juliana of duplicity, but still, wasn't that exactly what her friendship with his estranged grandfather was?

Meeting his own eyes in the shaving mirror, he had to admit that much of his ire stemmed from jealousy. He'd never forget the way his gut had clenched when he'd seen the portrait of Juliana. Even learning it had been painted with innocent affection couldn't erase those first feelings. He wasn't especially reassured to discover such possessiveness within himself, so how could he explain to Juliana what he didn't understand?

He looked across the room to see her silently struggling with the buttons up the back of her gown. Knowing she'd be too proud to ask his help, he crossed to her side and took over the task.

"Here, I'll do it," he said. She acquiesced, letting her hands fall to her sides.

Ruark silently cursed himself. He hadn't meant for his words to sound so curt. As he fastened the last button, he allowed his hands to stray to her narrow waist. He could feel her warmth beneath the smooth silk, and for an instant his fingers tightened. It would be so easy to turn her toward him, to apologize with kisses and words of love. And yet, a persistent pride simply wouldn't permit it. Sighing harshly, he took his hands from her waist and turned away.

"Ruark," she said in a hesitant voice.

"Yes?"

"If you prefer, we don't have to go to Moorlands tonight."

"I wouldn't dream of changing our plans," he replied, with a grim smile. "I have a special reason to attend your sister's ball." He avoided her eyes. "I wouldn't miss it for the world."

Gravely, she studied his averted face, wondering at the meaning behind his words. It alarmed her to think he might have something dangerous planned.

Before she could summon the courage to question him, he spoke again. "I'll wait downstairs, 'Liana."

She watched him leave the room, shivering in the chill left by his abrupt departure.

She was afraid she knew precisely what Ruark had meant: he was planning to stage a robbery at Moorlands. It would all be so simple. Sometime during the evening, he'd manage to slip away and don his gypsy garb, then return with his men to relieve Spencer's wealthy friends of their jewels and money. In the confusion, no one would notice his absence. Perhaps he was even relying on her assistance should an alibi be needed. After all, that had been a part of their original bargain.

Intuition told her that committing the intended robbery would be far too hazardous. There were too many ways for Ruark to be caught out. In a crowd, there was always the possibility of observant eyes. What if someone noticed Ruark slipping away prior to the holdup? What if someone recognized his face, his rangy build? It was too risky; she had to think of a way to stop him.

With a sinking heart, she realized it would do no good to reason with him. His anger would only make him more rash and reckless. No matter what she said, he'd be more determined than ever to flaunt himself, to punish her by subjecting her to paralyzing fear on his behalf. There was only one way she might be able to ruin his plans.

Quickly she donned her evening cape, then crossed the room to the secret door leading into the tower. Recently, she had laughingly bullied Ruark into showing her how to manipulate the spring that opened it. Now she thanked fate that she had.

With furtive speed, only taking time to light a candle, she ducked into the tower. Laying atop the scarred wooden dresser was the bundle of clothing Ruark wore as the Gypsy Highwayman. Without it, she knew he wouldn't be able to carry out his masquerade. She scooped up the shirt and black trousers, the red cummerbund and flat-brimmed hat, tucking them beneath her arm. Her one chance of thwarting his scheme was to find a secure place to hide his costume. Perhaps she could explain the situation to Essie and conceal the clothing in her room.

She left the tower, closing the door behind her. As she extinguished the candle and set it back on the nightstand, the bedroom door opened and in walked an impatient

Ruark. Guiltily, she turned to face him, grateful for the folds of her cloak which covered the clothes she carried.

"Is something wrong?" he asked. "We don't want to be late."

Struggling to keep her face impassive, she merely nodded and started toward the door. "I'm ready."

As they descended the stairs, Ruark took her elbow in his firm grip and ushered her out through the front door. There was nothing she could do but clutch the clothing beneath her cloak and pray he wouldn't become suspicious.

Blazing with lights, Moorlands was much larger and grander than Quarrystones. A row of glowing lanterns lined the curved drive to the front door and, inside, every room was bathed in the glow of thousands of candles.

After the silent ride in the carriage, Juliana was glad to arrive at her sister's home. Her mind had been churning, and she'd finally devised a plan for concealing the highwayman's costume. As they swept up the front walk to Moorlands, she stopped and exclaimed, "Oh, I've left my reticule in the carriage. It'll only take a moment to get it."

She whirled and flew back down the path. Pulika, the gypsy high up on the driver's seat, had been preparing to move the carriage to the stableyard, but he reined in the horses as she approached. Flinging open the door, she stood on tiptoe to reach inside, stuff the bundle of clothing beneath the seat, and emerge with the purposely forgotten handbag.

She exhaled in relief as she joined Ruark and they mingled with the other guests being received by Spencer and Mariette.

"Good evening, Ruark," Mariette said with a charming smile. Her gaze moved to Juliana, sweeping from her cloud of dark hair to the hem of her gown. "Juli, dear, can you possibly be wearing one of Mother's old gowns?" Her shocked tone carried easily to the couples nearest them.

Juliana felt the color recede from her face and knew she must be ashen. After the talk she and Mariette had shared, she wasn't prepared for such rancor from her sister. She struggled not to let her hurt show.

"It happens to be a favorite of mine," Ruark interjected, placing an arm about Juliana's shoulders. " 'Liana wore it at our wedding and looked so beautiful, I asked her to wear it again tonight."

Juliana cast a quick glance at her husband, gratified that he wasn't too angry with her to intercede on her behalf. He gave her shoulder a firm squeeze before dropping his arm.

"I must agree," said Spencer. "You look lovely, Juliana."

As though irritated that her jibe had been turned to Juliana's advantage, Mariette gave them a frosty smile and transferred her attention to the next guests.

Dodsworth and Eliza Lowell were sitting in the ballroom with a few of their former friends and neighbors. They greeted Juliana warmly and, even in her agitated state, she could see her mother was clearly impressed with Ruark.

Studying him covertly, Juliana had to admit he was exactly the sort of man any mother would choose for a daughter. Naturally his title and supposed family wealth were assets, but not to be overlooked was the fact that he was exceedingly handsome and personable, with correct manners and a genuine interest in those about him.

She found herself thinking that perhaps his recent show of temper and jealousy was a blessing in disguise. It belied the outward perfection of Ruark Hamilton and made him seem more human and vulnerable. For the first time all day, Juliana smiled. Every marriage had its first quarrel and no doubt there would be subsequent ones.

At that moment her father asked her to dance, and she lost sight of her husband as they moved out into the swirl of dancers on the floor.

Ruark stood talking with Eliza Lowell, finding that, despite her quiet manner, she was very little like Juliana. Indeed, she resembled neither of her daughters. She chatted about first one inane thing and then another, causing him to let his mind wander.

He was beginning to be overwhelmed by regret over the argument he'd had with Juliana. Meeting both her parents and seeing their shallow interest in nothing but themselves, gave him an insight into his wife's determination that he should know his grandfather. A close family relationship must seem very desirable to someone who'd never known it. Juliana must think he was willfully throwing away something precious. And perhaps she was right.

Ruark swept the dancers with a gaze that settled upon the slender figure of his wife, smiling at her father as they danced. Seeing her in the pale yellow dress she had worn for their wedding brought a rush of tender memories to his mind.

He swallowed deeply. She was beautiful, but he'd been the first to recognize it. It had been his privilege to prove it to Juliana herself, and now it was no longer a secret. She'd gained enough self assurance to let her true self show, and her outward beauty was only enhanced by genuine inner loveliness. His jealousy was unfounded. He couldn't expect to keep her entirely to himself. That would be as senseless as Juliana wearing only dull, drab clothing and scraping her hair into a tight knot. No, he'd taught her to shine; he had no right to subdue her.

Ruark took a long breath and started across the room to her. He wanted to dance with Juliana, to feel her in his arms and to look into her storm-grey eyes as he found some way to mend the rift between them. He'd only taken two steps when a feminine hand was laid upon his arm and a silky voice sounded close to his ear.

"Ruark, I need to talk to you."

He glanced at Mariette's seductively smiling face. "I was on my way to dance with my wife," he said.

"Don't be difficult," she snapped. "This is important, something you'll want to hear."

Ruark looked back at Juliana and found her questioning eyes upon him. He gave her a small, reassuring smile and returned his attention to Mariette.

"Very well, I'll spare you a few moments."

Mariette's eyes narrowed. "Follow me then. What I have to say can best be said someplace a bit more private."

The last thing he wanted was to be alone with Mariette, but she didn't give him time to object. She walked away, leading him toward the library. Inside the room, she pulled the heavy doors shut and turned to Ruark with a brilliant smile.

"What is it you want?" he asked bluntly.

"I think you know that," she answered evenly, moving closer to him. Her scarlet skirts brushed against his legs and the strong scent of her perfume filled his nostrils. She raised herself on tiptoe and leaned toward him, laying one hand on his shoulder. "I'm still available, just for the asking."

Ruark stepped back slightly. "I'm not interested."

"Really, I'm growing quite weary of your reluctance. But perhaps I've found the perfect means of convincing you to become my lover."

"And what method is that?"

"A very simple one, Ruark. I'm prepared to strike a bargain with you. You make yourself agreeable to me, and I won't tell anyone you're the Gypsy Highwayman."

Ruark's dark eyes showed only a flicker of alarm before he threw back his head and laughed loudly.

"Aren't you carrying things a bit too far this time?"

"I don't think so." She tapped him on the chest with a pointed forefinger. "You are the Gypsy Highwayman, aren't you?"

"You have a vivid imagination."

"Oh, no, it isn't my imagination. I should've recognized you immediately the night you broke in on Spencer's card party. But, to tell the truth, I didn't. It wasn't until the other day that I became certain."

"And what prompted your certainty?" he asked in a casual tone.

"When I dropped in at Quarrystones unexpectedly and saw you wearing an earring, something an ordinary man would never do."

Ruark was silent for a long moment.

"You needn't try to think of plausible excuses, Ruark. I wouldn't believe them. I'm as sure as I need to be that you are the outlaw."

"How can you prove your wild theory? Just because a man happens to sport an earring proves nothing."

"Only gypsy men and effeminate fops wear earrings. God knows, there's nothing effeminate about you." Her daring eyes raked his physique. "But you do have a certain foreign look to you. Some say the highwayman speaks with an Irish brogue, which marks him as an Irish gypsy, something rare in this district. You're an Irish gypsy, aren't you?"

"Why do you think that?"

"Your friend Chavo can be very informative when the incentive is strong enough." She laughed gaily. "And, believe me, I know precisely how to handle Chavo to find out anything I want to know. Do you still think I'm guessing?"

Ruark groaned inwardly. Curse Chavo and his dangerous weakness for this shrew. "So I happen to have gypsy blood. It proves nothing."

"Don't forget how powerful my husband is. All it would take to have you arrested is his suspicion you are the outlaw. The constable at Edensfield owes his position to Spencer and is bound to do his bidding."

"A court will still demand proof," Ruark began, but she held up a hand to silence him.

"Enough quibbling. Are you going to meet my demands or must I call in the constable and have you arrested?"

"My choices are public accusation or adultery with you?"

"Adultery is an ugly word," she replied. "I prefer to think of it as a love affair."

"Love would have no place in any arrangement we might make."

"Ah, so you do consider my offer?" A triumphant gleam lighted her aquamarine eyes.

"Consider and reject it in one split second," he said. "There isn't a strong enough reason on earth to make me do that to 'Liana. If you have sufficient evidence to have me arrested, go ahead."

"You'll regret this, Ruark," she spat. "You want to humiliate me by refusing my offer, but before I'm finished, you and your precious Juliana will suffer the real humiliation."

"Be that as it may, you still have nothing to offer worth the price of blackmail."

She raised her hand and dealt him a resounding slap on the face. A dangerous expression filled his eyes, but he remained motionless.

"You'll pay for that," she muttered, twisting away to

throw open the library door. Before he realized her intention, she called out, "Spencer! Constable Brodie!"

The two men who had obviously been waiting nearby stepped into the room. Ruark quickly decided his best chance was to face them boldly, with a show of confident arrogance.

"What is it, Mariette?" Spencer asked, looking from one to the other of them.

"Arrest this man," Mariette demanded. "Ruark is the gypsy highwayman."

"So your suspicions proved correct, Mrs. Hamilton?" The wiry constable had drawn a loaded pistol from beneath his frock coat and now he pointed it directly at Ruark's broad chest. Through the open door some of the guests saw the action and one or two ladies uttered sharp screams. The constable threw a quick glance at Spencer.

"Your wife invited me here this evening because she suspected the outlaw would be among your guests. That's why I asked you to wait with me outside the library door."

Spencer looked puzzled. "Mariette, are you accusing Ruark of being the Kentish Gypsy?"

"He has all but admitted it to me," she said, eyes flashing. "You're so simple-minded, Spencer, that you don't know evil when you see it."

"Evil?" her husband repeated.

"Ruark has badgered me for some time to have an affair with him. When I steadfastly refused, he became threatening. At first I didn't believe his boast that he was the highwayman, but the other day when I stopped at Quarrystones, he was wearing an earring." She shrugged her slender shoulders. "If you'll recall, the outlaw who robbed us at your card party was a big man, tall and muscular. Do you know of anyone else around here who fits that description so well?"

Spencer shook his head. "I hadn't thought of it, but you have a sound argument."

"Knowing Ruark would make the usual advances toward me tonight, I decided I had to put a stop to this whole thing. I didn't want to hurt Juliana, but what else could I do? He's a criminal who's terrorized all of us far too long."

"Aren't you being rather dramatic, Mariette?" Ruark asked casually. "I doubt there's anyone here who believes I've pressed you to have an affair. Your reputation has become common talk in the area."

"You shut your lying mouth," she cried. "Don't try to ease your own guilt by casting aspersions on me."

"Is this true, Ruark?" Spencer interrupted. "Are you the highwayman?"

"A ridiculous supposition," Ruark stated firmly.

"It's not!" Mariette appealed to the circle of men now standing around her. "It's known that the highwayman is an Irish gypsy. Ruark has already admitted such a heritage to me." She turned to her husband. "We should have guessed the night of the card party. For a man so adept at everything he undertakes, Ruark was strangely amateurish at playing cards. Maybe he was simply anxious about the robbery he had planned for later in the evening. He left early, remember? And the thieves appeared in about the amount of time it would've taken him to change clothes and meet his men. Think how he enjoyed making fools of us."

In the next room, Juliana's discussion with her mother was disrupted as several more guests crowded toward the library. She found herself swept along with them and when she saw Ruark being held at gunpoint, an icy fear gripped her.

"What happened?" she cried. Her father pushed his way to her side, a look of astonishment washing over his blunt features as he took in the scene before them.

"I say, Spence, what's going on here? Why does this fellow have a pistol?"

"There's reason to believe Ruark may be the highwayman who has caused so much trouble all spring."

"What are you talking about? The man's a duke. Why would he need to rob anyone?"

"Who knows why he did it?" remarked the constable. "That's for the courts to discover."

"Gentlemen," interjected Ruark, "might I ask why no evidence has been presented to substantiate this insane allegation?"

"Yes, you must have something to back up such an accusation," Dodsworth Lowell sputtered.

"Mrs. Hamilton recognizes him from the evening their home was robbed," Constable Brodie spoke up.

"Could you be mistaken, Daughter?" Lowell suggested.

Mariette tossed her head. "I'm not. I've been suspicious of Ruark for some time. If the truth were known, he probably came to the ball tonight with the idea of staging another robbery. He knew there would be several wealthy guests here."

Ruark laughed shortly. "Perhaps you'd explain how I intended to manage this somewhat difficult feat?"

"It wouldn't be impossible for someone with your cunning to slip away and, dressed as the gypsy, return to rob our guests. You've done it before, so you should be well-acquainted with Moorlands by now. No doubt your faithful wife would be standing by, ready with an alibi should you need one."

Ruark rounded on her with quiet fury. "Leave Juliana out of this."

Constable Brodie waved the pistol menacingly. "Calm down, Ruark."

"Did you have plans to rob us tonight?" Spencer asked, still looking rather uncertain.

"Of course not," Ruark flared. "Surely you don't believe your wife's wild story?"

"What if it isn't a story?" Mariette asked.

"Then you should be able to produce some sort of evidence to support your theory," he answered. He let his gaze drift toward Juliana and was stricken by the terror in her eyes.

"Very well," Mariette stated, turning to the constable and her husband. "Let's suppose that Ruark is the highwayman, and that he did have plans to stage a robbery this evening. There's something very necessary for his masquerade: the gypsy costume he wears. Wouldn't it be reasonable to assume that costume would be somewhere nearby in readiness for the holdup? I say we should organize a search for it."

"We'd never be able to find something like that," Spencer protested. "There must be a million places he could have hidden it."

"Perhaps," Mariette said with a sly smile, "but remember, he had no opportunity to hide the costume within Moorlands. It must be somewhere on the grounds, somewhere conveniently close to the house. It wouldn't hurt to look."

"What do you say to that, Ruark?" Brodie asked.

Ruark laughed. "I think it's a splendid idea."

"Very well, we'll search the grounds. If we find gypsy gear anywhere near this house, you'll be arrested on suspicion of robbery."

Ruark waved an impatient hand. "Go ahead. I'm telling you, I've nothing to hide."

The constable kept the pistol at Ruark's back as they moved out of the library toward the front hall of the manor house. Spencer and Mariette followed closely, and behind them came an assortment of curious guests.

Juliana's mouth was dry with fear. What if they looked inside the carriage? Ruark had no way of knowing what they'd find there.

"Wait," she cried, but her words were drowned in the excited murmurs. She cast a quick look at her father and knew there'd be no help from that quarter. He was as engrossed in the proceedings as the others.

Juliana was swept along with them, out the front door and down the curving drive. Constable Brodie designated several men to search the stables and grounds, and Spencer ordered one of his servants to bring Ruark's carriage around.

As they waited, Juliana frantically devised and discarded various schemes to distract attention from her husband. If only she could warn him.

She could hardly breathe as she watched Spencer climb into the carriage to begin the inspection. Ruark, confident nothing would be found, stood with arms crossed casually over his chest. Juliana struggled to get through the crowd to him, but found her way blocked immediately by one of the hard-bitten Londoners Spencer had in his employ. One glance at Mariette's smug face told her the whole incident had been well-planned.

Seconds later Spencer emerged from the carriage with the bundle of clothing in his hands. A gasp went up from those standing around and Juliana closed her eyes in despair. She couldn't bear to see Ruark's look of stunned disbelief.

"You must have concealed those things yourself, Mariette," he accused. "I didn't put them there."

"We hardly expect you to admit to it," she sneered, an excited light in her eyes. "But it proves your guilt beyond any doubt."

"It proves nothing," Ruark insisted. "It's a convenient ploy, nothing more."

Spencer shook his head. "Sorry, old man, but I can't support your innocence any longer. Constable Brodie, arrest this man."

Ruark took a step backward in preparation for flight, but two more men with pistols moved into the circle of lantern light and he stopped in defeat. His eyes sought Juliana's as though trying to convey some message.

"Put him in the barn, Constable," Spencer was saying, "and post guards. When your prisoner is secured, I want to talk to you in the library."

"Yes, sir," responded Brodie, suddenly bristling with importance as he gave brusque orders for Ruark to be taken away.

As two more of Spencer's hired hands seized him and began shoving him along in front of them, Ruark cast one last look back at Juliana. She stood in the dim light, eyes glistening with tears.

Oh, my God, she thought, *what have I done?*

"Spencer, I must talk with you," Juliana said, closing the library door behind her.

"Have you come to plead for your outlaw husband?" sneered Mariette. "If so, it won't do you any good."

"Mariette, let her speak," Spencer admonished. "Perhaps Juliana knew nothing of Ruark's activities."

"He's not the highwayman," Juliana firmly pronounced. "You've made a dreadful mistake. I was with him when we left Quarrystones, and he didn't put those clothes in the carriage. Someone is only trying to make him look guilty."

"A likely story," spoke up Mariette, her enjoyment of her sister's agitation evident.

"Do keep quiet, Mariette," scolded Spencer. "Now, Juli, I promise I'll look into the matter thoroughly. Ruark will have to stand trial at the Quarter Sessions, but if he's innocent, he'll be released."

"You can't mean to hold him until then?"

"It's the law. What else can I do?"

"Do you think he's guilty, Spencer?" Juliana asked quietly.

"I'm unsure." He cleared his throat. "It does look bad for him."

She turned to her sister. "Why have you done this, Mariette? Was it because Ruark was the first man who denied you? Is that what prompted your vicious scheme?"

"Why, sister dear, I don't know what you mean. Your husband has made improper advances toward me from the first time we met."

"You're a liar," Juliana said calmly. "He's never shown any interest in you. I believe that's what caused your wrath."

Mariette tossed her head. "Think what you like, but Ruark is going to be branded an outlaw." She came closer. "They hang highwaymen in this country, you know."

"You won't be able to prove anything against him," Juliana countered. "We'll fight this charge and win."

"I seriously doubt it, young woman." The voice came from the shadows where an elderly man was sitting, a glass of brandy in his hand. "Taking your husband's ancestry into consideration, as well as the fact the outlaw costume was found in his possession, I'd say it wouldn't be difficult to convince a jury the man is guilty."

"Juliana," Spencer said, "this is an old friend, Judge Harrison Martin."

"A judge?"

"Yes, and one who knows what he's talking about." Mariette's smile was icy. "Face it, Juli, there's nothing you can do for your beloved husband."

"Isn't there some way to prove his innocence?" Juliana looked from one man to the other.

"Spencer is the one you'll have to convince," Judge Martin said, putting the brandy snifter to his lips. "He's the one with authority to bring your husband to trial. Or to release him. As a Justice of the Peace, it all rests upon his discretion."

"Then would you mind if I spoke with him privately?"

"Not at all," Martin replied, getting to his feet. "But Spencer, don't let this beautiful woman talk you out of doing the right thing." He chuckled. "Whatever that might be." He shuffled toward the door. "By the way, it has been a marvelous party."

Spencer waited until the man was gone before he turned to Mariette, who stood her ground firmly. "Don't you think it would be a good idea for you to check on our guests, my dear? After all, this has been a rather unusual evening, to say the least."

"I won't leave you alone with Juli," she said. "If I know you, a few tears and a pretty plea or two will have you relenting and letting Ruark go free."

"Come now, Mariette, give me credit for some intelligence. Besides, I owe it to Juliana to hear her out. She is family, you know."

"All right, listen to her whining, if you must. But I warn you, you'll be making the mistake of your life if you release Ruark." With those venomous words, Mariette swept angrily from the room.

Spencer motioned to the leather chair in front of a large

desk. "Sit down, Juliana. Can I get you something to drink? You look very pale."

"No, nothing, thank you. I'm only worried about Ruark. What will happen to him now?"

Spencer perched his stocky frame on the edge of the desk and leaned toward her. "If he's innocent, as you claim, he'll be found so and freed." He spread his hands. "If not, there's very little I can do."

"You heard what Judge Martin said. As a Justice of the Peace, you have the authority to hold Ruark for trial or let him go. I'm asking you to please release him. I'll do anything if you'll only let him go home with me."

Spencer was clearly embarrassed. "No need for histrionics, Juli."

"Oh, but there is. I saw how easily the situation was turned against him tonight. It wouldn't be any different at a trial. Mariette has decided he must be punished for whatever purpose, and everyone else will agree because they want the highwayman caught. It isn't important to them that they have the right man. They'll want to make an example of Ruark. Spencer, you can't let that happen."

Spencer frowned. "What do you expect of me?"

"Use your influence to free him."

"And what do I get in return?"

"I'll find a way to make it worth your while," she promised desperately.

"Oh?"

She took a deep breath. "Spencer, when we were to be married, you were anxious to gain possession of Quarrystones." She looked down at her hands, clasped in her lap. When she looked up again, her eyes were bright with unshed tears. "If you drop the charges against Ruark, I'll sign Quarrystones over to you."

He sat back in surprise. "Why would you do that after all this time?"

"Because it's the only thing I have to bargain with," she replied honestly.

"Not necessarily, Juli." He leaned back in his chair and studied her. "Recently, I've had occasion to regret my hasty marriage to your sister. As I've watched you emerge a beautiful, as well as intelligent woman, I've often berated myself for throwing you over." He leaned forward across the desktop, close enough to lift a strand of her dark hair. "I wonder just how willing you'd be to bargain for your husband's life."

Juliana drew back. "I've already told you I'm willing to let you have Quarrystones."

"I'm afraid that's not enough to persuade me. Should your husband be convicted of his crimes, ownership of the estate will go to the Crown, and the Crown always rewards its most devoted servants."

"You'll have Quarrystones one way or another, won't you?" Juliana's voice trailed away. She felt as if her veins were filled with ice.

"There is another way you could help Ruark," he reminded her. "You may not have a home to bargain with, but you do have something in which I'm even more interested."

She met his appraising eyes with a level gaze. "What are you suggesting?"

"I think," said Mariette from the doorway, "that my esteemed husband is proposing a liaison between the two of you. Am I right, Spencer darling? Is that what you want? Juliana in your bed, at your beck and call?"

Spencer flushed. "Eavesdropping is not a particularly appealing habit, Etta."

"No, but a very enlightening one. Well, Juli, are you going to accept my husband's offer?"

"Don't be ridiculous," Juliana retorted.

"Then I fear he'll be of no assistance to you."

Juliana turned her back on her sister, concentrating her attention on the man before her. "Will you help me or not, Spencer?"

He shrugged. "There really isn't anything I can do."

"Then I have to tell you something that may influence the way you think."

"And what's that?"

"Ruark is your cousin," she stated simply. "He's the son of your Uncle Randolph."

Spencer looked appalled. "Randolph's son? Are you sure?"

"Yes. His mother is the gypsy woman Sara."

"My God, I never even suspected."

"You must reconsider. You can't send your own kinsman to the gallows."

"This definitely changes everything," Spencer said thoughtfully.

"Then you'll help him?"

"Give me time to think it over, Juliana. I'm rather taken aback by this news."

"Can't you release him tonight?"

"I don't want to be hasty. As a Justice of the Peace, I have more than myself to consider. Come back in the morning, and I'll give you my decision then."

Juliana breathed a tentative sigh of relief. "Please do the right thing, Spencer. I'm counting on your integrity."

"And I'm counting on his greed." Pulling a pink carnation from a bouquet on the library table, Mariette put the flower to her nose.

Tendrils of fear gripped Juliana again. "What do you mean?"

"Spencer may not have grasped the gravity of the situation yet." She faced her husband. "If Ruark is your Uncle Randolph's son, that means he's the legal heir to Moorlands. He won't be so easily handled as your grandfather."

Spencer's eyes narrowed speculatively.

"What better way to get rid of Ruark," Mariette continued, "than to have him convicted and hung as a highwayman?"

"You can't let Mariette talk you into misusing your position as a Justice," Juliana insisted. "You have a legal duty to be fair and impartial."

Spencer's smile was chilling. "And so I shall be, Juli."

"Now go home and leave us in peace," Mariette said. "We don't want you here anymore."

Juliana faced her sister, hands curled into fists to keep from entangling themselves in the cascade of perfect curls that graced her bare shoulders. "I wanted so much to believe you had some decency in you," she murmured. "After our talk at Quarrystones, I thought things would be different."

"How could talking change anything?"

"I thought we understood each other, that we'd settled all the old scores." She gave a short, mirthless laugh. "I'd hoped we could be friends for once in our lives."

"I don't want to be your friend, Juliana."

"I see that now. But even so, how could you do this terrible thing to Ruark?"

"You know the reasons as well as I do."

"Because he didn't want you?" Juliana whispered in dismay. "Because of childhood jealousies we should put behind us?"

"Don't be naive, sister dear. I may have told you why I act as I do, but I never promised to change. And even if I wanted to, it's too late. I've grown very accustomed to having my own way."

"Enough to destroy anyone who resists you?"

"Yes, exactly." Mariette stifled a bored yawn. "Good night, Juliana."

The library door was shut in Juliana's face, leaving her no choice but to go home.

Home, she realized, to a house as dark and silent as death without the presence of the man she'd come to love more dearly than life itself.

Twenty

Juliana paced the floor of her bedchamber, unable to sleep. She thought of Ruark and worried about his welfare. She'd tried to see him before leaving Moorlands, but the constable had refused to allow it.

She was haunted by the confusion she knew Ruark must be feeling. She'd have to tell him of her own guilt in hiding the gypsy clothing in the carriage, and after their earlier quarrel, he might not be able to forgive her.

She curled up in the window seat and looked out over the river. A fine, drizzling rain had soaked the lawn, and curling fingers of mist all but obliterated the watery moon. As she watched, a dark figure emerged from the shadows to toss a handful of small pebbles at the leaded panes.

"Who is it?"

On a gust of wet wind, she heard the faint reply. "Chavo. I must talk to you."

"I'll come down," she called softly, shutting the window.

Suddenly she was filled with the fear that something had happened to Ruark. She prayed silently as she raced down the stairs to the back door.

As soon as Chavo stepped into the kitchen, she grasped his arm. "Is something wrong with Ruark?" she cried.

"No."

She let out a trembly sigh of relief. "Thank God."

As her heartbeat slowed, she reached for the flint and a candle. The flickering light revealed Chavo's damp, disheveled appearance. His dusky face was anxious.

Fear gripped her once more. "Something is wrong! For heavens sake, tell me."

"They lashed him," Chavo burst out, his black eyes blazing. "That witch used a whip on him and no one stopped her."

"Mariette? But why?"

"He refused to answer the constable's questions and then, when he accused Mariette, she grabbed a whip and struck him with it. They just stood there and let her do it."

Juliana was filled with a fury of emotions, her fear for Ruark battling with a sudden, unrelenting loathing for her sister. "How badly is he hurt?" she asked in a quiet voice.

"She only struck him three or four times. He says he's unharmed and made me swear not to tell you about it."

"I'm so grateful you did, though."

"I did not swear lightly," he assured her. "But I thought you had the right to know."

"Thank you. Will you take me to him?"

"Wait," he cautioned. "I have more to tell you."

Juliana steadied herself. "Go on."

"After you left Moorlands, Mariette came to me with a bargain."

Juliana shivered. "Yes?"

The young gypsy stared down at the floor, hunching his shoulders uneasily. "She has convinced her husband that it would be best to rid themselves of Ruark."

"Because they learned from me that he's the rightful heir to Moorlands." She looked stricken. "It seems each thing I do only hurts him more."

"Don't blame yourself. Everything you've done has been out of love for him. If only I could say the same."

Alarmed, she asked, "What is it you've done?"

"I believed I was the one Mariette loved and wanted. But I was a fool. Tonight I discovered she was only using me to make Ruark jealous."

"My sister is very selfish. I'm sorry for you, Chavo. Sorry for all of us."

"She doesn't yet know I've realized the truth. She offered me money, as well as her continued favors, to take part in her plan to destroy Ruark."

"Destroy?" Juliana whispered. "What do you mean?"

"Just that. They're going to kill him."

She groaned, a desolate sound in the otherwise silent kitchen.

"They are afraid either the gypsies or the tenant farmers will march on Moorlands and demand Ruark's release. The old judge suggested they move him into Edensfield to the lock-up, and then, as soon as possible, on to London for trial. But Spencer and Mariette have a plan to assure Ruark never arrives in Edensfield alive."

"What are they going to do?"

"Mariette wants me to stage a rescue attempt somewhere along the road to town. Myself and Pulika are to stop the coach and demand Ruark's release. They'll pretend to comply out of fear, but as we ride away, the coachman will shoot Ruark in the back."

"Oh, God!"

"It will all come down to a criminal attempting to escape. Everyone's problems will be solved."

"I don't understand why Mariette came to you for help. Surely she knows you've always been Ruark's best friend."

"That's how certain she is of my loyalty." The expression

on his face was pained. "And lately I have been less than a friend to Ruark."

"In what way?"

"I've been careless enough to tell her things she wanted to know." He shook his head sadly. "All because I needed to please her."

Juliana laid a hand on his arm. "You're not the first to fall victim to my sister's deceit."

"And I doubt I'll be the last," he said bitterly. "To my eternal shame, I tried to prevent Ruark from marrying you. I told him he was mad to take such a wife, a country mouse who brought him no dowry. But many times he told me you were beautiful, that you meant more to him than anything."

"He said that?"

Chavo smiled briefly. "That and more. Now I know what he meant, for since your marriage, you are beautiful. And unlike your sister, your beauty lies not only in your face, but in your spirit as well."

"It means a great deal to hear you say that. It troubled me that you didn't like me. I thought I'd done something to offend you."

"No, you've never acted against me." He bowed his head again. "I wish I'd treated you as kindly. I brought the painting to Ruark, knowing it would cause trouble between you. I sorely regret my action."

Juliana touched his hand. "That really doesn't matter now. We have to think of some way to rescue Ruark."

"He knows nothing of the plot against his life."

"Then I don't think we should tell him about it. It would only be one more thing to worry him."

"I agree."

"When are they moving him?"

"In the morning. They want to get him away from Moorlands before anyone learns what is happening. I'm to meet them on the road to Edensfield."

"How can we keep them from murdering him?" she questioned. "There has to be a way."

"I've decided I must shoot the assassin before he has a chance to kill Ruark."

"And then?"

"We'll be forced into hiding. It may never be safe to show our faces again."

"As long as Ruark is saved, that's not important. Perhaps we can slip away to Ireland, or someplace farther, if need be."

"You'd go with him then?" Chavo asked with a half-smile.

"Only to the ends of the earth," she vowed fiercely.

"As he has told me so often, my friend is a lucky man."

"I hope his luck holds until we can ruin my sister's plan."

"We?"

"I'm going with you tomorrow morning."

"No, it would be too dangerous."

"I don't care about that," she said. "I want to be there."

"I cannot do as you ask."

"What if something goes wrong? What if he should need me?"

"Ruark himself would never allow such a foolhardy thing."

"He won't know about it until it's all over," she reasoned. "I have to go, Chavo."

He started to voice another protest, but she rushed on. "I won't be in the way, I promise. I know how to ride and shoot. I'll dress as one of your men and no one will even notice me."

"You'd be risking your life."

"Do you think I care about that?" The corners of her

mouth rose in a solemn smile. "Without Ruark, what would it be worth anyway?"

Chavo inclined his head as if acknowledging the wisdom of her statement. "Very well then."

"For now, I want to change into a warmer gown and ride back to Moorlands."

"They may not let you see Ruark," the gypsy warned.

"I'll think of something. Even beg Spencer, if necessary."

"I'll saddle your horse while I wait," Chavo said, vanishing into the dark of night again.

The misted forest dripped with rain and the only light came from the lantern Chavo held aloft. Shivering despite the old cloak she wore, Juliana slipped her free hand into the deep pocket to warm it. As she did so, her fingers encountered something rough.

She withdrew her hand and held the object to the feeble light. Her breath caught in her throat and tears stung behind her eyelids. She was holding the dried bit of gorse Ruark had plucked and presented to her the day they'd met. She'd barely worn the cloak since that time, and had forgotten she'd slipped the sprig into her pocket. Looking at its dusty yellow blossoms, she was filled with remembrance of a day that now seemed so far in the past.

She'd been unhappy and angry then, so preoccupied with her own misery that she'd never dreamed she faced a man she'd soon grow to love. He'd been so arrogant and sure of himself, swapping favors for kisses. A smile twitched at her lips as she recalled her own haughty refusal to kiss the gypsy highwayman.

Now, only short months later, she'd sell her soul for the chance to kiss him again. In spite of the rain and darkness, she urged her horse forward, impatient to see Ruark and tell him how very much she loved him.

As they rode into the stableyard, Juliana could see the armed guards posted at the door to the barn. One of the men signaled them to a halt and snarled, "Who are you and what do you want?"

"I'm the prisoner's wife. I've brought food and medicine for him."

"And a firearm or two, I'll wager," he sneered.

"All I have with me is this basket of food," she said calmly. "And a handful of gold coins for you."

"Are you offering me a bribe?" The outrage of his question was tempered by the avaricious expression that sprang into his eyes.

"Don't think of it as a bribe," Juliana remarked. "Let's say it's a reward for permitting a distraught wife to comfort her husband."

She tossed him the small bag that contained the coins, and he hefted it in the palm of his hand. "It's all I could scrape together," she hastily assured him. "You'll have to take it or leave it."

"Give me the basket," he commanded, stuffing the coin bag beneath his overcoat. When she held it out, he seized it and rifled through its contents.

"Looks safe enough," he finally said. "You can get down from your horse."

Juliana dismounted, handing the reins to Chavo. "I'll be all right," she stated. "Why don't you find a warm place to wait?"

"I'll be nearby in the stable. If you need me, call out."

"Thank you, Chavo. For everything."

He gave her an encouraging smile before leading the horses away. When he had gone, she squared her shoulders and addressed the sentry. "Can I go inside now?"

The man shrugged. "I'll have to search you first." He returned the basket, then ran rough hands over her body beneath the cloak, an amused leer on his whiskered face. Juliana bit her lower lip and stood impassively, knowing it was the only way she'd be allowed to see Ruark.

"You're not carrying a weapon," the man affirmed. "But it pains me to see such pretty company wasted on a damned outlaw." His calloused hand caressed her cheek, but she pulled away, struggling to control her anger.

"Let me pass, or I'll go up to the house and wake Spencer. He won't condone you insulting his sister-in-law."

"Even if I tell him you bribed me?"

"Aw, let her be," the other guard spoke up. "No sense in asking for trouble."

"You're right. I won't have any problem finding a woman more suited to me, anyway."

With a harsh laugh, he patted the coins in his pocket and gave her a broad wink. Pushing open one of the wooden doors, he indicated she was free to enter.

Her first glimpse of the scene before her tore at her heart and she uttered a cry of disbelief. Ruark was chained.

The faint glimmer of lantern light illuminated the corner where he was sitting in the loose hay. Metal bracelets encircled each wrist and heavily forged chains stretched into the shadows to brackets high on the wall, pulling his arms away from either side of his body. Each muscle stood out, painfully taut.

"Ruark," she cried, dropping the basket to kneel in front of him. "What have they done to you?"

Her arms went around his bare torso and she was instantly aware of his flinch of pain. "Your back," she murmured, feeling the deep weals beneath her hands. "Damn them!"

Ruark smiled faintly. " 'Tis of no concern, 'Liana. Are you all right?"

"Only worried about you."

He gave her a crooked smile. "There's no need to be."

"Chavo told me that Mariette struck you with a whip. Who let her do such a thing?"

"It doesn't matter."

"Oh, it matters to me." She slipped off her cloak and tossed it aside. "Are you cold? Where are your shirt and coat?"

"They removed my coat when they chained me. My shirt was torn by the whip—"

"And I ripped it away with my own two hands," came a sneering voice from the doorway. Mariette stood there, hands on hips. "It was a hindrance, you see. I hoped to inflict more damage without its protection."

She sauntered closer to them. "It's such a pity my weak-kneed husband had to stop me."

"Why have you come back?" Juliana asked.

"I didn't bring my whip this time, if that's what you mean." Mariette's chin went up. "But it'd be no more than he deserves. Your husband stole valuable property from me, don't forget."

"Do you honestly believe Ruark is the highwayman?" Juliana rose to her feet to face her sister.

"I can't believe he fooled us as long as he did. And after I knew for certain, I decided it was time the masquerade ended. Ruark was to be found out tonight, one way or another."

"One way or another?" Juliana repeated.

"It was a stroke of luck he grew careless enough to hide his gypsy garb in the carriage. It made it quite unnecessary for the constable to discover the clothes I'd so conveniently left in the stable."

"No wonder you were so sure of yourself," Ruark remarked.

Mariette moved closer to the chained man, surveying him with an amused smile. "My, it does seem strange to see the arrogant Ruark Hamilton so humbled. Who'd have thought my big, bold brother-in-law could look so pathetic?" She put out a hand to stroke his face, but Juliana moved quickly to grasp her wrist.

"Leave him alone."

"How dare you touch me," snapped Mariette, twisting free of Juliana's hold.

"I'm not going to stand quietly by and let you mock him." Juliana's eyes smoldered dangerously. "You've done enough to hurt him."

"What have I done?"

"I know you've pursued Ruark from the first."

"That's a lie," Mariette hissed. "He's hounded me, begging for my favors. He should never have married someone who doesn't know the first thing about pleasing him."

"Ruark's pursuit of you is only a figment of your diseased imagination."

"It's the truth! Why don't you ask Ruark what happened the day he lured me up to your bedroom while you were gone?"

"I already know. When I came home to the stench of your perfume in my bedchamber, I didn't need an explanation. I knew precisely what had happened. I trust my husband, Mariette. You're the liar."

Uttering a cry of anger, Mariette flew at her, hands curved into talons. Ruark cried out a warning, but Juliana had already stepped aside. She stuck out a foot to trip Mariette and send her sprawling in the hay.

"I hate you, Juli," she screamed, tears forming in her eyes. "I always have."

"I'm sorry you feel that way."

Mariette staggered to her feet. "I'll never forgive you for tricking me into marrying Spencer. You've been laughing behind my back all this time, haven't you?"

"You made the decision to marry Spencer before I knew anything about it. You're a grown woman, Etta. Don't you think it's time you stopped deluding yourself and faced the truth? You can't go on blaming other people for the things you do."

"But you are to blame. You've always been the cause of my misery."

"You bring about your own problems," Juliana admonished. "I think you know that."

"No!" Mariette flung herself at Juliana, clawing fingers catching in the neck of her gown, tearing it downward. Thin scratches on Juliana's neck welled with blood.

Stumbling backward under the onslaught of Mariette's attack, Juliana struck out. She landed a stinging blow to Mariette's face, causing her to begin chanting, "I hate you, hate you, hate you."

It seemed Mariette had gone mad, and her madness only made her stronger. She shoved Juliana against one of the stalls and, with a triumphant cry, snatched up a pitchfork leaning nearby.

Hearing Ruark's warning shout, Juliana dodged the

wicked tines that were driven into the wood where her face had been a split-second before. Seeing that Mariette was unable to pull the deeply embedded pitchfork free, Juliana sprang at her, knocking her to the floor.

Mariette's blond hair was matted with straw and manure, her nose streaming blood down the front of her ruined evening gown. Crouched and panting like a cornered wild creature, she began screaming.

The door burst open and the two guards ran into the barn, followed immediately by Chavo and Dodsworth Lowell.

"What on earth is happening?" shouted Lowell.

"She tried to kill 'Liana," Ruark told him. "Get her out of here."

"Yes, take Mariette away, Father," Juliana instructed, her breath coming in gasps. "She's caused more than enough grief."

"Are you hurt?" Lowell approached Juliana, but she held out a hand and backed away.

"I'm fine, but I don't want your concern now. Not when you stood by and let Spencer have Ruark arrested."

"See here, Daughter, there was a reason for that."

"Of course. You thought Spencer would be the victor in this particular battle and you wanted to align yourself with the winning side."

"You'll not speak to me that way, Juliana," Lowell began. He was interrupted by a sudden roar of anger.

"Take your slut of a daughter and get out of here, Lowell." Edward Hamilton strode through the door and into the center of the fray. He drew himself up to his full height and, putting an arm about Juliana's shoulders, glared at the man before him. "Mariette has caused enough trouble. If she isn't restrained, I'll hold you personally responsible."

Lowell pulled Mariette to her feet, releasing her grimy

hands with a look of distaste. "Come, Mariette. Your husband is the one to sort out this matter."

Mariette turned to Juliana. "I'm sorry I didn't kill you. I meant to, you know."

"Get out of here!" Edward bellowed. "Guards, see that no one else is allowed inside this barn tonight. My grandson and his wife want to be alone, do you understand?"

The guards shifted their feet and looked at each other. Finally one of them dared to say, "We take our orders from Spencer Hamilton."

"I don't give a glorious goddamn if you do. I'm not dead yet, and that means I'm still Duke of Hawkhurst. Do as I say or I'll see that you regret it. As for Spencer, let me handle him. I've put some things off for too damned long."

The guards shrugged and left the barn. Edward watched as Lowell and Mariette followed them, then turned to Juliana and said, "Will you be all right, my dear?"

Her eyes shone with pride. "Yes, Edward, we'll be fine. Thank you for coming to our aid."

"I've been watching Mariette since I heard what she did to Ruark. When she left the house again, I knew she was up to no good. Damn these worthless legs of mine, they kept me from getting here in time to stop her attack on you."

"But you came, that's what counts."

"Yes." Ruark's admission was somewhat reluctant. "If you hadn't interrupted, there's no way to know what Mariette would have done next. I don't know when I've ever felt so damned helpless." His eyes met and held those of his grandfather. "Thank you."

Edward stepped forward to rest a hand on Ruark's shoulder. "I'm enraged at the way Spencer has treated you. I'm going to demand he remove these chains."

"It's only for one night. Spencer's moving me to Edensfield tomorrow to await trial."

"That worries me," Edward said. "I don't trust either Spencer or his wife."

"I know," Ruark agreed. "But once I'm in the constable's custody, I should be safe enough until I'm tried."

"If Spencer wanted you in the constable's care, why didn't he send you with him earlier tonight?" Edward rubbed a hand over his eyes. "Something's wrong."

"You think he's only bluffing, then? That he's not really taking me to jail?"

"I'm not sure Spencer would risk you standing trial and possibly being acquitted. You're a member of the aristocracy, and he knows that's a class not often punished for its sins. Even if you were found guilty, you might only receive a rap on the knuckles. No, I suspect Spencer would prefer something more permanent than that."

"There's no sense in endless speculation," Juliana broke in. "We'll simply have to deal with matters as they arise. Right now, Ruark's more in need of food and medicine." She didn't want to reveal what she knew of Spencer's plans. The night ahead would be long and uncomfortable enough for Ruark without the added awareness of the danger he was in. She reached for the basket she'd dropped earlier. "I brought some of Essie's balm for your injuries."

"I'll go now," Edward said, "and try to talk some sense into Spencer. When I leave, bar the door from the inside. No one will disturb you."

"Have a care when you approach Spencer." Ruark's dark eyes held genuine concern. "He isn't going to take kindly to your interference."

"I realize that, and I'll be careful. Let me know when

you're ready to return to Quarrystones, Juliana, and I'll accompany you."

"There's no need for that," Chavo spoke up. He'd been standing by quietly; now he stepped forward from the shadows. "I'll wait and see her safely home."

"Very well. I'll come to Quarrystones in the morning, and we'll make our plans then."

Again, Juliana avoided mention of the plot against Ruark. She couldn't think of any good reason to involve Edward just yet.

"I'm glad you came to see Ruark." She gave his gnarled hand an affectionate squeeze. "It's nice that the two of you are finally speaking."

Edward and Ruark exchanged vaguely sheepish smiles.

"We'll talk more later," Ruark told her. "It's time we did."

"Your husband is a fine lad, Juli, though I know I don't have to tell you that." Edward patted her shoulder fondly. "Comfort each other now, and I'll see you tomorrow."

When Edward and Chavo had gone, Juliana barred the door behind them. She then went back to Ruark, dropping to her knees to put her arms about his waist. She rested her head on his shoulder and he turned his face to kiss her temple.

"God, I've never felt more useless in my life," he groaned. "Mariette could have killed you."

"Shh, it's all right." She drew back and said, "I sometimes wonder if she has gone mad. It's the only thing that explains her actions."

"I certainly could believe I saw madness in her eyes when she was holding that pitchfork."

They fell silent again, remembering the fearful scene. Finally, after a few minutes, Ruark said, "Mariette told me you offered Quarrystones to Spencer in return for my release." His obsidian eyes softened as they moved over her face. "I know you love your home more than anything in the world, 'Liana. Why would you give it up?"

"Do you have to ask?" A smile trembled on her lips. "You know, your grandfather once said that it's people who are important, not places. It was a lesson, he told me, that he learned painfully. At the time, I wasn't sure I understood what he was talking about. Back then I didn't think anything could be as precious to me as Quarrystones. I nearly worshiped its very stones."

He grinned. "I remember."

"But you came back from Ireland and before I knew it, I'd learned the same lesson as Edward. Though in a much more pleasant way." She leaned forward to brush his lips with her own. "You're more important to me than any mere house could ever be."

"I never expected to hear you say that, love. Nor did I imagine you'd sacrifice Quarrystones for any reason."

"I'm only sorry my efforts failed."

Ruark's expression grew more serious. " 'Liana, why didn't you tell me you knew Mariette had been in our bedchamber?"

"It didn't seem worthy of making a scene over," she answered gently. "Oh, I'll admit, I was furious at first."

A corner of his mouth lifted in a smile. "I'm glad you didn't keep quiet simply because you didn't care."

"No, I cared very much. The old jealousy was right there waiting to get a grip on me. But I forced myself to think rationally. The way you greeted me when I returned from Edensfield that day, the words you spoke—I knew you were asking for my trust. I also realized you didn't make accusations against my sister because you thought it would hurt me. As soon as I analyzed the situation, I guessed what must have happened. And, Ruark, I trusted you."

"Thank you," he said. "Though I feel like an ass for not returning that trust when I saw your portrait. I'm sorry my jealousy overcame my good sense."

She bowed her head. "Tonight may have proven me unworthy of your trust, after all."

"Tonight?"

"Please understand, I didn't mean to hurt you." She hunched her shoulders. "Actually, I was trying to help."

"What are you saying?"

Taking a deep breath, she confessed, "I put those clothes into our carriage."

When she dared to meet his eyes, she could see he was puzzled. "But why?"

"You'd made that comment about not missing Mariette's ball for the world, that you had a special reason for going. I knew immediately you'd planned a robbery and it terrified me. So I decided to keep you from acting as the highwayman by hiding your clothing. How ironic that by doing so, I caused you to be arrested."

"Why put them in the carriage, of all places?"

"I'd just come from the tower with them when you walked into the bedroom, impatient to be on our way. I had them under my cloak then, and there was nothing else I could do."

"Well, you couldn't have known Mariette would be devious enough to set her own trap." His smile was wry. "Or that I'd be so confident as to tell them to search wherever they pleased. It's almost comical."

"No, it's not," she exclaimed. "Look at the result of my

interference. You're chained in this barn like a common criminal."

"Sweetheart, I *am* a common criminal. I knowingly became one the day I first posed as the Kentish Gypsy. Don't blame yourself for what happened. It was a possibility from the start."

"I hate being the one who put you into this situation."

"If you hadn't acted in my best interest, things might have been worse. I did intend to rob the guests at Moorlands, so something even more drastic might have happened. Mariette had already alerted the constable, remember."

"I can't believe you were willing to take such a chance."

"I thought I'd planned it out so carefully. But who knows? Your innocent ploy may have saved me from a worse fate. Mariette might have hoped I'd be shot during the robbery attempt, as that would have been simpler and more effective than a trial."

"Still, I feel terribly guilty."

"Why should you, when certain others show no remorse? For example, my good friend Chavo."

"So you realize his part in all this?"

"Mariette made certain of it."

"What you may not know is that Chavo is truly suffering for what he did. He won't let Mariette influence him again. Don't blame him too much."

"In a sense, it's my fault Mariette chose him for her victim anyway."

"What do you mean?"

"It's not important. Could we discuss the food and wine you brought?"

"Sorry, I'd nearly forgotten." She uncovered the basket and took out a bottle of Will-John's homemade wine and several slices of buttered bread wrapped in a linen cloth.

"I hate seeing you like this," she said, lifting a cup of the wine to his lips. "Why on earth did they put you in chains?"

"It was another way to humiliate me," he stated. "I have two formidable enemies in your sister and her husband."

Juliana fed him bread and cheese and sips of the wine, relieved to see color returning to his face. When he declared he'd had enough to eat, she packed the remainder of the food away in the basket and brought out a jar of sweet balm.

"Let me put some of this salve on your back," she said. "We've used this for every kind of injury since we were children."

With an effort, Ruark got to his knees and, kneeling close behind him, Juliana examined his wounds. There were three lash marks across the breadth of his back, and one that curled upward to the side of his neck. She caught her breath.

"Damn Mariette! I wish I'd used a whip on her."

"I'm amazed at your ferocity, 'Liana." He forced a chuckle, though his body stiffened at her first touch of the cuts on his back.

With gentle fingers she massaged the marred flesh, smoothing fragrant balm along ridged shoulder muscles and down the corded length of his torso. Tenderly, she followed the line of each weal, covering it with a liberal amount of the herbal salve.

"That feels good, sweetheart," he murmured, his body warming and relaxing beneath her soothing touch. "You've taken away the sting."

She ducked under his arm and knelt in front of him. Dipping her fingers into the jar again, she carefully spread more of the medicine along the side of his neck where the lash had cut, stopping just short of his face. Thinking of the damage Mariette might have done, she felt weak.

"Right now it would be easy to hate Mariette."

"I regret being the cause of that," he said softly.

"It's not your fault. My relationship with my sister was never especially cordial."

Her fingers continued their soothing, circular motion, moving along his collarbone and down onto the planes of his chest. The curled black hairs growing there felt rough to her touch. She could discern the steady beat of his heart, see the throbbing pulse at the base of his neck. She leaned closer and put her lips to the sensitive point. A faint moan sounded deep within his throat.

Her fingers stroked and tenderly kneaded the bunched muscles of his arms. "Are you in pain?" she queried.

As her massaging hands moved toward his manacled wrists, her body pressed against his bare chest. His face close to hers, Ruark whispered, "The only pain comes from not being able to put my arms around you and hold you close. It scares me to think I might never experience that again."

"Shh." She placed her mouth against his to stop the words she didn't want to hear.

Her softly insistent lips seemed to kindle a flame deep within him, and his sensually molded mouth opened beneath hers. She used the tip of her tongue to trace its inner contours, delighting in the shudder that racked his lean frame.

" 'Liana, this is the worst torture I've ever had to endure."

She leaned back to look into his face, letting her errant hands stroke downward along his arms to his shoulders, then further, to his rib cage.

"A kiss from your wife—torture?" she teased.

"Aye, torture," he confirmed. "Thinking of making love to you takes my mind away from worry, yet such a thing is impossible with me chained as I am."

"I'm not chained," she softly reminded him.

She slid her arms about his waist and strained against

his body once more, feeling his tightly muscled thighs compressing her own. This time she placed a searing trail of kisses upward along his jaw, her breath hot in his ear as she whispered, "I love you, Ruark. And I'll comfort you in the best way I know."

"Now? In this place?"

"Why not?" she whispered huskily. "It wouldn't be the first time we've made love in a barn."

His laugh rumbled deeply. "No, it wouldn't."

It pleased her to be the aggressor for once. As she used her mouth and hands to rouse him to an impassioned state, she reveled in the knowledge she could so move him. Seeing and feeling his response to her advances only confirmed his declarations of love. It was sweetly thrilling to know he wanted her, that she could, for a small space of time, make him forget his dismal plight.

She knelt before him, allowing him to place warm, tingling kisses along her neck and into the hollow between her breasts. She glanced down at her torn gown, then began unlacing it to give his lips further access to her body. He kissed the scratches left by Mariette's nails, then moved downward to let his mouth caress the rounded sides of each breast, before dipping his head to capture first one tightened nipple and then the other, with gently teasing lips and teeth.

Her loosened gown slipped from her shoulders, bunching around her waist. Close to her ear, Ruark murmured, "You're lovely, sweetheart. I adore you."

Ruark's words, with their thin edge of desperation, increased her boldness. With no hint of shyness, she got to her feet and slipped off the gown, a hand on his shoulder to balance herself as she carefully stepped from the folds of fabric. Tossing it aside, she slowly removed her petticoat and chemise, never taking her eyes from his face.

As he watched her motions, a muscle twitched in one lean jaw and his gypsy eyes flamed hotly. His breath was ragged, his chest heaving with the effort of his breathing. Seeing such enormous energy held in restraint made Juliana think of a wild jungle cat, anxious to be unleashed and free. He looked dangerously violent, but she felt no fear. Now completely naked, she stepped close to him and placed her arms about his neck, bending to lay her head against his.

Ruark touched his lips to her satiny skin, burying his face in the sweetness of her. His warm breath created delicious spirals of sensation, moving along her spine and bringing a liquid weakness to her knees. She slid downward against his body and wrapped her arms about him, covering his mouth with a passionate kiss that left them both breathless.

As her kisses became deeper and more ardent, she let her hands stray to the waistband of his trousers. As the garment was loosened and her wayward fingers stroked the curve of his naked buttocks, she could feel the jolt of desire that rocked his entire body. He muttered a short Romany phrase and, though his words were strange to her ears, his meaning was clear.

Juliana fit her body to his, welcoming and warming him. Locked together, they gave their passions free rein, each thinking only to please and satisfy the other, and in so doing, finding an intense mutual pleasure.

Their world became the circle of lantern light within the dusty confines of the barn. The only sounds were their love-murmurs to each other and the rasp of their excited breathing. Their shadows moved erotically on the wall behind them, duplicating their frenzied quest for ecstasy.

As they reached the heights of pleasure and their joy burst around them like stars exploding in the black night, they stifled each other's cries with tender kisses.

Still intimately entwined, Juliana stroked the small of her husband's back, feeling the moistness of his perspiration beneath her fingers. "I love you, Ruark," she declared. "I love you so much."

"And I love you, 'Liana. Thank you for tonight. No matter what happens tomorrow, we'll always have this memory to hold onto."

Later, as Juliana crept through the mist-filled night to find Chavo and return to Quarrystones, there was only one thought in her mind.

She recalled the gypsy woman at the May Fair and the prediction she'd made. Her words seemed to thunder in the darkness: "You'll have to be strong, for there will be a time when you must protect your man. When danger threatens, you're his only salvation."

Juliana shivered in the chill night air. No matter the cost, she couldn't let Ruark die. He was good and decent and caring; the world had great need for a man like him.

She smiled faintly. And so did she. After knowing the sweetness of his love, she could never live without it. Nor would she want to.

Twenty-one

The horses pranced nervously, starting at each sound. They didn't seem to understand why their riders were idling there among the beech saplings that crowned the hill.

Chavo leaned forward in the saddle and strained his eyes southward, searching for any sign that the Hamilton carriage was drawing near.

Beside him, astride a second horse, was Juliana, her slender form dressed in gypsy garments borrowed from Chavo. She wore a loose-fitting jacket over the white shirt and black trousers, and her hair was pinned high and concealed by a flat-brimmed hat. Stuck into her wide leather belt was a heavy pistol.

"I see them," Chavo called softly. "They're getting close."

Juliana pulled the black mask hanging loosely around her neck upward to cover her face.

"Remember, stay on your horse at all times," Chavo instructed, adjusting his own mask. "If something goes wrong, ride like the wind. Don't stay to assist us. Ruark would gladly kill me if anything happened to you."

"Nothing is going to happen," Juliana said firmly, though her heart had begun to hammer in her breast. "As soon as Ruark is on his horse, we'll be off toward the seacoast and freedom. That's all that is important."

"There'll be shooting, so stay as low in the saddle as you can," he reminded her. "I'll try to bring down the coachman immediately, but if I should miss, be prepared."

"You won't miss."

As the carriage rolled into sight, they began their descent of the hill, Juliana holding tightly to the lead reins of a third horse.

She stayed at the edge of the road and watched as Chavo stationed himself, still astride his stallion, in the center of the narrow highway and waved the carriage to a halt.

One of the two men on the driver's seat flashed a confident smile and called out, "What's this? What do you think yer doin'?"

"Everyone out of the carriage," Chavo shouted, nodding his head at Juliana, who rode closer to the vehicle.

There was a brief murmur of voices before the door was flung open and Spencer Hamilton stepped down, carefully straightening the coat he wore.

"What's the meaning of this?" he demanded.

Juliana stiffened as his eyes moved over her face and body, but apparently, he didn't see anything familiar about her appearance, for he turned to Chavo and repeated the question.

The gypsy waved the gun he held and Spencer fell silent, as though intimidated by the danger. Juliana was sickened by the excited glint in his eyes that indicated he was enjoying the moment.

The second man out of the carriage was the elderly judge she had seen in Spencer's library. No doubt he was a somewhat more innocent party in this, brought along as a reliable witness to the attempted escape. He looked about anxiously, clearly frightened by the sight of the two armed men.

Ruark's large frame filled the door of the carriage for an

instant and then he was sprawling in the dust, shoved by the man behind him, Constable Brodie. Ruark's hands were tied behind his back, and he lay facedown for a long moment, as though reluctant to rise.

Juliana's heart went out to him. She knew he had to suspect his life was hanging in the balance. Even last night he'd realized it might not suit Spencer to bring him to trial, so he must have entertained the possibility of foul play. Juliana longed to be able to call his name, to reassure him he was facing friends.

Instead, her fingers curled menacingly around the butt of the pistol at her side and she derived great satisfaction from seeing the look of stark terror in the constable's beady eyes as she leveled it at him. Quickly, he leaped from the carriage and pulled Ruark to his feet.

Ruark squared his shoulders as though ready to face death, if it were to come, with dignity. Juliana saw the shock that jarred him as his eyes met hers. He had recognized her.

Chavo's voice cut through the deadly silence. "Constable, throw the pistol you have beneath your coat into the brush."

The constable did as he was told without argument.

Chavo looked toward Juliana. "Quickly, cut Ruark's bonds."

Thrusting her pistol into the leather belt at her waist, Juliana drew a dagger and, urging her horse forward a few paces, leaned down to saw at the rope binding her husband's chafed wrists. As the cords were severed, his arms swung freely and his knees nearly buckled beneath the onslaught of pain. The muscles in his upper arms began to twist and cramp as the blood forced its way through once again; the hours of immobility had taken a toll.

"Hurry, my friend," Chavo urged. "We must waste no time."

Drawing a deep breath, Ruark moved close to his stallion, and slowly, with visible effort, pulled himself into the saddle. Sweat glistened on his forehead as, teeth clenched, he struggled to regain control of his muscles. At last he was astride the horse, reins in hand.

Juliana studied the faces of the men before her. The judge seemed jittery, but Spencer and the constable stood calmly, with anticipation in their eyes. They made no move to stop the riders; obviously, they thought things were going as planned.

Ruark looked pointedly at her, and she read his expression without difficulty. He was making no move to ride away until she went first. She glanced toward Chavo and caught the imperceptible nod of his head.

Juliana prodded her horse forward, sensing Ruark close behind. As the animals began to lengthen their stride, a single shot rang out. Ruark reined abruptly, turning to look, and Juliana rode back to his side.

Behind them, Chavo had wheeled his horse and was starting to ride away. The coachman's body was sprawled across the driver's seat, and his companion was scrambling for the unfired gun in the dead man's hand.

Just as Chavo neared them, Juliana saw Spencer reach inside the frock coat he wore and bring out a pistol. She started to scream a warning, but Ruark's stronger shout masked her voice. "Chavo, look out!"

Spencer sighted the gun with accuracy and the report echoed against the hills. Chavo's features contorted, then drained of color as he slumped forward in the saddle.

"He's been hit," Ruark rasped. "Get the hell out of here."

Without waiting to see whether or not she obeyed, Ruark rode back to his friend's side. Swiftly he dismounted and, seizing the reins which had slipped from Chavo's fingers, swung up behind the injured man.

Juliana, too, had ridden back, her eyes sweeping over those standing around the carriage. Obviously, Spencer must not have another shot, but the second man on the driver's seat had managed to secure his companion's weapon, and she saw the morning sun glint off its deadly looking barrel.

"Stay low," Ruark ordered, leaning forward to shield Chavo's body. They spurred their animals to greater speed, and as they rode out of range, the pistol fired behind them, the ball falling short of its mark.

They had ridden quite some distance from the carriage before Ruark halted to examine Chavo's injuries. A spreading circle of scarlet stained the back of the white shirt the young gypsy wore.

"Thank God, he's unconscious," Ruark told her grimly. "It isn't wise to move him much farther. Where are we supposed to be headed?"

"To the seacoast near Rye. Pulika has secured us passage across the Channel."

"Chavo could never make it that far in this condition. We'll have to find someplace closer, where we can get a doctor to look at him."

Juliana struggled against the fear she felt. "We can hide at Quarrystones long enough to tend Chavo. It's taking a chance, but we have no better choice."

Ruark nodded. "Let's go. They won't be far behind us."

And as always, when disaster threatened, Juliana turned her face toward Quarrystones.

Will-John Clifton was in the yard as their horses clattered

across the causeway. Recognizing Ruark, he came forward quickly.

"My God, what has happened?"

Ruark flung himself from his horse, and he and the older man gently lowered Chavo to the ground.

"Chavo was shot rescuing me," he explained briefly. "He's badly wounded and we've got to find a place to hide from Hamilton's men."

"Hurry," Juliana cried as she slipped from her horse. "They'll be here any minute."

Will-John looked stunned. "Miss Juli," he gasped, taking in her deceptively masculine appearance. "What are you doing dressed like that?"

"There's no time to explain now," Ruark said tersely. "We've got to get Chavo inside."

"Go fetch Essie," Will-John instructed Juliana, easing his hands under Chavo's shoulders. "We'll carry the lad upstairs to one of the bedrooms."

Juliana hurried inside the house, shouting for Essie. She ripped off the mask she wore, as well as the hat, and was just shrugging out of the jacket when Essie came from the kitchen, wiping her floury hands on a cloth.

"What's all the fuss about?" She stopped short at the sight of Juliana in shirt and trousers. One hand went to her mouth and her black eyes grew round. "What foolishness have ye been up to now, Juliana? I thought ye were in yer bedchamber asleep. Where have ye been?"

"To help rescue Ruark. I'll tell you everything later. Right now, Spencer's men may be on their way here and we've got to hide Chavo."

"Chavo?"

"He's been hurt, shot in the back."

"Well, why didn't ye say so? Where is he?"

Juliana led the way up the stairs, Essie's spare form close behind.

Chavo lay on the narrow bed, his usually swarthy skin the same color as the linen sheet beneath him; his breathing was labored and slow. Essie knelt at his side and began a cursory examination.

"Will-John and I are going to turn the horses out into the pasture with the others," Ruark said to Juliana. "Get out of those clothes and into a dress. Spencer may not suspect your part in this morning's events, and it'll be up to you to convince him you know nothing."

She lifted her chin. "I'll manage."

Ruark put out an arm and drew her close against his chest. "My heart almost stopped beating when I recognized you on the road. Why'd you do something so foolish?"

"I wanted to help Chavo rescue you. They were going to kill you."

He nodded, then lifted a hand to her cheek. "I thought my life was coming to a swift end, until I looked into the most beautiful eyes I've ever seen. It was all I could do to keep from taking you in my arms right then and there." He pressed a kiss onto her lips.

Will-John shuffled his feet. "We'd better get on with it, lad."

"Aye, you're right," Ruark agreed, releasing Juliana. "As soon as we've taken care of the horses, we'll be back to move Chavo. Essie, do what you can for him while we're gone."

Juliana left Essie attempting to stop Chavo's bleeding and ran to her own room where she stripped off the clothing she wore and stuffed it hurriedly behind the tall bookshelves.

She washed briefly and slipped on a fresh dress, grappling with the fastenings. She had just finished brushing out her hair when Essie came into the room, panting in her haste.

"Quick, Juli, riders are coming up the lane. Ye'll have to stall them while Ruark and Will-John move Chavo."

Juliana swallowed her fear and hurried down the stairs. There was only time for a fleeting exchange of glances with Ruark as she passed the door of the room where Chavo lay. Her husband's dark eyes offered encouragement and she deliberately slowed her breathing. She wouldn't let him down.

She stepped into the yard and was calling Jakel when the six riders crossed the causeway bridge. She stood staring at them as though startled by their sudden arrival. Jakel created a bit of confusion by barking and leaping at Spencer's horse, causing it to shy nervously.

"Control your stupid dog, Juliana," he growled, "or I'll let my man shoot it." He inclined his head toward the ugly brute riding next to him. The huge man flashed a nasty grin and stroked the long-barreled rifle that lay across his lap.

"Here, Jakel," she said firmly, "come." The spaniel padded to her side and lay down at her feet.

She met Spencer's gaze directly. "What business do you have at Quarrystones?"

"We want your husband," spoke up Constable Brodie.

Juliana's grey-blue eyes grew wide. "My husband? What do you mean? He's already in your custody."

Spencer slid from his horse. "No, he's not, Juliana, as you probably know. We were moving him to Edensfield."

"You moved him?" she cried. "Why wasn't I informed?"

Spencer held up a hand. "Let me finish. We were moving him for his own safety, and halfway to town our carriage was waylaid by two highwaymen who took Ruark and made a run for it. I suppose," he added with sarcasm, "you'll claim to know nothing of the plot."

"As a matter of fact, I don't," Juliana said coolly, allowing a smile to curve her mouth upward. "But if he has escaped, I'm glad."

"His freedom is merely temporary," Spencer said with a frown. "At any rate, he can't go far without abandoning his dear friend Chavo, and I'm certain Ruark is much too noble for that."

"Chavo?" Juliana questioned. "What does he have to do with this?"

"He was the highwayman who held us at gunpoint and forced me to hand over your husband," stated the constable. "I'm happy to say Hamilton shot and wounded him."

Juliana turned a look of disdain on Spencer. "Is that true?"

Without apparent remorse, Spencer nodded. "It was no better than the damned rogue deserved. He killed one of my best men."

"We think they came to Quarrystones to hide out," the constable announced. "We want to search the grounds."

"I assure you, I haven't seen them," Juliana lied. "I was just preparing to visit Ruark at Moorlands."

"She's lying," suggested the big man. "I'll wager those gypsies are here somewhere. Let's begin a search."

Constable Brodie dismounted, motioning for the others to do likewise. "We stopped off at Moorlands long enough to get a few men and horses, but they can't be too far ahead of us. And your saying you haven't seen them doesn't mean they aren't here."

"Yes," Spencer said, "I think you'll have to allow us to look, Juli."

She inclined her head. "All right, if it will satisfy you, I'll give you permission to search the *house*."

Spencer was immediately aware of the slight emphasis in her voice, and he exchanged a quick look with Brodie.

"It seems to me," he said, "that it might be more sensible to look about outside first."

"I won't have these men tramping through my gardens and destroying my lawn."

"I'm afraid you have no choice but to stay out of our way," Brodie spoke up. "I'm getting tired of this foolish game."

She stood watching as the constable gave his men directions for searching the grounds. As two of them went off toward the stable, the others scattered throughout the gardens. Brodie himself walked along the front side of the house, his eyes moving over the rose-covered walls. As he neared the corner, Juliana began to follow him, careful to keep Jakel close at her side.

Behind her, Spencer said, "What is it you're afraid we'll find, Juliana?"

She gave a start. "Why, nothing."

Not really listening to her reply, Spencer let his own gaze roam across the front of the house. Slowly they came to rest upon the stone tower.

"What's this?" he asked absently, moving toward the small wooden door at ground level. "I say, Brodie, this wouldn't make a bad hiding place, would it?"

The constable glanced at Juliana. "Maybe we'd better have a look."

Cautiously, the man pushed open the tower door, pistol in hand, and stepped into the dim recesses.

Spencer moved closer. "Do you see anything?"

The constable reappeared. "Nothing. That hole is too damp and dark even for vermin."

Juliana tried to force herself to breathe naturally. She said a silent prayer that they wouldn't notice the overgrown staircase to the second story. She could do nothing to distract them if they decided to look there. There was no way she could warn Ruark.

The constable backed away from the tower, scanning it with inquisitive eyes. "Hmm," he muttered, "there appears to be another floor in this tower."

Juliana's heart twisted as she saw his eyes move to the tangle of vines at the base of the fragile staircase. How could she prevent them from at last discovering the highwayman's lair?

"That staircase hasn't been used within my memory," she said. "My father considered it dangerous."

"You don't expect us to believe that, do you?" sneered Spencer. "You're hardly going to be helpful."

The constable pulled aside the heavy vines and gingerly set foot on the first step, testing it. When it held, he continued upward.

Below, Juliana wrestled with a fury of emotion. Should she cry out and warn Ruark? Should she make some attempt to stop Brodie?

At the top of the rickety staircase, he paused briefly, then flung open the door. He stepped inside, still brandishing the loaded gun.

Spencer started up the staircase, but the eroded metal of one of the steps broke loose causing him to stumble. Shaken by his near fall, he paused at the base of the stairs and called out, "Is there anything up there?"

The constable retreated to the landing. "Not a damned thing. It doesn't look as if anyone has been here for years."

Juliana gave a small start of surprise. If Ruark and Chavo weren't in the tower, where were they?

Her relief was short-lived as Spencer growled, "They must be inside the house." He shoved his way past her. "Call your men, Brodie, and let's look. And you'd best not interfere, Juliana."

She was left to follow helplessly, fearful of what he might find within Quarrystones.

Constable Brodie made his way slowly down the tower stairs. Summoning the two men who had completed a desultory search of the gardens, he entered the house right behind Spencer. Essie Clifton's greeting was an angry tirade.

Kneeling on the stairs, scrub brush in hand, she spat, "What do ye think yer doing, tracking up my clean floor? Miss Juliana, can't ye get these clumsy louts out of here?"

"I'm sorry, Essie, but they seem to think Ruark may be hiding here in the house. We have to allow them to go through the rooms."

Essie sniffed audibly. "Well, it's a silly waste of time, but I guess we can't stop them."

Assuming from Essie's words that the fugitives were safely out of sight, Juliana stood aside and let the constable and his men conduct their manhunt.

She didn't follow them from room to room, but stood at the foot of the staircase and listened to their muffled movements. As the minutes passed and there was no cry of discovery, she began to relax a bit. She tried in vain to interpret the expression in Essie's black eyes, but it was impossible. Perhaps it was best that she didn't know where her husband was at this moment. At least she couldn't give him away by an inadvertent look or gesture.

Apparently satisfied their quarry was not to be found

within the upper floors of the house, a search was launched belowstairs. Spencer encountered Will-John in the stillroom, washing some of the bottles he used in wine-making. The old man's slow, deliberate answers to his questions obviously irritated Spencer, causing him to quickly determine nothing was to be gained by tarrying there.

"Well, Juliana," he said, coming back into the entry hall, "perhaps you were telling the truth when you said you knew nothing of your husband's whereabouts."

"He may not be here now," Brodie interjected, "but he'll turn up sooner or later. With an injured man on his hands, he's going to have to find medical help."

Juliana felt her composure returning. "Have you considered the possibility that Chavo may have died?" she asked. "If that's the case, he'd no longer be a hindrance to Ruark. It's possible my husband is already on his way out of the country." She let a pleased smile hover on her lips.

"If that's the case, Brodie," he snapped, "I'll have your damned hide. I want him found before he can get out of England."

"I'll need a larger force of men," the constable stated, "but we can block every road in the county to prevent his escape." He turned his sharp eyes on Juliana. "However, if Chavo's body isn't found, we'll assume he's still alive. And we'll come back to Quarrystones as many times as it takes to find them."

Juliana leaned weakly against the doorframe and watched as they left. By her side, Jakel growled menacingly until the horses had crossed the causeway bridge, then burst into a series of wild barks. She patted his head, soothing him with a calm she didn't feel.

When she was certain they wouldn't double back, she

entered the house to find the Cliftons waiting for her, both wearing broad grins.

"We fooled them that time," Will-John said proudly.

"Where are they?" Juliana asked. "I was certain the constable would find them in the tower."

"There wasn't time to move the lad that far," Will-John explained, starting up the stairs. "Fortunately, I remembered a closer hiding place."

About midway up the staircase he paused, letting his thick hand move over the carving in the oak paneling that covered the wall. As he touched the right spot, a section of the wood creaked and slowly opened to reveal a cramped cupboard where Ruark crouched, supporting Chavo's limp body.

"A priest's hole," exclaimed Juliana. "My God, I didn't even know it was there."

"Your father didn't want you children to know," Will-John said. "There's no mechanism to open it from the inside, and he was afraid one of you might get trapped in there."

"Not a pleasant prospect," Ruark assured her, carefully shifting Chavo into Will-John's waiting arms.

"Thank heavens you're safe." Juliana went into his embrace. "I didn't know where you were or what I should do."

"Ye did fine, Miss Juli," Essie affirmed. "Ye stalled the fools long enough for me to notice the bloodstains on the stairs and grab a scrub brush. That would've given the whole thing away for sure."

"That was too close for comfort." Juliana stepped back to look into Ruark's face. "Where will you hide now?"

"We'll have to put Chavo in the tower room and take the chance Spencer and his men won't come back today. I'll find a doctor to look at his injury, and by the time he can be moved, I'll have located some other hiding place."

"I'll go put sheets on the cot," Essie said. "Juliana, why don't ye bring me a basin of hot water and some cloths?"

Carrying Chavo between them, Will-John and Ruark started up the stairs.

The dusty tower room was bathed in candlelight, the black curtain across the slitted window once again. Ruark and Juliana stood helplessly beside the cot while Essie made her examination.

After removing the gypsy's shirt and the wadded cloth with which she'd staunched the flow of blood, she had Will-John turn him facedown. Chavo moaned, but his eyes remained shut.

The wound was bleeding sluggishly. When it was bathed, they could see the edges were blue-black and puffy. Essie laid her ear to Chavo's back and listened for a long moment. Finally, she shook her head.

"It's no use, Ruark. It's not worth the risk for ye to bring a doctor here."

"What do you mean?"

"From his labored breathing and the rattle in his chest, I'd say the ball has lodged somewhere in his lungs, probably close to his heart. I doubt there's a doctor in the area who could successfully remove the lead."

"He's going to die?"

She nodded slowly. "I don't see how he can survive. It'll be a miracle if he lasts the night. As the blood seeps into his lungs, he'll start to cough, and with the ball that close to his heart, there's nothing to be done."

"No," Ruark ground out. "I won't just stand by and wait

for him to die. Maybe you're wrong, maybe there is something a doctor could do."

Juliana put her arms around him. "Ruark, you know Essie is as skilled as any physician in the area. She wouldn't have said what she did without being positive."

"Would it help to bring a specialist from London?" he asked in desperation.

Essie's seamed face was sad. "No, lad, it won't help. I'm sorry."

After Essie gently bound Chavo's wound, Will-John turned him onto his back. They were startled to see his eyes wide open and staring.

"Chavo," Ruark murmured, dropping to one knee.

A warmth came into the young gypsy's eyes and he struggled to move the hand laying across his chest. Sensing his intent, Ruark carefully grasped the hand in his own larger one. "Rest, friend," he whispered.

The faintest of smiles lifted Chavo's mouth and he slept again.

They took turns sitting with Chavo through the night. Just before the earliest rays of sunlight marked the dawn, the gypsy opened his eyes again. Ruark, dozing in a chair beside the bed, heard Juliana speak his name.

"Ruark, Chavo's awake. I think he's trying to say something."

Instantly alert, Ruark knelt close to his friend. "What is it, Chavo? What can I do for you?"

"I-I know I'm dying."

"You'll get better," Ruark protested. "I swear it."

Again came the fleeting smile and a barely discernible shake of the head. "No."

"Chavo, please, you have to save your strength," Juliana said. As Essie had predicted, the coughing had begun and his condition was worsening.

"Home, Ruark." His black eyes were beseeching. "Take me home." He seemed exhausted by the effort of speaking the few words.

Ruark laid a hand on the dying man's shoulder. "All right, my friend. We'll go now, before daylight."

"Ruark," whispered Juliana, "he can't survive being moved."

"I have to try," he replied. "It's very important for him to die among his own people. A gypsy's worst fear is dying alone or with strangers. I owe this to Chavo."

Within a few minutes, Ruark had informed the Cliftons of his plan and, surprisingly, they offered no arguments. Will-John readied the carriage and brought it around to the front door while Essie swathed Chavo in blankets and gave him a spoonful of laudanum to ease his pain.

" 'Tis not a medicine I ordinarily hold with," she told Juliana, "but it may make the lad a bit more comfortable. It has taken a burden off his mind to know he's going back to the gypsies. I only hope Ruark can get him there in time."

Fastening her cloak, Juliana stepped through the front door and found Ruark waiting for her.

"I'm sorry, sweetheart, but I can't let you go," he said, putting his hands on her shoulders. "If the roads are being watched, we'll never make it to the gypsy encampment. I don't want you involved."

"But I can't let you leave like this."

"There's no other way. If I can get Chavo to the encampment, the gypsies will hide us until he gets better or . . . dies. I'll come back for you when I can."

"Do you promise?"

"I promise." He bent to kiss her and clasp her tightly to his chest. "I won't leave England without you, 'Liana."

"No matter what happens," she whispered fiercely, "I want us to be together."

The embrace they shared had to suffice for the words they wanted to say, but for which there was no time.

Ruark released her reluctantly. "I have to go before it gets any lighter. Will-John will return with the carriage if we make it safely." He stooped to gather a handful of flowers growing beside the path. "I've cherished our time together, and I want it to go on forever, too. But if fate decides against us, at least we've had these past few months."

"They've been the happiest of my life," she whispered, tears sparkling in her grey eyes.

"I love you, 'Liana."

Ruark pressed the flowers he held into her hand, then pulled her against him for one final kiss. She clung to his warmth and strength until he firmly put her aside.

Nearly blinded by tears, she watched the carriage roll away, cross the moat bridge and disappear down the tree-lined lane.

She glanced at the flowers she held and saw they were blue forget-me-nots. A smile trembled through her tears. As if she could ever forget the arrogant, yet gentle rogue she had married.

"Take care, my love," she whispered. "And please come back to me."

Twenty-two

Juliana endured an agony of waiting that day and the next. At least Will-John had returned to tell her of Ruark and Chavo's safe arrival at the gypsy camp where they'd been welcomed.

But, she wondered where the gypsies would conceal them should the constable's men come to search. Sara Hamilton had told Will-John they'd already been there once, and Juliana knew there was a distinct chance they would go back again.

In addition to her worry over Ruark, she was struggling with a growing concern about his grandfather. Instead of appearing at Quarrystones as promised the morning after Ruark's arrest, he'd sent the kitchen boy with an excuse. It had now been two days since she'd heard from him, and Juliana couldn't help but think something must have happened.

Unrelenting fear became a part of her every waking moment. She reasoned that there was no way for Ruark to avoid the manhunt indefinitely. Sooner or later, they were going to rout him out unless he found a way to slip past them and beyond England's borders. She realized he wouldn't go until his friend's fate had been settled and apparently, Chavo was lingering. Otherwise, she'd have had word from him.

Essie and Will-John shared her agitation, listening to her misgivings and encouraging her plans for the future. Her parents had left for London without a word to her. Whether their actions were caused by dismay at finding their son-in-law branded an outlaw or simply by their usual disinterest, Juliana didn't know. Stubbornly, she told herself it made no difference. Ruark was all that mattered.

The worst of it was that she could do nothing but wait. She wanted to pack food and clothing for their flight, but knew it might be discovered by Spencer or his men, who'd recently stopped to search Quarrystones again. The tenant farmers told her they'd ridden through their village, as well, turning everyone from their homes and ransacking the barns and granaries.

With each day that passed, Spencer would grow more and more anxious to lay hands on the fugitives, and Juliana already doubted that Ruark could sneak past the sentries posted on every county road.

On the third day, Sara Hamilton arrived to see her.

"Thank heavens you've come," Juliana cried, greeting her at the door and leading the way to the parlor. "I've been going out of my mind wondering what has happened."

"All is well with Ruark," Sara told her. "He's staying in your *vardo* with Chavo, and they're well hidden in the woods."

"How is Chavo?"

"The situation is very grave, I'm afraid. He sometimes awakes and speaks, but the fever grows worse."

Essie came into the room with tea. "The lead poisoning will make him weaker and weaker. 'Tis only a matter of time now."

Sara nodded grimly. "Our healers have worked over him

but there's nothing to be done but make him comfortable. Ruark is beside himself."

"He knows he owes his freedom to Chavo," Juliana pointed out.

"Chavo betrayed my son to Mariette," Sara said with a flare of anger. "Though Ruark doesn't seem to blame him."

"He knows my sister well enough to recognize who was really at fault. Besides, Ruark and I both have to be grateful for Chavo's change of heart."

" 'Liana, there's something I must ask of you." Sara spoke suddenly, as though her request was distasteful.

"I'll do anything."

"This isn't easy, nor is it pleasant," Sara warned. "Chavo wants to see Mariette one last time."

"Mariette? Why?"

"Apparently, he still feels love for her." Sara shrugged. "Perhaps the fever has confused his mind. But Ruark believes we should honor his dying wish."

"It would be very dangerous."

"It's a risk Ruark is willing to take for his friend. He knows that gypsies fear death more than anything, that they don't want to enter the world of the dead with sin on their hands." She reached out to pat Juliana's arm and her gold bracelets jangled musically. "We who know Chavo have made our peace with him, asking his forgiveness for sins we may have committed against him. It's to be expected that he'd also want to clear his own conscience."

"I'm afraid Mariette wouldn't go to him. Poor Chavo, he still hasn't learned how selfish she can be."

"He's too ill to think rationally, 'Liana. He only knows that Ruark promised you'd bring her."

"Ruark should never have agreed to such a thing," protested Essie. "How does he expect Miss Juli to convince Mariette to go with her without Spencer finding out?"

"Ruark trusts 'Liana completely. I offered to go myself, but he thinks she's more likely to be able to talk her sister into compliance. He has great faith in her strength and courage."

Juliana's eyes gleamed with determination. "Tell me what to do."

"Ride to Moorlands and conceal yourself someplace where you can watch the house. Don't go inside until you're certain Spencer and his men are gone. And when you approach Mariette, you'll need to be armed."

Essie gave a shrill cry. "Lord help us! What can he be thinking of?"

"Hush, Essie," Juliana scolded impatiently. "I can take one of Father's old pistols. You know I can shoot it if I have to. Go on, Sara."

"It's probable that you'll have to force your sister to accompany you. And because the roads are being watched, you'll need to ride through the meadows." She took a folded sheet of paper from her pocket and held it out. "Ruark sent this note to you."

Taking it, Juliana walked away to stand by the windows. She slipped on her spectacles and unfolded the message.

Dearest 'Liana, she read, *Please refuse this request if you want to. In fact, I almost hope you will, as asking you to bring Mariette here seems far too dangerous. I fear for your safety, and yet, how can I deny Chavo his dying wish after what he has done for me? If you decide to do this, don't take any chances. I love you, Ruark.*

She tucked the note and her eyeglasses into the pocket of her gown. "I'll go right away," she said quietly.

Sara stood, her expression filled with approval. "Yes, it would be best to get it over with."

"What will ye do with Mariette once she's seen the gypsy?" Essie inquired. "Ye can't just take her back to Moorlands."

"We'll hold her at the gypsy camp," Sara answered. "Once Chavo has died and Ruark is safely out of the country, we will release her. We'll be on our way back to Ireland shortly thereafter, leaving no one for Spencer to punish."

" 'Tis a fool plan" the older woman groused. "Ye're playing with fire."

"If we don't do this one last thing for Chavo," Juliana said, "I'm afraid Ruark will never forgive himself. He'll always be plagued by guilt over his friend's death."

"Ye may be right, but if ye're going to risk your neck for that husband of yers, at least take Will-John with ye."

"I'd be glad of his company," Juliana admitted. "If Spencer ever finds out, you can say I forced him at gunpoint."

"I'd best get back to the encampment," Sara said. She gave Juliana a swift hug. "God go with you."

Will-John and Juliana waited nearly two hours in the woods near Spencer's house before they saw a company of horsemen ride up to the front door. Within a few minutes, Spencer himself came out to join them, mounting the horse a stable hand brought around. After a brief discussion, all the riders galloped off down the lane.

"At last," breathed Juliana. "I thought they'd never leave."

"Let's hope they stay away long enough for us to find Mariette and get out of here," grunted Will-John.

They rode up to the manor house and Juliana took a heavy, old-fashioned pistol from her saddlebag. "While I get Mariette," she said, "would you try to discover what has happened to Edward Hamilton?"

They parted company in the entry hall and just as Will-John had disappeared up the curving staircase, Juliana heard her sister sharply rebuke a maid. She flattened herself against the wall in the shadow of a large grandfather clock as the tearful maid fled the front parlor. When she had gone, Juliana tightened her grip on the pistol and entered the room.

Mariette was sitting at a pianoforte looking through a book of music. At the sight of her, Juliana's temper flamed. "Isn't it nice," she said in a deadly calm voice, "that after causing everyone else so much trouble, you're free to while away the afternoon with music?"

Mariette's shock was evident as she whirled about. "For God's sake, Juli, you aren't going to kill me, are you?"

"I'm horrified to realize how much I'd like to be able to do that very thing. After all you've done to Chavo and Ruark, it's what you deserve." Her words came out stiffly through clenched teeth. "But even if I can't kill you, I won't hesitate to wound you if you don't do precisely what I say."

"What do you want?"

"I'm taking you to see Chavo."

"What makes you think I'd want to see that turncoat?"

"He's dying," Juliana said fiercely. "For some reason, he wants to see you, so you're going with me."

"I can't face him."

"You have no choice. Now, hurry up. We haven't got much time."

"Where are we going?"

"You'll find out soon enough. Start toward the front door and don't call out for help."

"Mother and Father will never forgive you for this," Mariette warned, rising from the pianoforte bench. Juliana nudged her with the gun she held and Mariette started across the carpeted floor.

"Do you think that makes any difference to me?" Juliana muttered.

Suddenly the front door was flung wide to admit Spencer and Constable Brodie, followed by two of his men. Seeing the gun in Juliana's hand, Brodie leaped forward and knocked it away, causing her to cry out in pain and grasp her wrist.

"What's going on here, Etta?" Spencer asked.

"My dear sister threatened to injure me if I didn't go with her. She says the gypsy Chavo is dying and wishes to see me."

"Dying, you say? A pity," Spencer sneered. "How fortunate you've already confessed to your shoddy affair with the man, or this could have come as a nasty shock to me." He turned to Juliana. "Where is he?"

Refusing to quail before him, she met his eyes directly. "I won't tell you."

Brodie raised a gloved hand and struck her a blow that sent her reeling against the wall and onto the floor. He stood over her. "Perhaps you'd consider telling me?"

Juliana put a hand to her bruised face, but pressed her lips firmly together. Ensnared by his evil gaze, she shook her head. "No."

Spencer reached out a hand to haul her to her feet. "It might be best if you'd tell the constable what he wants to know, Juli. He can be most efficient at extracting information, and I wouldn't want to see you hurt."

"I'll never tell either of you anything."

"Even if it means he has to kill you?" Mariette interjected.

Juliana shrugged, remaining silent.

"Don't tempt me," Brodie growled, capturing her arm and twisting it painfully behind her back. "We don't have time to waste. Where is he?" His grip tightened. "Is your husband with the gypsy?"

Juliana bit her lip to keep from crying out.

"Leave her alone!" The cry came from the doorway.

"Will-John," Juliana nearly sobbed, "why didn't you stay hidden?"

"I couldn't stand by and see this bully hurt you."

"Ah, the nobility of these country gentlemen," drawled Brodie. "How touching." He gave Juliana's arm another vicious twist, then pushed her onto the nearby couch. "Seize the old fool. I have a feeling he'll tell us what we want to know."

Juliana's heart sank as she watched Brodie's two burly henchmen drag Will-John forward. They held him between them as Brodie approached, his eyes narrowed.

"Where can we find the gypsy outlaws?"

Will-John sucked in a deep breath. "I don't know."

Brodie drew back his fist and smashed it into the older man's stomach. Will-John struggled for air, sagging in pain. The pair hoisted him upward and Brodie hit him again, the edge of his hand slanting downward across the bridge of Will-John's nose. The sound of crunching bone and cartilage wrenched a cry from Juliana.

"Damn you to hell," she screamed, launching herself at Brodie. "I'll tell you where they are. Just don't hit him again."

Brodie and Spencer exchanged satisfied smiles.

"They're at the gypsy encampment down by the river," she went on.

Mariette frowned. "How do we know we can trust her?"

"Yes, don't make the mistake of lying to us, Juli," Spencer cautioned.

"I'm not lying," she said in a defeated tone.

Will-John stirred, moaning, and she knelt beside him to cradle his shaggy head in her arms. His face was bloody and swollen, and the sight of his injuries filled her with blind fury.

"Get up, man," Brodie ordered. "We're going now."

"He's in no condition to go anywhere," Juliana argued.

"Then let him stay here." The constable motioned to one of his men who yanked Juliana to her feet, tearing her away from Will-John. She was shoved toward the door, then into the courtyard where the rest of the horsemen waited.

"As it turns out," Spencer remarked, "it was a stroke of luck that I forgot a weapon and had to return to the house. This way my sister-in-law can lead us directly to her husband."

Flung onto the back of her horse, Juliana clutched the reins with cold fingers. Silently, she prayed for a miracle. She was frantic with worry about Will-John, and terrified by the thought of taking Brodie to Ruark.

"Have a horse brought around for your wife, Hamilton," Brodie suggested. "I think we should comply with the gypsy's wish to see his erstwhile lover."

Juliana tried to calm her fears. It wouldn't do any good to panic, she told herself. Ironically, Mariette now held a pistol to her back, and it would take very little provocation to make her fire it. That would certainly end any chance of her finding a way to help Ruark. Her only hope lay in the possibility that she might warn him somehow before Brodie and his men rode in to surround him.

The group of riders stopped in the thick of the woods a small distance from the encampment, and Brodie issued orders in a hard voice.

"Mariette, you and your sister will go on ahead, as if the two of you are arriving as planned. It'll be up to you to kill her if she tries to shout a warning to her husband."

"We'll be close behind," Spencer added, "and as soon as Ruark has shown himself, we'll ride in to take him."

A light rain was misting down, drenching the forest and adjacent meadows. The steady dripping was a melancholy sound, matching Juliana's somber mood. She had never meant to let Ruark down, never intended to deliver him to the enemy this way.

"Slow your horse, Juli, so we appear to be riding side by side. If I look as though I'm meekly following you, Ruark will be suspicious."

As it turned out, there were few inhabitants of the camp visible when they rode into it. Most of the gypsies were staying warm and dry inside their caravans; only a handful huddled around a heavily smoking campfire.

Sara Hamilton, swathed in a long black shawl, came forward to greet them. Her dark eyes were anxious. "Did you have any trouble?"

Juliana shook her head, wishing for a means of conveying a silent message to Ruark's mother.

"Just where is this dying man you want me to see?" Mariette asked. "The rain is soaking me to the skin."

Sara was obviously disdainful as she viewed the younger woman. "Come, he is this way."

They dismounted and followed Sara down a path that

skirted the woods. Halfway along the footpath, she took a turn that led them through a grove of trees and into the clearing by the river where Ruark's painted gypsy wagon stood. Two men hovered over a fitful fire warming their hands. Startled by the women's approach, one of them called out to Ruark.

Juliana's heart began a slow, painful twist within her chest as she saw her husband emerge from the *vardo*. Dressed in gypsy clothing once more, he paused on the doorstep of the wagon. Mist glistened in his ebony hair and as he caught sight of her, his white teeth flashed in a relieved smile. He leaped agilely from the caravan.

He grasped Juliana about the waist and pulled her to him. As her mouth came close to his ear, she managed to whisper, "I'm sorry."

She saw the puzzled look in his eyes as they traveled from her face to Mariette, now holding the pistol in plain view. A muscle twitched in his cheek and his gaze grew flinty.

"What's this?" he questioned.

Mariette laughed gaily. "Poor Ruark, your plans do tend to go awry, don't they? I know this isn't what you expected, but how could you foresee that your wife would be so careless as to be found out by the constable and his men?"

Ruark glanced at Juliana, his eyes resting on the darkening bruise along the side of her face. He touched it tenderly. "Did Brodie do this?"

Juliana nodded. "I'm sorry that I let you down, but I was afraid they'd beat Will-John to death."

"It doesn't matter, 'Liana. Everything will be fine."

Spencer, Brodie, and their men chose that moment to ride into the clearing, their horses crashing loudly through the underbrush. At their arrival, the two gypsies backed away from the fire, sidling toward the caravan.

"Take them," shouted Brodie. "Don't let them alert the rest of the camp."

They were quickly surrounded by several men who dropped from their horses to subdue them. Sara Hamilton rushed forward to fling herself at one of the attackers, but seizing a handful of her long hair, he twisted it, forcing her to her knees.

"Damn you," exclaimed Ruark, starting forward.

Constable Brodie raised the gun he held. "Think carefully, Hamilton."

Juliana touched her husband's arm and he came to a halt, though his face was a mask of rage.

Spencer laughed softly. "You did well, Etta, leading us to our quarry so easily. Are you ready to surrender, Ruark?"

Ruark's eyes blazed, but his reply was calm. "Aye, I'll go with you. I only ask that I be allowed to say goodbye to my friend."

"The traitorous bastard who shot my coachman?" said Brodie. "What makes you think we aren't arresting him, too?"

"He's dying," Ruark asserted. "He'd never survive the ride into town. You have no reason to take him."

"He's wanted for murder and for abetting your escape."

"Take me and let him die in peace."

"Get the gypsy," Brodie commanded abruptly, and two more of his men got off their horses, striding toward the *vardo*. Ruark moved to block their path.

"Leave him alone," he raged. "He's beyond harming anyone."

There was sudden movement in the doorway of the

wagon. Chavo stood there, his weakened body supported by a priest.

"Chavo," cried Juliana. "What are you doing?"

Chavo's haunted eyes slid slowly over the people standing about the clearing, coming to rest on Mariette's face. Muttering in Romany, he lurched forward, raising his right hand. Within its grip was a dagger.

The priest looked shocked. He laid a hand on Chavo's arm and said, "You mustn't do this. Do you want to go to God with another's blood on your hands?"

Sweat beaded on Chavo's forehead; his face contorted. Time seemed to slow nearly to a standstill as he struggled to find the strength to stand on his own. The priest made no move to take the knife, but he began to pray aloud.

The dagger slipped from Chavo's fingers and clattered harmlessly over the side of the wagon. Tears streamed down his face as he mumbled, "I wanted to kill her." His eyes closed as he swayed, then toppled into Ruark's arms. The priest sank to his knees and continued to pray.

Gently, Ruark eased his friend onto the ground, supporting him with a strong arm. Spencer and the constable quickly dismounted to stand over the fallen gypsy.

"No need for your firearms now, gentlemen," Ruark snarled. "Surely you can see that for yourselves?"

Chavo's face was chalky and as he coughed fitfully, a froth of blood appeared in the corners of his mouth. Juliana knelt beside him, wiping away the blood with the dampened hem of her cloak. Her eyes met Ruark's, sharing his anguish.

"Priest?" Chavo's harsh whisper was strangely loud.

"He's right here." Ruark looked up. "Father?"

Clutching his black skirts, the priest scrambled down from the *vardo* and went to Chavo's side. "What is it, lad?"

"I want to confess," the gypsy panted. "Will you listen?"

"I'm here."

"I-I'm the . . . highwayman. Not Ruark."

"Chavo," Ruark broke in. "Don't tell them anything."

"Yes," Spencer agreed, "we aren't interested in the babbling of a dying man."

The priest leveled a reproving look at him. "Silence. Would you deny him the opportunity to ease his soul before death?"

"If what he says is true and Hamilton is innocent," Brodie said, "why did he rescue him?"

"He's my friend." Chavo's entire body tensed in a paroxysm of agony and again he coughed blood. "Mariette lied . . . he didn't want her."

"He's the one lying," Spencer protested.

"Ruark?" Chavo's whisper was agitated.

"Yes?" Ruark leaned closer, his free hand covering Chavo's cold ones. "What is it?"

"Do you forgive me?"

"There's nothing to forgive. Don't worry."

A brief smile lighted the younger man's face. "Re-remember . . . I was highway . . . man."

A spasm of coughing shook his slight frame and his face filled with a questioning expression of pain. The faint smile faded and was gone.

"Ruark?" Juliana whispered.

He nodded grimly. "He's dead."

Constable Brodie frowned. "I don't believe the gypsy's story that he was the highwayman."

The priest gently closed Chavo's eyes, then rose to his feet. "Would he have risked eternal damnation by dying with a lie on his lips?" he asked. "I'm a witness to his confession. No court of law will reject my testimony."

"Probably not." Brodie looked at Spencer and shrugged. "It appears we've found the Kentish Gypsy."

"No!" screamed Mariette. "Ruark is the highwayman. Chavo was lying to protect him!"

Juliana had forgotten that her sister had a gun until she saw it aimed directly at Ruark's chest. In that instant, the gypsy woman's prediction rang through her head. Ruark would die if she didn't do something to prevent it.

From her kneeling position beside Chavo's body, she struggled with her entangling skirts to fling herself at Mariette. Her clutching fingers closed around a fold of her sister's cloak just as the strained silence was shattered by the sound of the pistol being fired. A sound that echoed again and again in her stunned mind.

"Ruark!" Juliana's agonized cry rose upward, swirling through the treetops to be snatched away by the misty wind.

Twenty-three

Two months later . . .

Autumn had come to Quarrystones, gilding the trees and sending showers of golden leaves whirling along in the wake of a colder wind.

Juliana wrapped the woolen cloak more closely about her and, despite an involuntary shiver, breathed deeply of the crisp, cool air. Somewhere nearby someone was burning leaves, and the pungent smoke drifted lazily overhead.

Juliana's lonely figure moved slowly down a forest path guarded by ancient oaks. Through the trees she caught glimpses of the river, silent and slate-grey in the late afternoon light.

She sighed. Summer at Quarrystones had come to an end, as she had known it would.

At the termination of the path, she stopped to kneel by a gently rounded mound of earth. The only thing marking the spot as a grave was an unobtrusive stone, the carved letters on its face almost hidden by the ivy leaves scrambling over its surface. The glossy leaves were still undamaged by the early-morning frosts, she noticed, as she brushed them aside and traced the engraving with her forefinger.

A feeling of sadness gripped her as she laid the flowers she carried on the grave. The flowers, as lovely as they were, seemed inadequate. They could never express the words she longed to have said.

A shaft of chilly sunshine slanted down through bare limbs to caress blue Michaelmas daisies and white bellflowers, causing their deep colors to glow against the coppery leaves upon which they lay. The daisies were the symbol of farewell, and that was exactly why she had chosen them. Today had been a day for farewells.

And yet, before she could say a final goodbye to the events of the summer just past, she needed to think them through one last time. It had been the most unusual, the most exciting and wonderful summer of her life. But it had also been a season of painful discovery, of sadness, loss, and regret.

She let her thoughts stray back to that day at the gypsy encampment. So much had happened so quickly.

As if it were yesterday, she remembered the awful, immobilizing horror of seeing her husband shot down in front of her. She could hear the sound of her own muffled sobs as she'd thrown her arms around his still body, pressing her face to his heart and pleading with him to live. . . .

Mariette had fired the pistol, her face distorted by her triumphant hatred. Juliana shouted Ruark's name and threw herself over him, as if to protect him from further danger. For a few seconds, her low, keening cries masked the turmoil of noise that swept through the surrounding forest. But then, even she had heard it and looked up in time to see the clearing overrun by a howling mob of tenant farmers wielding pitchforks, shovels, and axes.

Edward Hamilton led the farmers, but as soon as he saw Juliana, he dropped the makeshift weapon he carried and hurried to her side.

"What has happened?" he cried.

"Mariette shot him. I-I don't know how badly he's hurt."

"Help me move him into the wagon," Edward ordered, his voice vibrating with new command.

It took every ounce of strength the two of them had to shift Ruark's motionless body and lift it into the *vardo*. As the farmers attacked and the fray came closer, she willed herself the stamina to accomplish the task. Once they got Ruark inside the wagon, they left him on the floor, draping a coverlet from the bed over him.

Juliana put her ear to his chest, praying for the sound of heartbeats, but all she could hear was the roar of noise from outside the wagon. She looked out the door in time to see Arthur Jacobson dispatch one of Spencer's London thugs with the flat side of a shovel. He then went after another one who was attempting to reach his horse and escape.

"Where did they come from?" she whispered.

Edward, a worried frown on his face as he studied his grandson, gave her a weary smile. "I brought them. It was the only thing I could think of to do."

"Will-John?"

"He'll be fine, 'Liana." Edward rubbed his jaw. "If he hadn't come to my aid this afternoon, I don't know what would have happened. After I so foolishly confronted Spencer, he had me held prisoner in my room. Will-John broke the lock and helped me escape, but when I started down the stairs, I heard Spencer and Brodie return." He shuddered. "Once you'd gone, I managed to rouse Will-John and he told me what had happened."

"Weren't you afraid to go to the villagers for help," Juliana queried softly, "knowing how they feel about you?"

"It was a chance I had to take. I couldn't let you and Ruark be killed."

He fell silent and as he moved to the doorway, Juliana turned her attention back to her husband.

"We've got to get him to a doctor," she said tersely. "He can't die now." Even as she said the words, ice encased her heart.

"It seems the gypsies have joined the fight," Edward reported. "Brodie has been subdued . . . my God!"

"What?" Juliana joined him in the doorway.

"Look at Spencer."

They were never to have a full explanation of Spencer's actions, but Juliana suspected he was driven by desperation and jealousy. She watched in stunned silence as Mariette flung herself upon a horse and prepared to flee the scene. Spencer, as if aware she wouldn't hesitate to abandon him, challenged his wife, gun in hand.

"Where are you going, Mariette? You can't mean to leave me?"

Mariette turned to look over her shoulder, her mouth twisted in derision. "What's wrong, Spencer? Afraid you'll have to be a man and defend yourself?"

"I am a man," he declared, "even though you've nearly made me forget how it feels."

"It's not my fault you're weak."

"Ah, but it is. And you deserve to be punished for it."

Mariette's mocking laughter turned to a scream as Spencer rushed at her, firing the pistol he held.

To Juliana, it seemed the noise of the discharging gun shook the very earth. Mariette's horse reared in fright and she sawed at the reins, fighting to stay in the saddle. But weakened by pain and blinded by the blood pouring over her face, she lost her balance and fell to the earth beneath the animal's thrashing hooves.

With a cry of anguish, Spencer threw himself down to

huddle protectively over her. The stallion's powerful front legs sliced through the air, coming down on the man with crushing force. Spencer's body convulsed, then stilled and he lay unmoving in the cold rain.

Two of the tenant farmers dragged him away from Mariette as she continued to scream hysterically. Juliana was filled with horrified sympathy for her sister, but she didn't leave Ruark's side to go to her.

The skirmish between Spencer's hired men and the farmers lasted only a short time longer. With Spencer dead and Mariette wounded, most of the men who worked for them voluntarily abandoned the fight. The constable, finding himself greatly outnumbered, called an official halt to the situation. Sweating and stammering, he promised to re-assess the commission of his public duties. He'd then ridden away amid the farmers' cheers; the battle had been won.

Now, months later, thoughts of that day could still make Juliana shudder. Kneeling over a simple grave in the quiet woods, she sadly reflected on the strange way fate had of coming to terms with people.

Spencer, ever selfish and weak, had discovered an inner strength that enabled him to save Mariette's life. Ironically, she'd been spared but had lost the one thing she valued most. The lead ball from Spencer's flintlock had torn through the flesh of her cheek and jaw, leaving a jagged, twisting scar that turned her once-perfect face into a travesty of evil beauty.

Eliza and Dodsworth Lowell had spent a fortune taking their daughter to first one specialist and then another, but the prognosis was always the same. No amount of salves or ointments or unique medical treatments would restore Mariette's former loveliness.

Having exhausted all hope in England, the Lowells were

at this moment escorting Mariette across Europe, seeking cures in every well-known spa and consulting with any physician who would see them. Juliana was afraid their efforts were in vain, but at least it gave them a purpose and filled their otherwise empty lives. However, as her desperation grew, Mariette became increasingly petulant and demanding. Without her extraordinary beauty, her parents were now the only ones who tolerated her shrewishness, and Juliana had to wonder how long their patience would endure.

Happily, they had sent her brother Jeremy to live with her while they traveled. She'd been very grateful for his cheerful company.

Essie and Will-John were there, as well, the warm and loving parents her own had never been. It had taken Will-John quite a long time to recover from his ill treatment at Brodie's hands, but thanks to Essie's good-natured scolding and her herbal concoctions, he was as good as new. Earlier, when she'd left the house, the Cliftons had been in the still-room arguing over ingredients for the latest batch of homemade wine. Jeremy, delighting in their bickering, egged them on, his carefree laughter ringing through the house.

Juliana experienced a poignant tug of emotion, as she always did when considering her dearly beloved Quarrystones. It was as much a haven for her as ever, perhaps more so. Secure in its ownership, she asked for nothing more than to live out her life there, finding peace and contentment within its boundaries. She knew she'd never lose her deep and abiding passion for the old house, for its rose-covered walls, its weathered tower, its tranquil gardens.

She rose slowly to her feet, the deep green folds of her cloak swirling about her. There was only one thing in her life she loved more than Quarrystones.

For that moment, she let her mind dwell on Ruark, recalling his lean, tanned face, the dimple that appeared so charmingly each time he smiled. The ardent gypsy eyes, the thick, slightly curling black hair. His voice, deep and masculine, yet edged with the intriguing lilt of Ireland.

" 'Liana!"

The voice became a reality as she heard her name called. She turned quickly and saw a tall, rangy form striding through a sea of autumn leaves toward her. At his heels romped a copper and white spaniel.

"Ruark, you're back," she exclaimed, running to meet him.

Strong arms closed about her, crushing her so tightly to his massive chest that she was breathless. Eager lips sought hers, midnight-black eyes smiled into her own.

"Grandfather nearly worked me to death." He laughed. "I finally told him I had to come home and get some rest."

Juliana traced his cheek with one finger. "He's determined to put Moorlands to rights before winter sets in. I think it's an admirable cause."

"So do I, sweetheart, so do I. But now that he and my mother have managed to reconcile their differences, she can help him make decisions. Besides," he admitted with a flashing smile, "instead of slaving the rest of the day away, I wanted to be here with you. Did you miss me?"

"I was lonely," she affirmed. "And a little melancholy. I've been thinking of Chavo and wanted to put some flowers on his grave."

"He was a good man, a true friend."

Together they approached the grave and stood over it.

"We owe him so much," Juliana murmured, memories churning again in her mind.

That day in the gypsy camp, she'd feared the worst when she'd seen her husband shot down in front of her. But, as she and Edward had eventually discovered, the ball had pierced his shoulder and not, as they'd believed, his heart. Her frantic grasp of her sister's cloak had spoiled Mariette's aim, saving Ruark's life and fulfilling the gypsy's prophecy.

Ruark hadn't been a good patient. His shoulder didn't heal fast enough to suit him. However, all he had to show for his brush with death now was an angry scar and a shoulder that stiffened somewhat when the weather turned damp and cold.

When he was well enough, a hearing had been held to determine his guilt or innocence in the matter of the Gypsy Highwayman. Spencer's old friend, Judge Martin, presided and eventually declared Ruark acquitted of all charges. After all, any number of witnesses came forward to testify they'd heard Chavo confess on his deathbed to being the outlaw, among them the local priest.

The judge announced there could be scant doubt that the young gypsy had been the culprit. He'd certainly had more motivation for robbery than a wealthy duke. Oddly enough, Constable Brodie wasn't in attendance, having left the district for a job up north. Without damaging evidence from him, the judge conceded there was no reason to continue to pursue the case. He even advocated clemency for the highwayman's two accomplices, as the role they'd played had been relatively insignificant.

"So," Judge Martin had stated, fixing a stern eye on Ruark, "as long as no further crimes are committed in this area, we can safely assume the Kentish Gypsy met a tragic and untimely death."

Now standing beside the grave, Ruark quietly said, "It seems we really did lay the highwayman to rest. With Spencer gone, Grandfather has assumed responsibility for his tenants, and there's no more need for highway robbery."

He crouched by the stone marker to touch the bouquet laying there. "And, thanks to Chavo, we can live our lives with no cloud hanging above our heads."

Juliana touched his shoulder. "I brought him Michaelmas daisies because they mean farewell. But the bellflowers symbolize eternal gratitude. That's something we owe Chavo."

"We must never forget him or what he did for us." Ruark stood up and reached for her hand. "Never."

The last rays of the sun fanned out behind the wall of leafless trees and Juliana shivered. "We should go inside," she said after a time. "Essie will have supper ready soon."

In her mind's eye she could envision the scene awaiting them. The lamp would be lighted in the entry hall, a cherrywood fire burning on the hearth. The wondrous aroma of Essie's cooking would waft through the house, beckoning them to the dining room.

As they passed through the parlor, Ruark would pause, as he always did, to admire the portrait his grandfather had painted of Juliana. It hung in a place of honor on the panelled wall, a prized possession. In the dining room, the table would be set for five, and the meal would be accompanied by lively conversation and laughter. Beyond the windows with their leaded glass, a frosted autumn moon would fling handfuls of diamonds across the icy surface of the lily moat.

Juliana sighed with contentment and snuggled closer to her husband as they walked.

Ruark looked down at her, at the face he loved above all others. In his mind's eye, he was picturing the long evening stretching ahead. In the dining room, once the meal had been cleared away, he'd spend a pleasant hour or so playing chess with Jeremy. Will-John would sit by the fire smoking his smelly old pipe and sipping black currant wine. Essie would be in the creaking oak rocker, darning "the husband's" socks or stitching baby quilts to be put away for the time they'd be needed.

Juliana would be curled up on the couch, reading spectacles perched on her straight nose and a book in her hands. When the chess game had gone on for a sufficient amount of time, she'd catch his gaze and with a smile, pointedly stifle a yawn with one slender hand. Silent laughter would lurk behind her smoky eyes as she'd watched him hurry to end the contest and override Jeremy's protests with the promise of more games tomorrow night. Then the two of them would bid everyone a solemn good night and hand in hand, run up the wide staircase to their bedchamber. There, within the intimate recesses of their curtained bed, they'd share a world of love and passion. A world that was theirs alone.

Ruark bent his dark head to hers and murmured a soft Romany phrase in her ear. She laughed and blushed rosily, lifting her mouth for his kiss. Though his words were strange, his meaning was clear.

The twilight deepened, a harbinger of night. They called to Jakel who dashed out of the forest and went bounding off ahead of them.

Arms entwined, Ruark and Juliana started up the leaf-strewn pathway to the warmth and light of Quarrystones.